KIRK'S SKIN
WAS SCORCHINGLY HOT

As if ignited by his nakedness, a searing flame coursed through Tracy, and a sweet taste gathered in her mouth as she responded to Kirk's searching kisses. Eagerly yet gently, Kirk slipped the nightgown off her shoulders, easing it lower and lower until Tracy lay naked before him.

"You're breathtakingly beautiful," Kirk whispered, his teasing tongue touching her whimsically in unexpected places, creating havoc with Tracy's senses.

Aroused to the very center of her being, Tracy wanted to open up to him, a wild primitive urge driving her. She reached out for him, running her hands through Kirk's tousled hair, exploring his body with an abandon that came from her deep feelings for him.

Her own body was alive as it had never been before. . . .

WELCOME TO...

HARLEQUIN SUPERROMANCES

A sensational series of modern love stories.

Written by masters of the genre, these long, sensual
and dramatic novels are truly in keeping with today's
changing life-styles. Full of intriguing conflicts
and the heartaches and delights of true love,
HARLEQUIN SUPERROMANCES are absorbing
stories—satisfying and sophisticated reading
that lovers of romance fiction have long been
waiting for.

HARLEQUIN SUPERROMANCES
Contemporary love stories for the woman of today!

Erika Fabian

SKY RIDERS

Harlequin Books

TORONTO • NEW YORK • LONDON
AMSTERDAM • PARIS • SYDNEY • HAMBURG
STOCKHOLM • ATHENS • TOKYO • MILAN

Published May 1984

First printing March 1984

ISBN 0-373-70116-0

Printed in Canada

My grateful thanks to the following people
for their help
Albert, Yvonne, Vladimir, Dr. Negussay
and Ayele Berhane.

COMING NEXT MONTH FROM
HARLEQUIN SUPERROMANCE

118 TO CATCH THE WIND, Margaret Gayle

No one in the chic Toronto fashion world she's
conquered knows that Miel McCrae's success has
been hard won despite her humble beginning. No
one, except Barth Tramande, the reckless lover she's
never forgotten, though she desperately longs to....

119 NEVER STRANGERS, Lynda Ward

When consumer advocate and author Sara Daniel
is challenged by controversial talk-show host
Ross Marshall, sparks fly. But having a very public
love affair proves almost impossible for two very
private people....

120 SANDCASTLE DREAMS, Robyn Anzelon

Lindsay Ashton's dedication to the family-counseling
center she heads leads her all the way to the San
Juan islands, following up casework on her own time.
Duty and pleasure never mix: that's Lindsay's
axiom—until she meets Mark Cavanaugh.

121 WINTER ROSES, Danielle Trent

After Haley Roberts's husband died in a tragic
accident, she threw herself into making her antique
store the best in the business. Love and men are
forgotten words—then football player Pete Thatcher
steps into her life.

THE DREAM LIVES LONGER
WITH SUPERROMANCE....

CHAPTER ONE

WITH THE TOP DOWN and her copper-colored hair flying, Tracy drove her red convertible much too fast toward her father's house. She was late for a meeting there and, risking being caught by traffic police, ran yellow lights at practically every intersection. It was too bad her car didn't have wings, she thought, as she dodged the crawling drivers on the road.

When she came to the top of Montana Avenue, as always, Tracy's heart skipped a beat at the sight of the Pacific Ocean stretching out like a blue canvas at the bottom of the road. For Tracy there was no other town like Santa Monica. Except for the time she was away at college, she had spent all of her twenty-six years there. She loved the small-town atmosphere Santa Monica managed to maintain even though it was next to the sprawling city of Los Angeles. She liked to tell visitors who came to her office, "Santa Monica occupies the last solid ground between Los Angeles and China." Turning right off Montana Avenue she raced through a quiet residential area, and managed to come to a squealing halt just before crossing the main thoroughfare of San Vicente Boulevard.

From there it was only a matter of seconds along a tree-lined street to her father's home, a stately, vine-covered colonial-style house. She pulled into the circular driveway, jumped out of the car and raced up the stairs to the front door. Using a well-established custom, she gave the bell three taps in rapid succession. It chimed out a melody that everyone inside would recognize as "Tracy's theme." Without waiting for someone to come to the door, she let herself in with her key. Clicking across the black-and-white tile floor on her high heels, she headed straight for the library.

Her father, Ray Nolan, and his business partner, Anne Weston, stopped in midsentence as Tracy entered. Anne was sitting in one of the large leather armchairs, and Ray was standing in the middle of the room, holding a glass of Scotch and soda in his hand.

"You're twenty minutes late," Anne said, her large hazel eyes accusing.

"I'm sorry." Tracy folded her tall slim body in the middle of the soft leather couch. "Alvin got sick and I had to fly his passenger to Mammoth Hot Springs this morning. It was quite windy there, so I just got back."

"I'd have just canceled the flight in that case," Anne said reproachfully.

"It wasn't that bad. Besides, I love the challenge."

"Well, I don't," Anne cut in sharply. "In fact, even while waiting for you, your father and I started to discuss this whole airline business of ours and I want to repeat what I said to him: I want out—now.''

I've barely stepped through the door and Anne is already at it, Tracy thought, irritated. Oh well, she'd known that this meeting wasn't going to be an easy one.

"But I thought you were willing to give us some time so we could buy you out!" Tracy's voice was full of indignation. Anne had promised not to push them, but apparently she just couldn't help herself.

"I'm not like you, Tracy. I was merely putting up with the airline business all these years. When the company got saddled with the Experimental Branch, for me, that was like adding insult to injury. I really hate planes. Always did," Anne said with stifled passion. "And after poor Eddie's accident...." Her voice broke for a moment and silence filled the room till she went on, "It's been over a year and I don't know why I should wait any longer. I mean, it's nothing personal against you, Ray, but having to deal with company business is just a constant reminder of him.''

"Now, Anne...." Ray went to her and put a conciliatory arm around her shoulders.

Tense as she was, Tracy couldn't help but notice the way Anne, even in her sorrow, snuggled into the curve of Ray's arm. At fifty-eight, her father was still a handsome man. Tall, suntanned, with gray hair that made him look distinguished. Could Anne be trying to charm him? Tracy wondered. For a second she entertained the thought that if Anne married her father, their financial disputes with her would be over. But she dismissed the idea, as Anne was hardly the woman Tracy would want her father to marry.

Tracy rose, went to the bar and poured herself a glass of Perrier. The ice cubes clinked softly as she stirred them to cool the bubbly water. Why couldn't Anne have stayed in Europe and let them get on with the work? Tracy thought, annoyed. But Anne was back, and this confrontation with her was inevitable, so Tracy straightened her shoulders and faced the room again.

It was a lovely room, a typical man's den. Dark mahogany bookshelves lined the walls, Persian carpets lay in muted red and beige tones on the polished oak floor. One part of the bookcase contained the built-in bar. Near the tall leaded windows stood Ray's claw-footed desk, and in the middle of the room the large leather couch and two equally soft armchairs suggested comfort and quiet meditation.

Ray had chosen to have the meeting with Anne here rather than in his office at Santa Monica Airport because he felt the explanations he and Tracy had to make would be better received in this soothing atmosphere. Now Tracy wondered if any place would have changed Anne's attitude.

"If poor Kathy were alive, she wouldn't put up with your crazy ventures either!" Anne pouted, pointing at the large painting above the old brick fireplace.

It portrayed a slim young woman with copper hair and warm brown eyes wearing a deep-rust-colored evening gown. One could have mistaken it for Tracy's portrait except for the different hue of the eyes and a certain softness in them.

"My mother loved planes," Tracy stated with increasing anger, fixing her intense green eyes on Anne.

"Forgive me for saying this, but she didn't live long enough to know better."

Tracy sucked in her breath.

"Anne!" Ray protested. "You're being unfair...."

"All right," Anne sighed, "let's get on with your explanation. Just what is this new project that you think will pull Westwind Airlines out of the hole?" She ran a small, well-manicured hand through her brown curls and looked at father and daughter expectantly.

"An organization called World Help has approached us, because they've heard through the grapevine that we custom-design planes. And they needed a couple of small planes for a special mission of theirs," Ray began.

"What sort of mission?" Anne interrupted dubiously.

"To airlift food to a remote, famine-stricken part of Ethiopia."

"Why do they need us for that? Why can't their government do that? Surely they have some small planes at their disposal!"

"Not for this particular mission," Tracy cut in. "And to meet their special requirements we've built the prototype of a modified light plane that can carry up to three hundred pounds of external load hooked under each wing!''

"You did that in just these couple of months I've been away?" Anne was incredulous.

Ray tried to explain. "You see, we took the design Tracy had originally made for the aerobatic plane, and working with Rob, the technical engineer, Tracy modified it to qualify the plane for this mission." Ray's eyes shone with pride as he looked at Tracy. "We tested it in California Mountains where the altitude is comparable to the high plateaus of Ethiopia. The plane can fly at extremely slow speeds, and because it pulls 9 g's—"

"Spare me the technical details," Anne cut in. "That's for you and Tracy. I'd just like to summarize where we stand with each other in the business at this point."

"Go ahead," said Ray, nodding patiently.

Tracy admired her father's way with Anne. He treated her as if she was his equal partner. But only Anne's husband, Eddie, had really been Ray's partner. As far as Tracy was concerned, just because Anne had inherited Eddie's share of the business, it didn't give her the right to interfere in how Ray conducted it. Even Tracy, working as head of the Experimental Branch, did not meddle with the Commuter Service, the other half of Ray's operation. As Ray's only daughter, it was assumed that some day she would take over from him. He included her in every important decision-making conference, and she was learning the ins and outs of the family-run airline. But Anne knew nothing of any part of the business! Never had. She'd left everything up to Eddie for twenty-two years. All she had ever cared about was his share of the profits.

Tracy forced her thoughts back to Anne, who was saying, "Before I left for Europe you told me you'd come up with the money. Now you're asking me again to wait to get my half out of the business. And to top it off you want me to okay this relief scheme of yours."

"Yes, because this project with World Help is almost sure to get us the government contract we've been looking for to finance the Experimental Branch. All we're asking for is six more months and we'll have the cash to give you your share," Ray explained.

Anne shook her head: "Ethiopia! Maybe if you had picked another country, like China, I could see it—it's in the news all the time. But who's ever even heard of Ethiopia? And who cares about what's happening over there?"

"Enough people to bring this project about." Tracy tried to keep her voice calm and free of her rising contempt for Anne. She'd always known Anne was spoiled and self-centered. Tracy could accept her on a small everyday level, but now they were talking about preventing a part of their company from being sold to strangers while doing an important international project, and Anne still couldn't see beyond her own nose.

"What about personnel on this mercy mission?" Anne's voice was scathing with sarcasm.

"We're supplying them," Ray explained. "We'll send over a team of two pilots and a technical expert whose job it will be to keep the aircraft fit."

"And where are you going to get those people? Or is Tracy going to be your chief pilot and expert rolled into one?"

Ray smiled. "Well, she could be. But I am selfish enough to want to keep her at home. I think she does more good for the company building planes than flying them. Don't worry, Anne, I have already found an excellent team of pilots and I've even got a technician lined up."

Tracy raised her eyebrow slightly, involuntarily. Her father hadn't told her he'd already located the necessary personnel. Ray caught the surprised look on Tracy's face and said, as much for her benefit as Anne's, "I didn't want to get your hopes up before finalizing the deal with the captain of the team. But I'm seeing him this afternoon, and if all goes well, we'll sign the contract."

"Who is he?" Tracy and Anne asked at the same time, exchanging a little laugh at the coincidence. It felt good to laugh together, despite Tracy's irritation with Anne.

"His name is Kirk Russell and he comes very highly recommended. He and his team worked together in Alaska for years. They operated planes for the smoke jumpers, so I'm sure they'll do a fine job for us."

"What's a smoke jumper?" asked Anne.

"They're people who jump out of planes to

fight forest fires," Tracy explained. "It's a rather dangerous occupation."

"For the jumpers, not the pilots, I assume," Anne asserted.

"For the pilots, too. They have to fly into the fire zones to drop the jumpers and their equipment."

"How come you know all this?" Anne queried.

"I had considered working up there before dad offered me the job at Westwind," Tracy said with a grin.

"Your father probably created the Experimental Branch just to keep you out of a crazy venture like that," Anne remarked sarcastically.

Ray laughed. "Maybe I did. In any case, if you want to meet this hotshot pilot, you're welcome to stop by my office after I'm through drawing up the contract with him."

"I'm afraid I'll just have to trust your judgment." Anne stretched lazily like a Persian cat, "I've got a hairdresser's appointment at Lalo's this afternoon and I wouldn't dare cancel it."

Tracy tried to sound as casual and disinterested as possible. "I'll be at the hangars. Bring him out there if you think it's worthwhile." But deep down she had to fight the twinge of jealousy she felt toward this pilot who came so highly recommended. Was he a better aviator than she? Tracy wondered.

"Talking about worthwhile," said Anne, "what if I wait six months and you still haven't got the government contract?"

"I'll either find you the money so you can get out, or sell the Experimental division of the business."

"That sounds good to me." Anne rose triumphantly and faced Ray. Her brown curls shook as she lifted her face to look at him with her large hazel eyes. "But remember, this is the last time I'll wait. When half a year is up, I must have my money."

"You will. I promise," Ray assured her.

Red-hot anger blazed inside Tracy. It sounded as if her father really meant what he was saying! Anne was pushing his back to the wall and he was going to yield. But maybe he was just playing for time, she thought, eagerly trying to excuse him. Even if they didn't get the government contract, Tracy couldn't see how Ray could let go of any part of the company, especially not the Experimental Branch! The Experimental Branch was the realization of a lifelong dream for them both.

When she was growing up she often heard Ray say with regret that he should have become an engineer instead of a pilot turned businessman. When he discovered that his daughter, Tracy, had inherited his love of planes and that her dream was to design them, he encouraged her to follow her inclination. During her years in engineering school, what kept Tracy going in times of difficulties was the promise from Ray that, once she got her diploma, she could come to Westwind and head up a new design department. How could he now so easily say that he was going to sell the Experimental Branch? What about her and the work she had put into it? What about Ray's feelings, his own admission that he was finally happy with his company because after years of stagnation he could see it growing again in a direction he'd wanted all his life? Why should he be willing to cast it all away for Anne's sake?

She stared at the well-preserved woman standing across the room and decided that regardless of what her father was telling Anne now, he did what he said merely to gain time. She did not really know the financial difficulties Ray was facing due to the expenses of the Experimental Branch. But whatever they were, she would find out and help, Tracy decided, as she stood facing the two people in the room. Even if her father had meant what he'd said, there was no way she would let him sell any part of the company. Anne was not going to destroy their dream, Tracy promised herself. She and Ray had six months in which to act.

Before they could go on there was a soft knock on the library door.

"Come in!" Ray called.

A tall slim woman in her early sixties entered the room. Her features were plain, but she had an imposing presence, accented by the tight chignon at the nape of her neck.

"Sorry to disturb you," she said, smiling pleasantly, "but lunch is ready...and you know how upset Esperanza gets when the food is just right and you're not at the table...."

"Of course, Irma, we'll come at once," Ray replied, smiling back at his sister.

"You are staying for lunch, of course," Irma said, turning her pleasant blue eyes on Anne. "I'd like to hear about your latest trip. I bet it was fun."

Anne laughed. "I hadn't planned on staying, but if I'm invited, I wouldn't miss a meal prepared by your housekeeper for anything. Of course I don't know how you've managed to put up with her bad temper all these years...."

"I can't stay, Aunt Irma," Tracy apologized. "I have some work to finish before five."

Irma sized up Tracy's slender figure.

"I know you like to keep your curves subtle, but I think you could use a square meal once in a while, young lady," she said, reproaching her niece.

"Tracy doesn't need food—she thrives on airplane fuel," Anne snapped.

Ignoring Anne's comment, Tracy hugged her aunt and said, "I'll pass through the kitchen and take a CARE package with me, okay? But I really must go."

She made her good-byes, avoiding her father's searching eye. He could always see through her, Tracy knew and even now he probably guessed that she simply didn't want to sit through lunch with Anne. Like a bird freed from the cage, she left the library, ran across the entry hall and entered the kitchen.

Esperanza turned her stocky body with amazing speed from the sink and clapped her hands when she saw Tracy.

"Ay, *niña*," the housekeeper said, "little girl, what did I not put on the table now?"

"As far as I know, everything's there," Tracy assured her.

"Then why aren't you in the dining room with the others?"

"Because if I had to sit at the same table with that woman, I'd throw up!" Tracy blurted.

"What a thing to say!"

"There she is, sharing our food while at the same time trying to pull the rug out from under us!"

Esperanza shook her head. "You mean Anne wants the airline sold again?"

"Yes! For twenty-two years Anne has enjoyed the money the business brought her and now she can't wait another year. She knows as well as anybody that it takes years to build up a company! But she doesn't like the Experimental Branch. She's afraid that we're spending too much of her profits from the commuter line in developing it. . . ."

"Maybe if you stayed and talked to her she'd listen to reason."

"I can't talk to her! I think, instead of brains, Anne's got sawdust in her head! Tracy sank down at the maple dinette table and picked an apple out of the fruit bowl before her. It was too much to explain, even to Esperanza.

"You're still behaving like you did when you were a little girl," the housekeeper commented. "You're always running out when you don't like somebody."

"It beats staying and getting more upset!" Tracy shrugged, biting into the apple.

"I know, that's how all you young people think." Esperanza shook her head and began preparing a sandwich. "Like you and that young man you married. You didn't even give him a chance! Six months, you had some arguments, so poof, the marriage is over."

"C'mon, Espe, you know it wasn't as simple as that. It wasn't the arguments that separated George and me."

"A man should be allowed his way now and then. They're made that way. In time you could have forgiven him."

"Is that how you and José stayed together the past twenty years, with him doing as he pleased and you forgiving him?" Tracy's voice was brimming with sarcasm.

"We had our share of problems when we were young." Esperanza's face clouded over. "But a woman has to learn to give a little."

"A little is fine. It's when a man wants you to give up everything you believe in that you get into trouble." Tracy sighed. "Whatever José did, he didn't interfere when you decided to continue working for us! He even agreed to live in the garden when daddy offered you the guest house. But besides wanting me to change my basic principles, George also wanted me to give up working for dad, and even flying! Now that's crazy!"

"On that one score he was right. I, too, wish you would give it up. Flying is dangerous."

"Oh, Espe, how can you have lived with us for so long and still say that?" Tracy exclaimed.

"Well, look what happened to poor Mr. Eddie—and after all those years of experience." The older woman made the sign of the cross over herself quickly, kissing her thumb afterward.

"It's usually the pilot who fails, not the machine," Tracy replied very seriously.

The two women were silent for a moment, thinking of Eddie. Often when a small plane malfunctioned, a skilled pilot could survive if he kept his wits about him. Unfortunately, investigators had never found the cause of Eddie's plane crash in the Sierra Nevada, en route to Mammoth on Westwind business.

"I've got to go now," Tracy said, breaking the silence. She took the neatly wrapped sandwich and hugged the housekeeper.

"Take care of yourself, *niña*," Esperanza murmured.

It made Tracy feel good to have stopped in to see her, even if Esperanza had brought up the subject of George. Esperanza had been with her family as long as she could remember. Between Espe and Aunt Irma, who had come to live with them when her mother became ill, Tracy felt as though she had gained not one but two mothers, when her own passed away. She had been only twelve then, and it had taken Tracy a long time to accept the love of the two women who were taking care of her. But now, at twenty-six, Tracy fully appreciated them both.

She swerved her Alfa Romeo out to San Vicente Boulevard and noted that the coral trees were all in bloom along the broad avenue.

Tracy hadn't thought of George for some time and wondered why Esperanza had brought up the subject of her brief marriage. Perhaps because it was hard for Espe to accept her fast divorce, Tracy thought, even though the housekeeper knew the reasons for it. But Tracy had been divorced for almost a year. That was longer than the duration of her marriage, so she couldn't see why Espe would even bother giving the past any thought. To her, George was like a quicksilver memory. She had met him, fallen in love and married him, all within a month. Six months later her marriage was over.

Tracy discussed aspects of her marriage with friends—but why she'd made the final decision to walk out on George was something she couldn't really explain in any detail to others. It was too deep a hurt, too humiliating for her as a woman and as a person of intelligence. How could she admit that George had been unfaithful to her without also admitting that it was largely her own fault? She fell in love and, blinded by her feelings, married George without understanding his true character. Why, she wouldn't fly a new plane without inspection, but she'd sure got into marriage without one! No wonder it crashed, she thought, smiling to herself at the comparison. George was basically a playboy. Initially, because of her own serious nature, it was his ability to have fun that appealed to Tracy. George had shown her another, lighter side of life and for a while she was enchanted by it. But fun without limits was not something she could live with. So she'd put a stop to it and borne the pain that went with the break. Since then Tracy had concluded that in California there didn't seem to be any men who shared her point of view.

Tracy made a right turn onto Bundy Drive, which led directly to Cloverfield Airport in Santa Monica. Then she continued her train of thought.

It was easy for her to meet people through her work, and after her divorce she had gone out on a number of dates. But she'd found the men she met sadly lacking. It seemed that all they wanted was "to have a good time without any commitment," and that was something Tracy couldn't accept. When she'd make it very clear during the course of an evening that she wasn't willing to spend the night with her date, he'd say he understood, but would not ask her out again. It seemed that there were enough available women; a man didn't have to try twice. Tracy didn't mind. It gave her un- limited time for work. *Maybe this is a part of me I inherited from Aunt Irma,* Tracy concluded. *She is perfectly content to be single, and so am I.*

Tracy overtook a silver Porsche and made a sharp right turn into the airport. She drove by the big sign that advertised "Westwind Airlines," and waved at Rosie, her father's secretary, who was scurrying back into the office.

Tracy drove to where the Ethiopia project planes were hangared at the northern end of the airfield, parked her car and got out. The little aerobatic planes stood silently in the middle of the hangar as if waiting for her. Affectionately she pulled her palm along the cool metal body of one of them. She loved planes, and these two were truly little gems. She raised her foot to reach the step on the side of the plane in order to climb into the cockpit, then realized that her fashionable tailored skirt wouldn't permit it. With a little laugh Tracy crossed to a closet at one end of the hangar. She removed a slightly crumpled white jump suit and, knowing that she was alone in the hangar, quickly slipped into it without even hiding behind the open door. She hung her skirt and silk blouse in the closet. Moving to close the door, she caught sight of herself in the narrow mirror nailed on the inside.

The one-piece suit emphasized her height and slim figure. Actually beneath the somewhat loose-fitting coveralls her lithe body was surprisingly curvacious and full breasted. But Tracy preferred not to call attention to her sexuality during work hours. She smiled as she recalled how worried Esperanza had been about her during her teen years because she didn't seem to be eating enough to round herself out. Aunt Irma had worried that Tracy was staying thin deliberately so she could become a fashion model as her mother had been. But that was nothing compared with how concerned both women became when they discovered that little Tracy preferred flying to food and clothes and even to the company of boys. It gave Tracy a sense of freedom to be up in the sky. She also gained a feeling of self-confidence at a time of life when most girls worry about their looks and acceptability by the other sex. Tracy didn't need any boy's approval. She had all her schoolmates' admiration, for she could fly. She never considered the possibility that her independent spirit might intimidate most of the boys around her and that her very independence was why she was seldom asked out. She kept herself busy in her free time by flying or tinkering with old plane parts around the airport and didn't miss going out. When other girls went on dates, Tracy went on solo flights. Even as a grown woman, in college and in engineering school, she dated only occasionally. Her time was too precious to waste on meaningless relationships. No wonder her family welcomed the change in her when she finally fell in love with George! They were probably relieved to see Tracy behave like other young women. Even Ray didn't try to persuade her to wait a while when Tracy announced her wedding plans. In fact, her family seemed to hurry her along, as though they were afraid she would change her mind. That was probably why Espe was still harping on her former marriage, she concluded. Since George, there hadn't been any permanent man in her life. Just as well, Tracy thought. She had other worries right now.

She pulled her shoulder-length flame-colored hair into a ponytail and fastened it with a tortoise-shell barrette that she fished out of her pocket. She shut the closet door, erasing her image. And as always when she wanted to think things through, Tracy headed for the cockpit of one of the little planes.

Balancing on the footstep, she raised the Plexiglas canopy. Then she swung her long legs over the side of the plane and climbed in. She felt at home inside the cabin. The instrument panel before her was like an old friend—not hard to deal with—as Anne was. Her father's promise to Anne made Tracy feel anxious. So much depended now on the successful performance of these small planes.

"Pegasus" was what Tracy had christened the line, after the mythical Greek flying horse. She'd chosen the name because her planes were to perform like that magical beast—flawlessly, under all circumstances, over any terrain.

Absently she lifted the copy of the flight plan that the test pilot had left on the seat next to her and studied it. From it she could tell the flight had been quite taxing.

Instead of sitting here worrying about the future, I should work for its success, she scolded herself. And a good start would be to check out the plane since its last test. Action always made Tracy feel better. Even now, just by making one simple decision she could feel her anger passing. It was useless to anticipate the future. Six months consisted merely of a series of days, each of which waited to be filled with work. Tracy had learned this at engineering school, when she found that, instead of worrying about grades, the secret to passing exams lay in one's ability to manage time and to concentrate on studying. Life of course didn't always flow in such an orderly fashion. To succeed, one needed a certain amount of luck, too. But she usually had that. So all she needed now was to put in her share of the work.

A quick check of the instrument panel before her assured her that all the switches were off. Then she clambered out of the cockpit for a walk-around. Normally this procedure was done by the pilot before take-off to make sure that everything on the plane was in top shape. But with the Pegasus line Tracy often did a double-check right after a flight. And she would do so now, especially since there was a chance that the pilot her father had hired would be coming to see the machines he and his team were to fly. Tracy wanted the aircraft to be perfect. She started by lifting the cowling, at the nose of the plane, off the engine. Everything looked clean, not a drop of oil or moisture showed anywhere. She pulled out the dipstick. There was enough oil. Tracy replaced the cowling and leaned down to check the landing gear. There was no leakage of the hydraulic fuel under any of the wheels. She straightened up and pulled her hand over the front of the left wing, called the leading edge because this was the part that sliced the air-flow. It had no dents or nicks. The wing tip was also fine. She moved to the rear edge of the wing to make sure that the aileron, the movable part of the wing that helps the plane bank and turn, and the flaps just inboard of the aileron were all securely fastened. Tall as she was at five-foot-nine, Tracy still needed to grab a stool and climb up on it to check the tail assembly for possible damage. She gently moved the elevator up and down. It moved smoothly. She pushed the trim tab up, checking to see that the elevator swung down as the tab went up. In flight, these parts, moving in opposite directions, helped stabilize the plane and kept it on course. Then she hopped off the stool and put it aside. She walked forward and followed through with her inspection on the other side of the plane, checking every detail.

On the leading edge of the right wing Tracy peered into a small flap—the stall-warning device. Even though the Pegasus line was equipped with the most modern avionic instruments, among them an electronic warning device that monitored the plane's angle in the air at all times, Tracy insisted that this gadget be well maintained. Considering the special function of a Pegasus, it was crucial that all stall-warning devices be operational. In Ethiopia, when on mission, the Pegasus was to fly low and at its lowest speed in order to drop the sacks without breaking them up on impact with the ground. However, even a small additional drop in speed could cause the plane to lose its ability to stay in the air. Thus it was essential that the pilot be warned of any change in the plane's speed or altitude. In case the electricity failed, this mechanical stall-warning device would still work. The air flow outside the plane would make the device warble a small reed inside the cockpit and alert the pilot that the plane was about to stall.

If Anne knew the potential dangers of this Ethiopian mission, she would probably be even more appalled, Tracy thought, smiling to herself. She probably wouldn't have given them even a month's reprieve, let alone six! In that sense, perhaps they had already won a minor victory. Who knows what could happen in six months, Tracy thought with sudden optimism.

She reached the propeller and carefully examined the blades. At high speeds even a small crack or bend in them could cause a lack of balance and such severe vibration that the engine could be shaken out of its mounting. And no pilot would want to be in the air then. But the propellers were flawless. As a final check she tested for water in the gas tanks.

The tanks in each wing were only half full. Normally this caused moisture condensation, creating a little pool of water at the bottom of the tank, which had to be drained. Often a plane's failure right at takeoff was caused by water in the gasoline mixture. Tracy liked doing this final step. Reaching for a plastic cup from inside the cockpit she fitted its special mouth into the drain under the wing and filled it with a small amount of gasoline. Through the clear plastic she could see the water settling on the bottom while the bluish-colored fuel floated to the top. She emptied the cup into a nearby container and repeated the operation till she could see that only pure gasoline filled the cup. Satisfied, she closed the drain and headed for the next tank. As she came out from under the wing, she passed by the hangar door and spotted her father walking toward the hangar. The sight of the man striding easily by his side sent a shock wave through her whole being. She stood transfixed in the shadow of the hangar, watching him approach.

He was inches taller than her father, who was six-foot-two. He wore a tan safari jacket and brown slacks, lending an almost military air to his broad-shouldered athletic body. And he moved with a graceful swing as though he owned the world. Tracy swallowed with a suddenly dry throat. It flashed through her mind that she ought to go inside, put her cup down and wash her hands, but she couldn't make herself move. *He is incredible,* she thought, and suddenly she was ready to run and change into her good clothes. But it was too late.

"Tracy! What are you up to?" her father asked, and then without waiting for an answer, added, "Meet Captain Kirk Russell. He'll be heading the Pegasus team for the food drop in Ethiopia."

Kirk Russell had a striking face, suntanned, with a commanding Roman nose, strong cheekbones and well-shaped, sensuous lips. His eyes were a remarkably clear gray under dark brows.

Outwardly Tracy composed herself, smiled and held out her palms, which smelled of gasoline. "I don't think we ought to shake hands, Mr. Russell."

She wondered how he would react and loved his controlled reserve when he merely smiled at her playfulness. The thought crossed her mind that he probably wouldn't have minded shaking her work-stained hand.

"Tracy is my chief engineer," said Ray, introducing her. "She can tell you more about the Pegasus line than anyone else, so I'll leave you two to get acquainted."

Her father's voice seemed to come from a great distance as Tracy's glance locked into the searching gray eyes of Kirk Russell. He seemed to be challenging her to look away first, and she decided it was important not to do so.

"I am sure we'll get along just fine," Kirk finally said in response to his new employer, and Tracy felt as though she had won a round when he shifted his eyes from her to look at Ray.

"Captain, I'll see you and the crew tomorrow." Ray shook hands with Kirk, then nodded toward Tracy. "I'll talk to you later."

When he had left, Kirk turned to Tracy. "So these are the planes?"

"Yes," said Tracy, suddenly feeling tongue-tied now that she was alone with Kirk.

She watched him eye the planes and wondered why she was so mesmerized by his presence. She never had any problems talking to strangers. But something about this man seemed to overwhelm her. It was more than his virile good looks. As he turned toward her again she suddenly realized what it was: he was fully in command. She had never met anyone before who seemed to be so much in charge of himself and everything around him. She felt a surge of relief; what she understood, she could handle.

"Would you like an introduction to them?" Tracy nodded toward the planes.

"I'd love it. First the planes and then you," Kirk said, and his face lit up with a roguish smile.

"I'm not included with the planes," Tracy retorted, her fighting spirit aroused by his comment. It annoyed her that he seemed to think that she might be as easy for him to figure out as the planes.

With an appreciative twinkle in his eyes, he asked, a challenge in his voice, "How about dinner then?"

"I'll see how we get along this afternoon," she replied, hedging. She decided she wasn't going to give in easily, because his attitude told her that he was a man who was used to hearing "yes."

"Let's start with the planes then," he laughed with mock resignation.

His graceful retreat pleased Tracy. A sudden good mood surged within her as she headed for the Pegasus plane with Kirk at her side. She secretly hoped that at the end of the afternoon he would repeat his invitation, because she felt that Kirk was a man she wanted to get to know better.

CHAPTER TWO

"THESE PLANES are equipped for instrument flying although we hope that you won't have to do much of that in Ethiopia," Tracy began to explain, sure that if she stuck to facts, she wouldn't betray the nervous excitement that Kirk's presence seemed to cause. Despite her effort, she found it hard to keep her voice level. Kirk's clear gray eyes had such a penetrating intensity that Tracy nearly stumbled over her own words. She wondered whether he was paying attention to her or was merely staring at her moving lips.

"Look," she said, stopping at the left wing, "these are the underwing supports for the loads you'll be carrying." She bent down to point out two trapezoid shaped metal pieces welded to the wing in parallel positions. As Kirk stooped beneath the wing next to her, she could feel his body heat. It radiated through her provoking a flush in her body that spread from her cheeks to her toes.

"There is another set of these under the other wing," she said, backing out and straightening her spine. The air in the hangar felt cool in comparison to her burning cheeks. "Each can hold up to 75 kilos, that is a total weight of 300 kilos, or

660 pounds, evenly distributed on the four hooks.''

Kirk nodded without commenting, and ran his fingers over the weldings as if testing them for solidity.

Tracy waited quietly for him to finish examining the attachments. She watched his strong, long-fingered hands probe the metal and wondered what it might feel like to have those sensitive fingertips roam over her skin. She was being ridiculous, she told herself, to be even thinking such thoughts. They had just met. Besides, any transaction between them had to be strictly business; after all, he was an employee. This realization raised a sobering question in her mind: considering Kirk's position how could she go out for dinner with him? But that was going too far, she decided. It was perfectly all right to have a meal with company personnel, especially a new employee. One could get better acquainted over a meal than during office hours, and it was important for her to get to know Kirk. The success of their Ethiopia project depended to a large extent on him. She had to find out for herself what kind of a man he was.

He was through looking and turned to her expectantly.

''Here,'' she said opening the cargo door on the left side of the plane, ''this space can be used for a third person, or even a litter in case of medical emergencies.''

''Maybe for a short person,'' laughed Kirk. ''But I'd sure hate to have to crawl in there.''

''How tall are you?'' The question slipped out

with such childlike curiosity that Tracy bit her lip for asking. It wasn't very professional.

"Just right for you," Kirk replied, smiling down at her. "How about you?"

Before Tracy knew what he was up to, Kirk's arms went around her and she was drawn to him so closely that her entire body pressed against his.

"What are you doing?" she stammered, taken aback by the swift gesture. She could feel the muscles of his powerful body against hers and was concerned that the violent pounding of her heart would be felt by him through the thin cotton of their clothes. She tried to push him away, but he held her tight.

"Relax," he laughed, "I'm just sizing you up."

"Mr. Russell!" Tracy protested, resorting to formality because she felt vulnerable. It was obvious that Kirk sensed her attraction to him and was taking advantage of it. She could feel her face flush. Her body was sending signals she hadn't felt since she first met George, and she knew that it was crucial for her to get released with her image as a professional person unblemished. To get angry at him would have just made things worse. "You're going about it the wrong way," she managed to say coolly.

"How so?" He loosened his hold on her just enough for her to be able to look up at him.

"You can't take my measure by my height," she reasoned, with deliberate calm. "Just as I'm sure you wouldn't want me to judge your competence by this silly thing you're doing."

"You're not only beautiful, you're clever, too," he laughed, releasing her.

"Let's get on with business," said Tracy, dismissing his compliment, though her heart had seemed to do a somersault as he held her.

"I think my getting to know you has also become a very important part of this business," Kirk murmured. Then sighing, he added, "But you're right. Let's get on with the planes first."

Tracy took a deep breath and brought her feelings under control. She went on for a while, describing the plane in a tone as businesslike as she could manage.

As though sensing the change in her, Kirk became serious and attentive. Even his clear gray eyes stopped teasing her as he concentrated on the information.

"Will you be going out tomorrow with the test pilot?" she asked finally.

"We have another commitment scheduled for tomorrow." Kirk rubbed his chin thoughtfully. "My partner, Bill, and I won't get to fly these things till Thursday."

From the wistful look in his eyes, Tracy could easily guess his thoughts. She glanced at her watch. It was nearly four o'clock. They'd have time, she thought. "Would you like to take a spin in one of them?" Her green eyes sparkled.

"How did you guess?" he laughed.

"Okay, I'll take you up."

"I thought you were an engineer...."

"I've been flying since my teens. Besides, this

plane is my creation; I should certainly know how to fly it!''

"Let's go!" Kirk exclaimed with great enthusiasm.

His electricity was contagious. Quickly Tracy telephoned the Flight Service Station to get the weather. It was clear everywhere in California. Then she called her father's office at Westwind. Ray was not in, so she left word with Rosie, his secretary, that she was taking Kirk up in Pegasus. She also asked Rosie to page the gasoline truck and send it to her hangar right away.

"I checked this one out before you got here," she said, patting the side of the plane. "It's ready to go.''

"You're the boss," said Kirk, bowing his head, but his playful courtesy didn't conceal the genuine delight in his eyes.

He waited by the hangar entrance looking outside while Tracy collected her handbag from the closet. With the open door hiding her from Kirk, she stole a glance at herself in the mirror. Her hair had come loose here and there and lay in soft ringlets around her oval face and on her neck. Her eyes had darkened to a deep emerald, and her cheeks were flushed, but not by the summer heat. It was an inner fire that gave her the color of a coral rose. She didn't mind her slightly disheveled looks. An excitement hung in the air between her and Kirk. She quivered inside with tension, as if this were the first time she had ever taken anyone up. Maybe it was the chance to show off her plane that caused it, Tracy rationalized as she shut the closet door. After all, Kirk was a well-known pilot and he was looking over her plane.

Searching around for her flight case she found it lying on the desk in a corner of the hangar. She opened it and checked its contents. The pad of flight plan forms and the red leather-bound book that listed her hours flown lay safely inside. She closed the case and looked for Kirk. He stood sharply silhouetted in the doorway and Tracy felt a strange pang as her eyes took in his broad-shouldered, lean-hipped figure. Even with his back to her, relaxing in easy repose against the doorframe of the hangar, he emanated strength. He had the secure grace of a mountain cat, Tracy thought. Sensing her eyes on him, he turned toward her and smiled. Caught, Tracy flung her flight case with unnecessary force into the plane behind the pilot seat.

"Shall we?" she invited.

Together they removed the heavy metal chocks that lay under the wheels to prevent the plane from rolling. Then Tracy took the tow bar out of the cargo compartment and fitted the U-shaped prong into the designated holes on the nose. wheel's steering strut.

"May I?" Kirk offered.

Tracy stepped aside and watched him thrust his powerful shoulders forward as he slowly, cautiously pulled the plane out of the hangar with the tow bar. He replaced the tow bar and waited for Tracy to shut the cargo compartment. The gasoline truck pulled up at that moment.

"Tom, this is Captain Kirk Russell," Tracy informed the sandy-haired young man climbing off the truck. "He'll be piloting these planes in Ethiopia."

"Good luck to you, sir." Tom saluted him lightly by raising a hand to his blond curls. "I wish I were in your shoes."

"Tom is working on his commercial pilot rating," Tracy explained, "and he is also employed part-time by Westwind."

"Yeah, flying is an expensive business." Tom said philosophically, then pointed at Pegasus. "Are you going out?"

"Yes, fill up both tanks, please," Tracy said.

"How is your time?" she asked Kirk while they waited.

"It's yours." The look in his eyes implied anything she wished to read into them.

Tracy decided to maintain a professional tone. "I mean, do you have any other appointments later in the day? I'd like to know so I can arrange our flight plan."

"Would I have invited you out for dinner if I had?" Then with a provocative smile playing around his lips, Kirk added, "I'm free till tomorrow morning."

"I thought you were joking about dinner." Tracy chose to ignore the second part of his comment.

"I would never do such a thing."

"All right, then I'll take you over the San Bernardino mountain range and Death Valley. If we feel like it, we can land at Fox Field; if not, we can just turn around."

"I'd go anywhere with you," Kirk said with mock passion, but his eyes were not laughing. Tracy's heart gave a leap as his eyes looked into hers, searching for her reaction.

"I won't even take you on this trip unless you cut that stuff out," she was smiling, but wanted him to understand that she meant what she said.

His attitude toward her made her wary. She sensed that beneath the jokes and teasing smiles he was really testing how far he could get with her and how fast. And while she felt greatly drawn to him, echoes of her ill-fated, speedy marriage to George prevented her from being at ease. She didn't want to fall in love again just because a man was bright and virile.

"What is life without romance?" he laughed, showing his even white teeth. "But if it really bothers you, I won't do it."

"I'm finished," Tom said, approaching them.

After she compared the gallons on the sheet with the meter on the mobile gasoline unit, Tracy signed Westwind's expense sheet, putting down the name and registration number of the plane.

"It's not that I don't trust you," she said, smiling brightly at Tom, "it's just a question of habit."

"I understand."

He took the pad, pulled off a copy of the expense sheet for her and saluting Kirk again, took off in his truck.

Tracy chose to ignore Kirk's remark about romance. She watched the gas truck roll out of sight, then turned to him. "Ready?"

They climbed into the plane, Tracy on the left—the pilot's side—and Kirk on the right into the copilot's seat.

"Belts, please," she requested. Preoccupied with flight preparation, Tracy's tone became impersonal. She didn't even glance at Kirk. Instead, she followed the checklist pasted on the instrument panel. The radios were off, both gas tanks were full and the mixture was set on full rich. Tracy set the flaps, then reached up, pulled the transparent Plexiglas canopy over them and locked it down. She yelled "Clear!" out the side window, though there was no one nearby. Still it was part of take-off, an old pilot custom, dating from the barnstorming days when gawkers in the field had to be warned that the plane was ready for take-off. Even today one never knew who might happen to be under the plane. So it was a good practice to give the warning. Tracy turned the key and advanced the throttle. As the engine came to life the propeller quickly became like a gossamer halo around the plane's nose. Tracy flashed Kirk a quick smile then forgot about him as she switched on the radio and contacted Ground Control.

The code names given to the letters of the alphabet for flight communication frequently amused Tracy. *Pegasus*' registration number was N1PT, but when she called it in, Tracy was always reminded of some fat gentleman trying to dance.

She spoke into the mike of her headset, and listening, Kirk could follow the communication between her and Ground Control over the radio speakers, mounted on the dashboard.

"Ground, November One Papa Tango, ready to taxi to the runway."

The speakers crackled as Ground Control replied, "One Papa Tango, taxi to runway two one." At the head of the runway Tracy did a run up: She revved up the engine and made a final check on all systems and controls to make sure they were in running condition. Then she switched to the control tower's frequency on the radio.

"Santa Monica Tower, November One Papa Tango, ready for takeoff."

The Tower replied, "One Papa Tango, you're cleared to takeoff."

Tracy pushed the throttle to full power. The tarmac beneath her became a blur. She pulled the yoke toward herself and watched the nose of the plane bear upward. No matter how much she had flown, the first moments of lifting off still gave her a sense of exhilaration.

"What does your registration number stand for?" Kirk asked as soon as they were airborne.

"The N of course is for the U.S.; then One, for the first in the series of these planes; P, or Papa, for *Pegasus*; and T, for Tracy, because I felt like rewarding myself by including my initial in the series."

"Pretty good," Kirk nodded. "You can hardly forget a registration number like that."

They headed west, over the sea, which glistened in the afternoon sun like molten silver. Then Tracy banked right, heading inland and within minutes they were passing over the northern end of the San Gabriel Valley, a landscape dotted with shake-roofed houses, greenery and sparkling pools.

"Almost every home seems to have a private pool," Kirk noted.

"They need it," Tracy laughed. "It gets above a hundred degrees around here during the summer. We're at four thousand feet and even up here the temperature is eighty-five degrees."

"And I thought it was being so close to you that made me hot," Kirk joked.

A sudden anger rose in Tracy. He was baiting her, she thought, treating her as he might any other "available" female in his life. Well, here was her chance to prove that she was not just any other woman. Tracy set their course for Lancaster on the instrument panel. Then she contacted Los Angeles Air Traffic Control and reported their position and destination, requesting radar following. She planned to fly an altitude of seventy-five hundred feet, and to land at Fox Field in thirty minutes.

"Okay, One Papa Tango, we have you on radar, proceed to Fox Field. Traffic at two o'clock, two miles, northbound."

"November One Papa Tango, we have him, thank you." Tracy replied.

She waited until the area was clear of traffic. In the meantime, her plane reached the reported altitude. Now she was ready. She stole a glance at Kirk. He was observing the landscape below them, his belt snug across his lap and broad chest. For a brief moment she scanned the sky for other aircraft nearby. When all seemed clear, she brought the power back, pulled in the yoke, and pushed the rudder hard to the right. The plane tilted and the ground filled the windshield as the plane rolled into a fast spin. Tracy caught the startled expression on Kirk's face but she suppressed her delight.

"Just want to show you some of the things this plane can do," she informed him nonchalantly.

"Go ahead," he dared her.

And she did. The horizon tilted, dipped and whirled about them as Tracy maneuvered the plane through a variety of spectacular loops and spins. She could feel Kirk's eyes following her every move at the controls, but to his credit, he stayed silent. She executed a flawless inside-outside figure eight and decided to end the demonstration by doing a three-hundred-sixty-degree turn, complicated by four slow rolls of the plane in the opposite direction of the turn.

"Doing slow rolls makes me feel like a chicken on a barbecue spit," Tracy commented to Kirk as she finally leveled the plane and set it on a straight course.

"You didn't tell me this plane was rated for aerobatics." Kirk's tone implied a quizzical surprise.

"*Pegasus* and I are both qualified. How could you think I'd do these things otherwise?" Tracy deliberately sounded indignant, though secretly she was delighted at detecting Kirk's concern. Where was his self-assured arrogance now, she thought triumphantly.

"I underestimated you." He was studying her with an amused smile on his lips.

His candor robbed Tracy of her secret feeling of triumph. "You couldn't have thought much in the first place if a few maneuvers in the air could raise your opinion of me," she commented sharply.

"I'm not talking about your flying ability," he stated with quiet intensity. "What you did made me realize that you are an even more formidable challenge than I thought."

Tracy didn't have time to ask what he meant for just then a male voice at Los Angeles control came on the radio to inform her that she was now leaving his area and should turn her frequency to 123.0 for Fox Field.

She did so and found she could hear voices on that frequency. It wasn't long before Tracy sighted the airfield and pointed it out to Kirk.

She contacted Flight Service and was directed to land using her own discretion since the tower at Fox Field was closed. Carefully Tracy began her descent, keeping an eye not only on the controls but also on the sky for possible air traffic around them. There were no other planes in sight, so she lined up with the runway and brought the power back. Her hands worked busily at adjusting the flaps, while her eyes were glued to the runway that was rapidly approaching beneath them.

If takeoffs were exhilarating, landings too had their excitement. Cutting the power to slow the plane, precisely adjusting the flaps to cut the airflow and finally executing the delicate touch-down on the tarmac required concentration—especially when an expert colleague was watching the operation, Tracy thought. She applied the brakes and taxied Pegasus One around the U-shaped runway. Working the foot pedals she lined up her craft in a row of parked private planes and came to a complete stop.

"That was quite a flight," Kirk said, grinning appreciatively. "You're not only a beautiful woman, you're also a damn good pilot."

His words made Tracy feel warm all over, as though Kirk had actually caressed her. She was annoyed with herself for feeling so good about his praise. Tracy knew that she was good. There was no need for a validation from him, she thought, frowning. Yet in a fleeting second of insight she had to admit to herself that for some reason she couldn't explain, Kirk's opinion really mattered to her.

The afternoon's scorching heat enveloped them as they clambered out of the plane. It was a dry heat. Not a breeze was stirring. Kirk spread his arms, took a deep breath and, closing his eyes, raised his face toward the sun. With his dark hair, strong profile and suntanned skin, he reminded Tracy of an Inca sun worshipper. She stood in silence, enjoying his abandonment of himself to the desert.

"I like this kind of heat," Kirk explained, when he finally dropped his arms and opened his eyes. "The summers in Alaska were filled with moisture and mosquitos."

They tied down the plane with the chains that lay on the ground, and headed for the Federal

Aviation Administration building, which housed the radio station.

A friendly operator greeted them, and registered their time of arrival on *Pegasus*'s flight plan, which had been forwarded to him from the Santa Monica Tower.

"Things are so tightly controlled around here," Tracy explained as they walked toward the restaurant in the next building, "that I must cancel my flight within half an hour of arrival or we'd get the air patrol out searching the mountains for us."

The air-conditioned restaurant seemed almost too cold at first, but once they settled into a booth, Tracy was glad of the cool air soothing her burning cheeks. A middle-aged, heavy-set waitress shuffled over to their table. They ordered coffee and two large orange juices.

"I love the color in your cheeks," Kirk commented. Raising a gentle finger he caressed Tracy's face. "Your skin is like a rose petal."

An electric current ran through Tracy's whole body at his touch. It was an innocent enough gesture, yet she pulled back. Even after all her efforts to show him that she was a professional, now that they were on the ground again, Kirk seemed to regain his powerful effect on her senses. She escaped into drinking her orange juice, creating a silence between them. But as she looked up and her eyes met his, Tracy felt as though she were being drawn into the very core of his soul. She would have liked to ask why he was doing this to her, but instead, she opted for trying a safe question.

"How long were you in Alaska?" she asked attempting to sound interested but distant.

"Six years."

"What kind of planes did you use there?"

"Cessnas, Cherokees, sometimes helicopters."

"Have you quit there for good or are you planning to go back?" His short answers didn't give Tracy much to go on, but anything was better than silence and looking into his eyes, which were so full of disturbing messages.

"I left for good. Six years is enough of that kind of life," he explained.

"Do you have a family?" She knew the question sounded awkward, but looking at Kirk in the bright afternoon light she judged him to be around thirty-five and she wondered whether or not he was married.

"I've got one," he said casually, "but I don't really keep in touch with them."

He caught the shock that flashed across Tracy's face and broke into ringing laughter. "You weren't asking me about my family, you wanted to know if I am married!"

Tracy could feel the blood rising in her face.

"I love to see a woman blush," Kirk commented, his eyes sparkling with mischief.

"Well, are you?" Tracy figured that at this point she might as well be direct about it.

"Of course not," he laughed. "No woman would put up with the kind of life I lead. What about you?"

"I am single." She wondered if she should add

that she had been married. But there didn't seem to be any need for it. Besides, she didn't know him well enough to reveal such an intimate matter as her failed marriage.

"Seems like we met at the right time in our lives," he said, his eyes searching Tracy's face for agreement.

"I don't know what you mean by the 'right time,' " she demured.

"That's because you're not listening to your heart." His gray eyes looked directly into hers.

"Do you always come on so strongly?" Tracy asked averting her glance.

"Only in situations where it's vital."

"What's vital about this one?" Tracy could feel her heart beating violently. She knew she was leading him on to an answer she didn't really want to hear, but it was as if she had entered a maze and was compelled to follow its intricate corridors to the end.

"You are. We are. And where we go from here?"

"You're too intense for me, Mr. Russell." Tracy tried to rise from the table, but he placed his powerful hands on her wrists, holding her back.

"I think you and I are made of the same fabric. But for some reason you're not letting yourself go."

"I barely know you!" she cried out, in protest.

"Fair enough," he laughed, "I shall have to give you plenty of opportunity to remedy that."

The waitress returned, wanting to know if they needed anything else.

Only my peace of mind, Tracy thought.

THE VAST SAND FIELDS of the desert glowed in the golden light of the late afternoon sun as they soared above them once again.

"It's wonderful to be floating in space with you, watching this storybook scenery below. It's as if we were on a magic carpet, and anything could happen." Kirk did not say what the "anything" he had in mind was, but Tracy could read the completed message in his eyes. It alarmed her to guess what he was referring to and she quickly averted her eyes. They fell into silence, but a sweet heaviness hung in the cabin between them, quickening Tracy's heartbeat. Fighting the feeling, Tracy fiddled with the controls. A quick side-glance at Kirk assured her that he too was preoccupied with his inner world, for he was turned away from her, staring at the passing cloud formations.

In the lazy afternoon smoothness of the air, the plane was practically flying itself, and Tracy could allow her thoughts to wander. Kirk intrigued her. In time, she could see them developing a friendship—or even a closer relationship she admitted, forcing herself to be totally honest about her feelings. The memory of his arms around her earlier in the day returned and she felt a sweet longing within her that bordered on pain. On the rare occasion that someone from the opposite sex attracted her, she was too susceptible to them, she thought, trying to pin down her vague yearning. Perhaps if she had dated as a young girl, the way her friends did, she would never have fallen for George. Or if after her divorce she had been willing to frequent "the single scene," she could have gained enough experience not to respond so strongly to a man like Kirk. But she could not take sex casually. To her sex was an integral part of loving a man, not something you did just to conclude the fun of an evening. That was where she and George had differed so much, as she had painfully found out too late. To George, sex was only for fun. And marriage meant one secured playmate alongside other, more casual ones. Kirk's approaches and innuendoes bespoke the same attitude. Their differences did not preclude Tracy's wanting to be with him, but she would just have to be extra cautious not to get caught in the vortex of Kirk's masculinity, she concluded.

The San Bernardino Mountains loomed ahead, rising out of the flat landscape like great big creases in a wool blanket. The low-lying sun stretched long fingers of light across their rims, accenting the deepening shadows of the canyons. Then they were across the mountain range and over the thickening cluster of houses and roads.

"There." Tracy broke the silence between them, by pointing out the Santa Monica Airport.

Kirk straightened in his seat and watched her get ready for landing. She contacted the tower and got clearance. Like a homing pigeon Tracy glided the plane over the familiar territory and alighted on the runway smoothly, effortlessly, in a perfect landing.

"That was a good flight!" Kirk exclaimed.

Tracy gave him a brilliant, appreciative smile. She felt they had reached a subtle balance of understanding.

They rolled the plane back into the hangar. Kirk waited outside while Tracy changed into her street clothes. She emerged in her aqua-colored skirt and cream silk blouse and with her hair, released from its bonds, framing her face like a fiery halo. Kirk gave a low whistle.

"You look great," he said, his eyes roaming over her from head to toe. He approached her and before she could protest, with gentle hands Kirk placed a couple of curls closer to her chin. Then he stood back, appreciating the effect. "I've wanted to see your hair down all day," he admitted. "The color is so Titianesque...though I suspect your body is just like those lithesome beauties of Boticelli."

"You make me sound like a composite painting," Tracy said, making light of his compliment. His assessment of her body produced a strange tension within her. "Listen, I'll go home now to change and meet you later."

"I wouldn't dream of letting you out of my sight," he joked with a certain firmness in his voice. "You look beautiful just as you are. So if you'll put up with me the way I am, we'll just head for dinner."

Tracy's eyebrow rose involuntarily when at the parking lot he opened the door of a silver Porsche.

"Borrowed it from a friend," he said shrugging casually.

"He must be a very good friend."

"He is."

Kirk obviously wasn't going to elaborate on the

subject and Tracy didn't press the issue. But it made her all the more curious about him.

He drove them to a small, quietly elegant French restaurant by the beach. They sat tucked away at a corner table amidst a profusion of hanging plants that created a feeling of privacy around them. Though the food was excellent, neither of them ate much. They kept the conversation light, talking about themselves and flying, but Tracy could feel a mounting tension between them. It grew dark outside and the flickering candle on the table cast a warm glow, drawing them into a web of intimacy. Kirk's hands brushed hers as he reached for his wine glass and his touch sent shock waves through Tracy. She felt as if the light table wine had made her tipsy, but knew full well that it was the sexual tension between them that was making her head spin.

After dinner Tracy asked him to drive her back to the airport so she could pick up her car. He did, but then insisted on following her home.

She lived in Marina del Rey, in an apartment she'd bought with money inherited from her mother. It was a spacious, two bedroom apartment that overlooked the beach. She used one of the bedrooms as her study and often her best designs were created there in the still of the night. Now, apprehensive about Kirk following her, she drove at a crazy speed in and out of the little streets that led toward her home, hoping vaguely that at some turn she would lose him.

"You drive a car as if it were a plane," Kirk

commented as he drew up beside her on the walkway to her apartment.

Tracy looked up at him, and he could read the message in her eyes, for he laughed lightly. "You can't get rid of me that easily."

A sixth sense told Tracy to say good-bye to him now, before she opened the front door, however impolite that might be. So she fitted the key into the lock and turned around to face him. As though he had been waiting just for this, his two arms shot forward on either side of her. She backed up against the door for he was leaning forward so close that if she had moved an inch, she would have been pressed right up against him.

"You know what you're like?" he asked, lifting her chin with his large, well-shaped hand, while his eyes studied her features.

"What?" she asked, laughing nervously to hide her growing agitation at his nearness.

In a husky voice that made the blood surge in Tracy's body like a hot wave, he began listing what he saw: "Your hair is like burnished copper and your eyes the color of an emerald lake with golden specks of sunlight. Your skin is like the first blush on a peach."

"How poetic," Tracy interrupted, not knowing whether he was making fun of her or not. But he put a gentle finger across her lips to hush her and went on unperturbed. "And your lips...your lips are temptation...."

He leaned forward and she could feel the heat of his body while he touched her lips with his, lightly at first; then unexpectedly his mouth possessed hers in a demanding, scorching kiss. His arms molded her against him with such force that she could feel every inch of his muscular body. A sweet ache arose within her, spreading from her lower body to her lips. She returned his kiss with a passion Tracy hadn't known she could feel. As though he had turned the key to a locked door, her feelings had become unguarded and her whole being poured into the kiss. One of his hands slowly glided up from her waist and cupped one firm breast. Tracy felt a sharp, almost painful sensation as his fingers teased the aroused tip beneath her silk blouse.

She let out a low moan, and opened her eyes into the glare of the hall light.

"Someone might see us," she whispered, feeling foolish.

Without releasing his embrace, Kirk's other hand twisted the key in the lock behind her. As the door yielded, he pulled Tracy inside, shutting the door behind them.

She reached out to turn on the light, but he arrested her arm as his lips hungrily sought out hers again. She wound both her arms around him, exploring the taut muscles on his back with her palms. She felt a sweet warmth flooding her body as his lips showered the tender skin of her neck with small kisses. He deftly unbuttoned her blouse, and finding the snap of her bra, he liberated her swelling breasts. Barely knowing what she was doing, Tracy arched back with a wild desire to offer her aroused nipples to his searing lips. She raked her hands through his thick hair, pulling him to her. Then as if they had a life of their own, Tracy's hands glided down the length of Kirk's body, feeling the ripple of his powerful muscles as he molded her against him. Tracy didn't know how or when they sank onto the soft rug, but suddenly she was lying on her back, with Kirk next to her, his hard body tightly pressed against hers. Leaning on one elbow, his free hand found its way beneath her skirt and began inching toward her most intimate secrets. She felt a strange languor as her thighs parted for his burning touch.

"I want you," he murmured softly in her ear, his hot breath making her skin tingle. "I wanted you the moment I laid eyes on you in that ridiculous jump suit."

That was only this afternoon! Tracy thought, her body growing rigid at the realization. What was she doing making love with this total stranger?

"Is anything wrong?" Kirk pulled back, but continued to run his fingers through her dishevelled curls, making her skin tingle with pleasure.

Tracy sat up and hugged her knees against her naked breasts as she turned to face him. She could see Kirk's face quite clearly in the moonlight that poured through the sheer curtains of the window.

"You're too fast for me. I...I don't really know you." She stammered, feeling awkward.

"Of course you do. People like us don't need years to recognize that we are the same kind!"

"I don't know...."

"But you do. You want me as much I want you, so why not?" he persisted and tried to pull her back toward him.

"I can't..." Tracy whispered. How could she explain that by pulling away from him she had stopped the magic and her past had come rushing up to remind her that she couldn't trust her own judgment when it came to men?

Kirk knelt behind her and planted a soft kiss on her naked shoulder. "You know, all afternoon, while I watched you fly, I felt that you were challenging me...that you were showing me in a subtle way that we could be equal not only in the outside world, but also in love...."

"Perhaps we could," Tracy whispered, "but not now...not yet...."

"Is there someone else?" Kirk asked suddenly, his voice hard.

"Is it so inconceivable to you that I might want to know a man a little longer than a few hours before I become intimate with him?" Tracy asked, bristling.

She was angry now. Why did men always assume that if one didn't make love with them on the first meeting it was because of a rival? Slipping into her blouse she rose and stood by the window with her arms crossed over her breasts. Through the sheer curtains she stared at the moonlit ocean beyond the sand, too upset to look at Kirk. She wanted him but something was stopping her and now she was angry at herself and even angrier at him.

"Moments like this are too precious to waste," he said firmly as he came to stand behind her.

"They're not wasted, just arrested at this point," she stated miserably.

"I don't want to play games. I'm leaving, remember?"

"I'm not playing," Tracy protested. "But I do need a little time."

"All right—" a challenging gleam came into Kirk's eyes "—I'll give you time. You have until the next time I see you—whenever you choose that to be. You call me. I'm staying at the Century Plaza for just a week. After that . . . ." He finished the sentence with a shrug.

Long after he had left Tracy tossed and turned restlessly in her bed. Kirk's voice echoed in her ears. Her body ached for his lost embrace but she wondered how he could expect her to call him when he had made it so clear that phoning him would mean a clear commitment to going to bed with him.

She never got a chance to find out.

CHAPTER THREE

THE NEXT DAY she was awakened by the insistent ringing of the phone.

"Tracy, are you all right?"

She recognized Rosie's voice on the line. "Yes, of course I am. Why?"

"Well, you didn't come in this morning. . . ."

Tracy stared at the clock radio on the dresser. Unbelievably the red digits blinked 11:00 A.M.

"I overslept," she murmured into the phone. "I'll be right over."

"Don't come here, honey. Mr. Nolan wants you to join him for a business lunch at the Beverly-Wilshire. He's gone out and said he would meet you there."

"Who is going to be there, do you know?" Tracy asked, trying to shake the cobwebs out of her head.

"He didn't say, just told me to ask you to be there at noon."

"I'd better get moving then. Thanks for calling, Rosie."

And thanks for efficient secretaries, Tracy thought as she hung up and swung into action. Somewhere in the back of her mind she knew she had to deal with something upsetting that had taken place the night before, but for the moment she pushed the nagging recollection into the background. Tracy had always had the ability to compartmentalize events in her life. Right now she needed to dress. The final effect, created in half an hour, wasn't bad, she decided, as she took a last glance at herself in the mirror. Business lunches meant a fairly formal look, so she chose a cream-colored linen suit and accented it with a bright orange silk shirt. The shirt matched the flaming color of her hair which fell in soft waves to her shoulders. The dark brown mascara Tracy applied to her lashes brought out the brilliant green of her eyes and a touch of lipstick in the same shade as her blouse outlined the delicate shape of her lips.

She liked lunching at the Beverly-Wilshire. The opulence of the thick Persian rugs and the Bohemian chandeliers surrounded Tracy as she entered the hotel lobby. The way to the restaurant led through a hallway full of expensive shops filled with exotic merchandise. She would have loved to have lingered and looked, but she couldn't, for her father had been very specific about the hour.

Arriving on time despite her late start gave an extra lift to Tracy's bearing as she followed the headwaiter to her father's table. But before she got there, her heart skipped a beat as her eyes met the clear gray stare of Kirk Russell. He was sitting at the far end of the table, on her father's left. She continued toward the table as if drawn by some invisible force behind his eyes.

"Tracy!" her father exclaimed as he spotted her

emerging from behind the dark-suited headwaiter.

Four men rose to greet Tracy, while Anne, sitting on Ray's right, just waved her red-nailed hand at her in a familiar gesture.

"Tracy Brooke, our chief engineer." Ray presented her to the two very formally dressed men, Mr. Johnson and Mr. Garett, executives from the World Help organization. She had met them before when they had come to look at the planes. Mr. Johnson was tall and slim and Mr. Garett a man of average height with dark brown hair and an unusually pale face. Both wore dark gray business suits and even their ties were dark. The third man was Bill O'Connor, Kirk's copilot for the Ethiopia project. Tracy shook hands with all of them, taking a closer look at Bill. He was a stocky man of medium height with light brown hair and pleasant features, a far cry from Kirk's dark intensity. She wondered how the two of them got along—probably with Bill giving in on every issue, she concluded as she registered the easy-going grin on his face.

"We met yesterday," she nodded formally to Kirk. He pressed her hand tightly in his, holding it just a fraction longer than necessary. His fingers caressed her palm as he withdrew his hand and Tracy hoped no one would notice the blush that rose under the delicate skin of her cheeks.

"We're celebrating the signing of the contract," Ray informed Tracy when they were seated again, and he handed her a glass of champagne. "I tried calling you last night, to make sure you came today, but it seems you were out very late."

"Now there's a worried father, if I ever heard one," Anne chimed in.

Three pairs of eyes turned on Ray, but the fourth, with its piercing light gray color, settled on Tracy.

"Brooke's Tracy's married name," Ray explained, responding to the surprised glances. "We thought it best to have Tracy use it to give her a separate identity from the head of the company's."

"And where is Mr. Brooke?" Kirk's voice brimmed with sarcasm as he leaned toward Tracy across the table.

Before she could reply, Anne turned to Kirk with her most charming smile and said, "Oh, he's been out of the picture for a while. If you ask me, he just couldn't stand having two people wearing the pants in the family."

"Anne!" Ray exclaimed.

She looked around with a guilty smile. "Oh, dear, I shouldn't have said that."

But the damage was done. Anne's comment had made Tracy turn as red as her own hair. She faced Kirk's searching gaze for a moment but couldn't read what thoughts lay behind his eyes. They felt as cold on her as though a wall of ice had descended between them.

She sat through the joviality of the lunch with a fixed smile, wondering what was going on in Kirk's mind while he chatted with calm courtesy with the men from World Help. She watched Anne toss her brown curls around and flirt with the men around the table and wondered why Anne had made such a careless remark in front of total strangers. *Was she dumb or deliberately vicious,* Tracy wondered, looking at the other woman's bright smile as Anne directed her attention to Kirk.

"But you must see that musical," Anne insisted as she laid a hand on Kirk's arm. "If you're free Friday night, I'd be happy to go with you." Anne's long red nails reminded Tracy of the talons of a bird of prey as they dug into the sleeve of Kirk's blue blazer.

"I'll consider it," Kirk smiled politely, his glance directed at Tracy.

She knew she would have no opportunity to say anything to Kirk during lunch. There was no way to explain why she hadn't told him about her marriage until they were alone again. Since his copilot, Bill, was along, Tracy suspected she wouldn't have a chance to see Kirk alone even after lunch. The thought of phoning him for a later meeting made Tracy recall his parting words of the night before. She feared that if she asked him to see her he might misconstrue the invitation—and assume that she wanted more from their meeting than the chance to explain her marriage and divorce. While her mind went around trying to untangle her dilemma, she was somehow also able to maintain the semblance of a serious conversation with the men from World Help. They too were important in her life and she just regretted that the luncheon had gotten tangled up with her personal affairs.

Tracy's expectations about Kirk proved to be correct. He left with Bill right after lunch, shaking hands with the men and smiling at Anne, who pressed her phone number in his hand. But Kirk gave Tracy only a stiff nod. She looked after his tall figure moving easily in his well-tailored suit and felt as though she had lost something precious.

TRACY AGONIZED FOR FOUR days over whether or not she should see Kirk. But when she finally made up her mind and called, resigned to the possibility of an affair, Tracy was informed by the hotel clerk that Mr. Russell and Mr. O'Connor had checked out the day before. With a mixture of disappointment and relief, she drove to her father's office.

There, Ray explained to her that since the two *Pegasus* planes were being shipped by air cargo, Kirk and Bill had opted for starting their journey earlier than planned. They wanted to be sure of being in Ethiopia before the planes arrived. "Look, Ray, I know you're handling the Ethiopia project as far as the actual procedures are concerned. But I'm in charge of the planes, so how come I wasn't informed of this change in schedule?" Tracy asked indignantly.

"Kirk asked to deal with John Morris," came Ray's answer.

Tracy paled. "John is only second in command on the Pegasus team. He works under me...why him?"

"Tracy, you know how some men are about dealing with women, even if the woman is as good as you. Since John is almost as knowledgeable about the project as you, I figured it wasn't worth it getting you and Kirk into a tense situation at the start of the project. So I let Kirk have his wish.

"There'll be plenty of opportunity for you to prove to him that you can stand your ground against anybody," said Ray.

Wordlessly Tracy walked out of his office. If only her father knew how bad the situation was already between her and Kirk, she thought ruefully. It hurt her to hear that Kirk didn't even want to see her. Over and over she pondered what possibly could have made Kirk reject her so suddenly. She relived the brief times they had spent together, her body aching for his, and her mind raking over every bit of conversation they had had, trying to find a key to him. The only possibility she could think of was that, once he had found out that she was a divorcee, he might have resented that she had stopped their love making. Maybe he resented that she wasn't a pushover, she thought, feeling a helpless fury toward him. If that was the kind of man he was, it was just as well that he had left, she thought, consoling herself. But despite her speculations and resentment toward him, an inexplicable sense of loss pervaded her whole being.

With iron discipline she continued her work, designing other planes along the lines of Pegasus and modifying luxury aircraft for those who could afford to outfit their plane with all the modern equipment it could bear, and tried not to think of Kirk. But her heart was restless. Despite the brevity of their encounter and her efforts to forget him, Tracy yearned for his touch, and his teasing smile. The memory of his eyes staring at her after Anne's cruel comment still created turmoil within her. Tracy wished she could turn the clock back and make good her mistake of not telling him about her disastrous marriage. In her mind's eye she could recall the very hour in the sun-drenched desert when it would have been so easy for her to talk about it. . . and she hadn't. She wondered if Kirk would have left so soon had she told him the truth about herself. But there were no answers.

Even her father noticed that she wasn't her usual self. "You look so pale, Tracy. Maybe you need a little vacation. Why don't you take some time off," he suggested, coming upon her once as she sat quietly in her office, bending over drafts with unseeing eyes.

"What would I do?" she shrugged. "I am better off working. I'm going through a phase, dad, it'll pass. Don't worry about me." How could she explain to her father that no matter what she did, or where she went, she'd still have to take her troubled inner self along.

Tracy was in her father's office when the call came in from Addis Ababa. It was Kirk. He informed Ray that Bill had had a slight accident and although Bill was all right, his plane needed parts they couldn't get locally. Ray kept taking notes while he listened and Tracy stood there transfixed, watching his pencil race across the paper. She couldn't believe that it was Kirk's voice, transmitted from half way around the world, that she could hear, only slightly muffled, through the phone amplifier on her father's desk. Kirk asked for new landing gear, a new propeller, and for someone to bring the equipment in person if it were at all possible. He explained that it would take forever to get the gear out of Ethiopian customs if it were shipped through the regular channels. Ray promised to call him back as soon as arrangements were made for the replacement parts. Kirk thanked him and assured Ray that, apart from the problem they'd discussed, the project was proceeding as planned. Then the line went dead without the mention of her name.

Tracy was still staring at the phone, not quite accepting that once again Kirk was out of her life. When she caught her father's glance on her. She smiled wanly and shook her head. "It's too bad about the accident," she said, not knowing how else she could cover up her painfully exposed feelings.

"Why don't you go?" Ray suggested and Tracy's heart began to race wildly. A part of her wanted desperately to be given a second chance with Kirk, but another part cautioned her to stay away. In time she would forget him. But if she went near him again, he might break her heart.

"This might kill two birds with one stone," said Ray, continuing his train of thought out loud. "You could get out of the office for a while, and at the same time prove to Mr. Russell that you're as competent in the airplane business as any male."

While Ray spoke, an amusing idea occurred to Tracy. If she did go, Kirk couldn't accuse her of "calling him," yet it would give her the opportunity to at least clear the air between them. "All right," she said, smiling, "if you'll have the supply department get the gear together for the plane, I'll get myself together."

Ray registered delight at her uplifted spirits. "Once you're there, take some time to enjoy your stay. Look around, travel a bit, see what the country is like. Have a real vacation," he encouraged her gently. Tracy leaned forward and planted a kiss on his cheek.

"Thanks, dad, but that might depend on Mr. Russell and his operation over there."

"If I know you, you'll get him organized before he realizes what's happening," laughed Ray.

"I don't know about that man," Tracy murmured under her breath.

WHILE SHE PREPARED FOR HER TRIP TO ETHIOPIA, Tracy frequently wondered what was happening to her. Often she felt a sharp stabbing pain in her chest and had to breathe deeply to get enough air. Her mood ranged from inexplicable elation to deep despair as she took care of every necessary detail before her departure. It seemed to her that it was taking the supply department of Westwind Airlines forever to obtain the necessary parts and to crate them. The polite diplomats at the Ethiopian Embassy in Washington D.C. appeared to stonewall her repeated requests for import permits on the equipment she was to carry.

"Call back tomorrow" was the response officials kept giving her till she was ready to scream.

Her father advised patience—after all, Kirk *did* have one plane left with which to operate and if they had to wait a while for the second plane—well, it would give Bill a chance to recuperate. Tracy gritted her teeth, and went about her business as methodically as her frayed nerves would permit. Among her other preparations she also had to get immunization shots and her resulant sore arms didn't add much to her already strained mood.

Her wardrobe also concerned Tracy. She spent a day going through her closets and decided that she had virtually nothing suitable for the trip. In all honesty she had to admit to herself that, were it not for Kirk, she would have just packed her everyday clothes and have gone without a second thought. But during the month of his silent absence Tracy hadn't been able to get him out of her mind, and now, for whatever it was worth, she wanted to look her best when she saw him. Tracy had no idea what she hoped for on meeting him again. She was still angry over his sudden departure and every instinct warned her to be cautious about him. She wasn't willing to analyze why every time she thought of him her pulse raced and why the mere prospect of seeing him left her breathless. But she decided that it would be best to present a cool and sophisticated exterior that would hide her inner turmoil. With this in mind she began to shop around for clothes. After a couple of days' frustrating hunting she realized that putting together a fashionable but businesslike travel wardrobe was more difficult than she had anticipated. In utter frustration she called upon her friend Judy.

Judy, a petite, vivacious brunette, was a professional fashion designer. Tracy and Judy had been close friends since high school, and neither their widely divergent college careers, nor Judy's marriage had affected the bonds of their friendship. Kenny, Judy's tall, lanky husband, was a "brain" for the Rand Corporation, and although he didn't talk much about his work, Tracy knew that he was involved in highly technical research for the military. Occasionally Kenny would ask her questions about the construction and handling characteristics of small aircraft—information he needed for his work. During the most trying period of Tracy's marriage, it was Kenny who had been able to assure her that not all males behaved like George. It was to her friends' house that Tracy had fled the day she decided that her life with George was over.

A month after their wedding George began to make remarks about feeling too tied down. He dropped little sentences about friends who had "open marriages," and fished for Tracy's feelings on the subject. He laughed at the idea of a monogamous life-long relationship, though when Tracy asked him point-blank why he had married her if he yearned for freedom, he backed down, saying he was merely testing her. They were married only three months when he began to suggest that she leave the Experimental Branch of Westwind Airlines and work elsewhere for higher pay. That way they could use the extra money for a trip around the world. "Life is too short, honey," he told her. "Let's enjoy it while we're young."

Behaving as though they were on a perpetual honeymoon, George insisted that they go out nightly and when Tracy tried to beg off because she was too tired or had a project she wanted to work on, he intimated that she didn't know how to have fun and that this was destroying their relationship. Tracy accepted his judgment of her because, indeed, she didn't know how to cope with the kind of fun George insisted on.

It was Kenny who pointed out to her that other couples didn't have to go out nightly to have fun.

"It's like you're on a double shift," he told her. "No serious professional could get any work done on such a grueling schedule."

Then of course came the ultimate insult to their relationship and Tracy walked out on her marriage. Too embarrassed to explain to her father and Aunt Irma what had happened, Tracy fled to Judy and Kenny's house. Because her friends were of her own generation, and she could see the way Kenny treated Judy, she trusted him when he told her that some men still believed in "closed marriages." It restored her sense of balance to talk to a male who had the same value system as she had concerning love and work, and who thought that neither were to be taken frivolously. Since Judy was busy with their year-and-a-half-old daughter and she was also having health problems, it was mostly Kenny who gave Tracy support during her divorce procedures and she was grateful to him.

After her divorce Tracy buried herself in her work at Westwind. Kenny was switched to another department and his new work took up most of his time. In addition to taking care of her child, Judy also began to work part-time for a large Los Angeles manufacturer, so Tracy had not seen much of her friends over the past year. Now she felt odd calling on Judy.

"I hate to impose on you," Tracy explained as they trudged from boutique to boutique. "It would be different if you were just a friend—but dressing people is your profession! It's as if someone were asking me to help them design a plane out of friendship."

"Don't be silly," Judy laughed. "It gets me out of the house. Between taking care of Kathy and designing clothes I seem to be locked up for months at a time. Besides, it's been ages since we played dress up together. Remember how after school you used to come over to my house and I'd make you try on all my creations? You were the best model I ever had!"

"That's because I was so skinny that clothes hung on me as though I were a hanger," Tracy replied, grinning.

"But look at you now." Judy pointed at the sky-blue jump suit Tracy was trying on. "If you pull the zipper low enough, it'll reveal just enough to show how shapely you are in the chest department. And because your hips are slim, the gather below the waist gives you just the right feminine curve. And to top it off, it looks like an outfit designed for a pilot! What else do you want?"

"What other colors do these come in?" Tracy asked the saleslady, who had just peeked into the dressing room.

"White and green."

"I want those too if you have them in my size."

"Why?" Judy asked, her eyes opening wide after the saleslady had left. "You don't want to look like you're wearing a uniform!"

"But you just told me how flattering they are! So why not get several? It'll save me from looking for similar stuff!"

"Tracy, you'll never change. Here, try this."

Judy handed her friend a deceptively simple, tailored emerald-green crêpe-de-chine dress. "With a scarf this could be used for formal dinners. Without one, you could wear it for daytime business meetings."

The green underscored the red of Tracy's hair and the brilliant hue of her eyes. The soft folds of the material clung to her seductively yet discreetly in all the right places.

"I should have your figure," Judy murmured with mock envy, as she looked in the mirror at her own curvaciousness next to the elongated slimness of her friend.

Tracy laughed. "I don't think it makes one bit of difference how we're built. You've got a man who thinks you're the world's greatest . . . ."

Suddenly Judy's eyes filled up with tears and she turned her face away.

"What's wrong?" Tracy asked, bewildered. They hadn't spoken intimately for some time, and now Tracy felt a twinge of guilt for having called on

Judy only when she needed her. "Come, I'll buy you a cup of coffee. I think we've done enough shopping for today." Tracy nudged her.

"It's okay," Judy sniffed. "Let's go on."

But Tracy wouldn't. She paid for the clothes, insisting, to Judy's dismay, on actually buying all three jumpsuits in addition to the green dress and some cotton tops. "I don't want to come back next month only to find that they haven't got my size anymore," Tracy explained. "These will suit me perfectly even after the trip. Anyway, you know how I hate clothes shopping."

Judy just shook her head.

Soon after, the two of them were sitting at a small table in a sandwich shop on Beverly Drive, and Judy was pouring her heart out.

"Sometimes I think Kenny doesn't love me anymore. He is so absorbed with his work, I barely see him. I think he buries himself in his projects so he won't have to be with me. You know he used to say that he wanted some years alone with just me, and didn't want any children until later. Then I got pregnant. Now Kathy is almost three, but to date I suspect that he hasn't really come to terms with having her! Kenny acts as though he believes I got what I wanted, so he's not needed anymore."

"Have you tried telling him how you feel?" Tracy inquired.

"I never seem to get the opportunity! He comes home so late at night, and spends his weekends working, too, so the little time I get to see him, I don't want to spoil."

"Maybe it's just a phase he is going through," Tracy suggested.

Judy stirred her coffee uneasily. "I haven't told you the worst part."

"What?"

"I'm pregnant again!" Two large tears rolled down Judy's round cheeks.

Tracy reached across the table and patted her friend's hand. "Judy, you must talk to Kenny. Maybe he doesn't even realize how buried he is in his work and you're mistaking it for something personal! I can tell you from my experience that when I'm involved with making a new design the whole world could come down about my ears and I wouldn't notice!"

Judy smiled at Tracy through her tears. "He should have married you. You're both so logical and scientific."

"Now you're getting silly," Tracy objected. "Logic has nothing to do with love."

Judy sighed, admitting that it was probably her nerves that were making her say such things.

"I'd like to see you straighten things out between the two of you by the time I come back," Tracy commanded her friend lovingly.

"Talking about your trip," Judy said, suddenly smiling again, "it isn't a bit like you to be doing all these careful preparations. Who's the guy you're dressing up for?"

Tracy tried to deny that she was trying so hard for any man. "I'll be representing the company over there," she explained.

However, Judy knew her too well to accept Tracy's lame excuses and finally Tracy conceded and told her friend of her exciting but all-too-brief encounter with Kirk.

But even Judy couldn't suggest any reason why Kirk had left without a word to Tracy. If anything, she just underscored Tracy's growing suspicion that Kirk was no better than the typical Californian swinging single—out for a good time without complications.

Yet somehow Tracy couldn't believe this about Kirk. For a long time after her conversation with Judy, she mulled over her impressions of Kirk and decided that he wasn't a lightweight as were the other men who had come her way. There had to be another explanation for the rift between them. She told herself that it was obviously the hope of solving this puzzle that made her so anxious to see him again.

Finally the equipment was cleared for shipping by the Trade Department of the Ethiopian Embassy and Tracy had even received the last of the necessary inoculations.

"Stay as long as you like, at least a couple of weeks," her father encouraged as he waved her through the gate at the Los Angeles International Airport.

That depends on Kirk Russell, Tracy thought, but she didn't share the thought with her father.

THE ADDIS ABABA AIRPORT looked just like every other international airport, Tracy concluded as she studied the busy luggage area. The early morning light filtered through windows placed high in the walls but bright florescent lights gave a cold, impersonal feeling to the hall. A large sign hanging like a tapestry above the crowd bore red letters saying Ethiopia Tikdem. The phrase was also used on the seals the Ethiopian Embassy had placed on Tracy's visa and import permits. She had learned that the words meant "Ethiopia First." The slogan had been the battle cry of the revolution that had deposed the former emperor, Haile Selassie, and had established the current Socialist government. But apart from this sign the airport seemed no different from any other she had been in. Tracy and her fellow travellers had walked into the large building directly from the plane and had gone through the passport check quickly without any trouble. Now, all around her, weary passengers were dragging their luggage across the marble floor to the long counters of the waiting customs inspectors.

Tracy looked around the luggage area and saw that Kirk was not there to meet her. She sighed in secret dismay at the prospect of having to pass customs by herself. Her scanning glance caught the attention of a porter. Tracy nodded vigorously as he pointed at her luggage and asked in broken English if she needed help. On second thought, Tracy wasn't sure she should have agreed to his assistance, for the porter was a short, slightly built man who looked too frail to lift more than an average-sized suitcase. But Tracy was mistaken. Deftly the man pulled along one wooden crate after another and hoisted them quickly and easily onto the counter in front of the customs official. The official's eyebrows arched in a questioning curve as he looked first at the two crates, then at Tracy. His eyes were large and dark behind his thin, gold-rimmed glasses and she could detect more than a hint of suspicion as he pointed a finger at her packing crates.

"What's in those?" he asked in mildly accented English, ignoring her suitcase, which Tracy was more than willing to expose to inspection.

"Landing gear in here and a propeller in this one. They're for a private plane," said Tracy, patting each crate in turn as though their contents were the most everyday items to travel with. "I have an import permit for them." Tracy sensed the man's hostility so she eagerly fished around in her travel bag for the envelope sent to her by the Ethiopian Embassy in Washington D.C. she handed over her permit with as bright a smile as she could muster.

While the officer took his time reading the letter, Tracy studied him. He wore a well-pressed khaki uniform and his slim body bespoke rigidity and discipline. She guessed that despite the letter it wasn't going to be easy to convince him to let her through. Once again her eyes swept over the luggage area in the hope of catching Kirk's reassuring presence. *How inconsiderate of him not to be here when I arrived,* Tracy thought, with rising anger. It was especially inconsiderate since Kirk had specifically asked that the parts be flown in this way instead of being shipped. She was aware that a line was forming behind her. It made her uncomfortable but there was nothing she could do. Without

someone who knew how to get her through, it was
going to take time to deal with customs.

"I'm sorry," said the officer, looking up at her
over his glasses, "but these crates look like they
could contain anything. You will have to open
them for inspection."

Tracy pointed indignantly at the bright red labels
pasted on each pine box. "It says right here on the
labels what they contain! And you even have a letter to confirm it!"

"Sure, but between the time our Embassy typed
this letter and you sealed the crates, you could have
put guns in them for all I know."

"Now why would I do that?" She was getting
really irritated.

"As you may know, miss, our country is not on
the best of terms with yours. Maybe the United
States would like to help create a counterrevolu-
tion."

"You don't think...."

"I am not here to discuss politics with you, miss.
You will either open these crates, or they will not
leave the airport."

"Well, you'll need special tools to open them,"
Tracy said, shrugging. She really didn't want the
steel strapping on the crates disturbed and was hoping to discourage the man.

"We can get whatever it takes, but it will have to
wait till we get around to it." He pushed his glasses
back on the ridge of his finely shaped nose and said
sternly, "Until then, you and your luggage will be
taken into our custody."

Before Tracy could protest, he motioned the porter who had helped her before, and in a rapid, flowing language she could not understand, instructed the man. The porter brought over his luggage carrier and loaded the two crates and Tracy's suitcase on it with ease. He motioned her to follow him.

Tracy felt like a captive giant as she trailed after the porter toward the far end of the terminal. Most of the people around her were of medium height or less. They were dark-skinned and delicately boned with fine features and large round eyes. All her life Tracy had been conscious of her willowy five feet nine inches. Now she couldn't decide if everyone was staring at her because she towered over them or because of her fair skin and copper hair, or because she was being so obviously ushered into custody.

A fine mess I'm in, Tracy thought as she settled down in the cluttered office after the porter had left. She was alone. She chose a chair by one of the desks, facing the door. There were three desks in the room, all piled high with paperwork. She was puzzled at the office being empty but a look at her watch reminded her that it was only six o'clock in the morning. *It may take quite a while for that customs man to round up proper tools,* she thought. *At least until eight.* Tracy also wondered whether she should try to phone the American Embassy and ask for assistance, or go on waiting and hope that Kirk would show up. She could not understand what was keeping him. *Unless he didn't receive my cable!* The thought flashed through her mind and for a moment panic gripped her. Kirk could be out flying somewhere, and even after she was released from the airport, Tracy wouldn't have any way of getting in touch with him. Trusting that Kirk would come to pick her up, Tracy had never bothered to contact him directly. Thus she had no idea what arrangements had been made for her stay in Ethiopia. Tracy knew how to reach him once she got out of the airport, but at the moment, that seemed a dim prospect. What a lot of trouble and heartache Kirk had been to her practically from the time she'd met him!

"Excuse me, ma'am, are you Ms Brooke?" A delicately featured, handsome man stood in the doorway, wearing the uniform of the Ethiopian Force. "I am Major Hadib. I was asked by Captain Russell to come for you. I am sorry to be so late. The Jeep ran out of gas and at this hour of the morning it was hard to find a place where I could fill it." The officer smiled apologetically, his even white teeth gleaming in contrast to his dark skin.

Tracy stood up, delighted at his arrival. "Nice to meet you, major, but I'm afraid we can't leave until the customs people see the contents of my crates."

"Why would they want to do that?" the major asked, frowning.

"They suspect me of bringing guns in from the United States." Tracy could not conceal the sarcasm in her tone.

"That wouldn't be a bad idea," Major Hadib grinned. "They might work better than the Russian ones. But I believe you are only bringing in airplane parts. Isn't that so?"

"It sure is." Tracy smiled at him. She liked his quick humor.

"All right, let me see what I can do," he sighed. "Come with me, please."

Tracy couldn't understand the conversation between the customs official and the major, for they spoke in Amharic, the dominant language of Ethiopia. But she could guess a lot of what they were saying by their gestures. Major Hadib showed the customs man a little blue book that looked like his air force credentials and the officer nodded as he looked at it. From the way he handed it back it was obvious to Tracy that the major's authority had been clearly established. They talked and gestured some more and then the customs man summoned another officer. Now the three of them seemed to go over the same ground again, looking at Tracy her papers her crates and then at the major's papers. This process was followed by more conversation. Then the second officer left then returned with some forms and handed them to the major, who filled them out and signed them. After that they all smiled and the first customs man summoned a porter. He pointed at the office where Tracy's luggage was still waiting.

Soon the man returned with her suitcase and the two crates. The customs official turned to Tracy and apologized in his broken English for delaying her at the airport and wished her a pleasant stay in Ethiopia.

"For a while I thought that Captain Russell had not received the telegram advising him of my arrival," Tracy said as they made their way through the airport terminal.

"That reminds me," Major Hadib said searching the pockets of his uniform, "he sent you a note."

Tracy's heart pounded as she held the wrinkled piece of yellow paper in her hand. She was almost afraid to unfold it. What was Kirk going to tell her, that after she left the supplies with the major, she was free to go home, or that he was waiting for her phone call?

The major held the door open for Tracy and she stepped out of the airport terminal into the crisp, sunny morning of Addis Ababa.

"Wait here, please. I'll get the Jeep," he said.

The porter too stopped and waited. Tracy slowly opened Kirk's note. Scribbled with a pencil, obviously in a hurry, it read:

Sorry I can't pick you up. See you tonight at five, at the hotel bar. Kirk. P.S. Stay at the hotel, don't go wandering about town on your own.

Tracy felt greatly relieved. At least he was civilized on paper. Kirk's last remark puzzled her, but she was not going to worry about it, Tracy decided. Slightly dazed from jet lag, her one wish at the moment was to get to the hotel and relax. Sightseeing could come later.

Major Hadib lined up his Jeep by the curb. The porter loaded her crates and suitcase into the back seat and soon they were rolling through the early morning traffic of Addis Ababa. Tracy noted the tiny adobe houses and the unpaved roads and wondered what the rest of the country was like if this was how the capital looked.

"Addis is nothing like your American cities," Major Hadib commented as if guessing her impressions. "I've been to America, so I know our capital must look really primitive to you."

"It's very different," Tracy agreed. But actually she was enjoying the difference. She caught sight of three women walking down the street in a shaft of light streaming down from the early morning sun. They wore full white skirts and the billowing white shawls that had fancy embroidered edges and lay draped across their shoulders. Two of them balanced large woven baskets on their heads, and the third, a water jug. Watching the women's swaying rhythmical steps, Tracy was reminded of images from the Bible.

"We like to think of ourselves as the descendants of King Solomon," Major Hadib informed her when Tracy told him her impression.

"How so?"

"You know the story in the Bible about the Queen of Sheba's visit to King Solomon? Well, according to our legends that visit was a happy one and it resulted in this nation."

"That's a great story," laughed Tracy. "But do you mean that you are all descended from that one visit?"

"Well, that was a long time ago; we have multiplied since. Look, if you believe the Bible, the whole world started with just two people, so why not a nation?''

"I hadn't thought of it that way," Tracy said nodding. She didn't know quite what to say since she wasn't sure how serious the major was about his story.

"This our main street," the Ethiopian pointed out as he turned into a wide, paved boulevard. It was a lovely street. Lined with trees and rows of stucco buildings painted in grays and beiges, it created the impression of a European city. The major pulled the Jeep to a halt along the curb. They had arrived.

The lobby of the Hotel Addis Ababa reminded Tracy of the kind of old-fashioned resort pension she had seen in Europe. The reception desk was made of wood polished to a rich gleam, and even the telephone switchboard behind the desk was wood paneled. Tracy noted that the telephone operator was dressed in the same kind of billowing, embroidered shawl and full skirt the women on the street had worn. *The outfit must be a native costume,* she concluded.

The reception clerk, a short and friendly man, gave Tracy a bright smile as she told him her name.

"We'll give you a lovely room, Miss Brooke," he promised.

"I could do with a quiet room," Tracy said sighing. "I didn't get much sleep during the past few days."

"All right, we'll give you a lovely quiet room," the clerk replied with a grin.

A bellboy took her up in the elevator. On the fourth floor Tracy was led to a corner room that looked out on an inner courtyard. It was neatly furnished with old, dark, European pieces.

"If you need anything, just call downstairs." The bellboy put her suitcase on a luggage bench and hauled her crates under the window. He waited a moment while Tracy searched her handbag for change. When she tipped him, he grinned as he folded the bill.

"American dollar. We don't see much of these any more. Mostly Russian people come here now."

After he left, Tracy decided to shower to refresh herself before getting on with what promised to be a long day. She adjusted the stream of water to be as hot as her skin could bear and let the spray flow over her body. Tracy hadn't realized till now, how chilled she had become in the cool air of the morning. While she relaxed her limbs under the hot stream Kirk's note came back to her mind. *What did he mean? What sort of danger is he protecting me against?* she wondered. Of course, as a red-haired Caucasian woman in an African country, Tracy would stand out were she to tour the town—but so what? Why couldn't Kirk be more specific, she thought, annoyed. Yet she couldn't allow herself to get irritated at him for such small things. If she did, her trip might be wasted not only from a personal, but also from a professional point of view. While she was there, Tracy intended to see the food drop operation, and it wouldn't do her much good to be at war with Kirk. From the brief encounter over lunch that she had had with Bill O'Connor, the other pilot, it seemed to her that Bill was an easier person to deal with than Kirk. But then, Bill wasn't in charge; Kirk was.

Thawed out and feeling refreshed, Tracy shut off the shower and dried herself on one of the large, rough-textured terry towels in the bathroom. She padded back into the room and dug her robe out of her suitcase. The newly purchased, peach satin dressing gown clung to her warm skin with cool sensuousness. Tracy looked at her other clothes knowing she should hang them in the closet but decided to do it later. The bed looked too inviting. She rolled back the bedspread and slipped under the blankets. As soon as Tracy closed her eyes she felt as though great rolling ocean waves were rocking her gently from side to side. She smiled as she recognized the long flight syndrome. The feeling of motion would remain with her for several hours, she thought, so she might as well relax and let the illusion of rocking lull her to sleep.

CHAPTER FOUR

WHEN SHE AWOKE her watch showed 3:00 P.M. She felt strangely disoriented and figured it was because she had slept during the day. *Or is it because at home it would be the middle of the night,* she wondered. A nap couldn't just erase the ten-hour time difference. Tracy lingered under the warm blankets, thinking again of what she wanted to accomplish during her stay. Topping her list was finding the right opportunity for a talk with Kirk, but she dismissed that as frivolous in the face of her other responsibilities. Her father did suggest that she make this trip a vacation, but even he would expect his chief engineer to find out what had caused the accident involving Bill's plane. Also, Tracy wanted an opportunity to test the planes under field conditions herself. Suddenly, she laughed out loud. If Kirk had left instructions for her not to leave the hotel, how would he feel about Tracy flying around the countryside on her own? Although he knew that she could fly, this was Kirk's territory and she could just imagine the kind of sparks her wish might provoke. *Take it one step at a time,* Tracy told herself. *It's like building a machine. When all the parts fit, it will*

*work. But right now, your clothes need hanging,
your stomach needs lunch and your brain needs to
get into gear again.* Tracy reluctantly rolled out of
bed and searched for her slippers on the floor.

She unpacked, removing the thin plastic sheets
layered between her clothes to prevent wrinkling.
She was glad that she had taken the time to coor-
dinate her wardrobe. She hung up the jeans and
two of the three jump suits she and Judy had
found. The jump suits would do nicely for flying
and touring. For city wear she had brought two
pairs of tailored slacks: a dark gray pair with thin
white stripes, and a tan pair. The drawers in the
old-fashioned dresser stuck when Tracy tried to
pull them out, but finally she managed to store
away her blouses and her cotton and knitted silk
tops which mixed and matched with all her slacks.
The cream-colored pants suit with the cobalt-blue
shirt, which Tracy had worn during her flight, had
a matching skirt that would instantly transform
the outfit into a business suit. Having learned that
in the summer the temperature in Addis Ababa
hovered around the seventies, she had brought
two sweaters. Her emerald-green crêpe-de-chine
dress, which she would wear with the Dior scarf
Judy had given her as a going away present, completed her wardrobe. Satisfied, Tracy closed her
closet door.

"It all fits so neatly together. Why, you haven't
got an extra piece in your suitcase!" Judy had
noted enthusiastically.

"Oh, I'll probably pick up some exotic outfits

while I'm there so why drag a lot of stuff halfway around the world with me?'' Tracy had responded.

As she recalled this conversation, Tracy thought about the billowing dresses of the local women. She decided she would ask the telephone operator where she could get one of the native costumes.

For her first meeting with Kirk Tracy wanted to look fairly formal but not overly so. Thus she chose her tailored tan slacks, a knobby, peach-colored silk sweater that buttoned in front like a blouse, and high-heeled sandals that matched the color of her slacks. With Kirk she didn't have to worry about being too tall, Tracy thought, smiling to herself.

It was after four o'clock when she went downstairs and the woman operator had gone. The operator on duty was a man. He explained that Miss Sarah, the operator Tracy was looking for, would be back in the morning.

The restaurant's kitchen was closed, but Tracy could get a snack in the bar if she wished, the reception clerk informed her. Tracy decided against that because it would mean going in to the lounge before Kirk arrived, and that might make her appear eager. *I'll wait another hour for a snack,* she told herself. *It won't kill me.*

''Do you think it would be okay for me to walk around outside the hotel a bit?'' Tracy asked the clerk.

''Of course. Why not?''

''Just asking,'' she said breezily, and leaving

her key on the counter, Tracy strolled through the revolving doors.

She felt a distinct pleasure in defying Kirk's note. But she didn't plan to go far—only for a walk up and down the street, to get the feel of the place. She stood still for a moment. Temporarily blinded by the bright sunshine, Tracy closed her eyes. She opened them to find herself surrounded by six or seven children of various ages, staring at her and talking animatedly in their native tongue. Some of the bigger ones reached up toward her hair, and one even touched it, causing Tracy to panic for a moment. She felt an urge to turn around and flee back to the safety of the hotel, but then she straightened her shoulders as her father's voice echoed in her mind: "When faced with adversity, a Nolan doesn't run." She smiled bravely at the youngsters and headed across the street, hoping they would stay behind. They parted their circle to let her pass but followed at her heels, their voices twittering like birds. Tracy scanned the street, trying to decide which way to go. But the buildings along the boulevard all seemed to be offices or apartments; she could not see a single shop window to explore. As she stood there trying to decide which way to go, several young men approached her, each holding a bunch of painted scrolls and waving them at her. One, who spoke English, explained:

"We are selling paintings of the story of Solomon and Sheba. But don't buy from the others; the quality of their work is not good. Look at mine."

He unrolled a scroll, and as if on cue, so did the

others, and instantly they started shoving their merchandise in Tracy's face and pushing at each other, trying to monopolize her attention.

"I am a poor student," the one who spoke English protested. "These others are just vendors, and they are selling machine-made paintings. But mine are handmade. I am putting myself through school with these."

Tracy scrutinized his work and those of the others but she couldn't see any difference between them. They all seemed to have been made the same way. Painted in a flat, Byzantine style, without perspective, they portrayed round-eyed people in Biblical robes in a series of situations. Tracy could not distinguish between the men and the women in the drawings, but she could see that some of the figures were white while others were dark skinned.

"Here, I'll explain the story." The one who said he was a poor student pushed the others away and ignoring their angry protests he started to explain the first picture on the scroll.

"Here is where the Queen of Sheba reads the invitation to come and visit Solomon." The man's finger moved to the next frame. "Here she prepares for her trip. The queen is taking gifts and a hundred servant girls to Solomon. Here she is crossing the desert, and here she is received by King Solomon."

"I thought I told you not to leave the hotel on your own!" roared a deep male voice just behind Tracy, shattering her concentration on the story—which she had been finding rather charming.

"Hello, Captain Russell. As you can see, I'm doing just fine, thank you," Tracy said, whirling around to face Kirk with a defiant smile. It was absurd the way her heart began to pound when her eyes met his gaze.

"You're lucky," he said, too angry to return her greeting. Then he turned to the vendors who hung around them like a pack of hungry wolves and spoke to them in Amharic. Tracy assumed that he had ordered them to leave, for they grumbled but began to move on—except for the student. "What are you waiting for?" Kirk growled at him in English.

"I was telling this lady the story of the scroll," the young man explained. "Are you her husband?"

"What business is that of yours?" Kirk snapped.

"If you are, maybe you would like to buy her this exquisitely painted work from a poor student."

It appealed to Tracy that the young man was obviously unperturbed by Kirk's temper.

"And how much are you asking for that 'exquisitely painted' work?" Kirk mocked him.

"Eighty birrs."

"Are you kidding!" Kirk laughed.

"That's only forty American dollars, and it would buy me food for a couple of weeks."

"I'll take it," Tracy cut in, reaching for the scroll.

"You're not a student!" Kirk laid his hand on

Tracy's and pulled it back, keeping his gaze on the young Ethiopian.

Tracy didn't know what to make of this exchange between Kirk and the young man. Her hand, trapped in Kirk's powerful grip, felt strangely at home. Despite the tension of the situation she began to feel the warmth that radiated from his palm to hers slowly creeping up into her face, painting it pink. She stopped concentrating on the argument between the two men and began to wonder what it was about Kirk that made her respond in such a way to his mere touch. But Kirk didn't seem to be distracted by Tracy. Something drove him to continue the fight.

"Admit it," he insisted, "you're not a student."

"So maybe if I am not, what difference does it make?" The young man seemed cornered and his English grammar suffered.

"You get your merchandise at the same place as these others," Kirk went on relentlessly, pointing at the vendors who were now following the argument with great interest even though they couldn't understand what was being said.

"Look, why don't I just buy this thing and you can stop arguing!" Tracy interrupted, freeing her hand.

"Because I hate liars. Besides, you'd be overpaying him," Kirk stated firmly.

"It's just a souvenir for me." Tracy was surprised at herself for pleading with him.

"I'll give you fifty birrs for it," Kirk offered the young man, pulling out his wallet.

"The price is eighty." The youth glared at Kirk.

"Then forget it." Kirk took Tracy by the elbow and started to guide her away.

"Stop treating me like a child," Tracy protested and stood her ground.

"Of course. I am sorry." Kirk said, his gray eyes mocking her. "I forgot that you are not a defenseless female, but Tracy Brooke, alias Nolan, the boss's daughter. You do as you please, Miss Nolan." He bowed, stepped away from her and waited.

Tracy noted the sarcastic way he had brought up her status and his use of her maiden name, but choosing to ignore it, said softly, "You don't need to wait for me."

"We'll go together," he informed her coolly.

Tracy turned to the vendor. "I'll buy that piece. But I only have traveler's checks with me. If you accompany me to the hotel I'll exchange some for local money."

The young man looked around him, obviously displeased. "I don't want to go into the hotel with you," he finally said.

"Of course not. Because there they'll recognize you as a vendor with a story as good as Solomon and the Queen of Sheba's," Kirk quipped. "So if you want your sale, I'll give you fifty birrs. If not, scat."

Before Tracy could protest the young man exchanged the scroll for the money.

"Thank you, madam. Thank you, sir. May you be as happy together as Solomon and the Queen of

Sheba were,'' he said with a grin, and bowed. Then he ran off, followed by the rest of the vendors.

Tracy's spine tingled with a curious shiver at the vendor's blessing but Kirk's face betrayed no emotion.

"Here." He pushed the scroll into her hand and took her arm to walk her across the street. "And next time stay where you're told to stay."

"I'm not used to being ordered around," she protested wriggling away from him.

"I'll bet you're not! But as long as I am head of operations here you'd better get used to it. You have no idea what trouble you could get into around here."

Tracy stopped in front of the hotel challenging him. "I wish you'd tell me."

"For starters, some Ethiopians are no longer fond of Americans and you could get stoned if they managed to get a crowd together. Or some Muslim male might decide that as a lone foreign female you wouldn't be a bad-looking addition to his household as a third wife."

Tracy shuddered. "Why didn't you explain this a little clearer in your note?"

"I had to fly to the base at dawn and had no time for lengthy notes. But when I give an order it's usually enough for my men."

"Vive la différence," laughed Tracy, looking up at him.

"I wouldn't suggest that you remind me of the difference—" Kirk's eyes met hers "—unless of course you want to make something of it." His suggestive smile flashed through Tracy like lightning and left her feeling somewhat shaken.

Kirk stood aside at the revolving door to let her go first. But then he quickly stepped into the same wedge as Tracy. In the tight space his body molded against hers.

"I've forgotten the delicious scent of your hair," he murmured above her head.

Tracy could feel his hot breath through her hair. Kirk's nearness caused an almost painful tightening in her chest and she had to breathe deeply as they came through to the lobby.

"Bill is meeting us in the bar," Kirk informed her. Only his curiously veiled eyes indicated that he too had been touched by their momentary closeness. His face betrayed no emotion as he led her toward the molded archway.

"How is he?" Tracy felt a bit guilty. All this time had passed between her and Kirk and she hadn't even thought of Bill. After all, the man had had a plane accident!

"Got away with just a little trouble," Kirk replied smiling. "He'll tell you about it."

"Is the plane badly damaged?"

"Not too bad. Let's settle down first."

The bar, like the rest of the hotel, was imbued with Old World charm. Handmade lace curtains covered the tall, shuttered windows, and wallpaper, flocked with a deep red rococo design, gave the room a sense of intimacy. On all the small, round tables, red tapers flickered. On the bar two large copper espresso machines gleamed, while on the shelves against the wall stood a colorful display of liquor bottles. But except for the bartender, no one else was there.

"I guess he is a little late," Kirk shrugged as he chose a table for them in the back. "What would you like? At this hour it's 'get it yourself' around here."

"Something light," Tracy requested. "What with the trip and the time difference, I feel a bit light-headed even without a drink."

Kirk nodded and left. While he was gone, Tracy leaned back against the soft velvet upholstery of the seat and closed her eyes. She wasn't kidding about feeling light-headed. Kirk's presence and the seeming unreality of the whole situation was beginning to have an effect on her. With her eyes closed, Tracy began to wonder, was she really sitting in a bar halfway around the world from Los Angeles, waiting to have a drink with a stranger who made her heart beat faster? Or was she just dreaming and as soon as she awoke would she be in her Marina del Rey apartment? Tracy opened her eyes and saw Kirk's tall, muscular body, which moved with controlled ease as he approached her. He carried a drink in each hand. *He looks more like a cowboy than a pilot,* Tracy thought. *Perhaps he is a cowboy, but instead of horses, he rides planes. A skyrider, that's what he is,* she thought, and the image of him in a small open-cockpit plane, with a white scarf streaming in the blue sky, made her smile.

"I got you a Dubonnet. It should hold you until dinner."

"I haven't had lunch yet. You don't suppose I could start with that?" Tracy asked, smiling up at him.

"You poor child, why didn't you say something! I'd forgotten how your schedule can go haywire in coming over. Did you do it in one stretch?"

"I went from L.A. to London. I missed my connection there, so I had to spend a night in a hotel at Heathrow. The next morning I flew to Rome and from there caught the night flight to Addis."

"That was only this morning. You must be exhausted."

"Not really. I took a nap when I got here."

Tracy was amused at his concern, which seemed genuine. It was a new side of Kirk. She rolled the liqueur glass between her long slim fingers—there were so many things about Kirk that she didn't know. She looked at him and, meeting his eyes, felt unsettled for a moment. To maintain her balance with him, it seemed best to keep up a light conversation. She turned to him.

"When you first spoke to the vendors outside, you talked to them in Amharic. Do you know the language?"

"A little."

"How come?"

"I make it a habit to learn at least some basic vocabulary and the grammar of the language of any country I travel to. When it looked like I really was going to take on this job, I began to study Amharic. That was three months ago and I'm pretty quick with languages. Being able to use it helps, too.''

Tracy couldn't help but admire the simplicity with which Kirk dismissed his unusual approach to a language.

''I had trouble learning even high school Spanish,'' she admitted, smiling.

''It's a question of determination,'' Kirk said, shrugging. ''If you had an interest in learning a language I bet you would. I do it because it helps me get around in out-of-the-way places. Also, I consider it common courtesy toward the natives of a country. If they came to the States I'd expect them to know some English, so why not the other way around?''

She really liked his attitude. When the sexual tension between them subsided and they just talked, she really liked Kirk as a person, Tracy decided. He seemed at ease now, charming, and approachable. Suddenly she wondered whether the mood wasn't right for her to have that talk with him. They were sitting together almost like friends—he might actually answer her question. Then she saw Bill O'Connor coming through the doorway. He stood still a moment, then spotting them, headed toward their table.

''I'm glad to see you in one piece,'' Tracy said, smiling as she watched him lower himself cautiously into a chair.

''I'm glad I'm in one piece to see you,'' Bill quipped.

"Oh, that Irish wit of yours," Kirk moaned. "I can't take another minute of it, so I'll go get you a drink. What do you want?"

Bill noted the Scotch in Kirk's glass. "Same as yours. But being as I'm sick, you can bring me a soda on the side, too," he said, grinning at his partner.

"Tell me what's wrong with you. Then tell me about what happened," Tracy urged Bill.

"It's better if I tell you about the plane first," Bill suggested. "Then you'll understand what's happened to me."

"Any way you wish," Tracy said obligingly.

"It was late afternoon and we were making our last food drop into a valley not too far from camp. As usual, I slowed down to a near stall so I could make the drop without splitting the bags. When I was done I hit the throttle to gain altitude, but instead of climbing, the plane started sinking toward the ground. All I had time for was to try to clear the rocks. Fortunately the kids and goats moved when they saw I was going to land. I wish rocks had the same sense. Some of the rocks were the size of small boulders. Of course I used all the braking power I had, and maneuvered the best I could, but I still hit a rock. It buckled the nose wheel and bent the prop out of shape, but at least I stopped without a ground loop."

Tracy wondered if it was engine, or pilot, failure that had caused the plane's inability to rise. But this was no time to ask. Instead, she concerned herself with Bill. "What about you?"

"On my last mishap, in Alaska, I got away with

just a dislocated disk. This time the doctors tell me I've got a cracked disk.'' Bill saw Tracy's eyes open wide so he quickly added, ''Just a hairline crack. I'm told it will heal if I don't strain my back and don't make any sudden moves.''

''That means you're safe from him,'' Kirk cut in, setting Bill's drink before him. Then, turning to Tracy, he said, ''I asked the bartender to make you some hors d'oeuvres, but this is all he could produce.'' He set a bowl of green olives before Tracy.

''I love 'em,'' Tracy beamed, pleased by his thoughtfulness.

''So what happened after you landed?'' She was eager to hear the rest of Bill's story.

''I had gone ahead by then,'' Kirk said, picking up the story where Bill had left off, ''but when I noticed that Bill wasn't coming into camp right behind me, I turned back to look for him. Fortunately the drop sight was only twenty minutes away.''

''He didn't just fly back,'' Bill interrupted, ''he came back with a stretcher and two men.''

''I figured, if Bill had crashed, I'd need the help,'' Kirk explained, shrugging.

''What did you do then? Land, too?'' Tracy's throat was so dry that she could barely get the words out. It was incidents like the one Kirk and Bill were describing that made her feel inadequate. There was no way to make a plane perfect, no way to prepare it for all errors and emergencies. Upset, she took a sip of her drink.

"We circled overhead while Bill directed the villagers to clear the larger rocks from an area so we could land."

"So you picked up Bill and left the plane there?" Tracy was jumping ahead of the story.

"We left one of our people with the plane with a tent and supplies. He is still there. That's why it was so urgent that we get the new gear," Kirk explained.

"I'm glad you weren't hurt seriously," Tracy sighed.

"Not Bill," Kirk looked at his friend with pride. "This man has nine lives."

"How many have you got left, though?" Tracy teased.

"With this latest accident I've used up my seventh," Bill replied, grinning.

"And how many have you got left?" Tracy asked, turning to Kirk.

He returned her joking gaze with unexpected intensity. "Just one. But I intend to live this one right."

Kirk's eyes telegraphed their message only too clearly. Tracy looked away.

"How about another round, for a toast to all of us live and lively people?" Bill said, breaking the silence.

"I'll get it." Kirk rose.

While he was gone Bill looked at Tracy's troubled face and patted her hand. "Don't take him too seriously. Kirk isn't a bad sort. But as he says, he wants to have things his way in life. And as long as I've known him, his way means to live dangerously and to just have fun—if you know what I mean.''

Tracy felt as though she had a sudden lump in her throat. ''You really are quite close to him, aren't you?'' Tracy asked, although she already knew the answer.

''Oh, yes. We were together in Alaska for five years, and we stayed partners when we came back. That's why we're doing this job here together, too. We're real good buddies.''

Tracy was suddenly thankful that she'd never got that call through to Kirk in Los Angeles. Knowing what she now did, it was no longer essential that she find out why Kirk had left L.A. so abruptly, or why he might have been angry with her. It hurt her, but she decided that even though he was the most exciting man she had ever met, he wasn't for her. Tracy had had enough of playboys with George. *This time I won't get involved,* she thought grimly as she watched Kirk returning to the table, balancing a small tray on his palm, mimicking a waiter. *If only he weren't so attractive,* she thought with an aching heart.

''To life!'' Bill raised his glass.

''To your stay,'' Kirk added saluting Tracy.

And to your staying away from me, thought Tracy, closing her eyes while she took a sip.

''Let's go have dinner,'' Bill proposed, and gingerly raised himself out of his chair.

They crossed the lobby to the hotel dining room. As the headwaiter led them to their table,

Tracy noted that most of the people eating there appeared to be European.

"Many of the guests here are Russian," Kirk explained to her. "They're ostensibly in Ethiopia as advisers, but in reality they're making sure that the government sticks to a socialist policy suitable to Moscow."

Tracy looked across the tables with open curiosity. At the far end of the room her eyes were met with an equally inquisitive look from a burly blond man who was dining alone. He smiled at her, a gold tooth gleaming in his mouth. For a moment it looked as though he was going to rise and come over to their table, but then Tracy shifted her glance.

All three of them ordered a simple but flavorful dinner of roast veal in lemon sauce, vegetables, rice pilaf and salad. Between bites, they talked mostly about flying and about each one's reaction to danger.

"When you're actually in trouble, you only think of ways to solve the problem—not about crashing," Kirk commented.

"It's only afterward, when you're hurt but alive that you really get scared," Bill laughed. "That's when it hits you that you could have died. Then you don't even care about being hurt because you're so thrilled to be alive."

A four piece band at the far end of the dining room struck up a dance tune.

Tracy's insides churned as she listened to the sensuous melody. She looked down and pretended to concentrate on her sherbet because she was afraid Kirk would detect in her eyes how much she yearned to be taken in his arms and move with him to the rhythm of the music.

"Even when my back wasn't cracked, I was no good at this stuff," Bill grumbled apologetically, guessing Tracy's desire to dance.

"What makes you think Miss Nolan would want to dance with either of us?" Kirk eyes sparkled as he waited for her response.

Tracy wondered why he had called her Miss Nolan again, but she didn't have time to ask for just then a shadow fell over the table. She looked up to find herself facing the burly man from across the room.

"May I have this dance with you?" the stranger asked in heavily accented English.

It only took a second for Kirk to catch the hesitation on Tracy's face. "She has already promised this one to me," he said stepping in and pulling Tracy up by her hand.

The Russian stood aside to let them pass and, with a friendly smile, asked, "Your wife?"

"What else?" Kirk replied with a shrug.

"She is beautiful. I am sorry to disturb you." And the Russian trotted back to his own table.

Tracy wished she could suppress the sweet ache that gripped her whole being when Kirk enfolded her in his arms. He held her so close that she could feel every muscle in his body. The faint odor of his shaving lotion, mixed with the aroma of his skin nearly made her dizzy. Kirk's powerful thighs pressing against hers made Tracy feel as if liquid fire was racing through her veins. He nuzzled her hair with his lips and Tracy could feel his soft kiss to the very tip of her toes. A deep sigh broke from her as Kirk's lips brushed against her cheeks and down the sensitive skin of her neck. Her body molded to his with a life of its own and a wild desire rose within her to touch his lips with hers. *I mustn't let him overwhelm me,* she thought frantically, fighting the urge. *It's just chemistry, and I'll only get hurt in the end.* But it was safe on the dance floor, and Tracy allowed herself to close her eyes and enjoy the magic of being in Kirk's arms as he guided her through the melting sounds of the music.

"What a wonderful dancer you are. Do you do everything so well?" Kirk murmured in her ear, his hot breath making her skin tingle.

"That's for you to find out." The words escaped before Tracy realized their full meaning, but Kirk's peal of laughter showed that he had not missed it.

"I didn't mean it the way you think," Tracy stammered, the color deepening in her already flushed cheeks. "It's just that I am getting a little tired and I wasn't paying attention. Now if you don't mind, I'd like to leave."

"Of course." Kirk was as solicitous as though he were conceding to a child. "How inconsiderate of me. But holding you close made me forget what a long day you've had. Come, I'll take you to your room."

"That's not necessary." Tracy tried to appear cool but her insides screamed "danger!" She remembered well what had happened the last time Kirk had escorted her home.

But he insisted. Tracy gathered her purse and the scroll from the table and said good night to Bill.

"I'll see you later." The copilot waved at her and added with a good natured smile, "And like I told you, watch out for old Kirk here, he's a lady killer."

"I am sure she can take care of herself," Kirk said, snapping at his friend with surprising sharpness.

Upstairs, Kirk asked to come into her room to look at the crates.

"It's a mess," Tracy protested.

"I've seen women's intimate wear before," he assured her.

"Stop making fun of me," Tracy was indignant.

"Then stop behaving as if I were interested in your housekeeping," he retorted harshly.

Without a further word Tracy opened the door and let him pass. Kirk spotted the crates right away. They were stacked against the wall beneath the window.

"They're a little big, but I guess we could squeeze them into the cargo compartment." He rubbed his chin thoughtfully. It was a gesture Tracy recognized from their first meeting. The familiarity of it pleased her. She watched him, realizing that he hadn't considered the steel cables wrapped around the crates.

"Those straps are designed so that you can hook a crate under each wing—like a grain sack," Tracy quietly informed him.

"I suppose you thought of that," Kirk's eyes lit up with admiration. "Clever woman!" Then, with a move so swift that she barely registered it, he was by her, his arms around her waist, pulling her close to him. "I was hoping you'd use this opportunity to come to me," he whispered, "though heaven knows I should keep away from you." Tracy was going to ask Kirk what he meant but there was a strange, brooding expression in Kirk's eyes that forbade her questions.

Instead, pressing her hands against his broad chest to pull away from his embrace, and using the coolest tone she could muster, she said, "I happen to be the chief engineer on this project. No matter what it looks like to you, I didn't come after you. My sole interest was the plane."

"Is that so?" A slow, deliberate smile broke around his lips as he studied her flushed face. "Let's see if you're telling the truth."

Before Tracy could stop him his lips crushed hers possessively. She struggled wildly against him, and against her own surging desire, but to no avail. His powerful arms pinned Tracy against him till she felt all resistance drain from her. She melted against him, returning his kiss, her lips pliant and responsive under his searching tongue. With a flash of insight Tracy realized that her body would betray her to Kirk as easily as he now lifted her onto the bed.

"Don't," she protested pushing his hand away as Kirk began to unbutton her sweater.

He stopped abruptly, his eyes filling with anger.

"Anything you say," he mocked as he moved away from her. "Just don't lie to me that your sole interest is in a plane."

"You're a beast!" she cried out, rolling off the bed.

"I told you last time, I don't play games." Kirk smiled almost menacingly. "And before you return to your safe little world, maybe you'll learn how not to, either." He headed for the door, adding, in a tone that was suddenly calm and impersonal, "I'll see you tomorrow at noon in the lobby. We have a lunch date with an official. His name is Colonel Teshome. He is the assistant to the Minister of Relief. It's sort of an unofficial official invitation to welcome you. Try to get some rest; later on, you might not get a chance." A fleeting smile crossed his face. Then he left and slammed the door behind him. Tracy told herself she would do the minimum, just to prove to Kirk that she had come to do a job. Then she would head for home. And the sooner that is, the better, Tracy decided.

CHAPTER FIVE

BY SIX O'CLOCK THE NEXT MORNING, Tracy was up and pacing her room. She knew her restlessness was partly jet lag, but also it was the memory of Kirk's touch that had kept her tossing and turning all night. Sometime between her fitful sleep and waking Tracy had decided not to run home, as had been her first impulse after Kirk had left her room. Instead, Tracy determined that she would learn how to handle both her feelings and Kirk's advances. She realized that although she was twenty-six years old, she was as inexperienced with men as a teenager half her age. It mattered little that she had been married and that George had taught her a few things about making love. Indeed, her marriage had made Tracy all the more vulnerable, for it had awakened her dormant sexuality. But George had also hurt her deeply and it was her pain, which still lingered, that had prompted her to want to run from Kirk and his dangerous magnetism. With a half smile Tracy remembered one of the important rules about flying: if you crashed and wanted to get over the fear of flying again, you had to get into another plane—as soon as it was reasonably possible—and fly. Could this same rule apply to love?

she wondered. Somehow, Tracy didn't believe it. Feelings were not the same as machines. Machines were predictable and, if you maintained them, quite reliable. Even with her limited experience with love, Tracy knew that feelings could be totally irrational and unreliable. But still, she wouldn't run.

She might not have the courage to pilot a flight of love again, but she would at least stay aboard and see if she could get along with the captain, whose every gesture etched itself into her nervous system.

Bill's casual remark about Kirk's attitude toward life bothered her. Tracy wished she had had a chance to explore it further. If indeed Kirk sought only fun out of life, the incident between them in Los Angeles was insignificant. She had merely provided him with a day's entertainment. Then in some way she had displeased him, so he had forgotten about her. She had been too much trouble. But if he didn't care, then why would Kirk want to prove that she was attracted to him? A shiver ran through Tracy at the memory of his fervent lips and powerful arms as he had held her tightly. Something was out of line. She needed to talk to Bill again. Maybe he could help her figure out Kirk. She would have to look for another opportunity during her stay.

Tracy sighed and looked at her watch. It was nearly seven. She recalled that the telephone operator was supposed to come back on during the morning shift, so she called downstairs to find out what time the young woman would be arriving. Much to her surprise Sara answered the switchboard phone. Tracy asked her where she could buy a native dress similar to hers. The young woman laughed.

"We buy the fabric and make it ourselves, or have a dressmaker make it," Sarah explained. "If you'd like, I get off work this morning at ten, and I could go shopping with you. You can buy the fabric and have the dress made at the same store."

"That would be wonderful," Tracy responded enthusiastically. Then she remembered her noon appointment with Kirk.

"If you have to return by lunchtime, you might want to go earlier," Sarah suggested. "You know, my husband is the night manager of the hotel, and he'll be getting off his shift shortly. If you'd like, I'll ask him to go with you."

Not knowing what her schedule would be like during the next few days, Tracy felt she should take advantage of this opportunity, so she accepted Sarah's offer and agreed to meet Ato Negussay, Sarah's husband, in a half hour in the lobby.

Tracy dressed with a sense of purpose, feeling very much like her old self as she rushed through the morning procedure. When she returned from shopping she would groom far more carefully for her lunch date, but for now, almost any clothes would do. She slipped into jeans and a crisp white blouse. She pinned her hair back in the hope that her red mane would attract less attention than if it were flying loosely about her face. A thin layer of mascara on her lashes, was all the makeup she needed. Tracy threw some traveler's checks into her handbag and buckled the straps of her open sandals. *Father was right,* she thought happily as she bounced out of the room, *it's fun to be able to take off some time away from home.*

Ato Negussay was waiting for her near the switchboard. He was a handsome man and he and Sarah made a good-looking couple, Tracy remarked, to the young woman's delight. Before leaving, Sarah's husband insisted that Tracy have some breakfast and she asked him to keep her company while she ordered a roll and coffee. The roll, similar to a Kaiser roll, was served with butter and jam on the side. Tracy found the coffee aromatic and far stronger tasting than the kind she normally drank in the States.

"Did you know that coffee originated in Ethiopia?" her companion asked.

"Really?" Tracy laughed, for she couldn't help thinking, that it was national pride that prompted his claim. But Ato Negussay was oblivious to the cause of her amusement.

"The story goes," he began, "that in the town of Kaffa, in the southwest part of Ethiopia, some monks observed that whenever their goats ate the berries of a certain bush, they would become very high-spirited. One of the more adventurous monks tried the berries himself, and discovered that they helped him stay awake during the long hours of night devotions. And that is how coffee came into usage. The Arabs claim that they came up with the idea of roasting coffee for fuller flavor. But that can't be proven. Wherever the custom came from, though, it's sure a good idea."

"I'll say," Tracy agreed.

Finishing her coffee, Tracy rose from the table and nearly bumped into the burly Russian she'd seen in the restaurant the night before. He grinned broadly and said in his heavily accented English, "Ah, the beautiful American lady. If I had known that you were eating breakfast alone, I would have rushed to keep you company."

"As you can see, I'm not alone," Tracy indicated her companion, who discreetly stayed a step behind her.

"I meant without your husband," the Russian said, grinning.

"Good day, sir." Tracy moved around him.

"My name is Alyosha, Alyosha Sergeievich. I am an engineer. If I can be of any service to you. . . ."

"Nice meeting you, Mr. Sergeievich. Now if you don't mind, I'm rather in a hurry."

"How long are you staying?" the persistent Alyosha called after her, but Tracy pretended not to hear him.

"They're everywhere," murmured Ato Negussay. "I know they're here to help us build a better economy but we sure don't like them as much as we liked the Americans. Even the Italians were better, I'm told. They mixed with our people. The Russians make us feel like strangers in our own country."

Not wishing to get involved in a political discussion, Tracy just smiled. Her company was in Ethiopia at the invitation of the Berg, as the ruling military junta was called. Tracy wasn't going to jeopardize the success of their mission by expressing any opinion on the prevailing conditions. She was here to help, not to criticize. Perceiving her point of view, Ato Negussay sighed and concluded his grumbling by saying, "I am wrong to tell you these things. So let's just forget I did and let's go about our own business."

They took a taxi to the marketplace. When they got there Tracy was surprised to find every stall locked and barred.

"It's Sunday," Ato Negussay explained. "But don't worry. The people I'm taking you to are my friends, so they will open for us."

They walked through narrow lanes between stalls built of wood that was ash-gray with age. Tracy could just imagine what it must be like bustling with people ogling the colorful merchandise on a regular market day. She and her companion stopped at one of the stalls and Ato Negussay knocked on the door. It opened a cautious sliver and Tracy could see a flash of white as a pair of dark eyes peered through the slit. A rapid exchange in Amharic followed between the person behind the door and her companion, and then like the door to the magic cave in the *Arabian Nights* that opened to the secret word, "Sesame," the door to the stall opened and they were allowed to enter.

Inside the store two smiling and bowing men received Tracy and Ato Negussay. Within the cramped space, a rainbow of fabrics were draped from ceiling to counter.

"If the lady would like a fabric, tell us what kind of dress it is for and we shall help you select," one of them said in fairly good English.

"How much fabric would I need for a typical native dress?" Tracy asked.

"If you'd like a *kamise*, as we call a whole dress, you will need about three yards of fabric. And you will also need a *shemma*, which is the shawl our women drape on their shoulders. That will take another three yards because you're tall. Normally we recommend two, but on you, two wouldn't drape properly. You must appear richly draped to be properly dressed in the *shemma*."

The other man, whom Tracy judged to be in his twenties, interrupted in rapid-fire Amharic.

"My cousin here says that you should select the fabric depending on whether you will use your dress for every day or for evening."

He had a point, Tracy thought. It was unlikely that she would use the fancy-bordered dress for daytime. She could just see herself going to work in it—the very idea made her smile. The dress would have to be worn either cocktail length or as a long dress for some very special occasion. It would be perfect for the victory party when they got the government contract and paid Anne off!

"I'd like a very special fabric," Tracy declared. Instantly, the shopkeepers swung into action, opening every drawer in their tiny store. One fabulous color was displayed after another. Tracy found it hard to make a selection.

"This is the finest cotton we have," the older

salesman declared as he displayed one more length of cloth. "It will last you through many years of washing and wear."

Tracy held the soft white cotton against her skin.

"Pardon me for being so forward," Ato Negussay said, "but that white makes your skin glow like a fine pearl. Other colors are good, too, like the turquoise, or a green to make your hair shine . . . but that white makes you look like a princess."

The other two men agreed with Ato Negussay.

"Here, look at the fabric that you could have for the *shemma*, the shawl," said the older salesman. He held up a gossamer-thin gauze with a wide, embroidered border along one edge. "Allow me," he approached her and with skilled hands draped the fabric around her shoulders so the bordered edge rested in a circle, framing her slender neck and face. The border was emerald-green, laced with specks of burnt-orange that brought out the vivid hue of the green and was thickly interwoven with gold threads, giving it a rich and regal texture. "You look like a painting of the Madonna," the salesman breathed in awe while Tracy took a critical look in the mirror.

"Truly, Miss Brooke, you must buy this piece," encouraged Ato Negussay.

"And for how much, if I do?" Tracy laughed, overwhelmed by the reaction of the men around her. She too thought the fabric and colors rather suited her, but of course she couldn't see herself with their eyes, so had to take their word that she looked good. Of course she probably didn't look as glorious as they said. After all, they had a sale to make, Tracy reasoned. But perhaps she looked good enough to dazzle Kirk. The thought popped into her head involuntarily. I'm being a fool, Tracy chided herself. When would Kirk ever see me in this dress? *You'll find a way,* an inner voice told her but she dismissed it as a childish wish. *Or maybe not so childish,* the voice said. *Surely he'll be at your celebration....* Suddenly, Tracy became aware that the salesman was quoting a price.

"It will be sixty birrs for the fabric and if you wish us to also make the dress, that will be another sixty," she heard.

Quickly Tracy calculated this into U.S. currency and found that the whole thing would cost her only half the local price. Tracy knew she should bargain, but she had no idea how much of a discount to ask for. Kirk had paid much less than the asking price for her Solomon and the Queen of Sheba painting, but that was on the street and she wasn't sure such local customs extended into a legitimate store, as well. But she didn't want to look foolish, either, if this was only a first price. So instead of bargaining she tried another tactic. Tracy needed to take some presents home and fabrics were attractive, different and easy to pack.

"How much for two fabrics?" she asked.

The two salespeople looked at each other and conferred in rapid Amharic. Tracy hoped that Ato Negussay was not merely standing by, but would serve as her ally and watch out for her interest—at least a bit. She looked at him, trying to convey an appeal with her facial expression. He nodded to her and closed his eyes as if to say, "Everything will be all right."

The older salesman turned to her, "Because you are brought here by our friend, and we hope you will become our client, we shall make a very special price for you. You pay full price on the first fabric and the dress we will make—because we really gave you a very special price on that—but after that we will discount you anything you want by twenty-five percent."

Tracy looked at Ato Negussay. He said something softly to his friends. The English speaking salesman smiled and turned to Tracy again.

"Okay, we give you fifteen percent off on the white dress, too."

There was nothing more to do except gracefully close the deal, Tracy decided. For her Aunt Irma Tracy selected a pastel blue fabric with a deeper blue border and for her friend Judy, a warm peach fabric that would make her stand out in any crowd. Esperanza would receive a shawl's length of hot-pink fabric that would remind her of a Mexican color called *rosa Mexicana*.

While the younger of the two merchants took her measurements, Tracy had a moment of inspiration about the style of dress she wanted. Explaining her idea to the older salesman, Tracy sketched a picture of a flowing, floor-length dress with bell-shaped sleeves that followed a gentle A line. Both the sleeves and the bottom of the dress were to have the same border as the shawl. Judy always said that the better the fabric the simpler the dress lines should be—so Tracy decided to give the concept a try.

"You pay us half now, and half if it's to your satisfaction when we deliver the dress to your hotel," the older salesman explained.

"And when will that be?" Tracy wanted to know.

"We can have it ready in three days."

"Wonderful."

It was only after she paid and left the store amidst a profusion of thanks, hugging the fabrics she had selected for gifts, that Tracy looked at her watch. She panicked. Somehow the shopping ritual was so timeless that she had spent over two hours in the store. Now she would have to rush.

By the time Tracy and Sarah's husband got a taxi and it delivered them to the front of the hotel, Tracy had only twenty minutes left to dress for her lunch appointment.

She had thanked Ato Negussay for his kindness on their way back, and then, having explained her situation, she dashed out of the taxi and into the hotel lobby like a whirlwind.

"Hold it," said a familiar, deep voice as Kirk caught her by her arm, cushioning, what otherwise would have been a painful collision. Before Kirk's powerful hands detained her, Tracy found herself pressed for an instant against Kirk's chest.

The sudden contact sent a sharp sensation through her and Tracy realized with embarrassment that the sensitive points of her breasts had hardened and were quite obvious through the thin cotton of her blouse.

"I'm sorry," she muttered, blushing and anxious to get away.

"I know you want me—but to throw yourself at me like this?" Kirk teased her, holding her at arms' length. Then his expression grew quite serious as he looked her over.

"Where have you been? Is this how you plan to come to lunch? We're seeing a high official of the government!"

"One question at a time, please," Tracy interrupted. His scolding tone was irritating, but it served to calm her down. "I was out shopping. Now if you'll excuse me, I'll go change, so I can be on time for our appointment." Tracy tried to peel his hands off her arm, but in vain.

"Have you been out alone again?" Kirk's voice grew grave.

"Out, yes. Alone, no. Now if you'll let go of me...."

"I am responsible for you, you know."

"Then act like it," Tracy snapped.

"What is that supposed to mean?"

"Take your hands off me, so I can go and change!"

"As soon as you tell me where you've been and with whom."

"I'm a grown woman; I don't have to give you an account!"

"Oh yes, you do! As long as you're in Ethiopia, you do, Miss Nolan."

"And stop calling me by my maiden name!"

"I am calling you by your rightful name. Six months of marriage shouldn't give you the right to use a man's name. What went wrong there anyway?"

"Would you like my life story, or would you prefer that I get dressed for our lunch date?"

"Both. But right now, I'll chose the latter. We'll have plenty of time for the other."

Kirk let go of her and without a word Tracy strode to the elevator with an angry toss of her head.

"And hurry up!" he called after her.

Was it laughter she detected in Kirk's voice? Was he really laughing at her? Tracy was furious with him. His fingers had left red streaks on her milky skin, but it wasn't her arm that was burning with pain. She wished she could tear from her soul the agony he caused by his mere presence. She felt a pain in the pit of her stomach every time he touched her, and wondered how she was going to survive being near Kirk while in Ethiopia. He teased her, but his wasn't the fun approach of a would-be lover. Instead, Kirk seemed to want to torment her, to wrench something from the very core of her being. It was as though he thought Tracy was hiding some important secret from him and he needed to know what it was. *That's ridiculous,* Tracy thought, as she mechanically dressed and made up her face for the lunch. It was Kirk who was hiding something. What had made him leave L.A., and what was the cause behind the anger he seemed to harbor against her? Was it really important? Tracy sighed. Not unless she planned on a real relationship with Kirk. And from the looks of things that was out of the question. No matter how attracted she was to him she would only be repeating the painful experience of the kind of uncommitted relationship she'd had with George. Tracy couldn't afford to fall in love again for purely physical reasons. First she had to get to know the man. Unfortunately, judging from her brief encounters with Kirk, that wasn't going to be easy. He was the wrong man for her in every way but physically.

Tracy blushed at this thought, which made it difficult to apply even a light coat of artificial blush to her cheeks. She shrugged. It wasn't important. She was wearing her cream-colored jacket with the matching skirt, and a silk blouse with a soft beige pattern that complemented her coloring. The bow tie of the blouse softened the businesslike lines of the suit. She looked just right for the occasion, Tracy decided, looking in the mirror. Feeling a perverse desire to annoy Kirk, she put her hair up into a French twist on the back of her head. *It serves him right,* she pouted with childish glee. Then to give the hairdo a modern touch Tracy pulled the front curls loose around her face and let a few strands escape at the nape of her neck as teasers.

"Pretty good," Kirk pronounced as soon as she stepped out of the elevator.

Tracy didn't probe whether he meant her quick timing, or her looks. His eyes roamed over her as though he was measuring every inch of her. With a

self-confident smile Tràcy accepted his compliment
and followed him out to the Jeep in front of the
hotel.

Colonel Teshome, their luncheon companion,
was a tall, corpulent man, with a dark face and a
broad smile that revealed a perfect row of white
teeth. He was already at the restaurant when Kirk
and Tracy arrived, and he welcomed them as
though they had come to his home. It was a pleasant place, with whitewashed walls and a simulated
thatch-roofed ceiling. Sisal rugs covered the floor
and the tables and chairs were made of wicker. The
light filtered through windows covered with soft,
flattering muslin curtains. It was moderately
crowded and Tracy noted that they were the only
foreigners there. That pleased her. They were
directed by a waiter to a corner table. Tracy was
seated across from the men. The little, round
wicker chairs on which they sat had soft cushions
but the table in front of them seemed to lack a top.

"That's because the food tray will become the
top," Kirk explained in answer to her questioning
look.

"You will try native Ethiopian food today, Miss
Brooke," the colonel explained.

The waiter wove through the other tables toward
them, balencing a huge, round, brass tray. He set it
before them and went to get the rest of their meal.
On top of the tray, covering it an inch thick, lay a
soft-gray spongelike substance. Tracy delicately
touched it with a fingertip. The mysterious delicacy
felt cool and springy.

"This food provides our basic sustenance. It is

called *enjera*. It is made out of *teff*—that's our word for 'wheat'—and we eat it together with a sauce called *wot*. Sometimes the *wot* also contain meat.'' He smiled, and his charmingly self-effacing tone wasn't lost on Tracy.

''You mean even today most people are very poor?''

''Why, of course. You can't change the course of history in a mere few years! When the emperor, Haile Selassie, was the ruler, a few were very rich and most were very poor. Since the revolution, our new government has been trying to raise the standard of living among the very poor. But it will take a long time. You will see, for I have a favor to ask of you.''

The rest of what the colonel wanted to say was cut off by the arrival of several steaming dishes. Their spicy aroma made Tracy realize how little breakfast she had really had.

''This is beef, this is chicken, this is lamb and this is a vegetable dish of chickpeas,'' said the colonel, explaining the contents of the bowls.

The meat dishes were covered with a thick sauce. The waiter ladled portions of each onto the *enjera* and set the bowls on a side table next to them.

''The sauce the meats are in, is our national dish,'' explained the colonel. ''It's the *wot*. It's a base in which one can cook any sort of meat, or one can have it without meat. For each meat dish the basic sauce is spiced differently. For today, I've asked them to tone down the pepper. I hope it will be to your liking.''

Tracy looked questioningly at the two men facing her. She had a plate before her but no utensils to eat with.

"You eat with your fingers," the colonel explained.

"I'll show you how," said Kirk, rushing to her aid.

Tracy watched his strong graceful fingers tear off a piece of the grayish *enjera* and form a little cone with it. He then dipped it into the beef *wot* and scooped up a piece of meat with sauce. Tipping it back so it wouldn't drop, he reached across the table.

"Open your mouth."

Tracy did so and Kirk slipped the food in, his fingers touching her lips lightly.

"Isn't it delicious?" he asked, his smile wickedly provocative.

"Couples and even good friends often feed each other," Colonel Teshome explained, easing Tracy's embarrassment.

To Tracy's surprise, the spongy, soft *enjera* was a perfect complement to the spicy *wot*. The *enjera* had a doughy, sourish taste, that reminded her of San Francisco sourdough, although the texture of sourdough bread was nothing like the cool, chewy *enjera*. And the flavor of the *wot* was similar to beef stew, even though the thick sauce was made mostly out of ground paprika. If Tracy was going to eat without Kirk feeding her, she had to dip in. She felt clumsy wrapping the *enjera* around a piece of chicken and scooping up sauce with it, especially since getting one's fingertips full of sauce couldn't be avoided. But the colonel just laughed, saying that such difficulty was to be expected the first time around.

"You must drink this wine with it," the colonel insisted and poured a golden liquid into their glasses. It was a honeyed wine, sweet and aromatic with a tangy, slightly bitter aftertaste that counterbalanced the food. "To a wonderful stay with us, and many happy returns," Colonel Teshome toasted.

"And to a successful mission," Kirk added.

"Talking about that," the colonel said growing pensive, "I've got a little problem in the Wollo region, and I wonder if you could help us out, Captain Russell."

"If there is a way, I'll do it," Kirk said obligingly.

The colonel leaned closer to Kirk. "I hate to even mention this to you, but you know how our bureaucracy tends to make a mountain out of every molehill. Sometimes, for efficiency's sake, we just like to get things done bypassing the system...." He cast a cautious glance around the restaurant but all the other guests were seated at a distance, and the waiter was nowhere around, so he continued in a confidential tone. "We have a trusted man out in Wollo who's been very cooperative with our government. We'd like to reward him, but we need a way to take his prize to him without a lot of publicity. We wondered if you...."

He broke off and looked at Kirk expectantly.

"How soon do you want me to fly there?" Kirk asked without batting an eye.

Colonel Teshome broke into a happy grin. "I knew we could count on you," he exclaimed brightly and raised his glass. "Here's to good friends!"

Clinking glasses, they drank. Then all three of them continued to eat while Colonel Teshome explained that the gift was a shortwave radio, to be taken to a certain sultan, the sovereign of two million souls out in the Danakil Desert, and that, preferably, the mission should be accomplished the next day.

Kirk responded that the only obstacle was that first he had to use his plane to drop the airplane parts at the site where the damaged, *Pegasus 2*, was.

"One of our army helicopters can do that with no difficulty. We will also pick up your mechanic and fly him to the plane," the colonel said waving away Kirk's problem as if it were a fly. "But you see, what you're doing is a sensitive matter, for the subjects of the sultan don't welcome people from the government. They mistrust us because they fear that we shall disrupt their way of life. So, we try to handle all matters with them through the sultan. The gift will allow for direct, unobstructed communication between him and us."

The waiter appeared and cleared away the remnants of the *wot* and *enjera*. He and the colonel got into a brief discussion.

"He asked if we'd like some raw meat for dessert," Colonel Teshome explained. "Raw meat is a great delicacy of our people and is eaten after a feast such as ours.''

"Did you order it?" Tracy wondered aloud, feeling apprehensive. How was she going to manage this unusual dessert?

"No, I explained that you would rather have fresh fruit and coffee.''

"You're right," Kirk laughed.

The waiter returned with fresh bananas and coffee—brewed like a European espresso. "In my country it's not customary to eat dessert the way Americans do," explained the colonel. "Even sugar wasn't in fashion until just a decade ago. Now of course, we use it too much.''

As if to prove his point he spooned three scoops into his coffee, then with a brief smile at Tracy, turned his attention again to Kirk.

Tracy found it interesting to listen to the colonel as he put his case to Kirk. She noted the ease with which Kirk accepted doing him a favor. But despite the colonel's promise to take care of *Pegasus 2* the next day, secretly Tracy wondered how well the damaged plane was going to fare, with the mechanic not under direct supervision. With increasing anxiety she also realized that by delivering the radio to the sultan they were going to lose a day, maybe two. Time was of the essence for World Help. With only one plane in operation, they were likely already behind schedule. The arrangement also meant having to pay the men extra time in the field. It was one thing for her father to suggest that she take a vacation, it was quite another for Kirk to take a day off from his job just to do a favor. Tracy was annoyed by the easygoing discussion between the two men. Didn't Kirk realize how important the completion of this project was to Westwind? Obviously not. *Well, I'll just have to explain it to him the first chance I have.*

AFTER LUNCH, instead of returning with Tracy to the hotel, Kirk offered to take her on a little tour of Addis Ababa. She agreed and soon they were off the main avenue and driving along unpaved roads. In the hardened earth deep grooves marked the carriage wheels that must have struggled through the wet clay during countless rainy seasons. The Jeep lurched from side to side despite the careful way Kirk drove it. Adobe dwellings lined the now dusty streets and people dressed in shabby clothing appeared in the doorways to stare at the strangers.

"It all seems so gray," Tracy observed.

"The color of poverty," Kirk said nodding. He pulled the Jeep close to a house and parked it. "Come, you'll enjoy this store."

It took Tracy a few minutes to get used to the semidarkness inside the dirt-floored room. But when she could see, Tracy cried out with delight. Hanging every which way were long narrow tapestries made of thick yarn. The storekeeper appeared, wearing a spotless white shirt and dark slacks but only sandals on his feet. Kirk greeted him in Amharic. Wanting to be friendly, Tracy imitated Kirk's way of saying "hello," and it brought a broad grin to the face of the owner.

"This is Ato Shimelis," Kirk said introducing the shopkeeper. "He runs the best rug store in town."

"I'm very flattered, sir," Ato Shimelis said and bowed a little. "What can I do for you today?"

"I thought the young lady here might be interested in some of your merchandise."

"Whatever you like, madam, I am at your service," Ato Shimelis bowed again.

Tracy was amused. She knew practically no people in Ethiopia, yet this was the second person she'd met in one day whose first name was Ato. She mentioned this to Kirk and both men burst out laughing.

"Care to share the joke?" Tracy wondered what she had said that was so funny.

Amidst chuckles Kirk explained that *Ato* simply meant "Mr."

"Ethiopians don't have two names like people in other Western countries," the shopkeeper explained. "I got a name when I was born and I can also use my father's name with it, if I want to. My father's name is Gabriel, so my full name is Shimelis Gabriel. But if you saw me across the street and called to me as 'Ato Gabriel' I would not react. My father would, if he were walking with me. Because people in Ethiopia are called only by their first names, adding a title such as Ato to it makes it acceptable as a formal address."

Feeling a bit sheepish about her ignorance, Tracy couldn't help but laugh too. After their merriment subsided, Tracy turned her attention to the fine fur rugs that were piled high on a chair. The rugs, which were about thirty inches in diameter, were sewn in circular patterns. Their color varied between light and dark brown. They would be wonderful decorations on a wall or furniture, or even in front of a fireplace, she decided.

"How much are these?" Tracy asked.

"Those are made of monkey, and therefore cannot be exported from the country," Ato Shimelis explained. "Some people buy them anyway, and hide them in their suitcases under their clothes. But if the customs agents find such rugs in luggage, they confiscate them."

"Then those rugs are not something I would want to buy. What about these?" Tracy asked turning her attention to the hanging rugs.

"These are handwoven. It's perfectly fine to take them out of the country. They're pure wool. We sell them by the square. I can cut as many squares for you as you like."

It was only now Tracy observed each square was separated by a wide fringe that could easily be cut. Some of the rugs were as large as two feet by two feet, while others measured only a square foot each. She chose one on which the brick-colored design was woven against an off-white background. One square depicted a house flanked by two palm trees, the next a lion, and the third a pair of birds. Tracy asked for six squares so she could have the design repeated twice.

"I'll hang it on the wall by my fireplace," she said, smiling at Kirk who was patiently observing her. "And if it's too long, I can always give a square or two away."

"Have you seen this one?" Ato Shimelis pointed at a fuzzy, brown-and-beige rug patterned with a series of lions and ostriches.

Tracy ended up buying six squares of that rug, too. She was surprised to see that Kirk hardly bargained this time. Ato Shimelis quoted a price. Kirk raised an eyebrow, the price was instantly reduced by 10 percent and the bargain was struck.

"You are still being robbed," Kirk jested, "but go ahead and buy it anyway. Once we leave Addis, you won't find this kind of stuff anywhere else."

With her purchases rolled up and tied with a string, one tucked under each arm, a happy Tracy clambered into the Jeep again.

"Thanks for bringing me here," she said beaming at Kirk.

"It's my duty to take you around."

He made it sound like such a burden that Tracy got angry. "I didn't ask you to!" she bristled.

"No, you didn't. But I'm hosting you, aren't I?"

"If it's such a chore, why didn't you leave it to someone else?"

"My staff is limited."

"It sure is," Tracy said icily. "In fact, I wonder how you could take on yourself so easily to fly around for Colonel Teshome when one of our own planes is grounded, along with the pilot, and you're the only one left to carry on with the project!" There it was, she had blurted it out.

With an impulsive gesture Kirk pulled the Jeep

over to the curb and glared at her. Tracy felt her insides wither under his angry stare.

"You've been here less than two days and already you're telling me how to run my business! You may be the boss's daughter, but you've got no right to criticize when you haven't the faintest notion of what's going on around here!"

Kirk's voice cut her like a steel blade, but Tracy was conscious of only two words: "boss's daughter." She could feel the blood drain from her face with anger.

"I may be the boss's daughter, as you call me, but I'm also the boss. Your boss." Tracy reminded him with a level look.

"I was hired by Ray Nolan as the man in charge and nobody told me otherwise," Kirk retorted.

"You just didn't bother to ask around," Tracy smiled sardonically. "It might have been too much for your male ego to bear to learn that the whole project lives or falls by my aircraft design!"

"In most companies the engineer is merely an employee. What put you in a power position, my dear, is that you happen to be the boss's daughter!"

"Stop calling me that!" Tracy shouted furiously. "I wasn't handed my job on a silver platter, I've earned it!"

By now, a curious group of natives had gathered around them, staring at their quarrel from a distance. The women and children watched with awe, but when Kirk glanced at the men, they laughed and shouted some words to him that made him, too, supress a smile.

"What are they laughing at?" Tracy demanded sullenly.

"The men are giving me advice on how to handle you. They tell me that a good beating always tames a wife!"

"Let's get out of here," Tracy urged irritably.

"Why, of course, Miss Nolan."

"Stop teasing me!"

"It's your name, isn't it?"

"No! It was legally changed and if nothing else, I expect you to respect the law."

"Whose law? Yours?"

"Whatever." Tracy sank back into her seat, her afternoon spoiled.

Kirk started up the car and waved a friendly good-bye to the people around them. They rolled down the street and he casually remarked, "Those Ethiopians might have a good idea there. Do you think a spanking would tame you?"

"If you behaved like a gentleman and also fulfilled your obligations to the project as you're supposed to, you'd find me quite tame."

Furiously Kirk swung the car into a side street and stopped the motor again. He turned toward Tracy, his face pale.

"As for my job, in this country one favor begets another. You yourself heard that the parts for the plane will be flown to the site by helicopter. That's a much better way to deliver them than we have at our disposal. Also, I'm not a mechanic, so first I've got to give my man a chance to work on the plane before I can fly it out of there.

"Secondly, we're in a hiatus right now. Since the new shipment of grain hasn't been delivered to our campsite, there is nothing for me to drop at the villages.

"And thirdly, if I behaved with you like a gentleman, you'd walk all over me."

Tracy was about to protest but Kirk raised his hand to stop her.

"Fourthly, this is the last time you will hear an accounting from me. If you don't approve of the way I run the operation, fire me."

Without waiting for Tracy's reply, he started up the Jeep again, lurching it through the twisting roads as if to take his anger out in the drive.

Tracy sat in stony silence next to him. The man was truly insufferable. She stole a glance at him. He was looking ahead, concentrating on his driving through the dusty streets. The muscles in his tanned arms were tense, and so were his hands, gripping the wheel. His jaw was set in a stubborn line. It was better not to question Kirk any more, Tracy decided. When the time came, she'd just do as she saw fit and would not discuss it with him in advance. Her father was right.

Kirk did not take to having a female boss. From a business point of view Tracy wanted to have nothing to do with a macho male even if he was the world's best pilot. From a personal point of view, he might just be too difficult a man to deal with. As soon as this project was over, she'd ask her father to fire him and look for someone else, she decided.

"I'll send someone up for the crates," Kirk informed her in a clipped voice when they arrived at the hotel. "And you'll have to be on your own for dinner. I suggest you eat lightly and turn in early since we'll have to get started at dawn. I'll pick you up in the lobby at 6:00 A.M."

"Who said I was going with you tomorrow?" Tracy objected.

"I just did. What else have you got to do in town? We'll fly there and be back by evening."

"What if I don't want to go?"

"This is one experience you won't want to miss, so no matter how mad you are at me, you'll come." Kirk's teasing grin lit up his face and Tracy's heart somersaulted—despite her anger.

With a defiant toss of her head, Tracy turned to go. "If I'm not down here by six, go by yourself."

"Wear something suitable for hot weather," Kirk called after her as she headed for the elevator.

CHAPTER SIX

BACK IN HER ROOM, Tracy wondered whether she should wait until Kirk sent someone to pick up the crates, or whether to simply go about her business. After the dusty roads of town she wanted to shower and change. It was already six in the evening so Tracy figured that after she cleaned up she would order room service instead of going down to the dining room. She didn't mind eating alone downstairs but she wanted to avoid any possibility of having to fight off the lonely Russian.

Kirk had not mentioned when he would send the people for the crates. With a slight feeling of apprehension Tracy realized that she didn't even have a way of contacting him. It seemed a part of his character not to bother about informing her of his whereabouts. This annoyed her. He could come and go as he pleased, tell her what time to be ready to meet him, but in case Tracy needed him, where could she get hold of him? Maybe he just assumed that she would know how to find him. Perhaps he was staying at the hotel and that's why he didn't bother. She called the operator and discovered that both Kirk and Bill were indeed staying at the Hotel Addis.

"Would you like me to ring Mr. Russell's room?" the operator asked.

Why not? Tracy thought, shrugging. She waited on the line while somewhere in the hotel Kirk's phone rang.

"His room doesn't answer, would you like to leave a message?"

"No, thank you. Try Mr. O'Connor's room please."

"Hello," came Bill's cheerful voice over the line.

"What are you doing for dinner tonight?" Tracy asked, without bothering to identify herself, laughter bubbling in her voice.

"For a sexy voice like that I'd give up whatever I was doing," came the answer.

"How about having dinner with me?"

"Where? And how do I recognize you?"

"Look for a redhead in the dining room in one hour." Tracy hung up, wondering if Bill was just joking with her or if he had really mistaken her for someone else. But it didn't matter. Tracy had a dinner partner and one from whom she might learn some useful facts about Kirk.

With a sense of purpose she dove into the shower. The hot stream dissolved the tension leftover from her afternoon's excursion with Kirk. She could handle him. In fact, she had handled tougher men than him when she was at university, she thought, her mood lifting. Of course it was easier to deal with men she wasn't attracted to—in that respect Kirk presented a new challenge. Both Tracy's thoughts and her shower were interrupted by a knock at the door. It was loud enough to hear even through the closed bathroom door and the hiss of the water. She shut the stream off and wrapped a towel around her wet body.

"Who is it?" she called out.

"We came to pick up the crates ma'am."

They would have to come now, Tracy thought wryly.

"Could you wait about five minutes?"

"No, the helicopter has to leave before sundown. We've got a special envoy waiting downstairs."

Tracy tensed up. That was not some deliveryman's voice; it was Kirk's. *Well he asked for it,* she thought defiantly. She straightened her shoulders and making sure the towel was securely fastened around her, padded to the door, leaving wet footmarks on the floor.

Kirk's eyebrows rose as he surveyed her bare shoulders, the beads of water on her skin and the strands of wet hair clinging to her moist throat.

"Come right in." Tracy's voice brimmed with artificial sweetness.

"Maybe we should wait." One of the two Ethiopian deliverymen said, and they both backed off. Kirk didn't.

"Wish you were always so obliging," he grinned, entering the room. "This will take but a minute."

Tracy watched his long-limbed figure stride across the room. She noted how efficiently Kirk supervised his two helpers as they loaded the crates onto their dolly. He exuded authority. Even Kirk's khaki safari jacket seemed more like a military uniform than a mere summer shirt. Tracy could see why he wouldn't tolerate a woman—or perhaps anyone—giving him orders. The men cautiously rolled the dolly with its cargo through the door. While they moved out into the hall, Kirk stayed behind. Turning to Tracy, he said, "You're lucky that I can't take advantage of the temptations you offer. But don't press your luck."

With that, he was out the door.

"I'm not offering a thing to you," Tracy called down the hall after him. She could hear his ringing laughter after he turned the corner.

The arrogance of that man, Tracy fumed. He insisted on walking in on her before she could get dressed and then, like all men, he just assumed that she was flirting with him! Had the situation been reversed, she wouldn't be making lewd comments about him! Although, to be honest with herself, Tracy had to admit that thoughts about his body frequently crossed her mind.

Dry now, Tracy chose to wear her gray slacks with the narrow white stripes and a white silk shirt—which seemed to make her skin glow like porcelain. Tracy tied a soft, black, leather belt around her narrow waist and noted with satisfaction that it made her clothes look festive. She brushed her hair out until it glowed like a halo around her head and quickly applied her usual light coat of makeup.

Probably, Kirk's reason for not being at dinner

was that he had to take care of shipping the crates. So Tracy went to meet Bill, feeling easy; she was sure that Kirk wouldn't be joining them.

Bill was waiting at the entrance to the restaurant, casting an anxious eye all around him. Then he spotted Tracy.

"So it *was* you," he said, grinning broadly as she greeted him.

"Were you hoping for another woman to show up?" Tracy asked teasingly.

"You never know," Bill joked. He turned red and Tracy wondered who was on his mind.

While the waiter served up a tasty cream of vegetable soup, Tracy started their evening by asking Bill about his health.

"It's coming along better than expected. In fact, the doctor told me today that, although I'll have to keep my back brace on for a couple of more weeks, if I'm careful I could fly again in a week."

Bill's mention of flying allowed Tracy to cautiously lead the conversation around to why he and Kirk had left Los Angeles so suddenly.

"Who knows?" Bill shrugged. "Kirk can be like that sometimes. I had expected to stay another week, but from one day to the next, some bug got into him and he decided we should leave."

"You didn't even ask why?"

Bill grinned. "When you've worked with a man like Kirk as long as I have, you learn not to ask. You just go along and eventually you see the reason."

"Did you? I mean do you know yet why Kirk left L.A.?"

"I think so. I believe Kirk saw a ghost . . . someone from his past, and he just ran like hell."

"You mean a former girlfriend?"

"No. Kirk's father wanted him to marry someone, but old Kirk ran away to Alaska instead. But it seemed to me that when we were in Los Angeles, echoes of his past began to pursue him. . . ."

"You mean the woman showed up?"

"In a way."

"Well, did she or didn't she?"

"Look, Tracy, Kirk never really told me what it was that chased him out of Los Angeles. It's not fair of me to talk about something I don't know anything about."

Tracy realized that she had pressed the point as far as she could. It was useless to ask any more. So she turned the conversation to Bill and his life. He told her he was divorced and had two little girls who lived with his ex-wife in San Francisco. When he was back there he spent his time with his daughters. But it was talking about his years in Alaska that made him really light up. Over roast chicken with a garnish of mixed vegetables and potatoes he told anecdotes about his past, then, returning to the present, told about how he and Kirk were trying to build something of value in their lives. "We're a team," he emphasized, "and that's rare these days. Kirk has a far-reaching vision of how flying small aircraft can help people. That's what I like about him. He is not just some two-bit pilot, trying to make a living. That's why I work with him, why I would do anything for the man.''

Bill's words made Tracy ache inside. While on one hand it was reassuring to know that the two men working for her company were trustworthy and supported each other as a team, on the other hand she didn't really want to hear about Kirk's vision or integrity or about how wonderful Kirk was. To her Kirk was the kind of man who looked at a woman only one way—and once he'd had what he wanted, he'd walk out on her. How he behaved in his own male world was only a part of the man. If Kirk couldn't relate to her world, all his other fine qualities made little difference to Tracy. Oh, he might be good as an employee—but then she didn't want him as an employee. The insight jolted her. What *did* she want him as? Tracy wouldn't let herself think through the answer.

"It's getting late for me," Tracy answered with an apologetic smile when Bill asked her if she wanted to have an after-dinner drink with him in the bar. "I've got an early call tomorrow."

"Oh, yes, you're going with Kirk," Bill said. "Well, sleep fast, for he'll expect you to be ready right on time."

"Thanks for the tip," she laughed.

After she returned to her room and went to bed, Tracy lay awake for a quite a while in the dark, thinking of what she had learned about Kirk and her own feelings toward him. Should she settle for just an affair with the man? After a year of almost complete celibacy her body ached with a newly awakened hunger. But no matter how much she desired Kirk, Tracy was still worried about what kind of relationship they would get into. She had tried a casual affair a few months after her divorce and hadn't liked it at all. She had felt empty and humiliated after making love, instead of elated and released. *What would it be like with Kirk?* she wondered. Would she feel the same let down? Or would it be as soul searing and wonderful as their brief physical encounters had been for her up to now? But how would she react if Kirk didn't feel the same way about their lovemaking? She asked herself. What would she do: suffer in silence, knowing she was truly attracted to Kirk on many levels whereas for him it was merely a passing affair? Was it better to have only a brief liasion with the man one loved, or not to have the experience at all? There it was, she had used the word love. Did she love Kirk? How could she when they had just barely met? What did she really know about him? Who was that woman in his past? What was his family like? Maybe that was the answer: to try to get to know him as much as she could before allowing herself to be drawn into the whirlwind of passion. Yes, that's what she was going to do. She would try not to get angry at him, but would let herself flow with the events between them and try to learn everything she could about Kirk. The resolution made her feel good enough to drift into a lighthearted, satisfying sleep.

Tracy thought she hadn't slept at all when she heard loud, urgent knocking on her door.

"What is it?" she called out sleepily.

"It's five-thirty, that's what. I hope you're up and ready for a cup of coffee," Kirk's voice boomed through the door.

"I'm neither!" Tracy responded. "Go away, I'll be downstairs at six."

She smiled as she listened to his receding footsteps. Kirk sure took his plans seriously. With a sigh Tracy abandoned the warmth of the covers and dressed in her sky-blue jump suit for the day's flight.

Kirk was in the lobby when she got downstairs. His eyes took her in from head to toe, but all he said was "Good, you're on time."

Tracy was pleased with Kirk's approval, whatever the reason was for it. It meant that they had a truce between them—at least for a while.

"Here." Kirk handed her a large Thermos and a plastic cup. "Have some coffee on the way to the airport. There is also a sweet roll for you in the glove compartment."

"Thanks." Tracy climbed into the Jeep, munched on the roll and sipped the strong breakfast brew quietly. She found herself strangely tense, sitting next to Kirk. She wished she could think of a way to start a conversation—especially since there were so many things she wanted to know about him. But given the circumstances, it just didn't seem like the right time to begin asking questions. Tracy didn't feel like making small talk, so she relaxed instead and watched the awakening city in the golden glow of the dawn.

Kirk, too, seemed absorbed in his own thoughts. He only broke the silence between them when they arrived at the airport. "We were given space for *Pegasus* at the far end of the field and we can just leave the Jeep parked there while we're away."

"That's convenient," Tracy said grinning.

She watched Kirk do the preflight walk-around and silently approved of the careful way he checked out every bit of the plane. Of course, Tracy was just aching to do the walk-around herself, but it would have been a grave error on her part to interfere with Kirk. She had to let him be in charge and act as his companion, not as his employer. That much she had finally learned.

Kirk gave her the go ahead and they both climbed into the cockpit. Unexpectedly Kirk reached across Tracy to make sure the door on her side was shut. His arm brushed against her breasts provoking what felt to Tracy like a mild electric shock throughout her body. *We're off to a great start,* she thought wryly. *We're locked into this tiny cabin together, with him burning me up with his touch.* Kirk's face did not betray any sign of noticing either his brush against her or the havoc he had created.

"Just making sure you're locked in," he said, grinning innocently.

"I can do my own belt, thank you," Tracy protested all too quickly.

"Why, of course." Kirk's expression turned blankly polite but there was a twinkle in his eyes and Tracy realized that he was poking fun at her. Of course he knew he had touched her in a sensitive spot! But since he chose to ignore it, so would she.

"This is the last place we'll have a control tower," Kirk informed her as he made radio contact and followed the instructions of Ground Control to taxi to the runway.

Their take-off was smooth. It was obvious to Tracy that Kirk handled the plane as if it were an extension of his body—comfortably and competently. He had a different piloting style from hers. Somehow he flew in a stronger, more forceful way. But the lift-off wasn't any faster than Tracy would have done it, nor was Kirk pushing the plane any harder than she would have. *Masculine* was the word that came to Tracy's mind. Everything he did seemed imbued with a masculine power. That's what makes him so irresistibly attractive, she mused.

"A penny for your thoughts?"

Tracy laughed. "Care to tell me what's below us and which way we're heading?"

"We're flying northeast, skirting around the city of Ankobar and we'll land at the doorstep of the spiritual shepherd of two million Muslim souls."

"How romantic," Tracy laughed.

And it was. The fields below them lay in a mosaic of varicolored greens, softened by the early-morning haze. Tracy could feel the air current beneath the plane carrying them like a swift river toward their destination. She wondered what kind of experience this was going to be, considering what she knew about the way Muslims felt toward women.

"Since you are a visitor, and white, our host

might be quite courteous," he said grinning. "Just because he lives in the middle of nowhere doesn't mean he is ignorant. Many upper-class Ethiopians are educated abroad, in Europe or the U.S. And even the current socialist system of egalitarianism can't erase that."

"What else should I know?"

"At least taste everything that's offered so you don't offend our host. And don't speak unless spoken to. I know this will be hard on you... but...."

Instinctively, Tracy's fist shot out and she boxed Kirk's arm. She had meant it only as a teasing reproach, but from her whitened knuckles, Tracy realized that she had hit him fairly hard.

"What a fierce temper," laughed Kirk, rubbing the spot where Tracy's fist had landed. "Suppose I were to retaliate?"

"I'm sorry. I don't know what came over me," Tracy stammered, embarrassed. "Perhaps your teasing triggered me to react like I used to when I was a teenager. I was a freckle-faced tomboy, and always got into fights with boys who tormented me about being a carrot head." She flashed him an apologetic smile. As she caught Kirk's searching eyes on her Tracy felt herself blush till her cheeks burned like glowing embers. She turned her face away from him to hide her color.

Suddenly the earth disappeared below them. Tracy's heart gave a violent leap and she leaned forward to see better through the front window. For awhile, she couldn't see land at all and had the odd sensation of having flown out into space, or of having dived into deep waters, where sometimes the earth dropped away and one was left floating in a bottomless sea.

"Scared?"

"Of course not," Tracy bristled, holding on to her dignity. "Just surprised."

"Yeah, that escarpment is a fun drop. For your information, we have now left the plateau of Addis Ababa. From here on we'll be flying over the Danakil desert."

Even without his explanation Tracy would have noticed the change in temperature. Suddenly it was warm and getting warmer. She watched the hot air shimmer beneath them. She commented, "flying is different when one is a passenger."

"Yes, you have to trust the pilot."

"Well, I pulled some stuff on you in California so I suppose you're entitled to play some games with me."

Tracy was trying to be fair to make up for her earlier misbehavior. But the moment she spoke, Tracy knew she had laid herself wide open to him, and sure enough, Kirk took her up on it.

"What I'd like to play with you is not a game." His tone was provocative.

"I don't want to play at all," Tracy fended him off.

"Oh, but you are playing. All the time."

"I don't know what you're talking about!"

"Shall I show you?"

Before she could object, Kirk put the plane on

automatic and leaned forward. His lips brushed Tracy's in an unexpectedly gentle way. Tracy opened her mouth in protest but his quick darting tongue left her no chance. A tremor ran through her as his tongue playfully explored her lips. A sharp sensation of desire rose in her, and she pulled her head back to get away from Kirk before she lost herself to her own passion. But there was no need. Kirk released her. Laughing, he turned his attention back to the plane.

"I don't know what you're trying to prove." Tracy felt so shaky after his touch that she could barely get the words out.

"That you're behaving childishly. That you came to Ethiopia responding to a call—"

"That's true!"

"I don't mean my phone call!"

"Mr. Russell, how about just flying the plane instead of insinuating that I came, not because of the plane's body, but because of yours?"

"I'm glad to see your sense of humor is returning, but why do you always revert to your position as employer, when we begin to discuss some basic truths between us?"

"I'm glad you credit me as your employer! In that case, please give an account as to why you ran away from Los Angeles?" There, she had said it. Not very subtly, but the question that had been plaguing Tracy for months had now finally landed at the only source that could satisfy it.

"What makes you think I ran away?"

"I don't know how else to describe your behavior. You dealt with John Morris instead of me. You left early. Why?''

''Were you upset that I did that?''

''You're not answering my question.''

''Okay, I will. I promise. But right now, if you'll excuse me, I've got a plane to land.''

Kirk tilted the plane toward the ashen, barren land under them till Tracy thought they were going to land nose first. But Kirk came out of the downward drift and pulled up for another pass.

''That was to scare the goats away and to let the people below know that we're coming in for landing,'' he explained.

Much as she had flown, Tracy had never landed among goats, trees and naked children who were running in circles with excitement. She couldn't help but admire Kirk's nerves. He maneuvered deftly among the moving targets and touched down on a clearing with hardly a bounce.

As soon as they had stopped, four men in a Jeep drove up to meet them. They wore short, white tunics and across their naked chests sported bandoleers loaded with ammunition. Long curved knives were stuck into the wide leather belts that girded their trim waists. Their dark skin glistened in the sun beneath the colorful beads that decorated their necks and muscular upper arms. But their fanciful attire in no way diminished their warlike appearance—especially since each one held a rifle in his hand, ready to point it at the visitors.

Kirk got out of the plane first and explained in Amharic that he and Tracy were expected by the sultan. By the time Tracy climbed out the men were relaxed and smiling broadly. On the ground Tracy was struck by a wall of heat such as she had felt before only in the California desert. The sultan's guards ushered them into a large, whitewashed adobe building where, due to the fortress-thick walls, the temperature was considerably cooler.

Tracy and Kirk were led through a narrow hallway into a large room. Draped in immaculate white robes from head to toe, cooled by a lazy fan, the sultan sat cross-legged on a couch at the head of the room. He was very dark and enormously fat. Flanking him on either side were guards, and by his left stood a skinny little man, who turned out to be an interpreter. Kirk stopped at a respectable distance, three feet from the sultan, and bowed. Tracy imitated his gesture.

"Welcome to my humble home," the sultan said, speaking through his interpreter.

"We are the ones who come to you humbly," Kirk answered with equal formality.

"Please be seated."

Tracy and Kirk took their place on the hardwood bench that faced the sultan's couch.

The sultan asked Kirk through his interpreter what brought him and "his wife" to this part of the world. Kirk explained that it was an honor to be able to visit the great sultan. Beside that, they had brought him gifts from the government in Addis Ababa.

The sultan smiled broadly, and it seemed to Tracy that he already knew what the gifts were.

A servant came in, bearing a tray, which he placed on the coffee table in front of Kirk and Tracy. On it stood two tall glasses of dark liquid and a large plate full of dates.

"It is *tamar*, the fruit of palm trees," explained the interpreter.

Tracy ate a date and was encouraged by the sultan to have more.

"Your wife is too thin," their host commented, grinning at Kirk.

"Prosperous people and women ought to be plump," Kirk explained to Tracy with twinkling eyes.

"I'll keep that in mind." Tracy could hardly suppress the urge to laugh.

The dark fluid in the glass turned out to be Coca-Cola diluted with soda water. Despite the fact that the drink was lukewarm, it refreshed Tracy. She felt like commenting to Kirk about the lack of ice, but decided against it for fear of offending their host.

Kirk and the sultan spoke for a while about the changes that were taking place in Ethiopia. The new government was dissolving the land ownership of the feudal lords and was distributing parcels to the peasants.

"My people are somewhat affected," explained the sultan, "for some of them are involved with agriculture. Now they will have the opportunity to keep more of the what they produce. Unfortunately, as you know from flying about the countryside, between the droughts and the floods we're having a hard time growing food. But most of my people are warriors who hunt, like my guards here, or nomads who tend to goats and live mostly on milk, or merchants who travel.''

''On the way back we might visit one of your villages,'' Kirk said.

''I am sure my people will welcome you.''

''I think we had better be on our way.'' Kirk rose. Tracy did the same.

''You might stay here in the cool of the house while I go get the packages,'' Kirk told her.

''Could I use the bathroom while you're doing that?'' Tracy asked.

She directed the question at Kirk, not knowing what the protocol was for addressing the sultan. Then she watched as Kirk repeated the question to the interpreter, who in turn translated it for the sultan. The sultan conferred briefly with the interpreter, then the interpreter nodded and escorted Tracy down the long hallway.

''This is a great honor,'' the interpreter said. ''You are the only woman who has ever been allowed in to the bathroom of the sultan.'' She was led to a large, clean room with a dirt floor. The narrow windows set into the thick adobe walls filtered only a minimum of light, keeping the room cool. Down at one end of the room was an old shower head rigged up on a pipe. Around it, there was a plastic curtain. In the middle of the room was a hole in the ground with a foot pedal to either side of it. Two buckets, full of clean water, and a cup stood at the other end of the room. Tracy poured some water over her hands and face. Patting herself dry with a paper tissue she extracted from her handbag, Tracy left the room feeling refreshed.

TRACY AND KIRK were in the air again, the heat slowly draining from the cockpit as they ascended. The land below was covered with dry grass, with clusters of live shrubs only here and there.

"So, what did you think of the sultan?" Kirk asked.

"Interesting experience. Do you think the new government will let him stay on as a religious leader?"

"Who knows? I understand that he's got two brothers who are rather progovernment. That might keep him in place. Although the next time we come around, his power might be somewhat curtailed."

"Are we going back to Addis?"

"Yes. But first I want to show you something."

Tracy didn't feel like pressing Kirk to tell her what he wanted her to see. They seemed to have settled into a comfortable truce and she enjoyed the absence of tension. She stole a glance at him. Kirk was looking straight ahead. His strong profile, etched against the sky, looked like the face on a Roman coin. A sweet ache spread through Tracy's whole being. She wanted so much to be close to him, to feel his arms around her waist, to mold her body against his—yet she was afraid. What kind of a person was he really? Did she want to get involved again with a man? With this man? She was tormented by the uncertainty of her own thoughts and feelings. Did it always happen like this? Did you always fall in love with someone first and only then search for what they were really like? She tried to imagine everyday life with Kirk. She could go as far as waking up next to him and having breakfast with him—in her mind's eye she had an image of him with tousled hair, his bronzed torso naked, throwing back a glass of orange juice at the kitchen counter—but that was as far as she could picture their togetherness. What would he be like as a husband? Wouldn't he try to dominate her, the way George had? Tracy shuddered at the thought. After a while he might become just like George in other things too. No, she didn't need that kind of heartache. It was easier to repress her feelings at the start.

"Look," Kirk said, pointing ahead of them.

Small rounded mounds of what looked like earth were clustered on the ground, each mound surrounded by a circular hedge—it looked more like a lunarscape than a landscape, Tracy thought.

They were descending with increasing speed but it took Kirk three passes to chase the goats away from their landing path.

"We're now in the village of Gawani," Kirk informed her as he placed his hands on her waist to help her climb out of the plane.

There was no time for Tracy to wonder why he was suddenly so accommodating. The heat enveloped her as though she had stepped into an oven. Children came rushing at them, shouting. The

younger ones were naked, the older ones wore bur-
lap skirts. They fell silent as they reached the
strangers. Bare-breasted women, wearing colorful
skirts wrapped around their waist and bearing in-
fants in their arms, stopped just beyond the circle
of the children and stared. The men formed a third
ring. As Tracy moved, the rings of people moved
with her.

"Hold it." Kirk raised a camera and took several
pictures of Tracy among the villagers.

"Where did you dig that up?" Tracy asked,
laughing at him.

"Oh, there is more on that plane than meets the
eye," he said, grinning back at her.

Then Kirk spoke to the village elder in Amharic,
and the man offered them a tour.

What had seemed like mounds of earth from the
air, were actually huts, built of poles tied together
with strings and covered with animal skins. Going
inside one of the huts, Tracy discovered that the
only light came through the seams between the
loose animal skins tied to the fitted poles. When
Tracy's eyes got used to the semidarkness, she
noted the primitive fireplace consisting of a ditch
and poles in the middle of the room. Animal skins
lay on wooden platforms around the walls.

"Those are for sleeping, and this is for cook-
ing," Kirk pointed out the obvious. Then he leaned
close to her and taking hold of Tracy's arm, he
murmured in her ear. "How would you like to
spend the rest of your life in a place like this?"

Tracy laughed, without answering. Kirk's warm

breath raised goose pimples on her skin and she moved away from him, freeing herself of his touch. In a crazy way Tracy wanted to tell him that maybe with him, she could live anywhere. But Tracy knew it was merely the cliché thing to say, for even if they were madly in love, neither of them would survive living conditions like these beyond their honeymoon.

Their guide led them outside. Leather pouches, shaped like gourds, hung by the doorway, thickly covered with flies.

"They're filled with goat's milk, the main staple of these people's diet," Kirk explained.

Tracy was secretly aghast because of the lack of sanitation, but she realized that it was merely her cultural background that made her feel this way. They were led to a hut that was the school building for the older boys. The boys held wooden tablets engraved with writing and each read the text out loud as their teacher called on them one by one.

"They're learning to read the *Koran*," the teacher explained through Kirk.

"Only boys study?" Tracy asked.

"Looks like it," Kirk said shrugging.

"Girls have other things to learn," their guide told them. "But now, with the new government, they, too, have started reading classes. But not from the *Koran*, of course."

"See, you just didn't know how good you women have got it in the States," Kirk said, grinning at Tracy.

Back outside in the sun, the trail of children and

women that had followed them on their village tour surrounded them again. Tracy's eye was caught by a wide scimitar-like knife one of the men held up for her to see.

"It's for sale," Kirk informed her.

"How much?"

"Fifteen birrs."

"Can you get it for me?"

"Full price?"

Tracy shrugged. "Bargain or not, as you see fit."

Kirk did, and she became the proud owner of the knife for twelve birrs. While Tracy held it admiringly, she felt a tug at the back of her neck.

A couple of young girls were touching her hair. Laughing, Tracy touched their hair. They wore a coiffure of tight braids, flat against the scalp, like corn rows. Ornaments of red beads and copper plates over small leather squares were woven into the crown of their neat braids. The same ornament, hanging as a necklace, graced the neck of one of the girls. She was quite lovely, wearing only a skirt as the rest of them, but covering her small shapely breasts and shoulders with a transparent red veil.

"Ask her if she would sell me her necklace," Tracy said as she turned to Kirk.

"She would, for sixteen birrs," he informed her.

The price seemed like far too much money to pay, in Tracy's opinion, but the girl wouldn't budge from her price. Through Kirk, and her own sign language, the girl indicated that she would sell her headdress for ten, but the necklace cost sixteen.

Finally, Tracy paid the price. The girl offered to tie it around her neck. As she extended it toward Tracy, the rancid smell of the piece penetrated Tracy's nostrils and she recoiled.

"It's treated with clarified butter to keep the leather soft," Kirk told her, seeing her reaction.

Instead of putting it around her neck Tracy just dropped the necklace into her purse. She hoped that once she got back to the hotel she would be able to scrub off the butter and get rid of the smell.

"Are you ready to head back?" Kirk asked, smiling at her.

"I think so."

Tracy and Kirk said goodbye to the villagers, who parted their concentric rings for them, so they could get back into the plane. Before doing so, Kirk pulled a wicker basket from the cargo compartment.

"I don't see any picnic tables," Tracy teased.

"We'll lunch in the air. I hope you don't mind?"

"On the contrary. What a great idea."

They climbed into the cabin and Kirk placed the basket by Tracy's foot. She was fascinated by the unruffled manner with which Kirk chased the flies out the tiny airhole in the window. Then he shouted "clear" in Amharic so the natives would get out of the way, and after a run-up to test that all systems were functioning, he lifted the plane off the nonexistent runway.

When they reached cruising altitude and the temperature had cooled somewhat, Kirk turned to her. "How about that food?" he asked.

"Ham and cheese sandwiches never looked so good," chuckled Tracy as she unwrapped the slices of limp bread with half-melted cheese between them.

She handed Kirk a sandwich and they sat munching their food, watching the desert below them stretch barren and pale as far as the eye could see.

There was an apple for each of them for dessert. But they had no cups or glasses for their bottled water.

"Go ahead," Kirk told her, "I don't mind drinking out of the same bottle as you."

Tracy drank deeply from the lukewarm water, and wiping the mouth of the jar, she handed it to Kirk.

"I shall know all your secrets," he teased her.

"How so?"

"Don't you know, that if you drink from the same glass that's what happens?"

"Does that mean I'll know your secrets too?" Tracy kidded back.

"No. I drank from your glass, so to speak, but you didn't from mine."

"We shall have to remedy that situation," Tracy replied, nodding with mock seriousness.

"I'll gladly share myself with you, Tracy." Kirk's tone was suggestive rather than playful.

"Thanks for the offer. I might take you up on it someday." Tracy felt like she was falling off a cliff, wondering and not knowing at all where she was going to end up.

"You name the day."

Without responding, Tracy stared out the window. As if the answer lay out there, in the blue sky, the truth came to her. She was in love with Kirk. That was the compelling need that prompted her to want to explore him and attract him, but at the same time made her reject Kirk because she was afraid of falling in love again. She looked at him. His eyes were on the horizon, but his concentration was on her. He was waiting for her answer. Her new realization drew her back from him. She needed time to come to terms with it within herself. Maybe it wasn't even true! Maybe it was just simple physical attraction and she was confusing it with love. In any case, she wasn't going to respond to his game.

"Tomorrow, are we going to the place where *Pegasus 2* is being repaired?" she asked.

"Chicken," he mocked her. "It's all right, Tracy, I know you'll come around."

"You haven't answered my question."

"Neither have you answered my offer."

"We're getting silly."

"Where I come from we call this getting serious."

"I don't consider hopping into bed with someone I barely know, serious."

"Aha. Is that why you got married two weeks after meeting your ex?"

"And who told you that?" Tracy was riled.

"I drank from your cup, remember?" He smiled at her, his eyes warm and probing on her flushed face.

Tracy was so aghast that Kirk knew so much about her that she didn't even bother to insist on knowing his source of information. "It's none of your damned business why I got married! I would thank you to stay out of my private life!"

"Then how do you propose we get to know each other?"

"You could start by talking about yourself!"

"I, too, am a very private person, Tracy. And I never make promises I can't keep. That, in the past, has included not committing myself to any long-lasting relationship. That's what you really wanted to know, isn't it?"

Suddenly the bubble they were sitting in, became too restrictive for Tracy. She desperately wanted out, to walk away from him, to shut out the steel-gray eyes boring into her secret depths. She didn't want Kirk to see how his words made her ache inside. Instead, she reintroduced the light tone of their earlier conversation.

"I believe I was asking you about tomorrow, not our future."

"Do you think we might have one?"

"If you keep your eyes on the instruments, instead of on me, we might."

Kirk laughed robustly. "One of the things I like about you, Tracy, is that you always manage to hide behind words! So to answer your frivolous inquiry, yes, we shall try to get to the plane tomorrow. As for the serious stuff between us—I told you—I intend for you to face up to a few truths before you leave this land. But all in good time."

His words created a gnawing feeling at the pit of Tracy's stomach, but there was no getting away from his powerful presence. It almost seemed as if he had projected his spirit over her, enveloped her in his power, so that she now sat immobilized by inner turmoil. She wanted to give in to him, and she wanted to pull away from him. Her palms were aching to touch the flat planes of Kirk's muscular chest, to feel the soft, dark hair that curled inside his open-necked shirt. Her breasts swelled with a desire for the touch of his large shapely hands that now held the yoke of the plane. Yet he had said so plainly that he merely wanted to teach her a lesson about her own sexuality. He didn't even want a long-term affair, let alone a lasting relationship like marriage. Marriage! The word felt bitter to her. Maybe Kirk was right. What good were the vows of marriage? Maybe it was better to take what the moment offered and not worry about commitment. Except, for that, it was too late for her. Without a doubt she was in love with Kirk and if she got any deeper into the relationship with him, Tracy knew she'd get hurt. Suddenly she realized that it wasn't marriage vows that concerned her, but the pain of divorce. She couldn't face another break with a man she cared about. Some day, if needed, she'd have to tell this to Kirk. This would be her weapon against his temptation. He only wanted a fleeting affair and she wanted one in which there would be no good-byes. Her needs and his were clearly incompatible.

Tracy could feel the plane tilting its nose toward

the earth. Looking ahead she saw the slate-colored rooftops of Addis Ababa. Suddenly, Tracy knew that from now on, her stay in Ethiopia would be a constant combat. It wasn't facing up to some truths that she and Kirk had to battle over—she knew the truth about herself as well as he did— Their fight was over his version of reality versus hers. She simply didn't want to get hurt again.

CHAPTER SEVEN

THE BEEPING of the alarm on Tracy's watch was high-pitched and insistent. Tracy held on for a moment to the darkness beneath her closed lids but she didn't really mind getting up. It promised to be a good day. Bill, Kirk and she would be flying to the damaged plane and then to the campsite where the food was being loaded for the drops. She rolled out of bed and stubbed her toe on the open suitcase that lay in her path to the bathroom. After they had returned to Addis from their flight to the desert, the rest of the day had been spent changing money at the bank, buying mosquito repellent and tissues in a pharmacy, as well as bread, cheese, salami and soft drinks in a small grocery store—all in preparation for their journey the next day.

"Bring your toothbrush, we'll stay overnight," Kirk had tossed the words at her. It was only after she had stared him down in stony silence that he added—"you might also want to bring along a change of clothes."

Kirk, Bill and Tracy had had an early dinner together, with Bill complaining about being stuck in Addis Ababa, and Kirk teasing him about the nurses he was trying to entertain himself with at the hospital. But Bill hadn't been in a good mood. Since they still didn't know whether or not the grain shipment had arrived at the campsite, he complained about Kirk and Tracy's plan to fly there the next day.

"You just want to get out of town and leave me to rot with boredom," Bill had pouted like a petulant child.

Kirk had let him talk on, but right after dinner he had suggested that after a nightcap in the bar they all retire early. Tracy hadn't minded. She was still suffering from jet lag, and the day's excursion had left her exhausted.

Now, holding onto her stubbed toe, she limped into the bathroom for her wake-up shower. She was slipping into her green jump suit when the phone rang. Expecting Kirk to be on the line, she was surprised to hear her father's voice.

"Just checking on how you're doing," he told her, sounding as if he were next door.

"Everything is fine at this end," Tracy assured him and gave him a brief account of her stay.

"Don't worry, honey, about Kirk not doing his job every minute of the day, just flow with it," her father reassured her.

"You mean fly with it?" She could see Ray smiling at the other end of the line.

"That too. Maybe he's doing you a favor, since you get to see some of the countryside this way. So don't fret over it. Enjoy it."

"You're right, dad." They spoke a little while

longer, and then telling Tracy to stay as long as she wished, Ray signed off.

I'm still his little girl, Tracy thought with a smile. When she was little and was sent away to summer camp, her father would always phone after Tracy had been gone for just a couple of days. Though she was no longer little, he was still doing it. Perhaps it was harder for Ray to get used to her absence than it was for her to be away from home. Tracy was on a trip, experiencing new and exciting things, while her father was immersed in the same routines as always but with a cog missing from his world. Oh, well, she wouldn't be missing for long. The call had taken up some of her carefully calculated time and now she would have to rush to get ready.

The first thing Kirk said when they met in the lobby was that there had been a slight change in their plans.

"I got an early call from the Ministry of the Interior. The Chief Commissioner of Relief, His Excellency, Ato Worku Adugni, wishes to meet you. I guess Colonel Teshome gave a favorable report after our luncheon. And while I love the way that green overall shows up your body, I wonder if you could manage to look a little more formal and less alluring when we meet him. After all, you've got to play the head of an important airplane company."

"I don't have to play it; I am head of it!" Tracy raised her chin in proud protest. "At least head of a part of it," she added with a grin in answer to

Kirk's quizzical smile. *Damn him,* she thought, *he flatters me till my heart pounds like a drum and then puts me down!* "What time is His Excellency expecting us?" she asked calmly.

"In an hour. Change and I'll meet you in the restaurant for coffee."

"Does that mean our flight is off for today?"

"No, just postponed a little."

It was too early in the day for Tracy's emerald dress, so she chose her cream-colored skirt and suit jacket again. This time she wore it with the cobalt-blue silk blouse, for color. She swept her hair up into a coil around her head that framed her face nicely and retouched her makeup.

Kirk was openly appreciative when she joined him at the dining room table. "Tracy, you're the most beautiful woman I've ever met. You look positively regal! It provokes a man into wanting to grab you, just to see if that cool exterior could be ruffled."

"What a way to talk so early in the morning," Tracy said, clucking her tongue in mock disapproval.

"You mean you'd rather hear it at a more opportune time?"

"I thought I was promised some breakfast." Tracy found it hard to keep up the flirtatious verbal battle between them without letting him see how much he affected her feelings. So Tracy opted for the easy way out by switching the subject.

Kirk laughed and solicitously ordered her coffee and a breakfast roll filled with melted Swiss cheese.

THE OFFICE OF THE CHIEF COMMISSIONER was a bleak, gray stucco building. The interior decor was just as plain as the outside. The commissioner's office contained a large, dark, executive desk, with two armchairs facing it. Off to one side was the obligatory conversation area, consisting of a nondescript leather sofa and two armchairs with a coffee table in front of them. A portrait of a handsome young officer hung on the wall. Tracy recognized it as that of Lieutenant Colonel Mengistu Haile Marian, the head of the military junta and therefore of the current government. Another wall was taken up by a large map of Ethiopia. A sign next to it said, Ethiopia Tikdem.

Tracy and Kirk sat by the desk, facing the commissioner. He was a man in his mid-forties, with a pleasantly round face and warm eyes.

"I wanted to meet you, Mrs. Brooke, to tell in person how grateful I am, along with my country, for the help you are providing. I've put together some information about the drought for you. But I thought you might better understand the problem if I also told you about it face to face."

The Chief Commissioner spoke English impeccably, with a soft accent and British pronunciation. His manner was serious but not pompous; as Tracy had expected. Knowing what a high position he held in the government, Tracy was aware that if he took this time with her, it was because the service provided by her company was considered important. As the chief commissioner explained the reasons for the drought, the true significance of their enterprise unfolded before Tracy.

"For three years, many of our provinces have not received their normal rainfall. In the districts of Wallo, Tigre and Shoa the only hope for raising a crop is the coming of the short rains, which we call Belg. These usually fall in February and March. Because the Belg failed to materialize again this year, those regions have been faced with an agricultural disaster. As in the previous two years, our government has been aiding them, but this year is the worst. Farmers, who fought valiantly to raise their meager crops, are now starving. Those who could, gave up their farmsteads and moved to the cities. Entire villages have become deserted. Livestock, especially the nomadic herds of cattle, are perishing for lack of grazing land. Then just these past weeks, the rains finally came, but in such large quantities that now some of those provinces are flooded. The floods have ruined what little crops farmers were able to raise, washed away villages and surviving livestock, and left even more people dependent on aid. The floods have destroyed roads and made some of our villages totally inaccessible. At first we tried shipping food in with helicopter, but that wasn't economically feasible. At this time, your planes seem to be the only ones able to reach those provinces with sufficient quantities of grain and food."

He stopped for a moment and Tracy felt he was waiting for her comment. "I am deeply moved by the enormity of the problem your people are facing," Tracy began, "and can only say, in the name of World Help, as well as my company, Westwind Airlines, that I'm happy that our planes can be a part of something as vital as delivering food to the needy."

"Your people, Mr. Russell here, and Mr. O'Connor, have been working round the clock, we must commend you on sending them to us."

Tracy swallowed in surprise. She glanced at Kirk and by now knew him well enough to catch the fleeting, smug smile he sent her from the corner of his lips.

The chief commissioner continued. "When there are delays in the operation, we are totally responsible. For example, we have grain that has been waiting in our harbor at Assab, but no trucks can deliver it to your campsite." He smiled bitterly. "I wish we were as organized as you people are. But some day, we shall be."

Tracy noted that they still hadn't got the grain to the camp and began to wonder if Kirk would cancel their flight. There didn't seem to be much point in going to the camp if the grain wasn't there. She was only half-listening when the word *flood* reached her. Her attention returned just as the chief commissioner was explaining that the night before, the Awash River had flooded the Province of Ausa and, at the town of Logghia, destroyed part of an important bridge that connected the highway to Addis. Since the grain was not deliverable because of the flood, he was now asking if she and Kirk could oblige his office by flying to Logghia and reporting back on the damages.

Despite her new understanding of the situation, Tracy couldn't help feeling anxious at the request. Her first reaction was that another day was going to be wasted flying around. Next, her pragmatism took over. Of course they had to help out. It was better than sitting at the campsite waiting for the grain to arrive. She smiled graciously at the chief commissioner and said, "Mr. Russell is in charge of operations here, so it's up to him to decide, but in my opinion, we must of course do whatever we can to help."

Tracy listened while the commissioner told Kirk which areas he wanted them to fly over. Then amidst profuse thanks and good wishes, they left His Excellency, Ato Worku Adugni's office.

On their way back, Tracy commented to Kirk, that it seemed to her that the main reason the commissioner wanted to see them was to explain that he needed their plane to survey this new disaster.

Kirk laughed. "Don't you realize that he was implying that our getting the grain at our camp depends on making this survey for him?"

Tracy swallowed with surprise. "I guess I'm just too new at this game to see through all this intrigue."

"Stick around and you'll learn soon enough."

"Considering the circumstances, do I still need to take an overnight case on our next trip?"

"We might not get to *Pegasus* 2, but I'm still planning for us to end up at the campsite."

Tracy and Kirk returned to the hotel where they both changed clothes for the flight. Then they headed for the airport.

SOON THEY WERE CIRCLING over the desert again, going in a northeasterly direction. But instead of the sere yellow planes of the sand, as far as the eye could see, water covered the land. Cows and houses were swimming among treetops and people huddled together on any elevation of the ground where they could stay dry.

"And it's only the first rains of the season." Kirk shook his head in dismay. He flew low, carefully scanning the ground for the bridge on which he was supposed to report. It was Tracy who finally spotted it in the distance ahead of them.

"But where are we going to land?" Tracy asked apprehensively.

Kirk smiled. "We'll see."

He circled over the area but Tracy could see no spot that met their requirements. There was a highway that lead to the bridge, but it was blocked by trucks, and there wasn't another spot of dry land. Then as Kirk trimmed the elevator and got ready to descend, Tracy realized with a sense of near panic that he was going to land right on the road!

"I suppose having been a bush pilot in Alaska comes in rather handy for you," she commented acridly. She resented the proprietory way he put her plane down just anywhere. What if something happened to her plane? Tracy could see that Kirk was skilled, but still she worried. He brought the small craft down smoothly, and ran it on the highway as if it were a car, until they reached the parked trucks.

"How's this for a landing strip?" he asked her proudly.

"Nice job," she granted him grudgingly.

The heat met them like a solid wall when they opened the doors of the plane. There was no wind, and the small thermometer Kirk kept inside the cabin registered a hundred five degrees.

"Think cool thoughts," he said, smiling at her. "We won't stay long."

A truck driver gave them a ride to where a group of men were standing at the near end of the broken bridge.

A tall, intelligent looking man in a military uniform came to greet Tracy and Kirk. "I am Major Imru Mekonnen, the governor of this god-forsaken district."

Kirk and Tracy introduced themselves and they all shook hands.

In fluent English the governor explained that his province was flooded in the subdistricts of Dittbari and Asaita, all the way to Lake Abbe. When he learned that this was Tracy's first trip to his province, he said, "Mine is the land of the Danakils, a nomadic people who live off their cattle. They use the milk for food and the animals for trade. Then of course, we also have the Galla tribe, who are farmers. It is densely populated where they live. Unfortunately, after every rain the soil from the farmlands is washed off to the desert—and only the Danakils and the stones of the earth remain. Looks like we're off to a bad start this year; the rainy season is just begun and we're already flooding. Will the government be sending me help, or have they merely sent you to look?''

Tracy could sense his desperate anger with the situation.

"We're here to report on the damage," Kirk said evenly.

"Well, as you can see, the bridge is not passable. I suppose the highway authorities will only do something about it when Addis begins to run short of gasoline because the supply trucks can't pass through. But besides having the bridge repaired, also, we need food and temporary shelter for the people whose houses floated away. Are you going to see the Minister of Relief?''

"We saw him this morning. We might see him again when we get back. In the meantime, I'll radio a report on the damage."

The governor turned to Tracy with a wry smile. "You know, miss, our country has been here since the Old Testament, and our way of doing things hasn't changed since then. Now the revolutionary government is trying to update us so at least we can come up to New Testament standards. But I'm not sure they're succeeding around here." The Ethiopian made a helpless gesture.

"I shall radio Addis as soon as we get back to the plane," Kirk assured him again.

"Aren't you going back to Addis directly?"

"I was planning on filling up at Dupti and then flying on to our campsite. Miss Brooke hasn't seen anything of our operation yet, and she is the engineer of our planes."

"What an honor to have you in our country," Major Imru said, bowing to her. "As you can see, we are far from producing women aviation engineers—but the day may come."

"Well, you're certainly doing your share to help it come about." Kirk smiled at him. "Just running this province must be quite something."

"It's better than sitting in prison," the governor replied, grinning. Then turning to Tracy, he explained, "I spent ten beautiful years of my life in prison for advocating that this country should have some reforms."

"You were arrested just for speaking up?" Tracy was astonished.

"That was under the previous government," Kirk said quickly. "Major Imru was one of the leaders of a coup d'état that tried to unseat the Imperial Government."

"You know, after the revolution I got out of prison and served four years on an agricultural committee. And I did nothing but argue with the people in the current administration." He gave a brief laugh. "Then they sent me out here, to run this province. I figure, I will run things my way till they put me back into prison." He shrugged, his row of even white teeth glistened as he smiled.

"How did you survive ten years in prison?"
Tracy really felt for the man.

"I have always had the feeling that I should
serve my country," said the governor, and his
dark eyes grew serious. "When I got arrested the
only thing I regretted was not having been of better service. But I didn't waste my time in prison.
After awhile they treated me in a somewhat civilized manner, so I was able to study law through
correspondence courses from La Salle University
in the U.S. I shall always be grateful to your country for giving me that opportunity."

Tracy didn't bother to ask the major where he
had learned to speak English. By now she had
realized that if the governor had been a major in
the imperial army of the former king of Ethiopia,
he must have come from an upper-class family.
Judging from his accent, Tracy guessed that he
had been to England. She wondered how long this
intelligent, belligerent man was going to last under
the current socialist government. But she didn't
voice her concern. She just hoped that he would
find a way to serve his people, regardless of
politics.

They thanked the governor for his time, and
Kirk promised to give a vivid report, in hope that
help would come quickly.

"Stop at the hospital in Dupti if you can,"
Major Imru suggested. "It's not wonderful and
modern, but at least we've got one."

When they were seated in the plane again, Kirk
activated the radio and sent his report to Colonel

Teshome, their contact at the Ministry of Relief.

"If I'd heard that report, I'd be out here with the National Guard," Tracy laughed.

"That's the idea," Kirk said, grinning at her.

"An interesting detail about the good major," Kirk added, "that while in prison, he invented a home spinning machine. Now that he is governor, he is starting a whole cottage industry in his province."

"How do you know all this about him?"

"When you're working in a host country, it's your job to find out who is who and what position they're in; otherwise you'd make all sorts of tactical and political errors."

Kirk's cleverness amazed Tracy. The more time she spent in his company, the more facets of his personality appealed to her. In a way Tracy resented him for this. *Why couldn't he be just a simple pilot,* she thought, *someone without the finesse of a diplomat?* It made it so much harder for her to accept the hopelessness of their relationship. Perhaps it was his very sophistication that made Kirk unavailable to her, she thought. It made him too complicated a man with too many choices.

She watched him turn the plane around so it was facing the open highway. He started up the engine and winked at Tracy. "Here we go!"

It wasn't often that, in an airplane, Tracy was concerned about her life. But this was one of those times. Kirk put the throttle on full power and, picking up speed, they raced down the highway. But, coming toward them, were a couple of trucks. Their headlights were on, shimmering in the heat. Involuntarily Tracy curled up her body, grasped her knees and ducked her head in expectation of a head-on collision.

"It's okay," Kirk reassured her. "They saw us and pulled off to the side."

With her eyes glued to the road and her heart pounding wildly, Tracy secretly prayed that they would encounter no more trucks. The lights of one emerged on their horizon just as Kirk lifted the plane off the ground. Tracy threw herself against the back of her seat with a deep sigh of relief.

"You really are taking some awful chances."

"Did you see any other way of getting out of there?"

"I guess not."

She lapsed into silence. Kirk was really an excellent pilot, with nerves of steel. Perhaps she had been too sheltered till now. Aerobatics were one thing, flying as a bushpilot seemed to require quite another kind of skill. Tracy wondered what she would have done if she'd been at the controls, but couldn't assess how she measured up as a flyer against Kirk. As if guessing her thoughts, he said to her, "Want to take over for a while?"

Taken by surprise, Tracy decided against it. "No, I'll take a raincheck on it. You're doing so well, it's a pleasure for me to watch."

"Is it?"

"Well, maybe not a pleasure. Let's say it's a thrill."

"I'm glad you find it so. Personally, I intensely dislike taking chances with a plane."

Kirk's honesty was disarming. But Tracy wasn't sure she believed him. He was too macho not to be exhilarated by danger. When Tracy told him her thought, Kirk stared at her with his clear gray eyes as though he was trying to look within her. "I find the ways between a man and a woman far more exciting."

"Then you admit it's the game you like."

"No, not the game. It's the possibility of a real contact between two people that I like."

"What do you mean by 'real contact'?"

"I can't explain it. I'll have to show you." Kirk smiled roguishly and Tracy felt as though a searing knife had cut through to the core of her being. It was obvious that Kirk was inching his way into forming a relationship with her, yet he avoided any clear-cut statement. Why was the courtship dance always so difficult? Why couldn't he state his feelings as openly as he did his intentions? It was easy to see that he'd jump into bed with her, given the slightest invitation. But why? Merely because she was an attractive female? Then why hadn't Kirk waited for her call in Los Angeles? What did he really want from her? Not knowing what his feelings were tormented Tracy, yet she couldn't really turn to him and ask. Even if she could, no matter what he answered, Tracy wouldn't believe him. She had to discover Kirk's emotions on her own, slowly, during these all-too-brief intimate moments.

"Will you let me show you?"

Tracy shook her head. "I'm afraid, Mr. Russell, that what you call 'real contact' would be defined by a completely different word in my dictionary.''

"How could such a cautious woman marry someone after two weeks?''

"Why do you think I'm so cautious now?'' laughed Tracy.

"Touché. Would you tell me about your marriage?''

"What would you like to know?''

"What it was like, and what went wrong.''

Tracy contemplated Kirk's invitation. *I can dismiss his inquiry with one sentence,* she thought, *and he would never ask me again. But should I?* She wanted to get to know him. Perhaps the way to do so was to start by revealing herself. Alone in the sky with him, in the sweltering heat, under the Plexiglas canopy of the plane, with only the blazing sun for a witness, it seemed like the perfect time for making friends with Kirk by exchanging confidences.

"George and I met at an air show. He too was an engineer. He was also the most fun-loving man I've ever met. He fascinated me because he had the ability to always look at the lighter side of life. I've always been too serious. Even as a teenager I never went out or did the things my peers did. But with George, my whole life changed. We went dancing every night and hang gliding at dawn and surfing...oh...yes...surfing.'' Tracy stopped for a moment, choked up with the memory.

Kirk waited in silence for her to continue. The plane droned on and the blueness of the sky reminded Tracy of the ocean and of the silhouetted figure of George, riding the surf in his glistening black wet suit like some Nordic water god.

"George actually hated being an engineer. His true passion was the surf. One of the things that began to go wrong between us right after we got married was that he wanted me to quit my job at Westwind. He kept saying, that with my skill as a designer, I could make far more money elsewhere. He wanted me to make more so he could quit his job and follow the surf around the world for a year."

"How did you feel about that?"

"You can well imagine. Obviously we fought a great deal over it. And I didn't leave my job. Then one day I discovered—" Tracy stopped, unable to go on.

"That he was unfaithful to you?" Kirk's eyes were on the skies ahead, but his voice enveloped her, his tone full of warmth and empathy.

"Yes," Tracy whispered. And then as though a dam had burst, she told Kirk the story she had never been able to relate to any of her friends or family members. Oh, her family knew that she left him because, among other problems, George "fooled around." But until this moment Tracy hadn't been able to bring herself to tell anyone about the horror and humiliation of that afternoon when she arrived home unexpectedly, because she'd forgotten a sketch in her study.

"I saw George's car in the garage and I wondered if he had come home because he wasn't feeling well."

She stole a glance at Kirk. He was looking straight ahead, but his concentration was on her. Tracy went on.

"I opened the front door and sensed immediately that something was wrong. I stopped to listen. Coming from the bedroom, I heard a woman's laughter mingled with George's. I was rooted to the floor. Still, like a fool I wanted to give him the benefit of doubt. What if she were just a visitor? Perhaps a co-worker or co-surfer had stopped by and he was just showing something to her in the bedroom. George hated me to be jealous. So I swallowed by suspicions and called out to inform him that I was home. There was a dead silence in the bedroom, followed by some frantic whispering, and finally George came padding out to the living room in his bathrobe. He demanded to know why I had come home. He accused me of spying on him! I headed straight for the door while he was trying to make up a story about having been out surfing and how he and this woman had returned to the apartment to shower—but by that time I was down the hall without a word to him. I went straight to my lawyer and filed for a divorce that afternoon."

Tracy slumped back against her seat, her energy drained completely from her body. Kirk put the plane on automatic pilot and turned to her. Tracy's hands were white from squeezing them into fists. Very gently Kirk took her hands in his. His gray eyes looked into hers, full of compassion. "That must have been a terrible shock."

Kirk's words provoked tears, but Tracy didn't feel she needed to hide them. He leaned forward, and tenderly kissed her eyes. Then in order to break the solemn mood between them, he smacked his lips with tender mocking and savored her tears. "Hmm, salty."

Tracy laughed and freeing a hand placed it on his chest to push him back. "Stop it you fool."

"I'm no fool," Kirk murmured, and reaching behind her he cupped the back of her head in his large palm. Holding her still, he forced her to withstand his deep gaze as he scanned her face, bearing into her eyes. "His loss is my gain."

"No, Kirk," Tracy cried out. "Don't you see why I'll never let myself in for a quick experience again?"

"Who's talking about a quick experience?" Kirk leaned forward and slowly, languourously brushed her lips with his. "We have all the time in the world." Then he pulled away from her. "But not now. Now we've got to land this baby."

While he gradually brought the plane down, Kirk told Tracy that the small town they were coming to was called Dupti. They would take on fuel there, and then head for their campsite. They landed in an open field in a bowl of dust stirred up by their propeller.

Kirk taxied the plane just a short distance across the field to a dilapidated wooden shack and stopped in fornt of it. He pointed at the building. "The gas station. The pump is inside."

"You're kidding," Tracy laughed.

"No. See for yourself."

An unrelenting heat surrounded Tracy as she clambered out of the plane. Kirk too climed down. He knocked on the door of the shack, but there was no one inside. Glancing at his watch, Kirk shrugged. "It's lunchtime. There is nothing we can do but wait."

He pulled their provisions from the plane, and suggested that they too have a bite.

Tracy wasn't hungry, only thirsty. She noticed that Kirk drank only a few sips of the water they had brought along.

"When it's this hot, I tend not to drink till evening. Just habit," he explained.

On the road that ran alongside the gas station, a Jeep emerged out of the dust. The windshield was so covered with fine powder that Tracy couldn't make out the person driving it until the car stopped. An attractive blonde jumped out of the car and ran toward them. She wore a white smock and had a stethoscope stuck into her front pocket. When she reached them the woman cried out, "Kirk!" and embraced him. He responded to her hug affectionately, then turned to Tracy.

"This is Doctor Helga Hense, from Switzerland. At present, the resident doctor at Dupti."

While they exchanged greetings and made polite conversation about being a long way from home, Tracy had a chance to assess Dr. Hense. She estimated the woman was in her early thirties. The physician's hair was a lovely strawberry-blond, more gold than red, and she wore it in a simple cut that fell straight around her face. Her broad cheeks were sunburnt and freckled. She wore no makeup and there was a healthy glow to her complexion. Her light blue eyes, framed by thick golden lashes, projected intelligence and warmth. Tracy wondered how well Helga and Kirk knew each other.

"Come I'll show you the hospital. I was on my way there when I heard the plane land." Helga smiled happily at Kirk. "It's better than your sitting around here for two hours!" Helga's open smile was directed at both of them and Tracy concluded that the other woman would not try to push her aside and claim only Kirk as her visitor. Tracy felt relieved. They locked up the plane and piled into Dr. Hense's Jeep.

"Beside the usual cases, we're now getting flood victims as well. Seems like it's one calamity after another in this country," Helga commented during the drive.

The hospital was a low building. It had a crowded, indoor-outdoor appearance because many of the patients were sitting in the hallways and some were huddled in the shade of the outside walls.

"When a member of a Danakil family gets sick, the whole family stays with him at the hospital," Dr. Hense explained. "They take care of the sick. All I have to do is tell them how. Of course if they don't like what I say, they don't follow my instructions, but that's part of the way they are."

Going inside, a beautiful dark-skinned young woman caught Tracy's attention. She sat on one of the beds in the overcrowded room, her head wrapped in a sky-blue gauze scarf. The sick woman stared at the visitors with large, indifferent eyes. When she caught Tracy's glance on her, her slim hands drew the scarf around her face and she looked away.

"A viral infection," Dr. Hense explained. "Essentially the only thing the desert people live on is cow's milk. If their cow gets sick, they get sick."

In another room, an old man's emaciated form was curled up on a mattress. "A famine victim," Dr. Hense said.

A mother held her child at her breast, while her husband, two other children and an old woman surrounded her.

"The baby had pneumonia when she brought him in. He's okay now."

"At least they know enough to come in," Kirk commented.

"The government sends them. I think they're told that the white doctor's medicine is more powerful than their own. They come and try it. Then they leave. And back at home they pay their own medicine man another fee—out of respect."

A nurse came over and asked Helga to go off with her. Tracy and Kirk wandered around for a while, working their way out of the hospital.

"I find it very depressing in there," Tracy confessed once they were on the street again.

"Think how much better off Ethiopians are now than they were before, when they didn't have any hospitals."

"How come Helga came all the way from Switzerland to work here?"

"An idealist I suppose."

An administrator caught up with them outside.

"Dr. Hense sent me to say she is sorry, but she will be tied up for a while. She wants you to take her car if you're going back to fill up your plane. She says she will meet you at her house later, and that you are welcome to stay for dinner."

He handed Kirk the car key.

"I thought we were leaving right after refueling." Tracy couldn't hide her irritation at this unexpected change of plans.

"I wasn't thinking of staying," Kirk said. "Let's get the plane in shape and go."

But their situation wasn't that simple. The gas station was still closed.

"It's the only one in town." Kirk rubbed his chin. "We'll just have to wait it out."

A villager came by and Kirk found out from him that the owner of the station had to go to a funeral in the next town, and the pump would be closed until he got back. Tracy was fuming. She felt they were losing their whole day. She was anxious to see if *Pegasus 2* was repaired and get to the campsite. She didn't want to spend the afternoon in a sleepy village.

"We're wasting time," she burst out in anger.

Kirk shrugged philosophically. "This isn't the U.S., my love. Time goes slower here. Everything happens at its own good pace."

"Don't call me 'my love.' That's a real put down!"

"I certainly didn't mean it to be."

"I am not in the mood for your teasing."

"I can see that."

"Stop being so damned agreeable!"

"You want me to fight with you?"

"Oh, go away."

Kirk smiled at her. "I'd obey but I don't think you'd enjoy the walk to Helga's house in this heat."

Tracy turned her back on him, furious with herself for behaving so childishly, and with him, for his good-natured tolerance of her. She didn't know how to respond to it. It disarmed her and she found it hard to stay angry with him. *Yet I should be angry,* she thought, her own restlessness welling up within her. Tracy fully realized that it wasn't Kirk's fault that the proprietor of the only gasoline station in town had a funeral to attend. Perhaps they had flown farther to reach the broken bridge than Tracy realized, yet she wondered why Kirk hadn't filled up sufficiently in Addis to make it to the campsite directly.

"You didn't tell me we were going to stop here," she complained. "Are you sure we can't go on without refueling?"

"The camp is too far from here and I won't risk it. My cargo is precious." Kirk smiled at her. "C'mon Tracy, be a sport. I know your father told you to take a vacation so why don't you relax and look upon this as an adventure?"

"How do you know?"

"We communicate. I call or he calls. I send him reports on the operation."

Tracy began to laugh and couldn't stop. Even her own father had conspired against her by letting Kirk know that she was supposed to have time on her hands. Gasping for air, Tracy thought, *Men have a special bond, and they will always tip each other off.* Through her uncontrollable peals of laughter she managed to get out, "You know everything, don't you?"

"Almost everything," Kirk grinned, watching her laugh.

Finally Tracy stopped, taking deep breaths to relax her cramped stomach muscles. "That felt good." She began to giggle again.

"Would you share with me what you were laughing about?"

"I'm not sure. Nothing funny, really. I sometimes have fits of laughter when I'm tired and frustrated. Maybe this is one of those times."

"I'm sorry you feel frustrated. It reflects badly on me as a host. Perhaps I could provide better entertainment."

They were standing in the only shade, near the wall of the small building that contained the office and the gas station. With a lightning-quick gesture, Kirk circled his arms around Tracy and pulled her against him. His swift move made Tracy lose her balance and she fell against him. The length of her slim body pressed against his from head to toe. The feel of his thighs against hers aroused a deep, sweet ache within her and she could feel a straining in her breasts as they came in contact with Kirk's muscular chest. His hand slipped into her hair at the nape of the neck and he leaned forward to meld Tracy's lips with his, in a deliberately slow, possessive kiss.

Tracy's first instinct was to push Kirk away, but as his lips and tongue languorously explored the warm, moist planes of her mouth, his teeth teasing, nibbling gently on the soft inner skin of her lips, it felt so right that Tracy closed her eyes and let the world disappear from her consciousness. Only their lips existed, responding to each other, demanding, giving. Kirk's strong arms held her tight against his firm body, and with a deep, sub-conscious yearning to become one with him, Tracy's arms reached around Kirk and held on to him. She caressed the taut muscles on his back, teasing the dark curls at the base of his neck. Lost in the searing pleasure of his embrace, when his lips released hers Tracy felt so weak in the knees that she was afraid to pull away from him. She stood still in his arms knowing that Kirk was aware of the shallow, fast breathing that betrayed the feelings he had aroused in her.

"I wish we were alone and someplace else," Kirk murmured, looking at her flushed face.

Tracy smiled, "I don't know about being alone with you, Kirk. You're dangerous." She moved out of his arms and leaned against the building.

He put his palm against the wall for support and

his extended arm gave him just the right distance to be near Tracy and still observe her face.

"I am! You're like a firebrand!"

"In that case it may be wiser for you not to be playing with fire."

"What do you think I was doing for five years in Alaska?"

"Ah, but there you were helping to put fires out. Here you seem bent on igniting one."

"I have a feeling you've stopped objecting."

"I'm going to level with you, Kirk. Earlier today I trusted you with the story of the true reason for my divorce. That was something I couldn't talk about before, even with my closest friends. Obviously I like you, and I'd be lying if I denied that I'm attracted to you, but I don't want to make the same mistake twice. I know virtually nothing about you, and what I do know is enough for me not to want to go any further with you."

"Tracy, what dark secret about me makes you turn away?"

"I'm not joking, Kirk."

"I'm sorry, but you sound so mysterious. Maybe if you told me what you want to know about me I could tell you."

"For one thing, you promised to tell why you left Los Angeles almost a week early, and why you sidestepped me and dealt with others in the company when you knew part of this project was under by supervision?"

Kirk was obviously taken aback by Tracy's unexpected question. He stayed silent, his gray eyes very serious now as they examined Tracy's face and finally met her gaze squarely.

"I guess I owe you an explanation, Tracy. The most direct answer I can give you now, is that when I found out that you were the boss's daughter, I thought it best not to deal with you again."

"But why!"

"It's a long story. Come, I'll tell it to you on the way to Helga's house."

She followed him to the Jeep in silence. Secret doors were opening between them and Tracy was afraid that if she uttered a sound they would shut tightly.

Kirk started up the motor and began a slow, puttering ride down the main street.

"My father owns a fairly large company," Kirk began. "From the time I was a young boy he had an understanding with a friend of his, another manufacturer in a complementary field, that when his daughter and I grew up we'd marry and the two firms would merge. Tress and I got along very well as kids. Judging from the marriages of our parents and others around us, we figured that if we did get married, ours would be about as good an arrangement as any—perhaps even better, since we had known each other all our lives. But what ultimately made me rebel against the idea was that if I married Tress I would have come under the domination of both our fathers for the rest of my life or theirs. That's when I ran off to Alaska."

Tracy's mind was racing. So that's the ghost Bill was referring to at dinner that night! Kirk saw in her another company owner's daughter and he just couldn't deal with the situation. "Did you love Tress?"

"I still love her. You don't stop loving a childhood friend."

"In that case, why couldn't you marry her and move away?"

"At that time I couldn't have done it. There was too much pressure from both our families. Besides, Tress wouldn't have wanted me to do that. Now, it's seven years later, and I'm building my own life."

"What about Tress?"

"She's married and her husband is working for her father's company."

"Do you regret it?"

"Are you kidding? I am my own boss! Most of the time, anyway," Kirk added, with a swift glance at Tracy. "Here we are." He pulled the Jeep up in front of a low-slung adobe house painted in pastel pink.

"Thank you for sharing your past with me," Tracy felt compelled to say.

"We both shared something of ourselves today." Kirk gave her a warm smile.

Tracy had a feeling of deep satisfaction. Their talk had created a glow within her, and she no longer minded that they were stranded. Had it not been for their situation, perhaps she and Kirk would not have been able to open up to each other. Tracy now understood Kirk's hesitation and anger. She had not answered for herself the question of whether or not she would leave her father's company if she and Kirk became serious about each other. It sufficed that for the first time since her arrival in Ethiopia, they had taken a step toward each other that went deeper than their physical attraction. Tracy wanted to preserve this new intimacy between them as a rare and precious gift that had been bestowed upon her.

DR. HENSE'S LIVING ROOM was large and rectangular shaped. Its lime-green walls were decorated with Ethiopian rugs and paintings. Surprisingly, it was air-conditioned. Tracy and Kirk settled on the sofa and a servant brought them tall glasses of iced soda water. Tracy closed her eyes for a moment. After the flight and the heat, it was wonderful to feel the silence and the cool air. When she next opened her eyes, the room was lit with softly glowing lamps and Helga was standing by her side, taking her pulse.

"It's normal," Tracy heard her say to Kirk. "She must have been exhausted. You do have a tendency to run people ragged."

Quickly Tracy closed her eyes again, not wanting them to know that she was awake. Helga's soft, intimate tone made her want to hear more of their conversation.

"Are you referring to Bill?" Kirk asked her.

"Him and everyone else. I wonder whether Bill would have had that accident had he not made that extra run."

"Helga, things happen to planes sometimes."

"I've heard that accidents are usually the pilot's fault, not the plane's. But I didn't mean to get into a discussion about this. I think dinner is ready. Shall we just let Tracy sleep, or do you want to wake her?"

"I am up," Tracy said, opening her eyes. "What's going on?"

"You fell asleep," Kirk said, coming to her side. "And I didn't want to wake you."

"What about our schedule?"

"The gasoline station won't be open until tomorrow morning, so we're staying the night."

"Here?"

"I'm sorry, Tracy," Helga cut in, "my guest room is already taken up by a couple. But the mayor of the town was here earlier and he insisted that you be his guests for the night. So we'll have dinner together, and then you two will go over there."

Tracy was speechless. She couldn't very well have a fight with Kirk in front of Helga, but she was quite angry. As soon as Helga went out to check on dinner, Tracy turned to Kirk. "How could you do this?"

"I didn't! I went back to the plane while you were napping, and found out that our man won't return to town till tomorrow. They do have a wake after the funeral, you know."

Tracy gritted her teeth without a word. It really wasn't Kirk's fault that they were stuck. Yet she held him responsible and resented him. With a clarity of mind that came from having rested,

Tracy realized that her eagerness to get to the plane and the campsite was due to the inner pressure she felt about the future of Westwind. It had been nearly two months since Anne had given them her six-month deadline. Every minute on this project counted! Even though her father told her to take a few days off, Tracy was eager to spend her free time on something useful instead of whiling away the hours. But she couldn't explain her difficulty to Kirk, especially not here, and not now.

Helga returned, bringing with her a young couple whom she introduced as Joyce and Steve Cameron, her houseguests. They were peace corps volunteers, recently arrived to teach English in Dupti. Joyce was blonde, somewhat plain, but pleasant to look at, and Steve's most distinguishing facial feature was a thick, brown mustache.

Dinner was a simple meal of a clear soup, roast chicken and baked potatoes. Helga explained that she had taught her maid to cook European style dinners because she found it easier psychologically. "It's like a bit of home after I come back from the hospital," Helga explained.

Conversation centered on life in the area, and Joyce and Steven described their excursion to a local market in Assayta, a nearby town.

The market takes place only once a week and it's on tomorrow. It's an experience you shouldn't miss," Joyce insisted, her pale features lit up by a smile.

"Especially if you're staying over anyway," Steve seconded her, stroking his mustache.

"What's so special about it?" Tracy asked skeptically.

"The people, the camels, the ride there—everything." Joyce bubbled.

"How long does it take to get there and back?" Kirk inquired.

"About an hour either way. I can lend you my Jeep. And Ali, my assistant, can take you." Helga offered.

"Can we decide in the morning?" Tracy balked at committing herself to the excursion.

"Sure. I'll send the driver to the mayor's house at 7:00 A.M. If you wish, you can go to the market; if not, he'll drive you to the plane."

"Fair enough," Tracy agreed, nodding.

After dinner the Camerons went off to their room, and Helga asked Kirk to come into her study for a moment. The doctor had a map there, and ostensibly she was giving Kirk directions on how to get to the mayor's house, but Tracy wondered what other things she wanted to discuss with him in private. She wondered about the relationship between Kirk and Helga and felt a deep sting of jealousy at the thought that it could be more than platonic. Yet there was nothing in the behaviour of either, as they emerged from the study, to indicate a greater intimacy than a good friendship.

"Ready to go?" Kirk asked.

They thanked Helga for her hospitality, and saying good night to her, Tracy and Kirk set out for the mayor's house.

CHAPTER EIGHT

WALKING WASN'T SO BAD, once they got used to the intense heat again. Following the precise directions given to Kirk by Helga, Tracy and Kirk picked their way slowly down the main street of town. The full moon lighted their way and cast eerie shadows on the small houses, which sat back from the road, dark and silent at that time of night. No one was around. They didn't even see any dogs, though occasionally they heard one bark at their approaching footsteps. Then down the street, another canine's voice would echo back. The hardened ground of the unpaved road crunched softly beneath their shoes.

Neither of them spoke. Tracy wondered if Kirk's thoughts were lingering on Helga. She would have liked to ask just how intimately they knew each other. They seemed so comfortable with each other, so much at ease.

Why was it, Tracy mused, that between she and Kirk there was almost always an undercurrent of tension. Even now, while they were walking silently alongside each other, she could feel a peculiar strain between them. It was as though invisible, cobweb-thin cords tied them together, and each time one made a move, the other could feel it. Or perhaps it was only she who felt this way because of her ambivalence toward Kirk. After the first day in Addis, Tracy had been sure that she would become disillusioned with him. Instead, beneath that hard exterior, she had discovered a caring, fascinating man. And now she had to face the fact that she had fallen in love. Yet Tracy knew Kirk was just playing with her, and considering his past, she knew his life goals would never include having a deeper, permanent relationship with her. Still, Tracy couldn't give up the hope that if Kirk wanted to, they could work out their lives together.

"What are you thinking of?" He touched her gently by the elbow, then released her.

"I'm wondering how well you know Helga."

"How well can you know anybody?"

"Stop teasing me."

"Then ask me directly what you want to know. If I didn't know better, I'd flatter myself by saying that you're jealous!"

Tracy was glad it was dark so Kirk couldn't see her blush. It was uncanny the way he always saw through her.

"Why would I be?" She could hear the falseness of her tone, and sure enough, Kirk heard it too.

He laughed out loud, his voice echoing in the night and setting off a distant chain of barking.

"I could string you on, Tracy, but I won't. It's Bill who's got something going with Helga, not me. She wanted to know when he'd be well enough to come and see her."

Tracy recalled Helga's accusation that Kirk worked his men too hard. Now she understood the other woman's concern over Bill. She felt relieved, but at the same time, Tracy began to speculate over who, then, held the key to Kirk's heart. After all, he was thirty-five, unmarried and too good-looking to be without love. If, as he had said, he did not want to make a long term commitment, it must be because his heart was already committed, she concluded. Despite the fact that Kirk had said he was over Tress, Tracy wondered if Kirk had been so hurt when his childhood love had married someone else, that he had closed his heart forever. *Or is he waiting for her to divorce,* Tracy thought with bitterness.

"I believe this is where we turn," Kirk said as they arrived at a wide crossroad.

"You're the navigator," Tracy said agreeably. Her own thoughts were not good company. She was relieved Kirk had broken their silence.

"Have you ever seen so many stars?" he asked, lifting his face toward the black sky, sparkling with millions of lights.

"I have, in the California desert. Out there the summer nights are just as hot as here."

"We must go there together to compare." Kirk's voice was as velvety as the sky. He put an arm around Tracy's shoulders. At his touch a sweet ache spread over her and regardless of earlier discouragement Tracy couldn't resist adjusting her steps, so that she and Kirk moved in unison. Their bodies walking in the same rhythm seemed so right, that she felt like holding on to this moment forever. At the same time her mind was racing. What had he meant by that remark? Did he mean that he planned to see her even after they got back to the States? Why would he say that if he didn't mean it? Tracy didn't ask aloud. Sadly, she suspected that Kirk had made the kind of comment he would make to any woman while he walked with her along a moonlit street with his arm wrapped around her. Tracy felt she was better off remaining silent and relishing the pleasure of his nearness, than speaking and igniting sparks between them.

"That must be it." Kirk pointed to the only house at the end of the street with lights on.

Tired as she was, Tracy was almost sorry that they had arrived because it broke the intimate mood between them. Helga had promised that the accommodations would be adequate at the mayor's house, but Tracy secretly worried that "adequate" might mean something different than "comfortable." If they were to leave early the next morning for another long day's flight, she, for one, would need a good night's rest.

The mayor received them with a broad smile. He was a tall man with a sizeable belly—a sign of wealth and respectability around this part of the world as Kirk had pointed out to her earlier. The mayor's English vocabulary was limited to "hello" and "welcome," so Kirk used Amharic to communicate. Their host offered them supper but Kirk explained that they had already eaten at Helga's house. But, knowing that they must accept at least a token of hospitality, Kirk agreed to a soft drink. They waited in the formal dining room, seated at a long table. The mayor returned, bringing them tall glasses of Coke, without ice. When they finished drinking, the mayor led Kirk and Tracy along a hallway, where a series of closed doors indicated that there were quite a few rooms in his house. At the very end of the hall he threw open a door to reveal a large bedroom decorated with western style furniture.

"This is where we'll sleep tonight," Kirk said, interpreting for Tracy.

"But I thought that we'd have separate rooms!" Tracy protested. "Doesn't he know we're not married?"

Kirk turned back to the mayor. Tracy watched their host's face light up with a bright smile as he listened to Kirk.

"What did you tell him?" she demanded.

"What I was supposed to," Kirk replied, grinning at her.

"And what was that?"

"I'll tell you later."

The mayor led them inside the room, and Tracy realized with alarm that Kirk had not explained their situation to their host. Not being able to express herself in Amharic, Tracy felt like a deaf-mute, but there was nothing she could do about it. Without a knowledge of the language, whatever she said would be lost on the mayor, who now was pointing with pride at the bed and at the air conditioner in the window.

"He says he imported the bed and the air conditioner from America," Kirk interpreted faithfully, and added, "give him a smile, Tracy; the man is offering you his treasures. Show some appreciation!"

Feeling trapped, Tracy tried to make the best of the situation by smiling at their host while she hissed at Kirk through clenched teeth, "I think this is outrageous."

Yet, while Kirk turned to the mayor again, Tracy had to admit to herself that the cool of the room after the heat outside, was pleasant. It was only the sleeping arrangement that was causing her anxiety.

The mayor showed them the private bathroom, pointing to the modern facilities, which included an imported plastic shower stall.

"This is all from Europe," Kirk translated. This time Tracy's answering smile was genuine. She was looking forward to a shower. With a gesture even Tracy could understand, the host bid them good night and left.

As soon as the door closed behind the mayor, she turned to face Kirk. His gray eyes seemed to be assessing her. As she had so many times in her life when she had been in a tight spot, now, too, Tracy was able to hide her feelings of apprehension, and present a calm exterior.

"Which of us will sleep on the floor?" she asked coolly.

Kirk burst out laughing. "You're wonderful, Tracy. You never let your hair down, do you?"

Tracy didn't rise to the bait. Instead, she walked over to the bed and examined it. There was no way to divide it. The king-size mattress sprawled in one enormous piece across the wooden frame, and the bedding consisted only of a light summer blanket and a sheet underneath.

"Even if we could separate the bed, I wouldn't advise sleeping on the floor," Kirk said, guessing Tracy's intentions. She lifted her chin at him defiantly. "All right, then, which side of the bed do you want?"

Tracy saw a light of admiration in Kirk's eyes and was pleased with herself. She sensed that they were walking a thin line between controlling the tension between them and sparking off the passionate desire, which was barely masked by their self-imposed courtesy. Tracy felt his pull. There was only a short distance between them as they stood facing each other, and it took all of Tracy's willpower to resist rushing to him, putting her arms around him and offering her lips to his tantalizing kisses. But she held her ground. By now she knew enough about Kirk to hold back her feelings. Ruefully she acknowledged that although she had an increasing love for him, he obviously did not feel the same way about her. While she wanted all of him or nothing, to him, she was probably just another adventure. If she allowed herself to get involved with him more deeply, he wouldn't get hurt, all the pain would be hers. And Tracy wanted to protect herself at all costs from this possibility.

"You take the side you prefer," Kirk said, smiling at her.

She pointed to the right side of the bed, and in return offered Kirk the bathroom first.

"I'll probably shower faster than you," he said, grinning. "After I'm done you can take as long as you like."

"A deal," Tracy agreed, smiling back at him. Then she dropped her overnight case on a chair, feeling as though her face would crack if she had to keep up the charade much longer. In a strange way Tracy was enjoying the surface coolness between them. She was also pleased Kirk had refrained from making one of his lightning swift moves for her. But another part of her was acutely aware of their true feelings and thoughts. The air was so heavy with sexual tension that she was relieved to have Kirk out of the room, however briefly.

When Kirk emerged from the bathroom, Tracy almost let out a loud gasp, for he appeared naked, except for a towel wrapped around his lean hips. A rush of physical desire washed over her as Tracy's eyes soaked up the beauty of Kirk's broad shoulders and lingered on his naked chest, which was covered with soft, dark hair. Finally she averted her gaze for fear that Kirk would read her feelings. But he showed no signs of being aware of her thoughts. Relaxed from the shower, he said to her, as though she were just a friendly stranger, "It's your turn, take your time."

Tracy lingered under the cool spray, letting the

water run over her body, the sensuous pleasure
heightened by the knowledge of Kirk's presence in
the next room. She couldn't help wondering what
it would feel like to have Kirk's hands run over her
as caressingly as the spray of water. But she
dismissed the thought, knowing that it would not
happen. From the way Kirk had handled things,
Tracy concluded that he would not take advantage
of their circumstances. He wouldn't touch her
unless Tracy indicated that she wanted him. And
that, she could not and would not do. Tracy knew
she couldn't cross the barrier she had set up for
her own protection. The realization filled her with
a pang of sadness. How near they were to each
other and yet how distant!

Tracy shut off the shower and dried herself with
one of the thin, rough towels hanging on the rack.
She had brought her overnight case into the bathroom. Tracy unfolded her nightgown, and slipped
into it, then stood in front of the mirror at a loss.
Through the fine lace her pink nipples were clearly
visible, and the peach-colored satin clung to her
body, leaving very little to the imagination. She
now regretted leaving her robe at the hotel in
Addis Ababa. "I've seen women's intimate wear
before," Tracy recalled Kirk had said. She
shrugged with a mischievous smile. Let him get an
eyeful.

She walked boldly into the bedroom, but to her
surprise, she found Kirk sprawled across the bed,
fast asleep. Relaxed in sleep, his face had all his
good looks without the hard set expression he so

often wore. Wrapped only in a towel, he reminded Tracy of a Roman centurion; his body lean, muscular, and perfectly proportioned. Tracy felt like touching the soft, dark fuzz on his chest, but knowing that she'd be playing with fire, controlled her impulse. Instead, she carefully lowered herself onto the bed in the space left by him and reached out to the wall above the headboard to shut off the light.

Sensing Tracy's presence, Kirk let out a deep sigh and turned in her direction. In the dark, as she pulled her arm back, she brushed against his naked chest. The touch of his sleep-warmed, fine-haired skin sent a curious pain through Tracy. She recoiled, then turning her back to Kirk, she slid toward the edge of her side of the bed. Again, despite the care she took, Tracy touched him. Now awake, Kirk must have misunderstood her touch, for he reached out and, putting an arm over her, drew Tracy to him, molding his body against hers.

"Tracy, my darling, how I want you," he whispered. And before she could protest, his lips began a gentle journey down the sensitive skin of her neck and shoulders. Kirk held her close with one arm while his free hand explored her body, brushing teasingly over her breasts and then down to her slim waist. Tracing the curve of her hips, Kirk's palm glided along her long, slim thighs, his fingers playing her nerve ends.

Tracy froze, fighting herself, wanting to pull away from him, but as Kirk's hand moved slowly, tantalizingly over her body, she began to tremble with an uncontrollable desire for him. With a great sigh of longing Tracy turned toward him, and no longer able or wanting to hold back, she sought out his lips. A searing flame coursed through her and a sweet taste gathered in her mouth as she responded to Kirk's searching tongue. Her breasts swelled into his stroking hand and her nipples grew hard, aching to be kissed. With eager but gentle hands Kirk slipped the nightgown off her shoulders, then pulled the garment lower and lower till Tracy lay naked before him. Her porcelain-white skin glowed in the moonlight. He gazed at her and she felt vulnerable, as though he could see through to her very soul, which was now so full of love for him. Tracy's eyes pleaded with him not to hurt her.

"You're breathtakingly beautiful," Kirk whispered, and he caressed her again with a feather-soft touch till Tracy's skin tingled. His teasing tongue touched her whimsically, creating havoc with her senses. She felt her body consumed by a smoldering heat. His hands, roaming, fondling, possessing, aroused the very center of her being. Tracy wanted to open up to him with a wild, primitive urge. Kirk's towel had fallen off, and she felt his bare skin scorching hers. She inhaled the warm scent of his skin with dizzying pleasure. Driven by some uncontrollable urge, she reached out for him and ran her hands through Kirk's tousled hair. She explored his exciting body with an abandon that came from her deep feelings for him. His lips, his tongue, his hands invaded her most secret places. Tracy moaned as sensations buffeted her. She arched toward him, her body alive as it had never been before. Kirk drew her beneath him. As their bodies joined, Tracy exploded with a pleasure that was almost painful. She was flying, soaring in the weightless ecstasy of their union.

Afterward, held in the warm circle of his arms, Tracy felt an unspoken love flowing between them as Kirk showered her with gentle kisses and stroked her hair till she fell asleep, snuggled against him.

WITH THE FIRST MORNING LIGHT, a warm glowing feeling slowly enveloped Tracy's consciousness. She knew something wonderful had taken place the night before, but didn't want to jarr the memory. She imagined she was hovering in a plane. She was surrounded by a wonderful pink cloud, but knew that if she stayed in the nebulous haze too long, she'd lose her sense of direction. In her fantasy Tracy feared that once she got out, the world would be all gray around her. Yet the cloud had already begun to disperse. Tracy didn't have to reach out to know the warm body that had held her in its magic circle through the night was now gone. She could hear the shower humming in the bathroom. It was time to get up and brave whatever the day would bring.

What made it so hard for her to face Kirk was that she didn't know how to behave with him now.

Her response during their lovemaking must have clearly revealed her feelings for him, and she was hoping that Kirk wouldn't comment on it or treat it lightly. Tracy was slightly embarrassed about her display of unbridled passion since Kirk had made no confession of his feelings for her. She braced herself, trying to bring the nerve-shattering effect their lovemaking had had on her under control before she had to face him. She suspected that it hadn't had the same effect on Kirk. Men could often make passionate love at night, and forget the experience the next morning—at least that was how it had been with George. Feeling lost, Tracy curled up in a ball and closed her eyes when she heard the bathroom doorknob turn. *Let him make the first contact,* she thought.

Kirk's lips gently brushed the curve between her neck and shoulder. "Tracy, it's time to get up," he murmured teasingly into her ear. His tone was playful.

Tracy opened her eyes only to meet his—smiling and warm. If she didn't know better, she would have thought Kirk's gaze radiated love.

She stretched, and suddenly, there was his warm, firm body for her arms to curl around as he pulled her to him, his naked chest moist against her bare breasts.

"Good morning, my love." Kirk kissed her affectionately. "Mmmm..." his kiss deepened but when he felt Tracy respond, Kirk pulled back almost abruptly. "Don't tempt me. As it is, we've overslept. Our driver is waiting outside."

Tracy leaped out of bed and past him, grabbing the sheet to cover her naked form. "I won't take long," she promised as she disappeared in the bathroom.

Everything will be fine, Tracy decided as she dressed with great vigor. Kirk wasn't going to embarrass her. She felt like celebrating by going to the market. *Even I am entitled to a day off,* Tracy thought wryly. It was the perfect day for her to take off. She had let love into her life again, and doing so had made her aware of how exciting and wonderful being alive could be. For once Tracy was going to take time and make it hers.

THERE WAS NO ROAD, yet Ali, their driver, seemed to find his way as easily as if he were on a superhighway. Despite the early hour, the heat was already intense. Tracy sat by the window, watching the cracked, arid land go by. Kirk, balancing between Ali and Tracy, with each bump in the road, placed an arm around her.

"I'd rather grab you than Ali," he declared, legitimizing his hold on Tracy in front of their driver.

Ali might have thought it was a joke, but Tracy knew Kirk held her for a reason other than achieving mere stability. The gentle pressure of his fingers on her arm felt reassuring and protective. His touch deepened Tracy's sense of excitement as she soaked up the vast open planes of the desert. Dust rose behind their track and ahead of them. A light wind rolled tumbleweeds along the baked surface of the earth, only to let them settle against the small shrubs that hugged the ground. In the distance they spotted a large lake surrounded by palm trees.

"It's only a mirage," Ali said, smiling at his passengers' excited cries of surprise.

"It can't be," Tracy gasped, "it looks so real!"

"You'll see."

They rode on and the lake receded, then disappeared.

"Now I can understand how people in the desert run toward a mirage," Tracy commented as over and over a lake appeared, gleaming in the distance, only to be gone when they reached the place they had spotted it.

The air shimmered with the heat and strange shapes loomed on the horizon. A line of people who seemed to be rooted to the ground against the far horizon turned out to be bushes. Thin, elongated horizontal shapes that glided across the desert, seemingly floating above ground turned out to be camels. "They are traveling to the market," Ali explained.

"Maybe this is where the expression, ships of the desert, originated," Kirk joked.

Heat, dust and the grayish-white land, seemed to stretch their journey into eternity. Nothing seemed to be real along the way. Then suddenly, something was. Ahead of them an ostrich appeared, then more, and more of the birds, until a whole flock materialized seemingly out of nowhere. They broke into a trot when they spotted the car.

"Want me to follow them?" Ali offered.

"Yes, let's get close to them!" Tracy begged, excited by the possibility of being able to see the exotic creatures up close in their natural habitat.

Ali stepped on the gas, and lurching over the uneven terrain, he caught up with the flock. The Jeep had to go forty miles per hour to keep pace with the ostriches, who ran alongside as though they were racing. It was comical to watch their featherless, gigantic thighs move up and down with mechanical precision. The sparse gray feathers on their backs were ruffled by the air as they strode along.

"Their movements are so even that they look like the oil pumps around Los Angeles," Tracy giggled.

"You're right," Kirk said, laughing with her. "I guess that's what makes them so funny. They look like machines, not live birds."

One by one the ostriches tired of the race. Increasing their speed, they began to cut across the front of the Jeep and Ali slowed down to make it easier for them. Soon the flock was gone, heading in the opposite direction to the market.

Exhilarated by the experience, the road now seemed less taxing to Tracy and Kirk. They craned their necks, looking for other surprises.

A THOUSAND CAMELS, looking like a sea of sand dunes, sat patiently in the burning sun while their owners bartered at the market place in the town of Assayta.

The people, especially the children, crowded around Tracy and Kirk as they walked around. Were it not for Ali's shooing the curiousity seekers away, Tracy doubted that they could have taken a step forward.

Ali explained that the shoppers at the market were all from the surrounding villages or members of the Afar tribes. Differences could be distinguished by the way people dressed. The villagers wore either western style clothing, or the typical Ethiopian garb of large pieces of homespun cotton draped around their shoulders and covering their heads. The Afar women wore long skirts of colorful fabrics wrapped around their slim hips, and scarves that covered their heads but not their shapely, bare breasts. Their men also wore skirts, but these were shorter and neatly pleated. While most of the women braided their hair tightly around the skull, the men sported fancy corkscrewlike curls that were heavily greased, and which obviously took hours to arrange. But there was no doubt about their masculinity, Tracy thought as she took note of their gunbelts, rifles and the feral look in their dark eyes. She watched three young warriors talking and laughing together and she was struck by the fact that all three had sharply pointed front teeth.

"That's an Afar custom," Ali explained, when Tracy commented on this to him. "They file their teeth down, so that in a fight, they can grab their enemy better. The Afars are very warlike. They believe that a man is not a man until he has killed someone. Often an Afar will target a victim, kill him, and cut off his testicles to present to his bride as proof of his own manhood."

"Friendly people," Kirk said, shuddering.

"It's nothing personal," Ali assured him. "The tribes often have wars, which kill far more men. That's a real loss to the tribe. But when it's for a test of manhood, the one who kills will go to the dead man's family and offer cattle to pay for the value of the lost life. This prevents a—how do you say it—blood feud between families."

"Not much has changed with the present government," Kirk said, shaking his head.

"We Ethiopians are like the leopard," Ali replied. "You can wash and scrub us, but we'll never lose our spots."

There was hardly any food in the market, Tracy noted. Everything was laid out on tarps on the ground. Goats, coffee beans, onions, medicinal plants, lengths of fabric and piles of rock salt were all the goods she saw. There were no vegetables and no fruit.

"I'm shocked at how poor these people are," she whispered to Kirk.

"Now you can see why an organization like World Help is essential in a country like this," Kirk said. "And these people at least have some items to trade! In the places where we make our drops, the villagers don't even have this much food. Without our planes thousands would die."

Tracy glanced at Kirk's earnest face, and her heart went out to him. How different this man was from the easy-going playboy he had appeared to be at their first meeting! Tracy wished she could reach out and touch him to let him know how much she had come to appreciate him. But she was too inhibited to reveal her feelings. Instead, Tracy said, "I'm glad to be here to see all this with my own eyes. I knew that getting involved with the project was a good thing but I had no idea how good."

"They could use a whole fleet of planes such as yours," Kirk suggested with a faraway look in his eyes.

"Maybe the government will eventually buy some planes from us. I shall certainly discuss this possibility with Ray when I get home," Tracy promised Kirk. She always used her father's first name in public, and Kirk's company was no exception to the rule. "Westwind could use the sales, and Ethiopia seems like a needy customer."

Kirk's eyes focused a curiously searching look on Tracy. Tracy wondered what thoughts were behind those clear, gray eyes but she couldn't read them.

"It's worth exploring," Kirk said, shrugging. Taking Tracy's arm, he began walking with her to the end of the market where their Jeep was parked. "How about a bite and then we'll start back."

Ali took them to the local tavern. Men were sitting along long wooden tables, drinking beer and *tej*, the traditional Ethiopian honey wine. The men looked up as the trio entered, and made way for Tracy and her companions to sit down. Ali engaged them in a brief conversation and after that the patrons stopped staring at Tracy and Kirk quite so openly. They ordered *tej*, and the spicy sauce, *wot*, with chicken, and ate it accompanied by the sourish dough, *enjera*. Tracy found the food as flavorful here as in Addis Ababa.

THE DRIVE BACK TO THE CITY didn't seem nearly as long as had the drive to the market. Fatigued by the heat, Tracy and Kirk sat like two joyous children, watching the shimmering air and counting how many mirages appeared along the way. Kirk's arm was around her again, and Tracy nestled into it with a new sense of trust. Once in a while, over particularly rough parts of the terrain, when the Jeep rattled and shook as though there were an earthquake, Kirk took advantage of the jounce. Holding on to Tracy with both hands, his fingers teasingly brushed the sides of her breasts, wreaking havoc with her senses. Had they been alone, Tracy would either have asked Kirk to stop, or to go on till he stilled her growing hunger for his touch. But in their present circumstances, Tracy pretended to ignore his gesture, though the blood racing through her veins made her even hotter than the weather. She wondered how their relationship would evolve from here on in. Nothing ever stood still. Since last night the sexual tension between them had vanished, and Tracy felt warmth and affection coming from Kirk. She attributed the change in Kirk to what had happened between them and did not see it as a sign of any commitment on his part.

"We'll go straight to the camp," Kirk told her when they arrived back in Dupti. But first they stopped at Helga's house. Standing under the shower, Tracy watched the pitch-black water run off her body. She had never seen so much dust accumulate in such a short time. Feeling refreshed and clean, Tracy twisted her hair into a bun at the nape of her neck and dressed in the jeans and the butter-yellow cotton top she had brought along. Then she joined Helga for a quick sandwich, while Kirk went off to change.

"Kirk is a good man, but you know, he needs a strong woman to tame him," Helga commented, as if she and Tracy were old friends.

"We'll just have to look for one," Tracy laughed.

Helga threw her a quizzical look. "I thought he'd found one in you."

Tracy blushed. "I think I'm just a passing fancy with him."

"Now, listen to me." Helga leaned forward, her manner suddenly intense. "Obviously we don't know each other and we may never see each other again—though if my plans work out, we may—" A fleeting smile crossed Helga's face before she became serious again. "But let me tell you something about Kirk. In the short time I've known him, I've come to realize that he is a profoundly lonely man. He buries himself in work because he's never found the kind of woman who was both loving and his equal in intellect. Of course if a woman is just a body, that's the way he's going to treat her! But I can assure you, when the right one comes along, he'll be hooked, gladly.''

"What makes you think I want him hooked?" Even as she said it, Tracy wondered why she resisted Helga's advice, when in fact her heart had leapt with joy at what the other woman had said.

Helga too was taken aback by Tracy's question. The doctor leaned her head against the chair back and sized Tracy up with her light-blue eyes as if she were doing a diagnostic test. "Tracy, in my job I see a lot of people. And my effectiveness as a physician depends partially on my ability to assess their character. Much of healing is not simply physiology but psychology as well, and I consider myself fairly gifted at my work. From the little I've observed, you love Kirk. And in my judgment you're the right woman for him to love. Don't let pride or some other foolishness stand in your way. And don't pit your will against his. If you try to establish how strong you are, Kirk might never admit that he loves you—just to prove that he is stronger than you. Then you'll both lose what you could have had. But if you give a little, you can get him to admit his love because strong men respond to a feminine woman.''

"How do you mean, feminine?"

"Don't be afraid to show him that you love him.''

"I can't fawn upon him!"

"Of course not. Just don't hide what you're feeling. And don't try to prove that you're better than him. Many American women, especially now with the feminist movement, try too hard to show their men that they are better than them."

"A lot of times, it's true," Tracy laughed.

"Of course. But we European women don't feel the need to rub it in." Helga gave Tracy a knowing, confidential smile. "If you're really smart, you don't need to prove it."

Helga's sincere attitude made Tracy feel a deep friendship toward her. Though Helga was very different from Tracy's friend, Judy, she had that same ability to cut directly through superficialities to the heart of things. It was strange, how one could meet a woman and within a brief time discuss such intimate feelings, yet the same thing was impossible with a man.

Tracy appreciated Helga's advice. The maturity of the other woman appealed to her. Perhaps they could remain friends even after Tracy left. "What did you mean when you said earlier that 'if your plans work out'?" she asked, hoping that the doctor was thinking of moving to the States.

Helga's smile was charming as she leaned forward and lowered her voice to almost a whisper. "Bill and I are in love. If all goes well, we might have a future together."

"You mean you'd get married?"

"Oh, it's more than that. He's got a very complicated life, what with his ex-wife and kids to support. And I have a contract with the hospital in

Dupti for another year. So we may have a long time to wait till we're both free. But if Bill's business plans work out the way he hopes they will, we could both...."

Helga didn't finish her sentence, for just then, Kirk walked into the room. His hair clung in wet waves to his head. He had the clean smell of after-shave lotion, which made Tracy's stomach tighten with desire. "You could both what?" Kirk asked, indicating that he had overheard Helga's last words.

"Never mind." Helga rose from the table. Tracy got up as well. Helga took Tracy's right hand in both of hers and pressed it warmly. "Don't forget what I said. Just follow your heart."

"What have you two been up to?" Kirk viewed them with mock suspicion. "Boy, you let two women alone for half an hour and they become thick as thieves."

"You men have your ways," Helga countered. "And speaking of men, when will you let that poor suffering slave of yours come to visit me?"

"If you're referring to Bill, he's got lost time to make up for. And us too." He turned to Tracy. "Ready to go?"

CHAPTER NINE

THE SKY WAS OVERCAST and the air moist, and as Tracy took in the campsite, it seemed to her that the name Soddo might well have been a play on the word sodden.

They landed at what Kirk jokingly called "the airport," a mere strip of grass and a small brick building. A hundred yards from it were "Airdrop Operation Headquarters," a large tent for office work, and three others that served as grainaries.

A happily grinning Bill met them as they headed for the office tent. "We've got the grain and we're filling the sacks. Also, we got word that *Pegasus 2* will be ready to pick up tomorrow morning. So all is going well."

"That's wonderful!" Kirk exclaimed.

"Did you have a good time in Dupti?"

Tracy could tell from Bill's expression that he was waiting for a word about Helga.

"How'd you know where we were?" Kirk teased him.

"When you didn't get here last night, we radioed Addis and Colonel Teshome told us."

"How's your back doing?"

"Who wants to know?"

"Guess."

"How is she?"

"Helga's fine. Sends her love. Would love to examine you at close range."

Tracy was enjoying the quick repartee between Kirk and Bill, yet she moved away to let them talk freely. She strolled to the other end of the field where three men, stripped to the waist, were filling the grain sacks. Each sack was carefully weighed and sealed. The sacks were made of a special impact-proof plastic, so they wouldn't burst when they hit the ground. A feeling of joy filled Tracy as she watched the men move in balletlike precision between grain, sack and scale. It wasn't so long ago that Tracy and her father had conceived of rebuilding an aerobatic plane to make what had become the *Pegasus* line. Here she could witness their dreams turned into reality—their planes were performing a service no other aircraft could with the same economy and efficiency. Maybe this was their future path, producing planes, not only for military purposes but for relief work—or for any work where because of the terrain and distance only a small plane of the calibre of *Pegasus* could travel. The possibility excited her. It would mean searching out places around the world that could use this type of transport, and also finding organizations that would have the necessary purchasing ability. But that wouldn't be too difficult a task. It would take time to develop the market, but once it was established, Westwind would be able to diversify and not remain dependent for survival on individual sales and military contracts. Tracy felt elated and wished she could discuss the idea with her father immediately. But there was no way to phone him from Soddo. Their talk would have to wait.

A pair of strong hands grabbed Tracy by the waist from behind, and she jumped with a start.

"Good reflexes!" Kirk laughed admiringly. "What were you so deep in thought about?"

Kirk was alone, so Bill must have gone off somewhere. Tracy was so overjoyed about her new idea that she wanted to share it. "Oh, Kirk, I just came up with a great plan for Westwind," she bubbled with excitement.

"Tell me about it!"

Kirk took her arm and while they slowly strolled toward the office tent, Tracy told him about the situation with Anne, and how observing the Ethiopian project had opened her eyes to future possibilities that would enable Westwind to survive even after Anne had pulled out her capital. "With firm orders from a few organizations, I'm sure our bank would finance us," Tracy added as ideas continued to whirl in her head.

Kirk listened to her quietly and intensely. Yet in the end all he said was, "Sounds great, Tracy. It might take a lot more work than you think, but I believe that with solid help around you, you'll make it!"

They had entered the tent and now stood by a desk loaded with papers. Kirk had absently reached for one of them but Tracy wouldn't let his attention waver from her. She was disappointed by the calm way he had responded to her. She had expected a more enthusiastic reaction. "Are you part of that solid help?" She leaned toward Kirk with a provocative smile.

"I could be." Kirk's expression was reserved, his eyes reflecting nothing.

"Is anything wrong?" Tracy was alarmed.

"What do you mean?"

"I don't know. Suddenly you seem so removed from me."

"I'm not. Everything is okay. But if you want your plans to succeed, I'd better check on what's been going on here in my absence."

Kirk had shut her out, Tracy thought, as she watched him reach for the papers on the desk, without giving her another glance. Feeling rejected, she moved toward the exit.

"Tracy, after I'm through here, I'll take you over to our lodgings. In the meantime why don't you wander around, to get the feel of the place. Bill is outside, in case you have any questions."

Tracy knew that she should stay in the tent with Kirk, and insist on looking at the paperwork also. After all that was part of the operation. But something in Kirk's attitude sent her away. Perhaps it was best to figure out on her own what had upset him.

She spent the rest of the afternoon watching the filling of the bags and chatting with Bill, who proudly told her his back was now "good enough to fly." Then they all had dinner at a local restaurant. Their meal consisted of *wot*, *enjera*, and a local beer, which tasted flat and bitter. Tracy had no appetite and merely picked at her food.

The house they used for living quarters had been built for one of the European aid programs. It was a modern brick structure, round, like a stylized Ethiopian hut.

Kirk led her to one of the bedrooms, and simply asked, "Will this do?" Then he waited, leaning against the door frame while Tracy surveyed it.

It was a sparsely furnished room with two single beds, a dresser and a large wooden closet against the wall. The tile floor had no rugs and the walls had no pictures. But the room was clean and cool and had its own bathroom.

When Tracy nodded, Kirk wished her a good rest as though they were strangers and left.

With Bill and the other men around, Tracy hadn't expected Kirk to be overly affectionate with her, but neither had she imagined that he would turn as cool and withdrawn as he had. She had had no chance to be alone with him without requesting it, and her pride prevented her from doing that.

As she lay in the dark of the night, with an aching heart and restless body, she asked herself again and again, what she had said that had struck Kirk the wrong way. She tried to recall every detail of their conversations, and analyzed his responses, picking them apart word for word.

The answer came to Tracy just as she was finally falling asleep, and it woke her with a start. Why should Kirk be enthusiastic about her ideas? Kirk was working for Westwind, but had no stake in the company! The more successful Westwind's experimental branch became, the further apart it could pull them. Likely, he did not have the funds to enable him to start a business of his own. If he had, Tracy reasoned, he wouldn't be working for her father's company—with her as one of his employers! She shuddered. No wonder Kirk had pulled away from her! "The boss's daughter." His phrase surfaced in her mind and Tracy realized that until Kirk regarded himself as her equal, he was not going to make a commitment to her. What was last night about then, she wondered angrily. A little taste of honey? Fun? The kind of lovemaking Tracy had shied away from at home? Resentment flared up within her. Well, this was the last time Mr. Russell was going to touch her! At least, it would be their last intimacy until he found his own way to her. It wasn't her place to reassure any man that she considered him her equal. After all, regardless of his current position at Westwind, he was really his own boss! He could make a contract with any company as a pilot, the same way he had with theirs! So this was Kirk's battle. Tracy would try to show him how she felt about him, but ultimately he had to come to her. In the meantime, they were back at war. She mulled over this last bitter thought before sleep took her over.

THE MORNING SUN ROSE BRIGHTLY, burning the haze off the ground. After having had a good night's rest, Tracy felt that the night's problems had been exaggerated. Kirk probably had other things on his mind now that they were back at camp, and she shouldn't take his every gesture and change of mood personally.

Because *Pegasus* was only a two-seater, Bill offered to squeeze into the cargo compartment while they flew to where *Pegasus 2* was, but Tracy wouldn't hear of it.

"I ought to learn what it feels like to sit back there," she rationalized. Removing the door she folded her long legs into the compartment.

It certainly was a different way to fly, Tracy mused, as, facing the tail of the plane, she looked down at the changing landscape beneath her. With the door off, the wind whistled by her. She enjoyed the unobstructed view even though she couldn't see what lay ahead. At first they flew over the high plateau, where the terraced land looked green and prosperous. Then the land dropped as they crossed over a canyon. At the bottom of the canyon, a muddy river lazily snaked its way south. Tracy recognized it from her map as the Omo River. Crossing the Omo they were over a plateau again. Round huts, like beehives, dotted the verdant fields. The farther inland they flew, the thicker the cluster of huts became. She could feel the nose of the plane dip, and she tightened her seatbelt for landing.

They found *Pegasus* N2PT standing on all three

wheels, its new propeller shining in the sun. In anticipation of leaving for the campsite, the mechanic and his assistant were folding up the tents they had been using while making the repairs. Tracy felt as though a sick child had been restored to her in good health.

"Let's try it," Bill suggested to Kirk.

"I'd like to go up with it," Tracy chimed in.

"Not until it's tested first," Kirk stated.

"I'll test it," Tracy offered.

"Not you. I will." Kirk locked eyes with hers.

"I flew it when it was still in its baby shoes, what makes you think I can't test it now?" Tracy was getting annoyed.

"I don't care what you do at home. Here *I* give the orders, and you're not going on the first flight."

"Of course I am!" Tracy lifted her chin defiantly.

Bill and the other two men had stepped back, forming a little group of spectators. Tracy was aware of their ringside presence but she didn't care. Her professional skills were being questioned by Kirk, and she wasn't about to give in.

"Tracy, don't provoke me into restraining you physically," Kirk warned in a low tone that sent chills up Tracy's spine. Little flashes of flame seemed to flicker in his narrowed, gray eyes.

But Tracy was beyond caring. "You'll have to tie me down before you can prevent me from going!" She met his gaze straight on.

"Then I will!" Kirk exclaimed.

"What's your objection?" Tracy said, trying a less direct approach.

"One, I'm in charge so I should go first. Two, Ray Nolan would never get over it if anything happened to you. Are those good enough reasons?"

Kirk was right on both counts, but Tracy ignored that fact because it upset her that Kirk hadn't said how it would affect him. "How come you're so concerned about Ray Nolan's feelings?" Her voice was brimming with sarcasm.

"Because you're his daughter!"

"Kirk, nobody gave me my pilot's license because I'm Ray Nolan's daughter. I earned it! I've been flying since I was a kid and I can certainly handle this plane. In fact, as the designer of it, I should be the one to test it. Now I don't want to spend any more time arguing with you. I want to go up!"

"You do that, and you've got yourself an additional job. You can take over from me." Kirk's eyes were smoldering. His tone was sharp enough to cut steel, though he had lowered his voice so only she could hear him.

Tracy realized with dismay that she had pushed Kirk too far, and that he would actually walk off the job if she pushed any more. Yet she wasn't going to back off, either. They stood glowering at each other. Then Bill called over to them, "How about going up together? That way if you both drop dead, I can take over the whole job here."

They turned to him, and Bill's broad grin cut through the tension between them like a knife through a taught cord. He was giving them a gracious way out and Tracy realized it was up to her to defer to Kirk.

"How about it?" she asked, smiling at him.

"I don't like it," he replied, "but it's an idea. C'mon."

As they climbed into the plane, Kirk remained clearly angry with Tracy. He conceded piloting to her, but Tracy knew that he would be ready to grab control of the aircraft at any moment.

"I've certainly seen what a skillful pilot you are, but suppose the propeller falls off or the landing gear buckles again," Kirk mumbled grudgingly as she prepared for take-off.

"You sure don't trust your mechanic!"

"Of course I do. But those things can happen to anyone."

"If they do, we'll both cope with it. There's nothing like learning on the job!" Tracy said, grinning.

She leaned out, shouted "Clear!" and locked the Plexiglas canopy above them. Then she primed the engine and turned the ignition key. The propeller began to whirr. Tracy let it run for awhile—testing it for stability. It did not vibrate. She looked at Kirk. He nodded to her. They were thinking alike. Tracy pushed the throttle forward to get the gasoline flowing, then turned on both ignition systems. At the same time she ran up the engine. She applied the breaks. They held. She switched off one of the ignition systems, then turned it back on, and shut down the other. So far everything seemed to be in order. She brought the power back to idle, and checked the ailerons and the elevator. Tracy could sense Kirk's approval as she went through the procedure.

Then she released the breaks, turned the nose into the wind and applied full power. She felt the usual thrill as the plane gained speed and lifted into the climb. They were off the ground well before they ran out of runway. She stole a glance at Kirk. He sat with his lips pressed together, watching her every move. But as the plane continued to climb, Tracy observed that Kirk had begun to relax. She headed toward the Omo River. When she reached it, Tracy banked, lining up her course with the river's. Then she descended, till the plane was practically gliding over the glistening, sunlit water. It was wonderful to follow the river and to feel the plane float on the air current just above it. Tracy flew lower still.

"What are you doing?" Kirk demanded.

"Testing it. I'll slow down as if I were making a drop and then come out of it—if it's okay with you," Tracy explained in a calm, professional tone.

Kirk shook his head and gave a short laugh, "You're a devil of a woman. I should stay as far away from you as I can!"

"I thought you were already doing that!" Tracy bit her lip, annoyed with herself. Why did she provoke him, when she knew it was useless to hope for anything lasting between them? She caught his raised eyebrow before re-focusing her attention on the flight.

"If I'm staying away, there's a good reason for it."

"I'm sure." A knot of pain swelled in the pit of her stomach at Kirk's admission. Why couldn't they be open with each other? Why couldn't she just tell him that she loved him and didn't care one bit about anything else? Her pride kept her silent. The flight had lost its thrill. She finished testing, then turned to Kirk and asked, "Want to take us back?"

"No, you can do it."

Tracy caught the fleeting warmth in his eyes and it made her feel curiously happy. *At least Kirk has forgiven me for wanting the first flight,* she thought wryly. It wasn't much, but it was better than nothing. She climbed out of the valley, returned to the field, circled, and landed, facing into the wind. A round of applause from the ground crew greeted them as they climbed out of the plane.

IN THE AFTERNOON Tracy asked Kirk to show her the operation's books. He was polite and cooperative, yet Tracy thought she could sense resentment on his part during the procedure. She knew that their relationship was an awkward one when put to such a test, but she chose to ignore that fact. Part of her reason for spending this time in Ethiopia, was to see how the relief work was done. She couldn't let their personal relationship or her own feelings deter her. If she wanted to be totally honest with herself, Tracy also had to admit that an oddly perverse streak in her gloated over the situation between them. If Kirk could insist on ordering her around when he was in charge, then she, too, could pull rank on him when the time was right. Kirk was the kind of man who would walk all over a woman if she let him, Tracy thought. But she was one woman who would prove to be his match. *He'll have to learn to deal with me as an equal,* she thought gleefully as she pored over the books.

Despite the tension between them, Tracy was happy when she found that Kirk's record-keeping was impressively thorough. He showed her the entries on the amount of grain that had been received and delivered, on the cost of making the flights and on the number of drops they had made since the start of the program. All were set down in his firm, masculine handwriting. He also kept a logbook of each day's activities and each man's work, including his own, and the salaries paid to everyone. Tracy saw that he had indeed spent most of his time running the project, and not doing favors or taking time off for other reasons.

Satisfied with what she had learned by looking at the books, Tracy thanked Kirk and left the office tent. Had he made one move toward breaking the ice between them, she would have melted into his arms. But he remained cool and aloof, cutting off any personal contact between them.

Forcing herself to ignore her aching heart, Tracy spent some time watching the men fill and weigh the sacks. She told herself that this too was part of her reason for being at the camp. Each empty sack was placed on a scale. The grain was poured into the sack through a giant funnel positioned over the scale. When the bag was filled to one hundred pounds two men removed it and replaced it with a fresh one. There was a hypnotic rhythm to their work. After awhile, feeling that she had seen enough, Tracy wandered away. She needed to be by herself to absorb what she had learned about running a project such as this one. She would have to have a thorough knowledge of all operations before she could offer her planes for other missions. She sat down at the far edge of the camp, on the bare ground, and sank deep into her thoughts.

Tracy didn't know how long she sat there, hugging her pulled-up knees and staring at the distant mountains. After awhile she stopped whirling ideas around in her head and just relaxed and enjoyed the landscape. The silence of the open fields matched her own feelings of isolation and sadness, yet Tracy felt at peace as she watched the shadows lengthen with the passing of the afternoon. The sun spread a golden blanket around her and lit up her Titianesque hair with a blaze. She loosened her hair, letting it fall over her shoulders, so that the wind could ruffle through it.

"Here you are!" Kirk folded his long limbs into the same position as Tracy.

She glanced at Kirk while he eased down next to her, then turned her face to the view again.

"Want to make peace?" Kirk asked gently.

Tears welled up in her eyes and Tracy was furious with herself for her vulnerability. Why should a kind word from him make her tremble inside? She was an engineer, a scientist, not a silly, dreaming female. How could she be so affected by a man's nearness? And affected she was. Her whole body went limp at the feel of Kirk's warmth next to her. She laid her chin on her knees, and pulled them tighter to her chest, so Kirk wouldn't notice how perturbed she was at his presence.

But Kirk knew. He slipped caressing fingers through her hair while his other hand cupped her chin and forced her to look at him. His serious, gray eyes studied her face and stopped when they made contact with her green ones. She felt like a doe facing a hunter, helpless and trembling. Her whole aching soul was laid bare to him through her eyes and she couldn't prevent him from seeing it. She had no power to resist the want within her, the overwhelming desire that unsettled her whole being.

"My wonderful lioness," Kirk murmured, fingering her hair. Then with a sudden, low cry, he gathered her mane in his hand, and with a fierce gesture, pulled Tracy to him, his lips hungrily plundering hers.

Kirk's embrace took Tracy's breath away with the force of its passion. His powerful body leaning over her eased Tracy back till they both lay on the ground, entwined. The world went blank for Tracy except for the wild quest of her lips, responding to Kirk's. Theirs was not a tender kiss, but a savage need to be satisfied. Their teeth and their tongues savoured and demanded as though they could say through their bodies, what they couldn't say with words. Kirk's hand had closed possessively over Tracy's breasts. He stroked each nipple through her thin cotton shirt till she let out a low moan and arched her hips toward him wanting to fuse her body to his. She could feel Kirk's desire as his hard-muscled thighs pressed against hers, slipping between her limbs. Almost unconsciously, driven by an exquisite yearning, Tracy wrapped her arms around Kirk and pulled him tighter. His weight pinned her against the ground but she welcomed it. Kirk unzipped her jeans and slipped a hand down her belly. Tracy ached with desire as his deliberate fingers sent a series of sensual shocks coursing through her. Tracy's own hand cupped over Kirk's tense male body. She wanted him to discard his clothes, wanted to touch his burning skin, but as she reached for his belt buckle Kirk arrested her hand. As suddenly as his passionate attack had unexpectedly begun, it ended. Kirk rolled away from her, panting.

Tracy lay immobile, suddenly as cold as if an electric blanket had been ripped off her. "What's wrong!" she exclaimed, hurt by the knowledge that Kirk could stop making love to her so randomly.

"I shouldn't come near you," Kirk whispered hoarsely. "At least, not until. . . ." He cut himself off and lay on his side, curled up, almost as if he were wounded.

"Until what?" Tracy demanded.

Kirk turned toward her again, his face tortured by self-imposed restraint. "Until it's right between us," he said, giving her a rueful smile.

"What's not right?" Even as Tracy protested, she knew she had to give him credit for bringing up the reality of their relationship.

"Nothing is," Kirk sighed, "unless you're satisfied with pure sex. In which case...." He reached for her in a half-jesting way and laughed as Tracy recoiled. "You see, I know how you would feel afterward and I'm not about to add that responsibility to my problems."

"Maybe if you shared your problems, we could solve them, together." Tracy marveled at her own need to make the offer. She had never before humiliated herself before a man, making him so aware of her feelings for him.

Kirk gently stroked her cheeks sending a ripple of need through Tracy's nervous system. "No, my dear, there are some things I've got to work out on my own." Then before Tracy could respond he changed to a lighter tone. "But listen, this is not what I originally came to you for. One of our mechanics, Petros, lives in a village not too far from here. He is the one who studied in the States. He tells me that his childhood friend, the mayor's son, is getting married this evening and he's been invited to the wedding. He said it would be a great honor if we went with him. That's what I came to ask you about."

"You have a strange way of asking," Tracy said, grinning as she clambered to her feet.

"It's your magic, Tracy. You make me lose control."

Secretly Tracy wished Kirk hadn't regained the control he spoke of when he had, but she kept her feelings to herself. Instead, she said lightly, "I think it would be fun to see a local wedding. Let's go."

THAT EVENING they took the Jeep Bill had driven from Addis Ababa to the campsite. Bill and Kirk sat in the back, while Tracy enjoyed the comparative comfort up front, with Petros, their driver. It was ninety kilometers from Soddo to Petros's village, Gidamo. A half-hour's plane ride at the most, Tracy thought, as she patiently lurched about in the front seat during the rough ride on the heavily rutted rural road. Pools of water, remaining from the rain of the day before, splashed the sides of the Jeep with the red mud so characteristic of the region. It was getting chilly, although the sun still had a way to go before it set. Noting the seven-thousand feet elevation of the central plateau, Tracy had had the foresight to bring a sweater along. Now she slipped into it and was warm again. The men, too, put on windbreakers. Along the road stood thatch-roofed farmhouses, looking like beehives. They were separated from each other by hedges made of thorn bushes. Here and there smoke rose through the porous walls of the huts and hovered over the sunlit land like a pepper-colored gauze, before dispersing.

"People are making supper," Petros commented.

Their driver was a nice looking young man, with small, round features and tan skin. When Tracy questioned him about his background, Petros explained that he had grown up in the village of Durami, where the wedding was to take place. But his parents had sent him first to Addis and then to the U.S. to get a better education. Petros had been studying in Los Angeles to become an aircraft mechanic when, on a visit home, he had decided to stay and help with the relief program. "They need all the technical help they can get to alleviate the suffering caused by the drought. Now we're coming into the rainy season, so everything looks green. But for the past two years, during December and January we've been hit with drought that killed all our crops. And as if that weren't enough, the crops that my people planted in expectation of the Belg, the short rains, have all been destroyed by a type of bug called the army worm. So were it not for the relief shipments of food and grain, people around here would die by the thousands."

The story confirmed what Tracy had been told before, and it fortified her conviction that her planes could fit well in a scheme to help the survival of people around the globe.

"Do you think you might stay home permanently?" Tracy asked Petros.

"After a year I will go back to the States to finish my training. Then, yes, I will come back because my country needs me more than yours," he said, grinning.

"Petros is already a wonderful mechanic," Kirk

commented from the back seat. "When he gets his degree, he will probably be head of a training program."

"That's the wonderful thing about a country like Ethiopia," Bill chimed in, "it needs so much improvement, that any skill you can bring is welcome."

"Sounds like you feel like staying here yourself," Tracy said, teasing him.

"I wouldn't mind," Bill said, shrugging.

"At least until a certain doctor we know is through with her contract, isn't that right?" Kirk asked, poking him in the ribs.

It took them over two hours to arrive in Durami. At Petros's suggestion they waited for the wedding party in a huge, green meadow. From where they stood they could see the mountain trail on which the wedding party was descending like a flock of white butterflies.

"The marriage was prearranged, of course," Petros explained. "This is the groom's village. The reception will take place at his father's house."

Children from the village surrounded the Jeep and Petros jumped out to join them in a song. He led the chorus of young, harmonious voices, in a new tune.

> *Haramba Kambatta*
> *Meteaman Hudjati.*
> Unity Kambatta
> Work together.

Like charging cavalry, the wedding party, now clear of the mountain, galloped toward the waiting visitors. Stopping by the Jeep, the bride and groom dismounted and greeted Petros and his foreign companions. The bride wore a lovely white satin dress and a headpiece complete with veil. The groom and his best men were all dressed in tuxedos. The bridesmaids wore pink, or light blue, dresses. Tracy found it somewhat incongruous to see the formally dressed crowd in the middle of a pasture—there was an air of unreality about the event.

"It is surrealistic, but only for us," Kirk said, echoing Tracy's thought.

"I wish I had brought my camera," Bill moaned behind them. "My kids will never believe this when I get back home."

After a brief discussion between the groom and Petros, the latter turned to them and said, "If it's okay with you, the Jeep will now be the official wedding transportation."

"By all means," Kirk agreed and Tracy enthusiastically seconded him. The bride and groom took their place in the back seat. Their best man rode in front and Petros drove, while Kirk, Tracy and Bill followed the slowly moving Jeep on foot, along with the wedding guests. Besides the wedding party a large crowd of well-wishers surrounded the Jeep. Riding, running, singing, and dancing like dervishes, the locals swarmed toward the bride-groom's house. Calling from the Jeep, Petros pointed out a singer who was running alongside the bridal couple improvising odes to them. "He's been doing that since the procession started at the bride's village. He has kept pace with the cantering horses all these miles without breaking his stride or losing a note." There was pride in Petros's voice as he talked about the man.

Tracy shook her head in amazement.

"Fun, isn't it?" Kirk said, taking her by the arm so she wouldn't be swept away by the crowd.

Bill also stayed close to her.

"You two make me feel like I'm with bodyguards," Tracy said, teasing them.

"If I had a body like yours, I'd be glad to have guards in this crowd," Bill quipped.

"Take heed and don't stray." Kirk's tone was friendly, but serious. "Women aren't worth a lot around here, and I'd hate to lose you to some tribesman who's taken a fancy to you."

As Kirk murmured into her ear, his warm breath sent little shivers down Tracy's spine. She didn't quite believe his warning, but Kirk's concern gave her a feeling of security nonetheless.

It was dusk and a full moon had risen by the time they reached their destination. The enthusiastic crowd that had gathered to gawk at the wedding party serenaded them all the way into the room where the feast was to be held. But instead of being allowed to stay, amidst good natured jesting, family members pushed the uninvited guests out through the back door into the open again. Oddly, the crowd didn't leave but continued their serenade outside, accompanied by the blaring sound of a bamboo trumpet.

Inside the room, Tracy, Kirk and Bill were invited to partake of the wedding feast. It consisted of the already familiar, *enjera*, several kinds of meats in *wot* and a homemade beer that tasted rather sour.

When the guests surrounded the table, Tracy noticed that the bride and her retinue of women were not seated among them. The groom, eating and drinking, seemed totally unconcerned by this.

"They are preparing her for the wedding night!" Petros shouted to her, across the table. The women you see here, who are doing the serving, are the groom's relatives."

It didn't make Tracy feel at ease when Kirk leaned to her adding, "I can assure you, if you weren't a foreign female, you wouldn't be sitting here either."

For dessert, a trayful of raw beef, cut into huge chunks, was brought to the table by the women. The guests would pick up a piece, carve it into bite size on their own plates, and dipping it into a spicy sauce, eat the bloody meat with relish. Polite or not, Tracy and her companions declined the dessert.

Petros's face shone as he relived his childhood memories through the celebration. Tracy watched with fascination as he rose along with the others to stamp out a dance to the beat of a native drum, a *kebero*, and a basslike instrument that had only two strings, the *kerar*. Each musician had pasted a birr on his forehead, indicating to the guests that they weren't adverse to tipping. After dinner the groom and his best men rose and left, while the dancing went on undisturbed.

Petros came to sit with Tracy and her party. He quietly suggested that this might be a good time for them to head back on the road.

"From here on the party will just continue the same way until the groom returns after the defloration."

"What do you mean, 'defloration?'" Tracy couldn't believe what she was hearing.

"Well, in this part of the country, women are required to be virgins. So during the wedding feast, the groom goes off to deflower the bride. The relatives of the bride give him a loaf of bread to take along. After he is through with his business he returns the bread. If everything was in order they'll find money tucked inside the loaf—usually about twenty birrs, that's about ten American dollars, and the groom continues to celebrate. However, if the bride was not a virgin the bread has no money and likely the woman will be returned to her parent's house. But that hardly ever happens, since to insure the virginity of the bride, it's an old custom to sew her genitals together with thin strings made of entrails." He saw Tracy's eyes widen and added with a broad smile, "This of course makes the groom's job rather difficult. If he can't do it, he asks his first best man. And if the first best man fails, the task goes to the second, and after him, to the third best man."

Tracy shuddered. The apparent cruelty of the procedure made her wonder about these ancient customs.

"Doesn't the bride have anything to say about this? After all you have a modern government now that preaches equality for women!" Wistfully, Tracy hoped that changes were taking place, however slowly.

Petros smiled at her and shook his head. "We've been here for five thousand years. Do you think the government can change our customs in five, or even ten?"

ATTENDING THE WEDDING had such a powerful effect on Tracy, that on her way home, she started a discussion by comparing her own wedding to the one they had just seen. Tracy told Kirk, Bill and Petros that during her own wedding she couldn't help thinking that the celebration surrounding her was a leftover from some barbaric custom in which a white-clad virgin was given away in a fertility rite. But she had never imagined that in other parts of the world that was in fact still the case. "I never saw any gesture or glance between the bride and the groom that spoke of love," said Tracy as she turned to Petros.

"You wouldn't," he explained. "Our marriages are for making babies and joining wealth. Life is too harsh in these parts to be romantic."

"But there is no divorce, either," Kirk said, joining in. "Or is there?"

"Very rarely. Since the union is arranged

through the families, they make sure that the couple is well matched. In the western world lack of love seems to be the cause of most divorces. Not expecting love, our people put up with each other for life.''

"That's my idea of marriage," Kirk put in.

"Is that why you haven't married?" Tracy couldn't stop herself from making the dig.

"How'd you guess," Bill roared with laughter. "Boy I feel sorry for the girl Kirk eventually chooses. 'Cause once he makes up his mind about her he'll never let her go.''

It was a good thing it was pitch-dark inside the Jeep, Tracy thought, as she felt the blood rising to her face, painting it red. She had an idea why Bill's comment would effect her so, but she did not care to face up to it.

CHAPTER TEN

THE MORNING SKY was filled with ominous dark clouds. They rolled like giant feather pillows above the chilled earth. But not even the prospect of rain could spoil Tracy's mood. She was truly looking forward to participating in the drop operation. During breakfast she and her co-workers agreed that Bill would fly with her while Kirk was to be in the lead plane. Now, hugging herself in the soggy chill of the morning, Tracy watched the men load up the planes.

They transported the grain sacks, which weighed precisely one hundred pounds, to the planes on stretchers. Using hospital equipment somehow heightened the sense of emergency, Tracy thought. The two men hoisted the stretcher under the wing while the load master hooked up each sack to the specially designed clasps. Soon a pair of bags were swinging gently under each wing. Tracy's stomach tightened with excitement. *The moment of truth has arrived,* she silently told herself. Of course Kirk and Bill had done many drops before, and Tracy herself had tested the drop procedure using dummies, in California. But tests were one thing, real fieldwork was another.

This was the proof that all those concepts Tracy had invented at the drawing board functioned even halfway around the world. It was her moment of truth, and Tracy was thrilled.

"Ready?" Kirk came to her side.

"Yes."

"Bill's in the plane already."

With a glance at Kirk to acknowledge the information, Tracy turned and headed for the second plane.

Kirk walked with her. "I'll make my drop and return to camp. After you make yours, follow me back."

"Yes, commander." Tracy grinned at him.

She circled the plane for the walk-around.

"I checked her out already," Bill said, leaning out of the cockpit.

"Thanks. But I'll be the one in the pilot's seat," Tracy quietly asserted.

"You're right," Bill acceded gracefully. "I would do the same thing."

Kirk climbed into his cockpit at almost the same time as Tracy got into hers. Bill watched her buckle in next to him, and said, "Don't forget, when we get over the village, you'll see a circle drawn by the locals, indicating where we should place the drop. I generally release the bags a second before flying over the circle. During their fall, the speed of the bags matches mine, so they hit the ground pretty much on target."

"Have you ever had any problem with the release?"

"Not so far."

"Good."

Tracy knew that if there was one truly critical point in their mission, it was the moment when the bags were released. In order to drop them without their bursting on impact with the ground, the pilot had to fly low and slow. To prevent stalling after the drop, the pilot had to pick up speed and altitude rapidly. If the bags were not released with split-second timing their weight could detain the plane just long enough to be able to rise. But this was no time for her to speculate on what could happen.

Ahead of her Kirk's propeller whirred and he began rolling down the runway. Tracy did a run-up test of all systems, and when she saw Kirk rise toward the sky, she followed. Bill sat in silence during their take-off. Ahead of them, Kirk's plane banked in a slow arc and headed toward the distant mountains. Soon she and Bill were flying alongside the other plane.

"There is the road we took yesterday," Bill said, pointing at the red ribbon below. "Except we never got this far in the Jeep."

Beneath them the land suddenly zoomed down to infinity as both planes skimmed over the ridge of the escarpment. Kirk took the lead again as they entered the narrow canyon of the Omo. They traced the silt-gorged river, flanked on either side by towering cliffs of green-covered walls. Bill pointed to the right and Tracy saw a waterfall cascading over the edge of the canyon above them.

As they descended farther into the canyon she looked back at the fall and got the impression that the thundering waters came directly from the sky. It was a thrilling sight.

"Do people live around here? I don't see any huts." Tracy turned to Bill.

"No one could survive here. The area is infested with malaria-carrying mosquitos and enormous river crocodiles. Besides, as you can see, it's surrounded by these walls of stone. They form an impassable barrier to the outside world. In fact, it was these cliffs that prevented any relief from coming to this area last year, when the famine became known in the other parts of the country. The way the government finally found out, was that some of the half-starved farmers managed to drag themselves across the range and reached a main road. Did you know that parts of southwestern Ethiopia aren't even charted? They're so impenetrable that they've never been explored."

Tracy shook her head incredulously. "I guess planes are the only answer in cases like these."

"Like old Kirk says, 'there's always a road in the sky,'" Bill said, grinning.

Reminded of Kirk, Tracy became conscious again of his plane ahead of them down the canyon. She could feel an invisible thread between them as she followed his route. Tracy saw Kirk begin to climb. She followed, and soon they were out of the canyon, on the opposite side of the plateau.

Tracy figured they must be nearing the drop site

for Kirk was flying extremely low. "It feels like we're practically skimming the treetops," Tracy commented to Bill as she followed Kirk with her eyes.

"It's just the view through this plastic bubble," Bill said, knocking on the ceiling. "But we are low, and the best is yet to come."

"I guess so," Tracy said, tensing up inside as she thought of the imminent drop.

Kirk banked sharply and Tracy followed suit. Directly ahead she spotted a clear field with a large circle drawn in its center. At the edge of the meadow stood a ragged group of natives huddled together, waiting. Kirk's plane dipped even lower. It was no more than fifteen feet above the ground. Suddenly, all four of his plane's bundles went tumbling toward the earth, then bounced, over and over, as they hit the ground. But Tracy had no time to observe them further. Ready for her drop, she reduced her speed to seventy miles per hour and descended. Red lights began to flash wildly in the cabin and the strident horn of the stall warning device alerted Tracy that her speed was dangerously slow and that she could stall in midair. As she had done so many times before when testing the release buttons in the California Sierras, with a wildly pounding heart, Tracy now pressed them as she neared the circle on the ground. At the same time she heard Bill cry, "Now!" Tracy glanced at him with a triumphant smile as without its load the plane jumped. But they were not out of danger yet. She pushed the throttle to the firewall and pulling the yoke back, put the plane into a climb. With a

last warble the stall warning device stopped
screeching and the red lights on the panel died
down. The engine hummed reassuringly as the
plane gained altitude.

"Well done!" Bill exclaimed.

Tracy took a deep breath. Despite all her training, Tracy felt as if she had just taken another test,
and she appreciated the grade Bill, as a fellow
pilot, had bestowed upon her with his praise. She
banked toward home, and in the process caught a
glimpse of the villagers, with the sacks already on
their shoulders, running toward their huts.

"It's very satisfying to do a successful run," she
admitted to Bill.

It was now raining softly. Tracy spotted Kirk's
plane not far ahead. With her wing tips practically
touching the walls of the canyon she followed
Kirk. Arriving back at the base Tracy glanced at
her watch. It had taken them only forty-two minutes from take-off to landing.

Kirk climbed out of the plane and came over to
Tracy and Bill, smiling broadly. "How did you
like it, Tracy?"

"She's one hell of a pilot," Bill answered in her
stead.

"Are you ready for the next run?" Kirk asked,
baiting her. "It takes the men just eight minutes to
load up, and then we can be off again."

"Sure." Tracy took up the challenge with a
pounding heart. Making several runs was more
than Tracy had bargained for, but that was something she wasn't about to let Kirk know.

"I'll try this next one if you don't mind," Bill

said. Turning to Kirk, he added, "With Tracy at my side, of course."

"What about your back?" Tracy asked.

"It's good enough," Bill assured her.

"It's time you got back to work," Kirk said playfully and walked away from them.

With a painful yearning, Tracy watched his broad shoulders swing in rhythm with his easy stride as he crossed the field to his plane. He never even gave her a second look!

They flew the rest of the day, making six more runs despite the rain, with Kirk in the lead and Tracy and Bill alternating at the controls of the second plane.

On the last flight Tracy piloted. She was tired but had that feeling of satisfaction that comes from a good day's work.

Through the repeated loading and flying procedure, the trio had fallen into a regular pattern, making their movements quick and efficient. Just before Tracy climbed into the plane for this last run, Kirk commented to her, "You make a regular team member, Tracy. It's a pleasure to work with you."

It made Tracy's heart sing that Kirk should have expressed his feelings. As though nature had wanted to match her mood, the late afternoon sun broke through the storm clouds, spreading its rays over the earth like golden fingers.

On the way back to the campsite, Kirk chose to rise out of the canyon just above the waterfall. Following him, Tracy and Bill discovered a rainbow that girded the cascading waters like a giant necklace of precious stones.

"What a great sight," Tracy laughed happily. "It's like a reward for a successful day's work."

Tracy was now feeling so elated that she decided to express it the best way she knew how. She brought the plane in as if she were about to land but instead, pulling up the aircraft again, and scaring Bill nearly to death, went into a three hundred sixty degree loop.

"What are you doing?" Bill shouted, hanging upside down for a second.

"I'm sorry," Tracy laughed as they descended. "I didn't mean to frighten you. I just couldn't help myself. Are you okay?"

"Now I am," Bill muttered as he watched Tracy come to a halt on the ground.

"Just what do you think you were doing?" Kirk demanded as Tracy walked away from the plane. He had come to meet her on the field and Kirk's face was darker than the clouds that had begun to gather above them again.

"We're down on the ground, walking safely," Tracy said shrugging. "What are you so worked up about?"

Kirk grabbed her by the elbow, and walking past the admiring grins of the workmen, led her firmly into the office tent. "You took an unnecessary risk. If there is one thing I won't tolerate in a pilot, it is needless exhibitionism!" he exploded. "What kind of an example do you think you're setting for the people working for you by acting on a whim like a child?''

Tracy knew Kirk was right but she, too, was angry. After all, they had landed safely, and knowing the plane as she did, Tracy really hadn't taken a big chance. It was more dangerous to make the drops than to perform the loop. ''I wouldn't expect others to follow my example! I had aerobatics training which they didn't! So I don't know what you're talking about!''

''You know exactly what I'm talking about. You're just too stubborn to admit when you're out of line!''

''I wasn't out of line!''

''If you were working for me I wouldn't put up with your behavior for one minute!''

''Well, lucky for me it's the other way around!''

The moment it slipped out, Tracy knew she had said the wrong thing. Kirk's eyes darkened, their gray resembling the color of the approaching storm clouds. He narrowed in on her, his gaze as penetrating as steel blades. ''That's right, Tracy, just rub it in. Nevertheless, I think you owe Bill and me an apology.''

Before Tracy could respond, the short wave radio at the other end of the tent began to warble. Kirk turned his back on Tracy, cutting her off as though she had stopped existing for him. He began to turn the knobs on the radio to find the channel through which he could receive clearly. Tracy stood indecisively in the tent. She felt terrible. On the one hand Kirk had no right to chastise her as though she were a child, but on the other Tracy had been foolish to pull rank on him. So if there was to be any apology it would have to be on both their parts, she decided. With Bill, it was another story. Tracy didn't want to alienate Bill, so she would go to him and explain her impulsive act. She would even apologize for putting him through the maneuvre despite his bad back. But with Kirk she would just bide her time. After all, despite the way *he* saw it, she really had done nothing wrong. Having made this decision, Tracy was about to stalk out of the tent, but the voice on the radio cleared and she stopped, curious to find out who was contacting them. It was Major Hadib and his message was for Tracy. A cable had come to his office from California, advising that Ray Nolan had suffered a heart attack.

With a jump Tracy was at Kirk's side. ''Can we radio back? I want to know how serious it is.'' Tracy's voice was thin with tension. Kirk managed to get her question through.

''We don't know,'' Major Hadib answered. ''But it might be best if you came to Addis as soon as you can. I shall make plane reservations for your return to the States.''

''We can fly back to Addis tonight,'' Kirk told the major.

''I'll do what I can at this end,'' Major Hadib promised. Then the transmission ended.

Tracy began to shake like a leaf. She had to steady herself against the desk for fear that her knees would give way. The shock was too great for her to control. Her mind was racing, wanting to bridge the distance and time gap between her ailing father and herself, but her body stood rooted to the desk, trembling.

Kirk came to her, and taking her face between his hands, he looked at her with soft eyes and murmured in a gentle voice, "I am truly sorry, Tracy. Now I want you to come outside with me. We'll find Bill and ask him to drive you back to our lodgings. He'll wait there while you pack. In the meantime, I'll get the plane ready. We'll leave for Addis as soon as you get back."

Kirk's tone was soothing but not soothing enough to allow Tracy to cry. Nor did he hug her. Tracy was grateful that he didn't. Instead, Kirk had given her something to do, a positive action that didn't allow her to whimper or fall apart as she felt like doing. Not trusting her voice, Tracy nodded in agreement.

Like a somnambulist, Tracy walked with Kirk to Bill, stood quietly while the two men discussed what had happened and then allowed Bill to guide her to the Jeep. She had the strange sensation that all this was happening to somebody else. Back in her bedroom, Tracy knew that she had to gather her things, but her hands and her mind seemed to be two separate entities. A growing fear and a sense of isolation gripped her as she went through the motions of finding her things around the room and throwing them into her overnight case.

Tracy just couldn't believe that the scratchy voice on the radio was real. Her father had always

been a tower of strength. She had never seen him
ill, or even showing the signs of his age—so she
had just taken him for granted, as a vital, active
man, who could always cope no matter what happened in both their lives. And now he lay in some
hospital. Tracy shuddered. She didn't want to
hold the image that kept surfacing in her mind's
eye—her father pale and helpless on a white
hospital bed, surrounded by medical machinery—
yet the image kept crowding into her brain.
Memories of her mother's illness surfaced and
tightened her stomach into a knot of fear. As
Tracy packed, childlike, she clung to the notion
that if she could only get to Ray's bedside fast
enough, everything would be all right.

Bill took her overnight case from her and
Tracy followed him mechanically to the Jeep. At
the campsite Kirk had the plane ready for take-
off.

Tracy climbed in and waited while Kirk left instructions with Bill for running the camp.

"Don't worry about a thing," Bill assured both
Tracy and Kirk as he climbed into the cockpit.
"I'll deliver the grain that's here and hold the fort
as long as it's necessary. I wish you the best,
Tracy," Bill added, squeezing her hand.

It was hard for him to know how to say good-
bye under the circumstances and despite her grief,
Tracy understood that. "Good luck to you, too,
Bill," she whispered softly.

Then Kirk locked the canopy down. Tracy
looked at his hard profile as he concentrated on

the necessary procedures. Since the news of Ray's heart attack, he had only spoken to her when it was absolutely essential and always in a gentle but firm tone. Tracy realized that his strength was helping her to hold herself together and she was grateful for his warm but unsentimental support. Feeling that she could trust Kirk implicitly, Tracy closed her eyes, and like a wounded bird, she huddled in her seat, letting Kirk take complete control of what needed to be done.

WHILE AT THE CAMPSITE, Tracy had left her large suitcase in storage at the hotel. If she could get a flight home as soon as they arrived in Addis all Tracy would have to do would be to pick up her baggage from the hotel and head for the airport again.

It was early evening by the time they landed in the capital. Major Hadib was waiting for them at the airport. After expressing sympathy over the unfortunate turn of events, he said, "Regrettably, there is no plane leaving tonight that would give you a connection for Los Angeles. So I booked you on a flight to London that leaves Addis tomorrow at 11:00 A.M. Tonight you'll stay at the Hotel Addis. I've reserved a room for each of you."

"But tomorrow might be too late," Tracy protested, her stomach tightening with apprehension.

"Tracy, if it were worthwhile, I'd fly you to London myself," Kirk said, reasoning with her. "But as you well know, that would take longer than waiting for tomorrow's scheduled flight.

Let's get to the hotel and put a call through to Los Angeles.''

Strangely, the familiar surroundings of the Hotel Addis soothed Tracy's raw nerves. Major Hadib said good-night to Tracy and Kirk, promising to come by the next day to drive them to the airport. Tracy went up to the new room she had been given and put in a call to Los Angeles.

She barely noticed that Kirk hadn't left her side since their arrival. He instructed the bellboy to leave her luggage by the door, led her to sit in one of the armchairs, and sat down across from her, holding her hands in his. She accepted it as a matter of course that Kirk should sit with her, his chiseled features still visible in the darkening twilight of the room, quiet and reassuring. The warmth that flowed from his hands was like a life force, transmitting itself through his firm palms, pulsating against her skin. Tracy closed her eyes, leaned back into the armchair and let the darkness and silence envelop her. She was trying hard not to think. Tracy just wanted to sit and wait, drawing strength from the touch of the man beside her. She dozed off and the shrill sound of a phone startled her. Kirk jumped for the receiver and handed it to Tracy in the dark. Then he switched on the table lamp and watched Tracy's face anxiously as she made contact with her Aunt Irma.

"It happened this morning," Irma was saying. "Ray had a fairly severe heart attack, but as far as the doctors can tell, he'll pull through. He's at St. John's Hospital. He's still in intensive care, but he's a strong man and all his vital signs indicate that he'll be okay. Of course no one knows how long it will take him to recover, but for the moment at least he's in stable condition.''

"I'm coming home tomorrow," Tracy informed her Aunt. "Please tell dad I'll be there as soon as I can get out of this place. And tell him, I love him." Tracy felt the phone tremble in her hand. Tears were streaming down her face but she didn't care.

"Don't worry, honey, he knows that," Aunt Irma assured Tracy. "I told him I had cabled you, so he knows you're on your way back. In the meantime Anne and I have been alternating at his bedside. So he's not being abandoned.''

"Anne? How come she is so devoted?" Tracy was shocked.

"Your father and Anne are old friends. Of course she is concerned.''

Anne's probably concerned about the business, too, Tracy thought bitterly. Anger flared up in her at the idea of Anne hovering over her sick father like a vulture. This was a poor time to be worrying about the business, yet Tracy suspected that Ray's illness would bring on complications Anne hadn't anticipated. But Tracy couldn't talk about it on the phone. "All right," she sighed. "I don't know when I can catch a plane from London but I'll be home within twenty-four hours. You can tell that to dad. And Anne too," Tracy added resentfully, her body tensing up as if to signal a warning to her father's business partner.

Irma, sensitive to the change in Tracy's tone, hurried to reassure her niece. "Don't worry about Anne, Tracy. She's been truly helpful in this emergency. Just get home, honey. Everything will straighten itself out, you'll see. Call from London before you get on the plane and we'll pick you up at the airport."

How like Aunt Irma, Tracy thought, to care for her comfort too. "Don't worry, Aunt Irma, I'll just grab a cab when I get in."

"As you wish. Have a safe journey home."

The line went dead. Tracy stood still till Kirk gently pried the receiver out of her hand and hung it up. Tracy repeated the conversation to him.

"I'm glad it's not as bad as it could have been," Kirk said with relief.

"Yes, but because of Anne, the situation is more serious than you think," Tracy confided.

"Don't worry about Anne right now," Kirk said, reaching out and folding her into his arms. "The main thing is that your father *will* pull through."

"Oh, Kirk, I'm so upset," Tracy whispered, dropping her head on his shoulder.

"Of course you are, dear," Kirk said as he pulled Tracy closer, his hand gently pressing her head onto his shoulder. "You'll have some tough issues to face once you get home. But I'll try to help."

Tracy sniffed like a young child and her nose caught the scent of Kirk's skin. Curiously, his scent made her feel warm and safe and easy about the future. "Will you?" she murmured, wanting to hear his promise again. Tracy needed Kirk. She needed his strength and desperately wanted his support in the battle that awaited her in Santa Monica. Yet Tracy knew that despite what he told her now, the battle was one she would have to face alone. Kirk had a job to complete here in Ethiopia and she was returning home by herself.

Yet at that moment, it was wonderful to hear him say, "Of course I'll take care of you, Tracy, to the best of my ability."

Tracy lifted her head and gave him a weak smile. "Thank you for saying it."

"I'm not just saying it," Kirk said, smiling back at her. "My first move is to take you downstairs for dinner."

"I couldn't eat a bite." Tracy peeled his arms away from her and stepped back.

"Then you'll just come and sit with me," Kirk insisted.

"I'd rather stay here."

"I'm not leaving you alone."

"Really, Kirk. . . ."

"You want me to make a spectacle of you by carrying you into the dining room in my arms?"

He would too, Tracy thought, as she studied his determined smile.

"All right, you win."

"Tonight we might as well relax, so I'll go to my room and change," Kirk informed her. "I suggest you change also. I'll meet you downstairs in fifteen minutes. By the way, my room is next door if you need me."

"I think I can survive the next fifteen minutes without you," Tracy said, smiling.

"It's nice to see your sense of humor returning." And then he was gone.

MUCH as she hated to open her suitcase, since it would have to be repacked anyway, Tracy decided to wash and change into something more attractive than the jeans she'd been wearing the past two days.

She was feeling a lot better since she had spoken with her Aunt. While the concern for her father was still uppermost in Tracy's mind, the knowledge that Ray was going to survive his heart attack calmed her somewhat. Kirk was right, under the circumstances she just had to wait it out till she got back home.

Tracy had not worn her emerald-green dress for any occasion, and since it was her last night in Ethiopia, it seemed a suitable time to do so. She brushed her hair out so that it fell in soft waves around her face and shoulders. She applied just enough makeup not to look pale against the vivid green silk of her dress. Then she tried the Dior scarf that Judy had given her but decided that she'd rather wear the dress by itself. She didn't feel festive enough for the scarf. Despite the ordeal she was suffering Tracy decided she still looked presentable. The ringing of the phone stopped her as she was going out the door. It was Miss Sarah, the telephone operator.

"Welcome back. I just came on the shift and

heard that you were here,'' Sarah explained. ''Your dress was delivered yesterday. My husband's been holding it for you in the storage room. Would you like me to send it up?''

''Thank you, but I'm going downstairs anyway. I'll get it.'' Tracy had forgotten about her dress. The remembered pleasure of her shopping excursion surfaced in her mind and Tracy was anxious to see what the vendors had produced.

When she had got to the desk, Tracy didn't want to take her dress upstairs to look at it. Instead, she opened the neatly packed brown paper wrapping, and unfolding the garment, measured it against herself in the lobby mirror. Even held against her, the dress fell in a smooth line from Tracy's shoulders. The length, too, seemed right. The dress fell to just above her toes. The green-and-gold borders contrasted beautifully with her skin and brought out the color of her hair and eyes. The white of the fabric made Tracy look superbly elegant. Amidst the approving looks and exclamations of the desk clerk and bellboys, Tracy reached for the gauze shawl that was part of the outfit. It was a yard wide and nearly three yards long. The shawl was supposed to be draped around the shoulders in a traditional way. Tracy had no idea how to make it look graceful instead of bunched up. ''I'm making quite a spectacle of myself here,'' she muttered as some of the hotel guests gave her curious looks on their way to the elevator.

''I'll teach you how to do that,'' Miss Sarah offered and came out from behind the counter.

"When can you do it?"

"In the morning if you'd like."

"I am leaving tomorrow so we'd better do it now while I have the chance."

"If you don't mind learning how to drape the shawl here. I can't leave the switchboard."

"It doesn't matter to me."

Tracy placed the dress on the counter and concentrated on learning the intricate way the shawl was tamed. When Sarah was finished, most of the *shemma* lay in smooth pleats around Tracy's shoulders with the leftover fabric falling freely toward the hemline. The embroidered edge fell on either side of the middle, giving even Tracy's emerald dress an ornate look.

"You look like a queen!" Miss Sarah folded her hands and tilted her head, admiring her handiwork on Tracy.

"I'll say she does," Kirk's voice boomed behind them. "So this is why you forgot all about me."

Tracy glanced at her watch. "Oh, Kirk, I'm so sorry. It's just that . . . ."

"With you looking like that how could I not forgive you?" Kirk's tone was light and mocking but his eyes danced with pleasure at the sight of her.

Tracy removed the shawl and folded it together with the dress. "Thank you for teaching me," she said, smiling at Miss Sarah.

"Send me a picture when you wear the whole outfit." Miss Sarah said as she returned to the switchboard.

"I will," Tracy promised, wondering whether she would ever get a chance to wear the dress, considering the problems facing her.

During dinner Kirk kept up a light conversation and Tracy was grateful that she didn't have to make an effort to respond. The distraction of her new dress had taken Tracy's mind off her concerns, but now at the table the complex problem of her father's illness rushed back to her. At first Tracy didn't want to eat anything at all, but at Kirk's insistence, she ordered and was surprised to find herself actually very hungry. She thoroughly enjoyed the chicken kiev, which was served with rice pilaf and vegetables, and followed by ice cream for dessert. The light white wine Kirk ordered for them helped Tracy relax. But when the musicians started to play, a great feeling of sadness came over her. How different this evening was from the excitement of that first night in Addis, when she had had Kirk's arms around her on the dance floor. Now Tracy was upset about her father and it suddenly dawned on her that part of her pain must also stem from the fact that this was the last night she would be spending with Kirk for some time to come. Despite their differences, Tracy's feelings had not changed toward him. With a sinking heart Tracy told herself that while she was rushing toward one important man in her life, she was giving up the other. She felt that if she were around Kirk, he might eventually overcome the real or imagined problems that kept him away from her. But once they were half-a-world apart, he would forget all about her. After the project in Ethiopia was completed, Tracy would probably see Kirk briefly when he and Bill returned the planes. After that, Kirk would probably seek other employment. This prospect plunged Tracy into an even gloomier mood. She looked at Kirk, who was watching the dance floor, and her heart ached with love for him. She wanted to reach out and trace the firm line of his lips, pull her fingers along his determined chin and place her palms against his strong cheekbones, just to feel the warmth of his skin.

Sensing her eyes on him, Kirk turned to her. "I'd love to take you in my arms out there," he said, smiling at her. "Would a slow good-bye dance be out of line?"

Afraid to speak lest her voice betray her feelings, Tracy shook her head.

"C'mon." Kirk reached across the table for Tracy's hand and pulled her to her feet.

With a pounding heart Tracy felt Kirk's arm wrap around her waist, enfolding her so that every inch of her body was molded against his. *How well we suit each other,* Tracy thought, as she and Kirk moved in the same rhythm slowly across the floor. It was both a pain and a joy to be in Kirk's arms again. His palm firmly pressed against hers, was hot. The familiar scent of his skin, a mixture of shaving lotion and his own natural body odor made Tracy want to bury her face in the inviting curve between her partner's neck and his powerful shoulder.

Tracy closed her eyes, letting Kirk lead her. He

too was silent, breathing occasionally into her hair. She could feel the fast beating of Kirk's heart as he pressed her against his chest. *It's as though desire and desperation are drawing us together,* Tracy thought. They were embracing, painfully aware that this was their last night together. Yet Tracy couldn't talk about their parting and it was obvious that neither could Kirk. When the music ended, Kirk took Tracy by the hand and pulled her off the floor. Without a word he led her out of the dining room.

At the door of Tracy's room, Kirk leaned down and kissed her. It was a gentle good-night kiss and Tracy returned it, her lips savoring his. As though it were an invitation, Kirk's arms tightened around her. For an interminable moment they revealed their feelings through their lips, giving and taking hungrily, passionately, yet knowing that they would stop before fulfilling their mounting desire.

"I'll see you in the morning," Kirk whispered hoarsely, tearing himself away from her.

Tracy knew it would be a long, restless night punctuated by disturbing thoughts but she couldn't make herself ask Kirk to stay with her and hold her. Spending the night with him would emphasize the loss that was awaiting her, for though Kirk would be at her side till the plane took off the next day, from there on she would have to cope with life alone again.

THE NEXT MORNING Kirk called her early to say that he needed to make some urgent arrangements, so he would not be able to see her till it was time to go to the airport. When they finally met in the lobby, the dark rings under Kirk's eyes, told Tracy that he had spent a sleepless night as well. He directed the bellboy with Tracy's luggage to the Jeep.

"No, no, you are the guest of our government," Major Hadib protested when Tracy went to settle her bill. "It's all taken care of."

Tracy thanked him, and asked him to convey her regrets to His Excellency Worku Adugni, for her sudden departure. "The drops won't be affected by it," Tracy said, smiling at the major. "So it's only my misfortune that I'm not able to stay in your beautiful country any longer."

"Well, we hope you shall return under happier circumstances."

Tracy took one last look at the hotel as they drove away. It was amazing how many memories could be crowded into so few days, she thought, already nostalgic. Despite her occasional clashes with Kirk and the uncertainty of what might happen in the future between them, Tracy would always cherish the memory of her trip to Ethiopia.

She looked back at Kirk sitting with his arm spread over the top of the seat. He wore his khaki safari jacket with short sleeves, exposing the dark hair on his muscular arms. Tracy would have liked to have reached back and feel the warmth of Kirk's skin and his soft hairs under her palm. But of course she didn't. Kirk smiled at her and she smiled back. *That's all that's left to us,* Tracy thought, *these friendly but distant few minutes before the steel door of the plane shuts, parting us, and the powerful engines carry me into a separate world, alone.*

Tracy's heart ached. *I have absolutely no luck with men,* she thought. First she had fallen in love with a frivolous man like George and now she had fallen in love with Kirk, who for his own reasons, seemed to reject her. Maybe it was something in her character that prevented her from holding onto a man. Like her Aunt Irma, maybe Tracy was too strong for her own good. But she *had* to be strong. Despite the lip service paid to equality, experience had taught Tracy that a woman still had to fight her way against prejudice if she chose to be an aeronautical engineer. And now with the illness of her father, Tracy would have to fight again, to hold onto Westwind. Inwardly she shuddered at the idea. She wished she could say all this to Kirk. But of course, that was impossible.

Major Hadib pulled up to the curb at Departures and let both Tracy and Kirk off.

"Why don't you check in, Miss Brooke. Kirk will take care of the luggage," the major suggested.

By the time Tracy's ticket and passport were processed, both Kirk and Major Hadib were at her side. Tracy expected her suitcase to be weighed in at the ticket counter, but Major Hadib told her that Ethiopians had a different system than she was used to.

"Our people check over everyone's luggage before it leaves the country to make sure that you're not taking out contraband. After that they send it directly to the plane," the major explained.

"But how did they know which flight I was on when I have the ticket?" Tracy asked.

"Because I told them," the major said, laughing.

"I'm getting a feeling of déjà vu," Tracy said, grinning. "You seem to be rescuing me from customs coming and going, major."

"That's the least I can do, considering the way your company is helping our country. By the way, you still have a little time—may I buy you a cup of coffee?"

"Of course."

"I'll be with you in a moment," Kirk said, waving them on.

The last thing Tracy wanted, was to waste her precious leftover minutes with the good major, without Kirk. But it seemed to be Kirk's choice, so resigned to what was happening, she followed Major Hadib.

Soon it was time to go to the gate. Kirk had not returned. Tracy tried to delay going through security by chatting with the major about keeping in touch. But when the third call for boarding came, Tracy realized that she had to leave or else miss her flight. And that she couldn't do. The "other man" in her life was still more important than Kirk. *What a coward, he is,* Tracy thought as, blinded by unwanted tears, she walked across the airfield.

"First class, please," the airline attendant said, pointing to the front staircase of the plane.

"But . . ." Tracy said, beginning to protest, and then looked at her ticket. It had been upgraded from tourist to first class, likely as a courtesy of the Ethiopian government. Normally the surprise would have given Tracy great pleasure. But now, feeling a gnawing emptiness at the pit of her stomach, she mounted the stairs to the first class compartment joylessly. The cabin was full except for Tracy's seat and the one next to her's. A friendly flight attendant helped Tracy store her traveling case and offered her a drink. After she declined a beverage the flight attendant moved to the back of the cabin. Tracy buckled up in the window seat and, turning her head to look out, finally allowed free flow to her feelings. She closed her eyes, and knowing that in this position others around her couldn't see her face, let the tears of anger and disappointment roll down as they wished. A part of Tracy ached as never before. Another part of her was almost removed from this pain, wondering how Tracy Brooke, Engineer Brooke, could be hurt so deeply by anything as trivial as love.

In the back of the cabin Tracy heard voices and realized that more passengers were getting on. That meant someone might sit next to her and no matter what she felt, it wouldn't do for a grown woman to be crying in public, Tracy decided. She quickly wiped her face with the back of her hand.

"Would you like to use my handkerchief?" said a deep, familiar voice above her.

Tracy turned her head only to meet Kirk's mocking grin.

"What are you doing here?" she stammered.

"I forgot something." Kirk leaned across the aisle seat and pressed his lips over hers in a measured, slow kiss.

"That's a very noble send-off," Tracy said, finding her voice. "Now how about leaving before they shut the doors."

"The doors are already closed." Kirk folded his long frame into the seat next to Tracy. "If you hadn't been so absorbed in your feelings, you'd have noticed that we're taxiing to the runway."

Tracy could feel herself blushing to the roots of her hair. Kirk, surprised by her reaction, burst out laughing. "Oh, now you really look like the lioness that you are, red, from head to toe!"

"Get out of here!" Tracy pushed him away from her side.

"As you know, that might be a bit difficult at this point," Kirk said, grinning. "Though if you wish, I could exchange seats with someone after take-off."

"Stop clowning, Kirk. What gave you the idea that you could just walk off your job and take the next plane out?"

Kirk's face suddenly turned serious. "I didn't just walk off my job, as you put it, Tracy. Bill is as competent as I am at handling things, and early this morning I arranged, with Major Hadib's help, for an Ethiopian Air Force pilot to fly in my absence. He's American trained, so you don't have to worry," Kirk said, anticipating Tracy's protest. "I told you I'd see you through this crisis—so here I am."

Tracy felt as though a lead weight had been lifted from her heart. She leaned her head back against the seat and looked at Kirk. "You evil-hearted man, why didn't you let me know you were coming along!" Tracy couldn't prevent the broad smile that spread over her face.

"I thought you'd like the surprise," Kirk said, grinning.

"Not in this case."

"The truth is, it took some doing to round up an extra ticket, and I didn't want to say anything in case I couldn't make it."

As though on cue, the flight attendant came over to them. "Mr. Russell? Here is your change for the upgrade. The ticket counter sent it after you but you had already boarded."

"Thank you."

Before Kirk could prevent her, Tracy took the envelope out of his hand and looked at its contents. Inside were receipts for the first-class seat for Kirk and for the upgrading of Tracy Brooke's ticket, all the way to Los Angeles. "Just what is this?" Tracy inquired, knitting her brows.

"Well, I didn't want the boss to travel economy while I sat up here by myself!"

"Kirk!"

"It's okay, Tracy, it won't break me to splurge on us a little."

"When we're back in Santa Monica, I'll pay you the difference."

"You can't accept anything from a man, can you?"

Tracy stared at him. The last thing she wanted was an argument, especially when she was feeling so elated by Kirk's presence.

"Okay, if it gives you pleasure."

"That's better."

Kirk reached over and put his arm around Tracy's shoulders. They were airborne. Together they watched the billowing white clouds through which they soared. Tracy knew that nothing had been resolved, either between them or back in Santa Monica, but being near Kirk made her feel so good that for the moment she just didn't care.

CHAPTER ELEVEN

"DAD, I'M HERE!" Tracy leaned over her father's bed, trying to catch the sick man's eyes.

"He can hear you," the nurse said, behind her, "but he may find it hard to respond."

"Squeeze my hand if you can hear me."

Ray Nolan gently closed his fingers over his daughter's hand.

Tracy sighed with relief. "Everything is fine," she reassured her father. "I am back and Kirk came with me and from here on I'll handle anything that needs to be done." Tracy saw Ray's eyelashes flutter and assumed the movement was in answer to what she was saying. That was good enough for now, Tracy decided. The doctor had given her permission for a five-minute visit and she had said just about everything that needed to be said, under the circumstances. "I'll be back soon," Tracy promised, and left the room with Kirk.

Outside, the doctor met with Tracy and Kirk. Dr. Lange was an eminent heart specialist. He had been recommended by their family physician, Dr. Keller. He assured Tracy that her father's listless condition was not unusual for a man in the second day of recuperation from even a mild cardiac arrest. "It will take him at least two weeks to be his normal, alert self again."

"And how long for him to recover completely?" Tracy asked.

"It's hard to say. That will depend on whether or not Ray can stay clear of any stress."

"I guess I'll have to deal with Anne on my own," Tracy said, then bit her lips.

"Let me know if there's anything I can do for you," Kirk offered on their way out of the hospital.

"How long were you planning on staying?"

"I'm not sure. Now that I'm here, I'll take care of some business of my own—without salary from Westwind of course. Kirk added with a smile. Then I'll head back to wind up the job in Ethiopia."

"Where will you be staying?"

"I've got some friends in town. How about giving me your home phone number so I can get in touch with you?"

Tracy scribbled her number on a piece of paper. "Thanks for coming back with me, Kirk. I'm coming to see my father tomorrow afternoon. Perhaps we could have coffee afterward?"

"How about dinner?"

"Fine."

"Where are you going from here? Can I give you a lift?" Kirk offered.

Kirk had rented a car at the airport and they had driven from the airport directly to the hospital.

Tracy hadn't even called her aunt, thinking that Irma might be at Ray's bedside. Now Tracy wondered whether she should go home first or to Westwind's office. It was only afternoon in Los Angeles but after their twenty-four-hour trip Tracy was bone tired.

"I'd appreciate it if you could drop me off at Westwind," Tracy said, finally deciding. More than anything, she needed to know how the company had been surviving during her father's illness. From Westwind, Tracy could call her aunt, and she could ask Rosie, Ray's secretary, to drive her home.

Kirk delivered Tracy to Westwind's main office.

"I'll see you at the hospital tomorrow afternoon," he promised, and drove off.

Tracy wondered, how after all they had been through together, Kirk could behave so offhandedly. Even under the strained circumstances, Tracy expected him to be more affectionate— perhaps by giving her a good-bye kiss or some other sign of intimacy. But what had passed between them did not seem to have affected Kirk. Apparently, from his standpoint, it brought them no closer than a casual friendship. *I'll never understand men,* Tracy thought as she shook her head. She picked her suitcase off the curb and walked into her father's office at Westwind.

"Tracy! Thank goodness you're back!" Rosie said as she jumped up to greet her.

Tracy hugged the secretary affectionately. "I've just been to the hospital," she informed Rosie, in order to prevent any outburst of sentimentality about her father. Rosie had worked for Ray for the past twenty years. She was married, had a son in college and never missed a day's work at the office. Tracy always felt that her small, round figure, pleasant face and thick glasses were as much a part of Westwind as the planes. Rosie removed her glasses, letting them hang around her neck by the string on which she had always worn them, and took a close look at Tracy's pale face. "It was quite a shock for all of us, honey, believe me. Such a vital, healthy man. . . ."

"What do you think may have caused it?" Tracy asked.

"I don't know of any particular cause. Business was going as usual."

"Has any important mail come in since his illness?"

"It's all in his incoming box, Tracy. You want to look at it now?"

"Not unless there is something urgent. I'm awfully tired," Tracy told the secretary.

"There is nothing urgent, as far as I could tell. Can I get you a cup of coffee?"

"No, I'll just call Aunt Irma and then go home."

Tracy liked the fact that Rosie automatically assumed that while her father was out, she would be handling the family business. It was as well for her to have Rosie's support in case Anne, also, decided to come into the office.

Rosie returned to her work and Tracy dialed

her aunt's number. Esperanza picked up the phone. She welcomed Tracy back, then told her that her aunt was at the hospital.

"Just tell Irma I'll come over tomorrow morning. I'm going home to sleep," said Tracy, yawning.

"I'll make a special lunch for you tomorrow," Esperanza suggested.

"Thanks, Espe. I'll be there."

Tracy hung up then realized that she had no transportation. Rosie offered to drive Tracy home as soon as she finished typing out a couple of letters. Tracy sat down behind her father's desk and casually began to glance at his mail. There were all sorts of letters. Some were from clients, thanking Ray for a great flight. Others were inquiries about remodeling planes—these she read with interest. Then Tracy's eye caught an official-looking envelope at the bottom of the pile. It was a manila envelope with the seal of the U.S. Air Force as a return address. She pulled out its content and first scanned the letter then read it over carefully. In clumsy official language Ray Nolan was being notified that his sealed bid had been duly entered, among others, for consideration for the defense contract regarding small reconnoissance planes, and that he would be notified as soon as a choice had been made. Tracy glanced at the date. The letter was two weeks old. Ray must have received it just after Tracy had left. Suddenly an idea occurred to her. Tracy searched the Santa Monica phone book, and finding the number, dialed the Rand Corporation.

"Kenny Davis, please," Tracy told the operator.

"Mr. Davis's office," a secretary announced in a practiced, nasal drawl.

"This is Tracy Brooke, I'd like to speak with Mr. Davis."

"Just a moment, please."

"Tracy!" Kenny's cheerful voice boomed into the receiver. "What can I do for you?"

"I'd like to talk to you about something as soon as possible."

"Well, c'mon over to the house tonight! No, wait, I won't be there till late. How about stopping by my office? I can always take a coffee break with you."

"I'm at Westwind but I haven't got my car. I just got back from Ethiopia."

"Ethiopia! I didn't even know you were away! How long were you there?"

"About a week." Tracy wondered whether Judy had neglected to tell Kenny of her trip or if he just wasn't listening when she did. Judy's husband did have a tendency to dismiss unimportant details from his mind.

"Kenny, would it be possible for you to come by and give me a lift home?"

"When?"

"Now."

"Is it that urgent that you see me?"

"Sort of."

"Heart trouble again?"

Tracy couldn't help smiling. Good old Kenny, he was ready to help out just as he had when her marriage was falling apart. Despite the seriousness of the situation Tracy permitted herself a bitter, little joke. "You might say that. But unfortunately this time it's not my heart, it's my father's." Tracy explained briefly what had happened and added, "I need some professional advice from you, and rather quickly."

"I'll be right over," Kenny promised and hung up.

While waiting for him, Tracy asked Rosie whether Anne had been coming in to take care of business.

Rosie told her that Anne had given instructions to refer anything of importance to herself. Otherwise, since the secretary knew the daily routine better than she did, Anne had just let Rosie run the business.

"From now till my father can take over again, I'll be here daily." Tracy informed the secretary. "So before anything goes to Anne I want to see it."

"As you wish." Rosie flashed Tracy an understanding smile.

Kenny's lean figure darkened the doorway to the office.

"I'll be here tomorrow," Tracy told the secretary, and picking up her suitcase, she followed Kenny out the door.

"I didn't want to ask you over the phone," Tracy began once they were in the car, "but I need to know, if several people are bidding for a government contract, is there any way to find out who they are?"

"That's a rather sticky matter, Tracy. I'm not sure. What is the bid for?"

"Reconnoissance planes."

"Why do you need to know?"

Tracy explained that with her father's illness, undoubtedly Anne would try to make trouble and she wanted to know just what the possibility was of the company getting the government contract. "I need to anticipate these things because I don't intend to have Anne take me by surprise," Tracy explained.

"I'm going to Washington next week," Kenny said pensively. "Usually these bids are confidential until the firm is chosen, but I've got friends in the right department, so I might be able to find something out for you."

Tracy's heart leapt with joy. "I'll be so grateful if you do."

"All I ask in return is that you look in on Judy while I'm gone." Kenny looked at her. "She's been so moody lately, I hate leaving her alone, but...."

"I know," Tracy laughed, "but work comes first."

"It shouldn't," Kenny rubbed his already tossled, brown hair, "but when an important project is on deadline, I just have to give whatever it takes to get it done."

"I'll explain it to her," Tracy promised.

"The odd thing," Kenny added with a puzzled look on his face, "is that I'm trying to do a good job not only for my own sense of accomplishment, but for Judy and Kathy too. But Judy doesn't see it that way. Why doesn't she understand that if

I do well at work, we'll do well as a family?''

"Because it's hard to look at it that way when your man spends more time with work than with you!" Tracy responded.

"But do you see what I mean?"

"Somewhat. I'll do my best to explain it to Judy." Tracy climbed out of the car. "Thanks for the ride. And call me collect as soon as you have some information."

Tracy felt strange being back in her apartment. *It's as if I'd been away a year,* Tracy thought as she pulled back drapes and opened windows to air out the place. She considered what she had been able to accomplish in the few hours since her return to Santa Monica and felt satisfied.

At the office she had established that she was taking charge at Westwind. With Kenny's help she might be able to fight for the government contract that was now more essential for the survival of her father's business than ever.

Moreover, her father's condition wasn't too bad. Obviously Ray would need intensive medical care for awhile, but as the doctor had assured her, he would pull through. And though Kirk was so strangely distant, still he was around. Tracy had a dinner date with him tomorrow to look forward to. Without bothering to unpack she lay down on her bed and fell into a deep sleep.

FEELING SOMEWHAT DAZED from jet lag, Tracy nonetheless managed to keep her promise and was at Westwind's offices by nine the next day. She started work by reviewing what had gone on at the Experimental Branch—her usual job—while she had been away. Then, she was about to get a briefing from Rosie on her father's area, the Commuter Line, when the phone rang. It was Patrick Robbins, Westwind's lawyer.

"Tracy, I know you've been through a lot lately, but I need to see you this morning," Robbins said by way of good morning.

"Fine, come by the office," Tracy offered.

"Anne would like the meeting at her house."

"Anne?"

"She is your father's partner."

"I know who she is. Why don't you give me a little hint about the reason we're meeting." Tracy was irritated by Robbins's arrogant tone and she wasn't going to make the call easy for him.

"The company, of course."

"Well, I didn't think it was to be a social hour," Tracy mocked him. "What about the company?"

Tracy had never really liked Robbins. After the senior partner, Jay Lacombe of Lacombe and Bush retired, Ray had accepted Jay's suggestion that he employ Patrick Robbins, a junior partner, as Westwind's lawyer. Robbins was in his mid-forties. He had a forceful personality, which he managed to hide most of the time behind his classically handsome face and studied smile. Ray thought that his polished manner might be an asset in the corporate world and was willing to keep Robbins on, at least for awhile. *Now, of course, we're dependent on him for who knows how long,* Tracy thought, not pleased with the idea. She would have preferred an older, mellower lawyer to deal with—someone who didn't feel that every transaction was a personal challenge.

"Tracy, can you make it by eleven?"

It was ten o'clock. "I've got an appointment for lunch at noon."

"If you can, cancel it. In any case, we'll try to make it quick."

"You still haven't told me what we're meeting about."

"I don't think we should spend the time on the phone. I'd just be repeating what you'll hear when you get to Anne's."

"I'll see you there." Tracy hung up abruptly, feeling good about being rude to the man. It was obvious that Robbins didn't give her the same courteous treatment he gave Ray and probably Anne. *He must think I'm just on the sidelines at Westwind,* Tracy concluded. *Well, I've got a surprise for you, and Anne too,* Tracy thought smugly. She was almost looking forward to the meeting.

ANNE LIVED IN BEVERLY HILLS, in a spreading villa above Sunset Drive. As Tracy drove up the hill to Anne's house, she remembered the discussion her father had had with Eddie and Anne about moving to Beverly Hills. Her father had chosen the opulent but less notorious residential area of Santa Monica while Anne had insisted on Beverly

Hills. "Finally the company is making enough
money for us to be able to choose our neighbor-
hood," Anne had said. Anne liked to use money
for her own comfort. Tracy preferred to create
new projects with it. As Tracy's Alfa Romeo came
to a stop at the gate of Anne's house, she braced
herself for the clash of their philosophies.

"It's me," Tracy said through the grill of the in-
tercom.

The tall iron gate opened and Tracy drove in.
Robbins's Mercedes took up the space directly in
front of the double doors of the house. Tracy
parked just behind the Mercedes, almost touching
Robbins's bumper. A uniformed Japanese maid
led Tracy through the marble-floored hallway into
Anne's combination study and morning room.
Tracy had to admit that Anne had a cheerful
place. The turn-of-the-century style chairs and
sofas were covered in yellow-flowered chintz and
the drapes matched the upholstery. A baby grand
stood under the open window, its ivory keys looking invitingly exposed. The view from the bay windows extended beyond the well-kept lawn to the
San Fernando Valley.

"Would you like some coffee?" Anne offered.

"Yes, thank you," Tracy responded politely.

Patrick Robbins waited patiently while the two
women dispensed with the ritual of serving, and
settled down, each holding a delicate porcelain
cup filled with the steaming black brew.

"I know this is a poor time to put more burdens
on you, Tracy," the lawyer began, "but unfortun-

ately it's precisely your father's illness that has caused us to call this meeting. As you must know, the company has two problems. On the one hand, you're invested heavily in the Experimental Branch and it's still losing money. It depends on the Commuter Line to keep it alive. On the other hand, Anne, who is an equal partner with your father, would like to withdraw her capital from the company.''

"You're not telling me anything new, Patrick," Tracy interrupted. "We had a meeting about this with Anne just a few weeks ago! Why did I have to cancel all my plans to hear it again?"

"Because the situation has been aggravated by your father's illness."

Tracy directed her words to the lawyer, but she was staring hard at Anne, who huddled unusually quiet in her wing-backed armchair. "Anne gave us six months leeway at the last meeting. We've used up no more than two months of that. I don't see how my father's illness could in any way affect that agreement."

"Tracy, Anne tells me that the six month timeframe was a verbal agreement you three had. Now with the change of circumstances, Anne is concerned about the company's future."

"What she is concerned about is getting her money out—just in case!" Tracy cut in angrily.

"I am sitting right here," Anne called out, "so don't talk about me in the third person!"

"Then don't have a lawyer talk for you!" Tracy was losing her temper, not only with Anne, but

with herself. Tracy knew that she should be
calmer. She would have liked to tell Anne and
Patrick about what a great future she could fore-
see for the company if only Anne would cooper-
ate. But now, Tracy was so riled that all she could
do was fight.

"I represent the company, not any one of you in
particular," Robbins pointed out.

"Then how come you're defending Anne's position instead of telling her that she'd made an
agreement, and whether she likes it or not, she'll
have to stick to it till it expires!" Tracy fumed.

"Your father is obviously not in charge at this
point," Anne responded. "Therefore as his equal
partner, I have to make some decisions."

"Don't bury him yet," Tracy spit out, her green
eyes narrowing on Anne. "What's more, if Ray
chooses to retire, *I* might take over his half of the
business. So at this point you can either wait till he
gets better or deal with me. And you know where I
stand."

"Tracy, let's try to get a perspective on the
situation," Robbins said, trying to calm the two
women down. The narrowed eyes of both Anne
and Tracy were locked, and neither woman broke
her angry stare. "As soon as the news came out
about your father's heart attack, the accountant
and I started getting calls. The bank and most of
your suppliers wanted to know how they were going to get their payments from Westwind. Some
callers also wanted to know if and when Westwind
was going up for sale."

Tracy muttered a curse under her breath.

"Those are the facts, my dear," Anne said in a saccharine tone. "You should also realize that I can sell my half of the business to anyone who makes me the right offer. If I haven't so far, it's only been out of consideration for your father. On the other hand, even you must admit that he won't be able to work for some time to come."

"And you don't trust me to run the business," Tracy retorted.

"Let's just say that I don't care to have a business partnership with you."

"Not even if I could guarantee that within a few months the Experimental Branch will become a profit maker?"

"That's a pipe dream, Tracy. Without your father at the helm the government would never give you that contract."

"I've come up with a much better deal than the government contract," Tracy said, trying to appeal to Anne's greed.

"What, you struck a gold mine in Ethiopia?" Anne mocked.

"You could say that." Tracy made herself sound as mysterious as she could.

"Care to tell us what it is?" Robbins asked, reentering the discussion. "After all, we're all trying to solve the situation together."

"No, we're not," Tracy said, shaking her head. "All I want from you, Patrick, is the original partnership agreement between Eddie and my father. I'd like to see in black and white what provisions were made in case one of them wanted out. And as for you, Anne, for my father's sake, I think you should stick to your promise.''

"For your father's sake, I think I should take the best offer I can get for Westwind. That way he can retire with a decent amount of money and live to be a hundred without worry.'' Anne sounded so sincere that Tracy could almost believe that she meant it.

"I've got the original contract right here, Tracy,'' the lawyer said. He put on a pair of dark-framed glasses that Tracy thought made him look very official, and read:

> Either partner shall have the right to purchase the share of the other partner. In the event that funds are not available for said purchase, the partner wishing to sell shall have the right to do so, provided that he or she obtains approval of the sale from the other partner.

"Aha!'' Tracy felt she suddenly had an edge over Anne.

"Wait, I didn't finish,'' Robbins insisted.

> Said approval is not to be unreasonably withheld. In the event of an emergency, incurable illness, or other catastrophe, either partner shall have the right to act independently in the best interest of the company, without consent or approval from the other partner.

"That's the vaguest contract language I've ever heard!" Tracy exclaimed.

"It's clear to me!" Anne said triumphantly.

Tracy rose. "I don't believe that the normal recovery period of any curable illness would qualify as a catastrophe in a court of law. My father suffered a heart attack, not brain damage. Presumably he'll be able to make decisions as soon as he is over his present crisis. Until then, I am handling his half of the business. If you don't like it, then let's go to court."

"Don't get so dramatic, Tracy," Anne said with disdain.

But Tracy was beyond caring. "Patrick, if you have trouble handling our creditors just send them to me. Have a good day, both of you."

Tracy gathered her handbag and strode out of the room. She could feel Anne and Patrick's stunned silence as she went by them. Perhaps it was wrong to walk out. Yet instinct told Tracy that only this shock tactic would show Anne how determined she was to keep Anne to the agreement she had made with Ray. The maid materialized, seemingly out of nowhere, and smiling pleasantly, let Tracy out of the house. Tracy breathed deeply and got into her car.

As she drove down the hill, Tracy realized that she was shaking all over. Despite the brave show she had put on in front of Anne and the lawyer, Tracy knew that Anne had a lot of power on her side. Her father very likely *would* have to retire and Tracy wasn't sure Ray would let her run the company without him. Even if he would, Anne would not. Tracy would have to look for a large loan, or build up her business very quickly to cash Anne out or Anne would sell her share to some unknown partner. She was now glad that she had cancelled her luncheon visit with her Aunt Irma and Esperanza. Before going to the hospital, she needed to return to Westwind, just to get the feel of the company around herself. It was her work place and the place where Tracy felt she could build her dreams. She could comprehend Anne's need to get out but Tracy simply couldn't allow it to happen.

WHEN SHE ARRIVED AT THE HOSPITAL that after-noon, Tracy found her Aunt Irma sitting in the waiting room. They hadn't seen each other since Tracy's return, and now the two women embraced affectionately. Their embrace was more than a greeting marking Tracy's return. Ray's illness made them feel closer to each other.

"He's asleep," Aunt Irma said, indicating the closed door to Ray's room.

"How is he today?" Tracy whispered.

"Better. Can you stay till he wakes up?"

"Of course."

The two women sat down on the plastic sofas to wait together. Irma studied Tracy's face and patted her niece's hand. "You look well, Tracy. A little tired, but well. How was your trip?"

"Interesting. From a business point of view very promising, I think." Tracy was eager to share her ideas with her aunt.

But Irma had something else on her mind. "Kirk Russell came to see your father a little while ago. Tell me, Tracy, what do you think of him?"

Tracy was taken aback by the directness of the question but she tried to sound nonchalant. "Why should you bother about details like how I feel about an employee?"

Aunt Irma's blue eyes looked sharply at Tracy. "C'mon, young lady, I know you were having problems with him! And he is far more than a mere employee."

Tracy blushed, wondering how much her aunt had guessed about her relationship with Kirk. "All right, so he is an independent contractor with us. And he is okay."

"Really?"

Under her aunt's quizzical glance Tracy found it hard to pretend. "Actually, we've had some clashes, but all in all, he's a good man for the job."

"Tracy, I must be getting really old, because apparently I'm no longer able to phrase a question right. I didn't mean, how do you rate him on the job, but how do you rate him as a man!"

"What can I tell you? He's like all other men—out for what he can get."

Irma shook her head sadly. "I wonder where I went wrong with you. I was so looking forward to your getting married and settling down."

"Don't be so conventional, Aunt Irma. You never got married and you don't seem to have suffered for it!"

"I did get married," Aunt Irma interrupted, then stopped abruptly.

Tracy stared at her. "I never knew that! What happened to your husband?"

"He was killed in a car accident—along with our nine-month-old son." Aunt Irma sighed and looked away.

Tracy sat in stunned silence. It was strange how during all the years her aunt had lived with them, Irma had never once hinted at her past.

"How long ago was that?"

"A couple of years before I came to live with you."

"So you came to take care of dad and me instead of starting a new life for yourself, is that it?"

"Not quite, dear. I welcomed the safe harbor your home offered and the chance to raise you as though you were my own."

So that's what her aunt had done, Tracy reflected, finally learning what had made Irma stay single. Tracy knew that her aunt had been attractive. She had seen photographs of her relative and Irma had looked quite lovely in them. Why, her aunt was still a good looking woman! But apparently Irma wasn't the great independent spirit she seemed, not at all a woman who had purposely stayed clear of the enslavement of marriage, the way Tracy had fantasized all these years. On the contrary, Irma had opted for safety, mothering her brother's child instead of finding a life of her own! Tracy reached out and placed her hand over her aunt's.

"Aren't you sorry that you never remarried?"

"How could I be? I look at you and I'm proud of the way you've turned out. My only wish is that you find the kind of happiness I had when I started out in life."

Tracy didn't respond directly to her aunt's implication. Instead, she asked, "Why didn't you tell me about this before?"

Aunt Irma sighed. "It didn't seem necessary. But now, as I watch you closing your heart to what may be a real chance at love for you, I wonder if I did the right thing. I guess growing up with what could count as an old maid didn't teach you anything about love."

"Oh, Aunt Irma!" Tracy felt a sudden rush of warmth for the older woman. She moved over to sit by Irma, and embraced her. Then like a child, Tracy put her head against her aunt's shoulder and whispered, "It's not me, Aunt Irma. Kirk Russell has never said anything about love, so what do you expect me to do?"

"Have you shown him how you feel?"

"I tried, but I don't think he noticed."

"If you're not sure, how about trying again?"

"How could I? He would just laugh in my face!"

"Tracy, my child, sometimes, if you want something really badly, you've got to take risks. If he did laugh at you—and I'm sure he wouldn't— you could always find a way to save your dignity. But if you don't try, you'll never know what you could have had."

"What makes you think that I should try?"

"A little bird tells me," Aunt Irma said, smiling.

"Maybe after dad is better..." Tracy sighed. "I really can't right now."

"What's more important than your own life?"

"Aunt Irma, love is only a part of one's life! The other part is work and right now...." Tracy's eyes filled with tears and she couldn't go on. The memory of her morning meeting with Anne and Patrick Robbins came back to her and she swallowed a sob.

"Tracy—" Aunt Irma's voice was full of alarm "—what's going on with you!"

"I'm scared," Tracy whispered, closing her eyes and leaning back against the hard plastic seat.

"Of what?"

"That Anne will take away not only her share, but all of Westwind and all my hopes with it."

"It won't happen, Tracy. You know that!"

"I don't know anything anymore." Tracy briefly told her aunt about the morning's meeting.

"Well, Anne was just pushing a little too hard, that's all. Your father will get better in no time and then everything will get straightened out."

"I wish I could be as optimistic as you are," Tracy sighed.

Before Aunt Irma could reply, the nurse came to tell them Ray was awake.

Tracy's father was not only awake, he was looking like he was on the road to recovery. Ray smiled at the two women as they entered his room, and said in a weak voice, "I really gave you a scare, didn't I?"

Tracy rushed to his side. "I'm so glad to hear your voice!"

"Kirk was here a little while ago. We had a talk. He is a good man, Tracy. I like him," Ray informed his daughter.

"Aunt Irma mentioned that he was here," Tracy replied. She didn't ask what the two men had talked about, assuming that Kirk's visit was a courtesy call. She also didn't tell her father how Kirk's visit had made her aunt reveal a life-long secret, that in turn, had made Tracy admit her feelings for Kirk. But Tracy was glad of their talk. It brought them much closer at a time when both she and her aunt needed mutual emotional support because of Ray's illness. It didn't make Tracy feel much better about Kirk though. He had come and gone without waiting for her when he had known she would be there. Also, he had called that morning and cancelled their dinner date and had left no way for her to contact him. It could be that he was so gracious during his visit that both her father and Irma had mistaken his manner for real concern. Despite what Aunt Irma had said outside Ray's room, it sure didn't seem to Tracy that Kirk had any love for her, even any interest in her! While all this was flashing through Tracy's mind, she smiled and patted Ray's hand.

"Yes, Kirk is okay," Tracy managed to say for Ray's benefit.

"How are you doing?" her father asked. "Tell me what's going on at Westwind."

She wondered if it might not upset him if she talked of business matters, but decided to risk it. She watched his face carefully while giving him a brief account of how she'd been handling Westwind's affairs. Tracy didn't want to tire him. Nonetheless, Tracy knew he was interested in her news and she needed to let him know that she was in control. At her father's first sign of fatigue, Tracy stopped, saying, "That's about it. As you can see, everything is under control. You don't have to worry. Just take care of yourself and get well."

"I'm glad you're doing so well." Ray closed his eyes.

Irma asked if she could do anything for him but Ray just thanked her, saying he was getting such good care, he couldn't think of a thing.

"Want to stay at the house for a few days?" Aunt Irma offered as she and Tracy left the hospital.

"Thanks, but I've been away from my place too long," Tracy said. "I'll be over soon, though, to deliver your presents."

"Why not come for dinner?"

"Not tonight. I've got to catch up with the work."

"You choose the day then."

"I will. And Aunt Irma?"

"Yes?"

"I'm glad we talked."

"Me too, Tracy."

The two women hugged. At the parking lot, they separated, each going to her own car. Tracy drove back to the airport. She had the rest of the afternoon and evening free for work. Instead of brooding over Kirk, or the fate of Westwind, this was a good time to learn as much as she could about how her father ran the company, she decided. Tracy knew that Anne would try to prove that she wasn't qualified to handle the airline. And she intended to prove otherwise.

IT WAS MIDNIGHT when Tracy finally got to her apartment. Rosie had returned to the office after dinner and the two of them had pored over the books till they could barely see. As far as Tracy could tell, Westwind was doing very well as a commuter airline. However, the Experimental Branch was a definite drain on the company's profits. Considering how much Anne loved money and hated planes, Tracy could understand why the woman would not wish to see her income diminished by creating more of them. Tracy asked Rosie to make an appointment for her in the morning with Westwind's accountant, Mr. Morris, so he could explain the company's tax structure to her. There just had to be some way to get rid of Anne and still keep Westwind afloat. And Tracy intended to find it.

About two hours later, Tracy was in bed, finally through with worrying about the business and Kirk, and was falling asleep. Then the phone rang.

"Tracy, it's me, Judy. I am bleeding, and Kenny is out of town."

"Call the paramedics. Then lie down. I'll be there in fifteen minutes!"

Tracy jumped out of bed, and as rapidly as she could, got into a pair of jeans and a gray sweatshirt that happened to be hanging on the first hook in her closet. After her meeting with Kenny, Tracy had called Judy. The two girlfriends had promised to get together, but that was all. Judy knew of Tracy's problems with Ray's illness and with Westwind and thus she hadn't insisted on getting together immediately. As Tracy was racing through the deserted streets of Santa Monica she felt rather guilty about Judy. She wondered whether she should have gone over to her house that evening instead of working. It was hard to know where one should draw the line between work and friends and Tracy had never been very good at putting personal pleasure before duty. *But when it comes to duty, I am always there,* Tracy thought, laughing at herself. But why did it have to be an emergency before Tracy would allow herself to see the people she cared for? She couldn't suppress the thought that maybe Kirk had gone to see someone he cared for and that was why he had cancelled on her. Tracy shut Kirk out of her mind and parked her car in the visitors' spot at the building where Judy lived.

The paramedics arrived just as Tracy was about to take the elevator. She asked them to follow her to the Davis's penthouse condominium. Judy opened the door for them. She was pale, and had tears in her eyes. "I'm so worried about losing this baby...."

Tracy calmed her down and gathered a few items for her overnight case. The paramedics had brought a wheelchair and Judy looked like a scared little girl as she sat in it and huddled under a pink blanket.

"I'd like to go with you, just to hold your hand," Tracy said, smiling at her friend to calm her, "but I believe you have a sleeping child somewhere in this place."

"Yes, stay with her, please," Judy begged. "I'm sure these gentlemen will take care of me." Judy gave the two competent-looking young men a wan smile.

"Which hospital would you prefer ma'am?" one of them asked.

"Please take her to St. John's," Tracy requested. "That way I can visit both you and my father tomorrow." Tracy winked at Judy.

"You're one busy lady," Judy tried to sound funny.

"I'll manage." Tracy squeezed her friend's hand. "Call me from the hospital as soon as you can, or if you can't, have one of the nurses call. I won't go to sleep till I hear from you. And don't worry, everything will work out fine."

A heavy silence surrounded Tracy after Judy left with the paramedics. She went to check on Kathy. Using the light shining from the hallway through the half-open door, Tracy tiptoed to her bed. The little girl was sound asleep, her hands clutching a corner of the blanket. The room smelled sweet, like a mixture of baby powder and candy—a rather warm and friendly odor. Tracy made a mental note to comment on it later to Judy. It might amuse her friend. She watched the child for awhile, listening to Kathy's even breathing. Then leaving the door slightly ajar, Tracy returned to the living room. She sank into an armchair near the phone and with a magazine in hand, waited for the call from Judy.

CHAPTER TWELVE

TRACY FELT SOMEONE tugging at the sleeve of her sweatshirt. "Where's my mommy?" a child's plaintive voice asked from a great distance. *I must be dreaming this,* Tracy thought. She heard the voice again and opened her eyes.

It was broad daylight. She was sitting stretched-out in a living-room chair in Judy's apartment and before her stood Judy's child, Kathy, her blond curls dishevelled from sleep. For a moment Tracy thought she was still dreaming, then the events of the night before crowded into her mind and Tracy rose with a start. Her first thought was that she had not heard from Judy. The next, that she now had a child to take care of.

"Where is my mommy? I'm hungry."

Tracy picked up Kathy and hugged her. "Let's get you some breakfast. Your mommy had to go out for a while."

"To work?"

Tracy realized that Kathy was used to baby-sitters. The easy way would be to tell her, yes. But Tracy didn't always choose the easiest path. "No, Kathy, your mommy had a tummyache and she had to go see a doctor in the hospital."

"And when is she coming back?"

"First let's get your breakfast. Then we'll call the hospital and find out. Okay?"

Kathy nodded. Tracy sighed with relief. The child promised to be easy to handle. Tracy lowered her to the floor, and taking Kathy's tiny hand, walked with her into the kitchen. Tracy stopped. "Shouldn't we change your diaper first?"

"I already went potty," Kathy informed her.

Tracy felt foolish. She had no idea how competent a two-and-a-half-year-old could be. She'd just have to wing it, Tracy told herself.

With Kathy's help Tracy found the cereal and milk and set breakfast before the little girl. There was a phone in the kitchen. Tracy dialed the hospital and asked to be connected to Judy. The head nurse answered the phone at the maternity ward. She informed Tracy that Judy was still asleep and that visitors would be permitted in the afternoon. On pressing the nurse further, Tracy was told that Judy was still pregnant and though the bleeding seemed to have stopped, her friend was being kept under observation.

I ought to reach Kenny, Tracy thought. However, she had no idea where he was staying in Washington. She called Kenny's work place. They couldn't give Tracy any information, but Kenny's secretary promised to get in touch with him.

"I'm finished," Kathy announced, and hopped off her chair.

"All right, let's get you dressed."

Tracy found it an awkward but rather nice experience to help Kathy wash and get into her clothes. She enjoyed the child's sweet voice as Kathy chattered non-stop about her friends at nursery school. Tracy wondered where the school was. She would have to find out so she could drop Kathy off there. After some searching around in Judy's desk, Tracy found her friend's phone directory. Sunny Day Nursery, said one of the cards. Tracy called the number on the card and indeed, they were expecting Kathy.

"School is from 10:00 A.M. to 2:00 P.M.," the teacher informed her.

Shortly after, Tracy dropped Kathy off at a brightly painted building on Montana Avenue. "I'll pick you up after school," Tracy assured Kathy.

"Will my mommy be home then?"

"I don't know, honey. She might be."

Tracy looked at the little girl as Kathy walked off, so self-possessed and calm. A strange new longing arose in Tracy, a wish to have a little girl like Kathy, of her own. She had never desired to have a child before. During her brief marriage to George they had only spoken about starting a family once. George had told her that he didn't want to have children for awhile, and Tracy had easily agreed. She had seen how babies occupied the lives of her married friends and she hadn't been ready to give that kind of time to anyone or to anything but her work. But now Tracy thought of Kirk and her stomach tightened with yearning

for him. She felt an overwhelming surge of desire
for a child who would look at her with Kirk's
smile.

Tracy became aware that she had been sitting
still ever since Kathy had left the car. Her hands
were gripping the steering wheel and she was staring blindly at the thin line of the horizon on the
sea. *A fine character I am,* Tracy mocked herself,
dreaming instead of going to work! Yet during her
drive to the airport Tracy couldn't stop herself
from anticipating Kirk's call. She missed him. In
the brief time they had spent together she had
come to regard Kirk's presence as part of her life.

Tracy would have liked to discuss her meeting
with Anne and Patrick Morris with Kirk. She
would have liked to tell him about the added responsibility of taking care of Judy and Kathy.
Though Tracy didn't expect Kirk to help her solve
her problems, the fact that she could tell him
about them would be reassuring. Of course she
could talk about her concerns with Aunt Irma,
and even with Rosie, to some extent, but somehow
Tracy felt that Kirk would better understand what
she was facing. Or would he? Apart from her personal involvement with Kirk, an objective look at
the way he handled his job at Westwind made
Tracy wonder about him. To her best knowledge,
no one at Westwind had ever agreed to his taking a
leave of absence. Tracy had accepted his return to
the States because it was with the understanding
that he came to stand by her during this time of
trouble. But since they had come back Tracy had

not seen him, nor did she have any way to contact him. Kirk *had* visited Ray, but that, of course, counted as a courtesy call, not business. Blinded by her own feelings for Kirk, perhaps she had been too lenient as an employer. The next time he calls, instead of making a date I'll schedule an appointment, Tracy decided. No matter what she felt for him, Tracy couldn't afford to have him take advantage of the situation. Even if the people Kirk had left in charge in Ethiopia *were* competent, he still had to go back and complete the job.

Kirk had not called in, Rosie informed Tracy when she returned to Westwind. Angry with him now, Tracy decided that when Kirk did call, she would give him an ultimatum about the job. She could not run a business with undisciplined personnel.

Tracy looked at her calendar and realized that Mr. Morris, the company accountant, was due in her office in a half hour.

Tracy was still dressed in the jeans and sweatshirt she'd worn the night before. *I'm not going to impress him with my businesslike appearance,* Tracy thought. But she shrugged off the problem. Dave knew her well enough not to be concerned with appearances. She pulled out Westwind's records for the year to date, so they would be ready to hand in case the accountant needed them, and waited for him to arrive.

He arrived right on time. Dave Morris, or Mr. Morris as he liked to be called, was a man of indeterminate age. He was slightly built with a bent back, and even in the heat of the summer, the accountant wore a dark suit, a white shirt, a vest and a tie. He combed his thinning brown hair to one side. Dave Morris's spectacles sat squarely on his fleshy nose and when he smiled his row of ivory-colored teeth reminded Tracy of horses with their lips pulled back. But he was a wizard at accounting and Tracy's father had employed him since Ray and Eddie first opened the doors to Westwind. So Morris knew the company's financial position better than anyone. Tracy trusted him implicitly.

Morris sat down opposite Tracy's desk, and placed his black, leather attaché case neatly by his chair. "Mr. Robbins, your lawyer, called me right after your father fell ill," he began. "He also called me yesterday, after your meeting at Mrs. Weston's house."

"What did he tell you?"

"That Mrs. Weston would like to sell the company before your management causes her to lose all her profits to the Experimental Branch." Mr. Morris gave Tracy a wry smile.

He certainly doesn't mince words, Tracy thought. That was one of Dave Morris's best qualities. "What do you think, Mr. Morris?"

"What do I think about what?"

"Do you think we should sell the company?"

"That's not the issue. I don't wish to sell it, Mrs. Weston does."

"Mr. Morris, let me tell you where I stand with this company. It was my father who built it, and were I to take over managing it, I would never do anything to hurt Westwind. Obviously, my interests go beyond running a commuter airline. While I was in Ethiopia I could see clearly that the Experimental Branch could become a big profit maker if our planes are marketed properly. Many areas of the world have a crying need for the special planes we are able to design and I fully intend to fill that need.''

''That means you'll need to build more planes and hire more personnel. And that takes money.''

''The way I see it, is that first we should contact the organizations and governments that could use our planes. Once they buy our services, we can use their money for expansion.''

''That's not bad thinking. But who is going to do the initial work?''

''I will.''

''And head Westwind too?''

''If dad can no longer handle it, we can always hire a manager to help me.''

''Mrs. Brooke, I like your ideas. But let me tell you what you're up against. Based on what you tell me, Mrs. Weston is right in the thinking that if you take over the company, you will spend money. She won't stand for that. Mrs. Weston will want to sell. If she sells her half, we don't know who the buyer will be. And even if you approve of the new partner, you won't really know how the arrangement will turn out till after you've worked together for awhile. It's like a marriage. Your only other choice—if you want to keep the company—is to find the money on your own and buy Mrs. Weston out. I know Mrs. Weston gave you six months to do just that, but at this point there isn't a bank in town that would lend you the money. They all know that Mr. Nolan is ill and that you have relatively little business experience. That's two strikes against you.''

''We might still get the government contract.''

''You might. Unfortunately before they award it they'll investigate the company. If they find that the head of the company is too ill to manage his business. . . .'' The accountant broke off with a telling gesture.

''What about applying for a loan as a female business owner?''

''You have to prove you've operated successfully on your own for three years before they will consider you.''

''Are you telling me that my back is up against the wall?'' Tracy rose from behind her desk, angry.

''I am afraid so. Who do you know with money?''

''Nobody with millions. Do you?''

''Not to loan.''

Tracy folded her arms and stared at the accountant. ''Well then, what do you suggest?''

''You might have to accept that this company is not yours, but your father's. That he has to sell it and that you'll have to start again on your own.''

The words hit Tracy hard. She knew Dave

Morris was right, but she had never even considered his final pronouncement as a possibility. Now it struck her as a staggering reality. If the entire company was sold Ray could retire with a large profit. Why should he give away what he had earned during a lifetime of hard work?

But Tracy just couldn't look at it that way. Though Ray had never actually told her, she had always assumed that eventually he would let her take over from him. After she got her degree, the dream that had brought her back to Westwind was to create new planes and eventually manage the airline. Her father had even established the Experimental Branch, just to get her to come and work for him! So how could she now accept that she had no future with Westwind? She had grown up at Westwind and had put her life and soul into the company! Granted, Ray could not make her a gift of his company even after he retired, but she thought they had a silent understanding, that she would stay on and manage it! Even now, it wasn't Ray who had changed his mind. It was Anne, who, because of her demands, was turning Tracy's life upside down!

"Do you think Westwind would survive the time it would take me to learn to run it?"

"If you don't take too long and you don't try to expand the Experimental Branch too fast," Mr. Morris said, smiling. "But that isn't your problem, Mrs. Brooke, Mrs. Weston is."

"I'll just have to find a way to get around her," Tracy muttered, more to herself than to the accountant. "Thanks for your time, Mr. Morris."

He nodded, wished her luck, and left.

Tracy felt like the world was slowly caving in on her. Kirk, despite his promise to help her, still had not called. She didn't expect him to solve her problems, but she had hoped he'd be at her side. *Well, I might as well forget about him,* Tracy shrugged, deeply hurt. What good was a man or even a friend, if he was only available at his own convenience? That went for him as an employee, too, Tracy thought with a sudden feeling of vengeance. Just as he could easily find another pilot to take his place at the food drops, so she could give his position to another, more reliable man. If Tracy had to be alone in this fight, she was going to take full charge of all that needed to be done. It was better for her to accept that she had no one to turn to than to rely on empty promises. The thought made Tracy feel as though her insides were being ripped out and that a great hollow had been left in the place where her heart had been. But her world had never revolved around a man before, and now especially, there could be no place in her heart or her life for love. It just brought grief and distracted her when she needed all her strength to preserve the most important aspect of her life—her work. Men could come and go but her work was something that nobody could take away from her. Or could they? A cold fear gripped Tracy as she realized that short of a miracle, Anne had the power to rob her of even this.

TRACY PICKED UP KATHY at the nursery school and took the little girl to stay with Esperanza while she went to the hospital. Kathy found it hard to understand why she couldn't just go home. Tracy did her best to explain, but it was Esperanza's offer to make cookies with the child that finally made Kathy forget that she missed her mother.

At the hospital, Tracy headed first for the maternity ward. She found Judy lying in bed.

"They won't let me get up for anything," her friend complained. Judy told Tracy that she had spoken to Kenny.

"He said he was upset at not being able to be here with me but I think Kenny could have come home had he really wanted to. I don't think he considers this a real emergency," she pouted.

"Of course he does," Tracy assured her. "But you can't expect Kenny to make an announcement like 'Generals, my pregnant wife is bleeding a little so I've got to rush home!' "

"Oh, Tracy, how do you always manage to make me laugh?" Judy held on to her bouncing stomach. "I think you're better for me than Kenny. Would you like his job?"

"You might be easier to put up with than my worries with Westwind," Tracy joked.

"I have to lie flat, but I can listen."

Tracy briefly told her friend what she had been going through since her return from Ethiopia.

"If I were you, I'd ask Ray to let Anne know that he has decided to let you manage the company—at least on a trial basis," Judy advised.

"Three months are not going to run it into the ground but they may give you a foothold against Anne."

"But how can I discuss this with Ray now?"

"Don't talk about everything. Only ask him to give you a vote of confidence by telling Anne to hold off till their agreement is up."

"That sounds good."

"I've got another suggestion for you, as well. Forget Kirk. He is bad news."

"That's what we agreed on before," said Tracy, laughing despite the pain she felt at Judy's advice.

"Well, we're still agreeing. So do it. Forget Kirk at least until you've sorted out the situation with Westwind.

"Now I've got a favor to ask you. If all goes well, I'll be home tomorrow afternoon. I'll hire a nurse then, but in the meantime, I'd really appreciate your staying with Kathy."

"I enjoy her. And your daughter might be just what I need to keep me company at night," Tracy said, grinning at her friend.

"Great. Now go away, so I can get some rest and you can straighten out your life."

Upstairs Tracy found that her father had been switched from intensive care to a pleasant private room. Ray was reading some papers when she entered but he quickly put them aside.

"Tracy, how are you?"

"I should ask you first, but it's obvious that you're much, much better," Tracy said, laughing happily. "Don't tell me you're working!"

"No, no." Ray patted the papers at his side. "Just some stuff I wanted to look over. Patrick brought it."

"You really shouldn't."

"I know. In fact Dr. Lange tells me I have a choice between getting another heart attack and retiring. What do you think I should do?"

Tracy swallowed. She hadn't expected her father to bring up the subject so abruptly but Tracy was ready with her answer.

"Obviously you must retire and let me take over."

"How can you handle the whole company?" her father asked dubiously.

"What if I asked for a three-month trial period to show you how?"

"What would be the sense of that?"

"I'd like the challenge," Tracy stated quietly.

"Actually, I don't think I have a choice," Ray chuckled. "Somebody's got to keep things running till we get a buyer. And you seem to be the best person for the job. Unless you think Anne could...."

Tracy heard only the word "buyer." "Are you planning on selling the whole company?" She could feel butterflies gathering in the pit of her stomach.

"I may be forced to."

"Dad, I don't want to discuss business with you right now. I'm sure you'll do what's best. But could you hold off for the next three months? That's all I ask."

Ray studied his daughter. "What do you hope to accomplish during those months?"

"I've got some ideas. Please give me a chance. And hold Anne to your agreement until then."

"I trust you, Tracy. And obviously, I am already relying on you to manage Westwind. Anne knows that too. But with all the other pressures on me, I can only promise that I won't make any irreversible decision without consulting you. How's that?"

"Thanks."

Ray closed his eyes for a moment and Tracy felt sorry for him. They shouldn't have discussed business at all, but she was desperate. Now at least she had won some time. And time was essential. She was going to use these months to the best of her ability to prevent Anne from selling the culmination of their lifelong dream to some stranger.

Before leaving her father's room, Tracy casually mentioned that she was somewhat concerned about Kirk's whereabouts. To her surprise, Ray told her not to worry, because Kirk had been in contact with him. At the moment, Ray told her, Kirk needed to be out of town on some business but he would be in touch as soon as possible. On hearing this, Tracy felt a surge of real anger. How could Kirk be so callous as to not call *her*! Why was he avoiding her? Why should he still turn only to Ray, when the man was ill and Kirk must know that Tracy was handling Westwind? But Tracy didn't want to upset her father by sharing her thoughts. Instead, she thanked him for the information and left. Tracy thought of her conversation with Irma and smiled bitterly. So much for letting Kirk know how she felt! It was possible that Judy didn't know how to deal with her own marital problems, but Tracy's friend might be more correct than her aunt had been about how she should handle Kirk, Tracy thought as she headed for her car.

DURING THE FOLLOWING DAYS Tracy felt like she had accidentally gotten on a treadmill and couldn't get off. Judy continued to bleed and she had to stay at the hospital. Kenny could not get back from Washington. Not wanting to upset Kathy's life any more than it had been already by the absence of both her parents, Tracy volunteered to stay with the child. That meant adjusting her work to Kathy's schedule. When Judy worried about this, Tracy assured her friend that she actually enjoyed taking care of Kathy.

"It's like playing house for awhile," Tracy said to soothe Judy. And that was true. But "playing house" also meant that Tracy had to run from Judy's apartment to Kathy's nursery school, and from there to work, then back to the nursery school and back to work—it was a good thing that Esperanza offered to baby-sit in the afternoons or Tracy wouldn't have known what to do with the little girl after her school. In between errands Tracy also had to stop at her apartment for changes of clothes and make daily visits to her father and Judy at the hospital. Her father was getting visibly stronger. In fact, Dr. Lange was saying that if Ray continued to mend, he would be going home in a few days. But Judy still needed to remain under doctor's care.

In addition to her hectic personal life, with Rosie's help, Tracy was learning how to head Westwind's Commuter Line. It didn't leave Tracy time for detailed supervision and new planning at the Experimental Branch, but she didn't mind. Tracy hired a college student to research the name of every organization that was involved in aiding third world countries with food or other products. She asked Rosie to screen her phone calls and told the secretary that she was definitely *not* available to Anne. Tracy decided that before she would deal with Anne she'd have to have a ready-made plan to present to her father's partner. Tracy felt good about her current mad schedule. It didn't leave her time to think about the fact that Kirk seemed to have disappeared without a trace. In Kirk's absence, concerned about the Ethiopia project, Tracy telephoned Major Hadib, and in turn, he had asked Bill to report to her as well. Both men assured Tracy that the planes were in top condition and that the drops were being made on schedule.

"We'll be able to wind up our first three-months program on time," Bill told her. Bill also mentioned to Tracy that Kirk had cabled him that he'd been delayed in the U.S. on urgent business. Bill said he had not heard from Kirk since.

"Very strange," Tracy said, expressing her own unease.

"He's never done such a thing," Bill told her over the phone, "so it must be a real emergency in his life. But the air force pilot I'm working with is excellent, so you really have nothing to be concerned about at our end."

Asking him to keep in touch, Tracy hung up. She didn't want to think about Kirk except in the context of work. If Kirk had troubles and didn't share them with her then Tracy didn't want to know what they were. As it was, Tracy had just about all the trouble she could handle. Instead of wondering what Kirk's problem was, she preferred to just think that he had proven to be irresponsible, after all. He had walked off the job without an explanation. That was enough cause to fire him. Tracy was just lucky that Bill had stuck it out and at least the project had not suffered because of Kirk. As for her feelings for Kirk, she simply refused to deal with them. Whenever thoughts of Kirk surfaced in her mind, she forced herself to substitute them with work related ones.

After her call, armed with the knowledge that her Ethiopian team would deliver the grain on time, Tracy made an appointment at World Help.

The World Help offices occupied two floors of a high rise in Los Angeles, on Wilshire Boulevard.

Tracy looked very professional as she entered the executive offices on the building's top floor. She had combed her hair into a French twist and wore a navy-blue business suit with a navy and white, striped silk blouse under the tailored jacket.

A very polite Mr. Garett received her. His tone

became a lot warmer after Tracy explained that despite Ray's illness the project was doing fine.

"I have received very favorable reports from the Minister of Relief, Ato Worku Adugni," he told Tracy. "That was of course before Mr. Nolan's unfortunate emergency, so frankly we were a little concerned around here. Of course Mr. Russell contacted us on your behalf not long ago, and assured us that all was under control. Still, it's nice to have you come by as well, Ms Brooke."

Tracy was rather surprised to hear that Kirk had contacted World Help on his own. It was good of him of course, to take care of public relations even unasked, but Tracy couldn't understand how he could be so considerate on the one hand and so irresponsible on the other. But this was not the time to speculate on Kirk's character. Tracy filed away this new information, then turned her full attention to Mr. Garett.

He was saying, "We are glad everything is going according to schedule. In truth, if it weren't, we couldn't continue to finance your planes staying there. The only way we can get the funds we need is by proving to our sources that our operations are efficient and cost effective."

"Are you working on a number of such projects?"

"Oh, yes. All the time. The world is a very needy place, Ms Brooke."

"Well, I hope we'll be able to continue contributing to the fine work you're doing."

"Yes, we'd like to consider other projects for

your planes after the conclusion of this one," Mr. Garett said, smiling at her. "But tell me, is it true that your father will retire and put Westwind Airlines up for sale?"

There it is, the rumor is spreading like wildfire, Tracy thought. She forced an easy smile to her lips, while her insides congealed with apprehension. The way she handled this situation might seal the fate of Westwind's future collaboration with World Help. She looked Mr. Garett straight in the eye.

"My father might retire—" Tracy said, emphasizing the word "might" "—but that doesn't mean that Westwind will change hands. I'm in charge of the company now and if my father retires, I believe I will stay on as general manager. Frankly, Mr. Garett, I see a great future for our *Pegasus* line in the kind of work we're doing for you. It is inspiring work and I believe that is the direction the company should take. And I can assure you, if it stays within my power, that's the direction the company *will* take. But for now that is strictly off the record."

Tracy saw the satisfied smile on Mr. Garett's face and felt that she had won his approval.

"I hope you do stay with the company, Ms Brooke," Garett said as he extended his hand to her. "I think we share a vision and could work together." His handshake was firm as if to confirm his words.

As Tracy drove back to her office, she felt for the first time in a week that there were chinks in the dark clouds that had been obscuring her horizons. *My plans* will *work,* Tracy thought, suddenly full of confidence.

"It's Mr. Davis on the line," Rosie told her as soon as Tracy walked into the office.

"Kenny! What's up?"

"I'm coming home tonight. Can you come over to the house? I've got something for you."

"Instead, you should be asking me to get out of your house now that you're coming back," Tracy said, laughing.

"Oh, I'm sorry, I forgot! How stupid of me!"

"You'd better not forget to let Judy know that you're coming home!"

"Could you call her for me? It takes ages to get through on that hospital line and I've got to run or I'll miss my flight."

"I guess I can."

"Thanks."

Tracy hung up, shaking her head. Even for an absentminded scientist Kenny was too much. How could he have forgotten that she was staying with Kathy? And how could he not let Judy know that he was coming home? Judy was right, something was definitely amiss on Kenny's part when it came to the marriage. It saddened Tracy to see it and she hoped that somehow he and Judy could work out their problems before it was too late.

It was almost midnight when Tracy heard the keys rattle at the front door to the apartment. She had been watching Vivaldi's, *Four Seasons* on television, in a live performance by the New York Symphony Orchestra. Tracy was so taken up by the music that she hadn't even realized how late it was.

"I went to see Judy first," Kenny explained, apologetically. He dropped his small suitcase in the middle of the room and gave Tracy's arm a light squeeze in greeting.

"How's Kathy?"

"Asleep, I hope."

"Mind if I take a quick look?"

"Of course not."

Tracy waited till Kenny tiptoed back from the nursery. "She's so cute," he said, beaming. "I really missed her."

"Judy really missed you," Tracy couldn't help saying. No matter how unsubtle her words, she had to let Kenny know how upset Judy had been about his absence.

"Couldn't tell from the reception," Kenny muttered. "I'm sorry Tracy. It's just that I had a long day and Judy wasn't in the best of moods. She asked me in this sarcastic tone, how come I came back so soon, and from there things went from bad to worse. I think she really hates me." Kenny threw himself into an armchair and looked at Tracy helplessly.

"What makes you say that?" Tracy sat down opposite him.

"I think Judy resents the kind of life she is forced to lead due to our circumstances. Because of Kathy, she can't work full time, and I work such long hours that even in the evenings we have virtually no social life. That must make Judy feel very isolated and I think secretly she blames me for all of it. And now, even though she is trying to save this pregnancy, I believe Judy is doing it out of a sense of obligation toward me, while all the time she's thinking that a new baby will just keep her at home six more years.''

Tracy was aghast at Kenny's perception of Judy's feelings. ''Has she ever told you any of this?''

''No, but any fool can see how angry she is at me all the time.''

''Kenny, I don't usually meddle in other people's lives, but as a friend, I must tell you some things. Judy doesn't resent staying home with Kathy, she chooses to. With her earning power she could easily hire a nanny but she likes raising your child. What she believes, though, is that you bury yourself in your work because that's more important to you than your family. And Judy is fighting to keep this pregnancy because she wants to have another child, despite the fact that she thinks that you resent having the kids come between you and her and that you don't love her any more.''

Kenny stared at her in disbelief. ''When did she tell you all this?''

''Before I went to Ethiopia.''

''How come Judy didn't tell me any of it?''

''It seems that you've never given her a chance.''

''What a fool I've been!'' Kenny slapped his forehead with his long, bony hand. ''I wish I

could rush back to her and have a real talk! For
years now I've avoided a confrontation because I
thought Judy would ask for a divorce! Instead, I
stayed longer hours at work!"

"And is that why you didn't rush back from
Washington, D.C.?"

"No, that was truly required of me. When I
found out that Judy was having problems I really
wanted to come immediately to be by her side, but
I couldn't. But talking about Washington...."
Kenny reached for his briefcase. "I've got a nice
little list for you."

"Oh, Kenny...."

"Yep, all the companies that bid. Surprisingly,
there aren't that many of them."

Tracy took the white envelope from him. "I
don't know how to thank you."

"You've done more than your share already,"
Kenny said, smiling. "Thanks to you, first thing
tomorrow I'm straightening my life out."

Tracy felt wonderfully warm inside. How little
it took sometimes to help someone gain insight.
She wished her own concerns could be resolved as
simply as those of her friends.

Kenny walked Tracy down to her car, and for
the first time in days, she headed home to sleep at
her own apartment. Tracy wasn't sure that she
welcomed the solitude that awaited her. But as she
glanced at the white envelope on the seat beside
her Tracy hushed any thoughts that could cause
her pain. Work awaited her. She had no time for
personal matters.

THE NEXT MORNING Tracy rose early and headed for the library. With the help of the librarian she found the business directory that listed all pertinent data about the companies whose names Kenny had given her. There were only thirty-five names, which meant that her competition was extremely limited. Tracy was pleased that so few companies manufactured the kind of rugged, small aircraft that she provided. Now it was a question of finding out on what scale her competitors produced their planes. After that she could research the types of planes each company turned out. Armed with this knowledge Tracy could probably write the kind of letter to the Pentagon that would make those who were in charge of deciding which bid to accept, look twice at her offer.

Tracy was copying information on each company, when halfway through her eyes caught on a name. Sky Safari. President: Kirk Russell. She stared at the name in disbelief. It must be a coincidence, she told herself. Tracy looked again and ran her eyes feverishly up and down the list of information. Sky Safari was a medium size, California-based company, with a manufacturing plant in Oakland and corporate offices in San Francisco. It produced airplane parts, chiefly for lightweight aircraft, although it also manufactured a small reconnaissance plane called the *Safari*. For awhile Tracy sat, too stunned to move. A heavy weight seemed to have settled on her chest and she had difficulty breathing. Why was Kirk working for her when he had a company of his own? Tracy could easily guess the answer. The term, *industrial espionage* was not a new addition to her vocabulary. Were it not for the obligatory silence in the reading room, Tracy would have laughed out loud at the absurdity of Westwind's position. Little things about Kirk rushed into Tracy's memory now. She recalled the afternoon in Ethiopia when Kirk had told her he had to resolve his problems on his own. Sure—how else was Kirk not going to tell her his true identity! Tracy scoffed at the sophisticated way Kirk had handled himself in all situations. No wonder he was so self-assured, so commanding. He was no Westwind employee, and never had been! And Tracy had thought Kirk had paid for her first-class ticket out of his savings! She couldn't sit still anymore. Quickly she copied Sky Safari's address and phone number in San Francisco, then returned the book to the reference desk.

Outside the sun was shining and Tracy wondered how the day could be so beautiful when her heart was breaking and her company had been laid bare to a predator. Kirk must have gone straight back to San Francisco, Tracy thought, as she drove absently toward her office. *Very considerate of him to leave Bill behind to finish the job.* She was filled with bitterness toward Kirk. What else was Bill reporting on, while dropping food for the starving? Oh, it was all her fault, Tracy thought, for not checking out Kirk's background before he ever laid a hand on her plane! But that was her father's responsibility, Tracy thought, defending herself. But she was her own hardest judge. When it came to planes, Tracy should never have trusted anyone but herself. That was the first rule of industrial survival. She had broken it, and now Westwind would have to pay the price. Tracy shuddered in the blazing sun as she got out of her car.

Walking into the office, she announced, "I'm going to San Francisco for the day. I want you to know it, but please don't tell anyone else. Tell father I had to make a flight and if I don't get back in time to today, I'll see him tomorrow."

Tracy wasn't going to upset Ray by telling him about her discovery. First she would confront Kirk on her own. She was going to just walk into Kirk's office and surprise him. That way he would have no recourse, but to admit what he had done. Tracy's love for him turned into bitter hatred with the speed of flipping the page to his name, and she was looking forward to the expression on Kirk's face when she stood before him to demand an explanation.

CHAPTER THIRTEEN

"YOU'RE FROM WESTWIND, aren't you?" asked the young man at the ticket counter, smiling at Tracy.

"How do you know?"

"I have a Cherokee Piper parked at Cloverfield, and I've seen you there. You're the kind of woman a man remembers after just one look."

"What a nice thing to say," Tracy said, pleased at his compliment. It didn't hurt her to know that she would look good when she walked into Kirk's office.

"You're leaving from gate six-hundred. The plane is boarding now. Have a nice flight. And say, I'll look you up next time I'm at Cloverfield. Maybe we could have coffee? My name is Paul."

"Sure, Paul. Nice meeting you." There was no point in telling him that the last thing she wanted was a new date. He would forget about going for coffee with her by the time he came to the airport, or Tracy would be busy when he called.

During the flight Tracy sat with her eyes closed, thinking of how she was going to get into Kirk's office without being announced. If indeed, he headed a company as large as the records showed,

there was sure to be a line of secretaries to pass
before she got through to the boss. Yet Tracy
needed the element of surprise so he would be
caught off guard.

On her way to the car rental counter Tracy spotted a ladies room and stopped for a final check on
her appearance. She wore a rust-colored linen suit
with a burnt-orange silk shirt that matched her
hair. Her hair was the way Kirk liked it, in loose
curls framing her face. She had made-up carefully, accenting the brilliant green of her eyes with
dark mascara on her lashes. For what Tracy had
to tell Kirk, she could have worn a pair of old
jeans and her hair in braids—but instinct told her
that the more beautiful she looked, the more advantage she would have over Kirk during their
confrontation. Men were susceptible to the way
women looked. Kirk might disclose more of what
he was up to if he desired her and didn't want to
lose her. Tracy had no idea where this knowledge
came to her from, but she felt it was true. Or was
it that she was making a last, subtle appeal to him
as a male? Tracy asked herself. She brushed the
idea aside as foolish. Why would she want to have
anything to do with Kirk after his betrayal? They
were competitors in a limited business and, as
such, could only be enemies in any area. Still,
Tracy wasn't sure she had the answer to the nagging inner question about what she really expected
from Kirk.

The road to San Francisco was well marked.
Tracy drove the rented Falcon with her usual speed

along the Bayshore Freeway, which stretched all the way from the airport to downtown San Francisco. The view of downtown, as she approached it along the snaillike curves, surprised her. Tracy had not been to San Francisco for years and could hardly believe the number of glass and steel high rises that lined up against the sky along the route. Strange, how on leaving a place one always expected to find it unchanged when returning to it, yet nothing ever stayed the same. Or some things did, Tracy thought happily, upon discovering that she could still park her car under Union Square, and head out on foot on the narrow, downtown streets.

The headquarters of Sky Safari occupied several floors of an office building on Montgomery Street, in the financial district. The top man's office would be on the top floor where the best view was, Tracy figured, and pushed the elevator button for the twentieth floor. Sky Safari's corporate area was a male-dominated world Tracy decided when she reached her destination. The hallways were lined with walnut-wood paneling and the rugs were a plush brown. Along the walls hung a series of prints of early planes in Florentine finish brass frames. At the end of the hallway a double door carried a discreet copper plaque that read, Sky Safari.

Tracy pushed the door open and entered. A dark-haired receptionist looked up from her typing. "May I help you?" she asked impersonally.

"I'm here to see Mr. Russell," Tracy an-

nounced. She knew that everything depended on
first impressions. If Tracy sounded self-assured
and assertive regardless of her violently pounding
heart, and her voice remained even and firm,
despite the dryness in her throat, then she would
get a chance to walk in on Kirk.

"Who shall I say wants to see him?"

Tracy wondered how she could get out of giving
the receptionist her name, but decided it would
just delay the procedures. She handed the woman
a business card.

The receptionist checked the card against a list
of names in a brown, leather-jacketed book. She
had pale white skin and large dark eyes and wore
her hair in fashionably layered curls. Tracy judged
her to be around twenty-eight.

"I don't see your name down here," the receptionist said as she looked up at Tracy.

"That's all right. Just give him my card, he'll
see me."

"His secretary stepped out for a moment.
Would you mind waiting?"

"Yes, I would. I flew up from Los Angeles for
the day and my time is limited. Just take the card
in, please."

The receptionist still hesitated, but Tracy stood
her ground. She stared steadfastly at the young
woman, forcing her to obey through sheer willpower.

"I'll be right back." The receptionist removed
her headphone and slipped through a set of double
doors behind her.

Tracy knew this was her moment. She gave the receptionist about thirty seconds. Tracy figured that was enough time for the receptionist to reach Kirk. Then Tracy followed her. Tracy found herself in a large office with a secretary's desk to one side and filing cabinets on the other. The rest of the room was arranged with armchairs and coffee tables strewn with magazines. No one was in the room. The door leading to the executive office stood ajar. Tracy walked right through it, almost colliding with the receptionist.

"Sorry," the woman said. Tracy wasn't sure whether the receptionist was apologizing to her, or to the person in the room, for Tracy's entrance.

"Come right in, Ms Brooke," a male voice called to her. He was momentarily blocked by the receptionist, who now slinked out of the office, obviously embarrassed by her inadequacy at keeping Tracy out. Tracy stood rooted to the floor, wondering where Kirk had gone. She was facing a tall man who, judging by the shock of white hair, must have been about her father's age. From under his bushy, salt-and-pepper brows his lively black eyes looked at Tracy with interest. "What can I do for you, Ms Brooke?"

"I am looking for Kirk Russell," Tracy stated as calmly as she could. She wondered if this man was Kirk's assistant, and how Kirk managed to slip out of the office.

"You're looking at him."

"But...."

A broad smile spread over the man's face. He

came around his desk and approached Tracy.
"You must be looking for my son, Kirk Russell
Jr."

"I don't think so. The man I'm looking for
doesn't have a junior after his name."

"Of course not," the older Kirk Russell roared.
"Can you imagine my son wanting to be called
junior by anyone?"

"No, I can't," Tracy admitted and she couldn't
help laughing. Tracy liked Kirk's father—if indeed that's who he was. Somewhere in the back of
her mind she recalled Kirk mentioning that his
father owned a company. Sneakily he had never
told her what kind. *Despite what he told me, is
Kirk working for his father,* Tracy wondered.

"Is your son a pilot who flew smoke jumpers in
Alaska?"

"He is that," Mr. Russell nodded, thoughtfully
sizing Tracy up. "And are you actually Tracy
Nolan, Ray Nolan's engineer daughter?"

"You know my father?"

"I don't know him personally but I know of
him, of course. As you get more into the business
end of it, you'll find, Ms Brooke, that the aviation
world is a fairly small one. How is your father?"

"Getting better, thank you." Tracy was surprised that Russell knew about her father's illness.
It was a small world, indeed, if the news had
traveled so fast.

"I'm glad he is. It can happen to any of us old-
sters who are still working as though we were in

our twenties.'' Kirk's father stayed quiet for a moment, then, brightening again, turned to Tracy.

"So, you're looking for that no good son of mine?''

"I guess you know him,'' Tracy said, laughing.

"Well, Kirk did come to see me a day or so ago, but I'm not sure whether he is still in town. In fact, I don't know where he is. Kirk doesn't work for me, you know, and even on the rare occasion that he comes to me, my son keeps very close-mouthed about his business. So I have no idea where he is hunting.''

"Hunting?''

"Figuratively speaking, Ms Nolan. Don't take it the wrong way from an old man like me, but looking at you, I can understand why he would have more than a business concern regarding your company!''

"What do you mean by that?''

"Well, I think Kirk has more in mind than merely getting involved with your company.''

Considering that he had walked off his job, Tracy couldn't understand what Kirk's father was implying. Wanting to get a clearer answer from him Tracy repeated her question. "I still don't understand what you mean.''

"Well, it's not my place to talk for him. I'm sure he'll tell you in his own good time.'' Mr. Russell smiled at her. "I wish you two luck.''

"But . . . .'' *What a strange thing to say,* Tracy thought. Mr. Russell appeared to be talking in puzzles about Kirk. If Kirk had told him something Tracy should know, why couldn't he come out with it directly?

She was about to rephrase her question when Mr. Russell said, "I'm sorry I can't spend more time with you right now. I am late for a meeting. But here." He scribbled on a piece of paper and handed it to Tracy. "Here are Kirk's addresses and phone numbers—both for business and home. I can't imagine why Kirk neglected to leave them with you. He must have assumed you had them."

As Kirk's father spoke, it occurred to Tracy that Kirk had probably put his telephone numbers down on the forms he filled out when he was hired by Tracy's father, but she had never even thought of checking. Realizing now that it was his father's company and not Kirk's whose name was on the list of bidders, Tracy was no longer sure whether Kirk was an industrial spy or not. After all, Kirk didn't manufacture planes, he just flew them as a contract pilot. Maybe Tracy was accusing him unfairly. Perhaps Kirk's only sin had been not letting Tracy know that he was taking some days off to fly up to see his father. Now that she had his phone numbers, Tracy would find out what he was *really* up to. And if indeed it was Kirk's father who had bid for the government contract, there was hardly anything Tracy could do. All people in the aircraft business had a right to send in their offer. She thanked the older Russell for his help.

"Don't mention it," he replied, smiling somewhat sadly. "Kirk and I don't always get along and so it's a rare occasion that I can be of some help. It's my pleasure. Good-bye, my dear. You are a lovely young woman. I hope we shall see more of each other." He shook Tracy's hand and his firm touch reminded her painfully of Kirk's.

On her way to the car Tracy thought about the elder Russell's words. She wondered if there was something Kirk had omitted to tell her or if his father had mistaken her for someone else. Tracy couldn't understand his warmth and his implication that he had helped her or Kirk out in some big way. People were strange sometimes, Tracy thought. The important thing was that she now knew how to locate Kirk. According to what his father had written down, Kirk's offices were across the Bay at the Oakland airport and his apartment was located on one of the hilly, narrow streets of the Telegraph Hill district. Before going anywhere, Tracy decided to phone both places. At Kirk's apartment, Tracy got an answering machine and Tracy hung up without leaving a message. At his business number a secretary answered, "Kirk Russell's Team."

Tracy asked to be put through to Kirk and was told he was out. "Would you like to leave a message?"

"No, I'll call back. When do you expect him in?"

"He's out of town, miss, and we don't know for how long. Would you like to leave your name and phone number?"

Tracy decided to do so. When the secretary

heard her name, she exclaimed, "Oh, Miss Brooke, he went back to Los Angeles this morning!"

"My luck," Tracy muttered after she hung up. They had probably crossed each other in the sky or walked by each other at the airport, Tracy thought, annoyed. No, she would have sensed Kirk's presence had they been near to each other. Then she dismissed the idea as foolishly romantic. She only tensed up when Kirk was visibly near, not when he was in the radius of a mile. So he had returned to Los Angeles, Tracy mused. Kirk obviously had some business with his father and that's why he disappeared. Maybe on seeing how fragile the human heart is, Kirk had rushed to make peace with his own father and hadn't wanted to tell her about it, Tracy thought. If he was back in Los Angeles, ready to make amends, Tracy would forgive him and let him return to Ethiopia. Now that she had met his father, Kirk too was allowed to have a few quirks of personality, Tracy decided. Nobody was perfect and she really preferred to have Kirk finish the Ethiopia project to having to look for a new crew.

With a lightened heart Tracy headed for the garage to pick up her car, so she could drive to the airport. She heard someone shout her name from across the street. Tracy looked up and spotted George, her ex-husband, waving to her. She stopped, feeling a strange little twist in her heart watching him approach. George looked good. His dark-blond hair still fell in unruly curls and he had a tan that made his eyes appear as blue as corn-flowers.

"How are you, babe?" He was also his usual ef-fusive self, Tracy noted as George bent down and kissed her on the cheek. "You're looking great!"

"So are you," Tracy replied, grinning at him.

"What brings you to sunny San Francisco?"

"Business."

"What else?" George said, laughing.

His teeth could still be in a toothpaste commer-cial, Tracy thought sarcastically, but she had to admit that his was an infectious smile. Her ex-husband looked like a man who had never out-grown his healthy, boyish charm. Tracy felt a certain fondness for him, but the strong physical attraction that had formerly drawn her to him was gone.

"Come, I'll buy you a drink for old-times' sake," George suggested, and before Tracy could protest, he had taken her by the arm and begun walking with her to the St. Francis Hotel on the corner of Union Square.

"So what's your business here?" George asked over their drinks. He had ordered a Scotch and Tracy was sipping a campari soda. "It's with Rus-sell Jr., right?"

Tracy's heart skipped a beat. How did George know about Kirk and what did his question mean? She needed to find out.

"What do you know about it?" Tracy pretend-ed to be coyly denying whatever George was im-plying. He took the bait.

"C'mon, everyone knows that young Russell's going crazy trying to borrow enough on his business to buy your company!"

The world gave a violent swirl around Tracy.

"Tracy, are you okay?"

"I guess I'm not used to drinking in the middle of the day," she said, smiling wanly. Tracy tensed up her body so she wouldn't betray that every part of her was trembling.

"Where did you get this idea that Kirk Russell is trying to buy Westwind?"

"I work for the airlines, too, remember. He's even gone to reconcile with his father just to see if the old man would lend him enough."

"Did he?"

"You should know that, it's your company he's buying!"

"Tell me George, what's Kirk's company worth?"

"Well, he's got a fleet of those *Safaris*, and those are worth quite a bit...but I don't know. He has a tendency to go off and do crazy projects with his teams. One of them is off in Nepal doing airlifts for some mountain climbers, and another is in South America, doing something equally crazy, and Russell himself was in Africa somewhere.... It's hard to say what he is earning on these projects. But I'd say he's not suffering."

"Is he big enough to borrow a couple of million?"

"I imagine so."

The already bitter taste of the campari turned

into poison in Tracy's mouth. So that's what Kirk was really up to! Tracy recalled the afternoon in Ethiopia when she had told Kirk of her future plans for the *Pegasus* line. No wonder he had shut her off! She had been telling him about something he was already doing! She was going to compete with him! With a sinking heart Tracy realized that Kirk indeed must have accepted the Ethiopia job to study her plane. And like a fool, Tracy had even demonstrated it for him! All along Kirk had been learning how to improve his planes by working with hers! And now he was rounding up money to buy Westwind! Why, Kirk wouldn't even have to bother to improve his planes. He could just use hers!

"Tracy, are you sick?"

"Yes, I think I'm going to be." Tracy rose from the small marble table. "I'll be right back, George."

Tracy barely made it to the bathroom. She could empty her stomach but not her mind. Tracy leaned against the tile of the bathroom wall, staring at herself in the mirror. She was as white as the tiles. Not even when she had discovered another woman in her marital bed had Tracy felt as physically revulsed as she did now. So that's what his father had meant when he said that Kirk was hunting! Hunting for funds! Who knows what Kirk had said to make his father think that Tracy was actually being helped by Kirk buying Westwind. And why did Russell senior imply that Kirk was doing both of them a favor? He must have given

Kirk some funds. Tracy's head was reeling. If Kirk could raise a couple of million, he could surely pay off Anne. For that matter, even her father could sell his half of the business for a down payment and receive monthly amounts on the rest, as retirement income. And what would she do? Work for Kirk? Tracy's stomach gave another leap and she rushed to empty it again.

Finally there was nothing left inside her except a deep, aching hollow. That's why Kirk had the audacity to assure the World Help people that everything was under control. *Kirk was planning on controlling it, so he should know!* Tracy now wished she had answered those calls from Anne. Anne had probably wanted to inform her of what was happening. Tracy could have fought back right there in Santa Monica, instead of rushing up to San Francisco. How ironic it was that she had found out through George what Kirk was up to.

Tracy washed her face and reapplied her makeup the best she could to hide her deathly pallor.

"I was ready to go in and get you," George joked when Tracy returned to the table. "Are you feeling better?"

"I must have eaten something rotten. I'm sorry to have spoiled our meeting."

"It's okay, honey, I'm sorry you're feeling sick. Would you like to finish your drink, or shall we get you a lemonade?"

"I think I'd better go, George. I need to get back to L.A."

"How are you getting out to the airport?"

"I have a rented car."

George insisted that Tracy was in no condition to drive. He offered to drive her and helped Tracy return the rental car downtown.

To take her mind off her problems, Tracy forced herself to query George about his life. She found out that her ex-husband had given up surfing and taken up golf as an antidote to his job—which he still found as dull as ever.

"At least you meet the right kind of people on the links," George said, grinning at her.

"I'll call you if I ever get to Los Angeles," he promised Tracy as he dropped her off.

"Do. And thanks for doing this for me," Tracy said smiling at him. George really wasn't a bad sort, Tracy thought as she headed for the ticket counter. Maybe she should have tried harder to make a go of their life together. But Tracy's mind screamed "no." George had introduced her to one kind of deception. Now Kirk had introduced her to another. She was through with men forever. She needed to put all her energy into what mattered, namely, the fight for her future. Perhaps her father would listen to reason. Tracy had to convince Ray that she could manage Westwind profitably enough so he would have an income to retire on. Then perhaps her father wouldn't sell his share. As for Anne, the government contract was still a possibility. Tracy wondered whether she too could be as aggressive and unethical as some businessmen seemed to be and if with Kenny's help she could pull some strings where it would count.

THE NEXT MORNING Tracy phoned Judy.

"I can't thank you enough for what you have done for me," Judy gushed. "You took wonderful care of Kathy and I don't know what you told Kenny, but we are now talking—just like we used to when we first met. I don't know how we're going to resolve some of our problems but at least we're discussing them!"

"I'm happy for you," Tracy responded. It was strange how the magnitude of her own problems made it hard for Tracy to feel enthusiasm about anything. Still, she was glad for her friend.

"I'll ask Kenny to call you tonight. Will you be at home?"

"Where else?"

"C'mon Tracy, you'll find another guy like Kirk."

"I hope not," Tracy said with mock horror. Tracy was tempted to tell Judy that Kirk was plotting to buy Westwind. But the hospital gynecologist had told Judy that she had to spend at least another week in bed, and Tracy decided this wasn't the right time to burden her friend with details of her latest discovery about Kirk.

"I'm glad to see your sense of humor returning. Everything will work out in the end, you'll see."

Tracy wished she could share Judy's optimism. But it was only fairy tales that always had a happy ending. Tracy was going through the second great crisis in her adult life and figured that, since the first one hadn't had such a great resolution, she had every right to be skeptical about the outcome of this one.

Her father, too, worried Tracy. Ray didn't seem nearly as upset as Tracy about the information concerning Kirk's plans. "I am aware of his interest in the company," Ray told her. "But there is usually a wide gap between interest and buying ability. So until Kirk shows up with a certified check, I wouldn't worry."

Tracy tried to pry out of her father whether Ray was planning to sell his half as well or to let her manage the company. "I don't know yet, but please trust me to do what's best all around," her father requested.

Considering Ray's condition that was all Tracy could do. He was improving daily, but she really couldn't push Ray to make business decisions from his hospital bed. She simply kept up her visits and only asked him questions about Westwind when it was absolutely essential to the company's everyday operations.

Despite Tracy's grief and her almost constant feeling of apprehension about the future, she got a certain pleasure out of managing both the Commuter Line and the Experimental Branch. At this time her job was really just a question of maintaining both offices, since Tracy wasn't making any changes or planning new developments until the company's future was resolved. Tracy's sober, cautious nature prepared her for the possibility that she would lose the company, after all. As that was the case, Tracy wasn't about to contribute any of her new ideas to the future owner, regardless of who he was.

It wasn't at all definite that Kirk would be the buyer. Tracy called Anne and was told Mrs. Weston was looking at several proposals and was going to choose the best offer.

"You can't be sentimental about business," Anne lectured Tracy when they finally spoke. "No matter how charming Kirk Russell is, if another buyer offers me five hundred thousand more that buyer is the one who's going to get Westwind."

"What about my father's approval of the person?"

"It's too late for that, Tracy. Ray can either approve or find a buyer for his share."

"You don't care one bit about Westwind, do you?"

"Let's face it, Tracy, your father must retire. So logically Ray should no longer worry about Westwind either. You're the only one who doesn't want to let go. And in my opinion, you're a little young to be given a company! If you were my daughter, I'd let you earn your own business, not inherit mine."

Thank God, I'm not your daughter, Tracy sighed to herself after they hung up. Tracy tried to envision what it would be like to manage Westwind if a stranger owned a part of it. She desperately wished that her father would get well enough to discuss these matters but Tracy knew that no company was worth risking Ray's recovery—so she struggled with her thoughts and feelings alone.

Tracy's last trump card at this point was the money Westwind might get from the government contract. Kenny had called her back and had promised to contact some of his friends in Washington to see if they could lobby for Westwind. That was at least a step in the right direction, Tracy thought.

Kirk still had not called her or reported back to work, but by now Tracy had stopped expecting him to. It was obvious that Kirk was going to let Bill finish the job in Ethiopia while he pursued more profitable goals. Kirk didn't have the nerve to show up and face her, Tracy finally decided.

What hurt Tracy most was that Kirk had made love to her, while all that time he was also spying on her company. She realized that Kirk could not have had it in mind to buy the company till after they had returned and the opportunity presented itself. But Kirk *did* take the job at Westwind under false pretenses to obtain information. And on top of that Kirk had made Tracy believe that he cared for her. *That* was what Tracy could not forgive. If Kirk had kept his distance, perhaps Tracy could have reconciled herself to the fact that in the business world this kind of piracy went on all the time, and that the next time Westwind hired a stranger they would just have to be more careful. But Kirk had also stolen her heart and that was harder to bear than his stealing trade secrets. Tracy could always come up with a better design for the next series of planes. But she would never trust another man as long as she lived. Kirk had robbed her of love forever, Tracy felt. The loss filled her with a searing ache, as though a great knife had cut across all that was vital in her. And the wound just wouldn't heal.

Every time Tracy accidentally tuned her radio to a love song, tears welled up in her eyes. When Judy gave her a detailed description of how she and Kenny were repairing their lives, Tracy could only compare it to the broken pieces of hers. In addition, whereas after her divorce at least she could throw herself into her work, the present circumstances had taken the heart out of that for her as well. The only thing that kept Tracy going was the hope that in the end Westwind would receive the contract from the government and she would triumph over Anne.

The researcher Tracy had hired to find other organizations like World Help was uncovering valuable data. Tracy could see that with the right approach at least a dozen groups would pay large sums to use her planes. But Tracy didn't even want to begin to work toward this goal. *Why should I build up the business for someone else's sake?* she asked herself.

One afternoon, when her father was feeling better, Tracy outlined her ideas to him as briefly as possible. She did so to show Ray where the company could go under her direction. Her father listened attentively and commended Tracy for her thinking. But he remained noncommittal about the future of Westwind. Tracy left his hospital room discouraged.

Kenny called to say that he had spoken to his friends in Washington but, he said, they could only make promises. Kenny didn't know how much influence his contacts could actually exert over the choice of contracts. Tracy thanked him.

Tracy tried to bury herself in administrative details. Because she was feeling so low, she refused to substitute on flights, thus denying herself the last vestige of pleasure available to her. But Tracy didn't think it was safe for her to fly. She wouldn't even go up alone. She knew that with her troubled state of mind, she could easily make an error and cause a crash. No matter how badly Tracy felt she needed to fly, she also needed to be responsible and to stay in one piece physically.

Instead of flying, after her work hours, Tracy took long walks along the beach by her apartment, watching sunsets and listening to the rhythmical crashing of waves against the shore. There was something soothing about feeling the salt spray on her face and listening to the incessant murmur of the sea.

Sometimes during her walks Tracy wondered whether she shouldn't just go on a trip and let everything resolve itself without her. Perhaps Anne was right, why should Tracy want to fight for Westwind? With her training and skill she could always find work! Or else she could start her own company, just like Kirk. Tracy smiled at the possibility of their positions being reversed. Kirk would own Westwind, and she would be on the outside with her planes for hire. But Tracy knew that this was merely idle daydreaming to ease her pain. Where would she find the means to beat Kirk at his own game, especially if she had to work for a living at some other company. No, it was better to put up a fight now, so Kirk, or anyone else, couldn't take away what she already had, Tracy told herself, and waited.

CHAPTER FOURTEEN

ONE MORNING Tracy woke to a deep state of self-doubt and depression. The emptiness of her existence, the feeling that her entire world was being uprooted, made Tracy feel totally anguished. Why should she continue to fight for Westwind, she asked herself. Maybe it was better to live the superficial way Anne did instead of struggling to hold on to what seemed to be basically just a job? Why should work be more important than play? George had brought up this question years ago. At the time Tracy had had no problem with George's question. She had been certain that work was more important. Now she wondered if she had been right. Feeling a bitter taste in her mouth, Tracy considered just taking the day off instead of going in to the office. Then she splashed cold water on her face and confronted herself in the mirror. The pale, green-eyed woman looking back at her was far too serious for play. Tracy might as well admit it, she couldn't take the day off, no matter how she felt. Tracy had a commitment to Westwind, and she was going to see it through.

Shortly after she arrived at her office, Rosie brought in a brown manila envelope and handed it to Tracy. It was a certified letter from the Defense Department. Tracy waited until Rosie had left, and then with trembling hands, she cut open the envelope. Her eyes scanned the stiff formal language of the letter. Then she let it drop on her desk. The letter informed Ray Nolan that while the *Pegasus* was certainly a very fine aircraft and reports of its Ethiopian mission had proved its versatility, this time the contract was to be awarded to another company. Tracy absorbed the contents of the letter. Then, like a plane that finds itself in the middle of a cloud, she felt her mind enveloped by a blank whiteness—and nothing else.

Tracy had no idea how long she sat there before the phone startled her out of the white fog of semi-consciousness. It was Irma, reporting joyfully that Dr. Lange would allow Ray to go home that afternoon. They would take him home by ambulance, but would Tracy like to come over to celebrate?

"That's good news, indeed," Tracy responded. She decided not to tell her father any bad news. There would be time enough after Ray had settled back home again.

But Tracy hadn't counted on Anne. Her father's business partner must have received a copy of the letter, for when Tracy arrived at the house that afternoon, it was Ray who took her hand and patted it, full of sympathy. He understood what Tracy must be feeling. What Tracy couldn't understand was why Ray didn't seem to be upset by the news at all. Instead, her father again asked

Tracy to trust him and assured her that everything would work out for the best.

But when she tried to get Ray to explain what he meant, Ray just said that, since he didn't want to anticipate things, it wasn't appropriate to say anything as of yet. "But its time to make some decisions," Ray added. "I'd like to call a meeting here for tomorrow afternoon."

Tracy spent most of the night pacing her apartment. *Strange,* she thought, *just a few months back I was so full of optimism.* She had been so sure they would find the funds for Anne and so sure Kirk was the kind of man she had been looking for. Now Anne seemed to have gained the upper hand with the company and Tracy's relationship with Kirk had turned out to be a farce. *It just proves what a rotten fortune teller I am,* Tracy thought sardonically. *I'd have done better to stay with what I know. From now on there will be no men in my life, just planes.* Tracy stood by the window, staring at the moon reflected on the ocean, and weighed her future possibilities.

If only Anne sold her half, and Ray didn't sell his, then depending on who the new partner was, she might give it a try, Tracy finally decided. But if Ray decided to sell as well, then Tracy would have to look for employment elsewhere. It would be too painful for her to continue to work at Westwind. If Kirk bought the company, regardless of the circumstances, she would have to leave. For Tracy could never live down the humiliation of exposing her feelings to him. Surely Kirk knew that Tracy would never have let him touch her had she not been in love with him. Yet he hadn't loved her. It had all been an act to gain her confidence and trust.

Vaguely Tracy recalled that Bill, Kirk's partner, had warned her about Kirk. She just hadn't known what Bill had meant when he said that Tracy shouldn't take Kirk seriously. Maybe this was what Bill had been trying to tell her! *But I guess when a woman is in love, no one can warn her,* Tracy thought bitterly. Well, that love was over, ended by a rather rude awakening to the realities of life. From here on in, Kirk would have no further hold on her. She would show him that feelings like love and trust are fragile and could easily be destroyed. In the process of using her, Kirk had created a determined adversary in Tracy. Even if he gained access to Westwind, she would find a way to get back at Kirk and fight him with his own weapons. If he tried using *Pegasus* for rescue work, she'd find a way to get to the job first. If he wished to continue the Commuter Line, she would link up with a competitor to provide an even better service. She was only twenty-six. Perhaps Anne was right. She *should* build her own future, and there were plenty of other companies that she could use as stepping stones.

It was a pale but determined Tracy who entered her father's library the next day. Anne was already there, looking bright in a powder-blue designer dress. She greeted Tracy with all the condescension of a victor. If there had ever been a time when Tracy felt like striking someone, it was now. She would have loved to have wiped that smug, happy smile off Anne's well made-up face.

Ray lay on the couch, a light blanket covering him, despite the summer day. He looked a little tired and Tracy hoped that they could get the meeting over without exhausting him. Her father came right to the point.

"We have several offers for Westwind. Three firms are willing to buy us outright, and have made fairly reasonable offers. With small variations in the amount, each one is offering a price below the actual market value for the combination of Westwind's Commuter Line and Experimental Branch. But any of the bids would be sufficient to pay our creditors and leave each of us a sum on which to live comfortably. Now the fourth offer is an excellent one. It would pay the fair market value for Anne's share and leave my half of the company intact."

"That means a new partner," Tracy interjected.

"That's the hitch," Ray said, smiling. "Now the problem is that, frankly, I am tired of shouldering the company, and I was hoping to retire in a year or so in any case. Now, with my current health problem, I think I ought to obey the doctor and retire right away. That leaves us with two choices. We can sell the company outright, or I can ask you, Tracy, to manage my half."

"Dad!" Tracy leapt to his side and hugged him. "You know that's exactly what I want so why have you teased me all this time?'' Tracy asked. ''If you approve of the deal I shouldn't have trouble getting along with the new partner—unless he is a monster.''

''No, he is Kirk Russell.''

Tracy sat back on her heels feeling the blood drain from her face. ''That's different,'' she said. ''I can't work with that man. You might as well sell the company.''

''Are you going to tell me that you're forcing your father to take a heavy financial loss for some personal whim of yours?'' Anne's voice was scathing.

''Are you worried about Ray's loss or yours?'' Tracy replied, her tone equally sharp.

''Frankly, both our losses.'' Anne rose and stood over Tracy. ''But beyond that, I'm worried about you, Tracy. How can you be so ungrateful? Your father is offering you the opportunity to take over his company and for some odd reason you throw a temper tantrum!''

''It has nothing to do with being ungrateful,'' Tracy countered coldly. ''If you two had a decent offer for the sale of the whole company, you'd probably take it. So I too must look out for what's best for myself. Had you sold Westwind, I would have left anyway. So in this case my decision makes no difference; Kirk can buy your half and dad can hire a manager who will get along with Kirk.''

''And what will you do?'' Ray asked as he searched Tracy's face.

"I can always get a job."

"There is one minor detail you haven't taken into account," Anne pointed out acidly. "When a company is sold, all its assets go with it. You and your designs are one of Westwind's assets. It is stipulated in all the contracts that you, as chief engineer, will stay on for one year after the sale."

"Is Kirk aware of this clause?"

"I would assume so." Ray answered.

"No buyer is stupid enough to let you go. If they did, what would prevent you from building the same plane for someone else?" Anne pointed out gleefully.

Tracy hated Anne's cheerfulness. The realization that no matter which way the sale went, she would still have to stay with Westwind, hit Tracy hard. She felt her stomach churn. The idea that she would be working for strangers or with Kirk, sickened her. She couldn't decide which eventuality was worse.

Tracy looked at Ray, observed the rings under his eyes and her heart contracted with sorrow for him. Still, it was her own life that was being decided upon along with the company's. "I need some time to think this over."

"Big choice." Anne laughed. " Either you remain as an employee, or as head of Ray's half. I can see it's a real tough decision, Tracy," she taunted sarcastically.

"We don't see things the same way," Tracy reminded Anne. How could she explain to Anne that if she had to stay on as an employee it would mean merely biding her time for the year. On the other hand as someone in charge, she would have to contribute. And she'd have to work closely with Kirk. Besides, why should she give Anne the satisfaction of getting more money through the sale to Kirk? If Ray didn't want Westwind, why should she want to hold on to it? *Let them both get their money and I'll survive the year somehow,* Tracy thought resentfully.

"Of course, take your time." Ray extended his hand to his daughter. Tracy took it and felt his gentle, supportive squeeze on her fingertips.

"But don't take too long," Anne chimed in. "Big money doesn't have to cast long—there are too many fish out there."

"You'll have my answer by tomorrow at this time." Tracy straightened up from her crouching position next to her father.

If looks could kill, Anne would have been dead by the time Tracy left the study. But Anne was fortunate. Nothing affected her. Tracy could hear her laughter as she crossed the hall. She wondered what Anne found so funny when she herself was feeling sick over the whole prospect. Tracy couldn't face visiting Esperanza and fortunately Aunt Irma was out shopping, so she simply left the house. She didn't bother to open the door to her convertible. Instead, Tracy swung her long legs over the door and plopped into the front seat. Her wheels screeched as she pulled out of the driveway.

Tracy had some serious thinking to do, so she

headed straight for the hangars at the airport. She wasn't going to take a plane out, but at least in the silence of the cockpit she hoped to sort out the situation fairly. She needed to calculate how much her father would stand to lose if her choice was to opt for Ray's selling out and how it would affect herself if that happened. She also had to consider the alternative. If she stayed on to manage Ray's half, what would it be like to work alongside Kirk? In effect Kirk and her father would own the company, while Tracy would be merely an employee of her father. Would she want to put herself into that position?

Moreover, every design Tracy made, would enrich Kirk. The way he had maneuvered his way into their company made Tracy's blood boil. She couldn't tell her father about her brief love affair with Kirk, nor about Kirk's spying because Ray's health was far more important than the past. But she could never forget what Kirk had done, or forgive him for it. So how could she work with him under such a strain?

As Tracy drove down the familiar road to the hangars, she noted that the airport was full of activity. Of course, Tracy thought, it was after six. That meant that every private pilot was out for a spin before dark. Well, it wouldn't affect her, she decided. Tracy parked her car by the hangar and, opening the small side door, walked into the cool semidarkness. Her heart ached as she remembered the first two *Pegasus* planes, which were now halfway around the world from her. A third *Pegasus* was ready to be tested, and it was for the cockpit of this one that Tracy headed.

She was wearing a pair of green, cotton slacks and a flowered blouse, which had a color scheme that matched the pants. Tracy stepped up cautiously so that she would not rip the skin-tight pants or the underarm seam of her blouse. But something stopped her from climbing into the plane. She sensed a movement in the shadows of the hangar. She was not alone. Someone was definitely in there. With her heart pounding Tracy waited for the person to move again.

"Where are you going, Tracy?" A familiar male voice echoed from the other side of the plane.

She jumped off the step to the ground. "What the hell are you doing here?" Kirk's mere presence made her furious.

He came around the plane and Tracy's heart gave a violent leap as she faced him. He looked better than she remembered, and she hated him for it.

"I knew you'd come here this afternoon, so I was waiting for you." Kirk gave her a knowing smile.

Tracy's blood surged to her head. Kirk had probably known that she would be told of his offer that afternoon, and he had just sat at the hangar counting on the fact that eventually Tracy would seek asylum there. *How dare he know her so well that he could anticipate her moves and spy on her feelings!* Tracy was so overwhelmed by sudden fury that she couldn't even respond. She turned on her heels and ran out of the hangar.

"Tracy, wait! Let's talk!" Kirk ran after her.

In a blind rage, Tracy jumped into her car and fumbled for her keys. She turned the motor on and raced off.

She was slowed by the cars coming and going on the main thoroughfare of the airport. Because it was only a two-lane road, she couldn't even pass anyone. Quietly cursing under her breath, Tracy rolled along. As far as Tracy could tell she had left Kirk behind. But not knowing what kind of car he drove, she couldn't be sure. Kirk knew the way to her house, so as soon as Tracy left the airport road, she headed the other way. She zipped through side streets till, reaching the Santa Monica Freeway, Tracy turned left, toward the Pacific Coast Highway.

She wasn't sure where she was going. All she knew was that she had to get away from Kirk. Seeing him again, Tracy had realized that he still had the old emotional pull on her. Yet now her feelings were mixed up with the fate of Westwind and she suspected Kirk's motives. It was all too much to sort out in Kirk's overpowering presence. She had to get away.

It was at the traffic light at Sunset Boulevard that Tracy recognized him behind her. Kirk was driving the same classic, silver Porsche that he had used on their first date. When he caught Tracy's eye in her rearview mirror he waved at her, indicating that she should turn right and stop on Sunset. There was a park off the road and he probably wanted her to go there with him. His wish just gave Tracy the incentive to aggressively step on her gas pedal as soon as the light turned green. She wasn't going to do his bidding! She shot out ahead of the traffic and raced toward Malibu, exceeding the fifty-five-mile speed limit. Kirk followed right behind her, and Tracy increased her speed. *He won't risk a ticket,* Tracy thought and pushed the pedal down farther. The wind tore into her hair, loosening it in a red stream behind her. Small pebbles on the road bounced off her car with more noise than damage as she pushed her speed toward the seventy-mile mark, and wove in and out of the two lane road to pass the bewildered drivers along the way. Tracy knew she was going too fast and consequently drove with that extra alertness needed to stay away from others on the road, but she did not reduce her speed. She was finally out of town and on the stretch where the cars thinned out. Now she could really take-off. Suddenly she heard the wail of a police siren. *They'll get Kirk first if he keeps chasing me,* Tracy thought with malicious glee and she drove on without reducing her speed. But Kirk didn't slack off and neither did the siren. The few cars in the middle lane of the road had pulled over to the right to let the police car advance. In her rearview mirror Tracy could see the speeding patrol car catching up to her, with all of its lights flashing. When the patrol car pulled abreast of her, the officer who was driving waved at her to stop, then pulled ahead of her.

Tracy's peripheral vision caught sight of a parking lot across the road. Instead of pulling over to the side, she waited an instant for the opposing traffic to clear, and then with a quick jerk of the wheel, crossed the road into the parking lot by the beach. A second later with sirens blasting, the police pulled up by her side. Tracy sat rigidly by the wheel.

A huge, uniformed officer swaggered to her side. "You've been speeding, miss," he said, stating the obvious.

"I guess I have," Tracy agreed amiably.

"May I see your driver's license and car registration, please?"

Without hurry, Tracy handed both documents into the beefy hands of the law. Out of the corner of her eye she saw Kirk pull into the lot, close to the exit. He got out of his car and headed toward her.

"I will have to give you a ticket."

"I guess you will," Tracy said, agreeably.

"Do you realize that you could have been killed driving at that speed, and that you also put the lives of other citizens into jeopardy by your reckless driving?"

"I'm sorry, officer."

"Did you consume any alcoholic beverage prior to getting on the road?"

"No, officer."

"Then why were you driving so recklessly?"

Tracy wished the policeman would finish his educational sermon. But he just seemed to be gearing up. She desperately wanted to get away from Kirk. But Kirk was by her side now, acting as a bystander, observing the officer at work.

The policeman noticed Kirk's presence and knitted his brows. "You were the guy following this lady. What were you two doing, racing?"

"Of course not," Kirk protested. "I was keeping up with traffic."

"You were the next one we were going to get," the officer said, "so you might as well hand over your driver's license and car registration."

Tracy couldn't help the satisfied smile that spread over her face. She was glad that Kirk was also getting a ticket. Who had asked him to race after her? It served Kirk right to get caught.

With agonizing slowness the officer examined both their papers, then wrote out a ticket for each of them. Before leaving, the officer warned them that if they were caught speeding again, he'd take both of them into the station.

No sooner had he turned his back than Tracy switched on the ignition again. Kirk reached down, and before Tracy could prevent him, he shut the motor off and pulled out the key.

"What are you doing?" Tracy gasped with surprise.

"You are through running. Now we shall have our little talk."

"No we won't! I've got nothing to say to you!" Tracy kicked her high-heeled shoes off, burst out from her car and headed down the beach, running. Kirk was right behind her. She changed directions and picked up speed again, but not for long. Tracy could sense Kirk in her tow, so she switched directions again. But this time he had anticipated her and followed with ease. It was almost like a cat and mouse game during which Tracy got the feeling that anytime Kirk wanted to catch her he could. But for some reason he let her run on. They were alone on the whole stretch of the beach, so Tracy couldn't even threaten him by calling out for help. As Tracy ran she wondered how long she could keep up her pace before getting thoroughly exhausted. But perhaps that was Kirk's intention—to let Tracy stop of her own accord. She ran on.

Finally, Kirk got tired of the game, and he ordered Tracy to stop and be reasonable. Tracy didn't heed him. But then she heard his heavy breathing right behind her, and suddenly she felt his hand grab hold of the back of her blouse. Kirk pulled on it. A button popped off and as Tracy caught at the opening in front, she gave Kirk the second he needed to get hold of her arm. He swung Tracy around and as she furiously raised her free hand to strike him, Kirk grabbed that arm too. Hooking her ankle with his leg, he forced Tracy down on the sand. He shielded her fall with his arm and went down with her, crushing Tracy tightly against himself. She fought him fiercely as they rolled together on the sand, their bodies thrashing and straining against each other. The sand got under Tracy's clothes and into her hair but she didn't care. Furiously, silently, she pummelled Kirk's back. She tried to push him away and tried to pull her nails across his face. Kirk grabbed Tracy's wrists, and finally got on top of her, pinning her body under his. They were both panting. Holding her still with his weight, Kirk raised his head so they could face each other.

"Let me be," Tracy demanded furiously.

She must have become aware of Kirk's body pressing against hers at the same second as he did, for suddenly Tracy could feel the spark between them ignite and the breath caught in her throat as Kirk's lips swooped down on hers. She wanted to protest but she was unable to stop the strange sweet ache that spread through her body. She felt powerless. Her stomach tightened, her back arched toward him and with a desperate longing Tracy offered her lips to Kirk's warm, firm mouth. His kiss deepened. Kirk's teeth hungrily nibbled Tracy's lips with an almost painful demand. Her body shuddered with a fierce yearning as Kirk's hands slipped under her blouse, the warmth of his exploring palms bringing fire to her skin. With fingers eager to touch him, Tracy raked Kirk's thick dark hair, moaning softly. In answer his hands cradled her breasts, teasing each sensitive nipple till suffused with pleasure, Tracy trembled beneath him. Her hands slipped under Kirk's shirt, stroking the rippling muscles on his back. Tracy's insides contracted as she felt his hardness press against her limbs, which lay imprisoned beneath him.

"My wonderful lioness," Kirk murmured softly

into her ear as he trailed his warm lips down Tracy's neck, planting little kisses with possessive tenderness along the way.

The phrase entered Tracy's consciousness. It stirred up memories of another time, of another world, in which she had let herself be seduced by the pleasures that only Kirk seemed capable of arousing in her. Slowly Tracy became aware of her body, crushed beneath his in the sand, of her arms, around Kirk and of her skin, responding with hunger to the caresses of his lips and hands. With consciousness Tracy's anger returned. By means of a gesture so fierce that it startled Kirk, Tracy managed to shove him off her, and rolled away from him.

"How dare you," Tracy hissed, sitting up, buttoning her blouse.

Kirk looked at her, the sharpness of his gray eyes veiled by passion. "Because I want you. I want you more than anything else in the world," he whispered hoarsely.

"Liar," Tracy cried jumping up. "You want Westwind more than anything else in the world! And you have used me to get it!"

Kirk's eyes cleared, and his face hardened in an instant to a stone mask. "Don't you ever say that again," he warned her.

"Then how else are you going to explain what you have done?" Tracy asked acidly.

Kirk scrambled to his feet and stood above Tracy, facing her green eyes which now blazed with anger. "What are you accusing me of?"

If this was their moment of reckoning, Tracy might as well let him have it all! "You took on the Ethiopia project to spy on our planes, and on top of that you made me believe that we actually had something going between us! When my father got ill you came back, pretending you were going to help me out. Then you disappeared for weeks. And where were you? Hunting for money so that you could take advantage of the situation and buy Westwind!"

"Tracy, what do you take me for?" Kirk towered over her. "It was you who told me of the trouble your company was having because of Anne. When we got back, I realized that you were in even more trouble than you knew. So I went off to raise the money to buy Anne's shares. And as for you and me, how could I ever pretend to feel something as electric as what you know exists between us if it weren't truly there? Or have you forgotten what happened a minute ago?"

"For a businessman you sure have a way with words!" Tracy didn't want to hear any more. Kirk had managed to twist everything around, so that she could now almost believe him. But not quite. Tracy tossed her last line of defense against him. "And so you are buying Anne's share, out of sheer altruism? What about the fact that your company does exactly the kind of work I spoke to you about in Ethiopia? How come you didn't tell me about it then?"

"Because by that time you had become more important to me than my company! I was afraid that if I told you that we were competitors, I'd lose you. But your father knew.''

Tracy felt his words penetrate her deepest emotional defenses and move with a slow, warming glow toward her heart. She let Kirk's words sink in and take their course, while she chose to respond to his second statement. ''What did my father know?''

''Everything about me. That my men and I were building up just the kind of customers that World Help is typical of. And that I took the job with you because I was interested in the *Pegasus* line. I was going to place an order for a dozen planes if they proved to be what your brochure advertised.''

The beach began to reel around Tracy. ''How come my father never mentioned any of this to me?''

Kirk shrugged. ''How should I know? Maybe Ray didn't think it was important.''

''Are you aware that my father wants to retire and leave me to manage his half of Westwind?''

A slow grin spread over Kirk's face. ''Without you doing that, I wouldn't buy the rest. Why should I rescue a company I don't need? It's you I need. Knowing that Westwind is such a part of you, I figured it would take buying the company to get you!''

''But you're mistaken,'' Tracy said. Her whole body was trembling with tension by now because she finally could see that as either daughter or lover she was just a pawn in this game between men. Her father had first led her to believe that Kirk was just an employee. Then Ray had pretended that Kirk was simply another buyer for Westwind, and not a man interested in his daughter. Tracy didn't quite understand why her father would do all this, but she was not going to play into his hands any longer.

"Since you and my father will own Westwind together, I'd simply be an employee running it for you two. And as such, I am handing in my resignation to you both. Right now."

Kirk stared at Tracy in disbelief. "You're being ridiculous." Then suddenly he flared up. "Now you listen to me!" He grabbed her by the shoulders so Tracy couldn't wriggle away. "From the first time I met you, I knew I wanted you—and only you—as I've never wanted a woman before. But you were the boss's daughter, and I couldn't see myself getting involved in a situation similar to what I'd left behind in San Francisco.

"I also realized that even if I told you how I felt, you wouldn't leave Westwind for anybody. All through our travels in Ethiopia I tried alternately to stay away from you or to figure out a way to transfer my company to Los Angeles. I wanted to come to you as an equal. Then this thing happened with your father and Anne. I realized that this was my chance. I staked everything to buy into Westwind. But only on the condition that you become my wife and partner. If I can't have you, I certainly don't want Westwind."

The tension broke within Tracy. Her eyes filled

up and all the strain and misery of the past weeks seemed to burst like a pent-up dam as she let out a choking sob and her eyes became blinded by a torrent of tears.

"Tracy!" Kirk took her in his arms, and held her. He rocked her gently without a word, letting her body shake with sobs, caressing her hair and allowing her crying to spend itself.

Finally the storm within Tracy subsided and she became aware of the approaching evening around them. A cool breeze swept the white-capped waves toward the sand. Tracy shivered slightly.

"Let's head back," Kirk suggested.

Tracy raised her face to him and Kirk gently kissed her slightly swollen lips. "Your place or mine?" he asked as they stopped by her car.

"Who said anything about continuing this discussion?" Tracy smiled teasingly.

"I can think of lots of other things we could do."

"Just follow me then." Tracy got into her car.

"Please stick to the speed limit—just this once," Kirk said, smiling at her. "I'd rather we didn't spend this night in jail."

EPILOGUE

IT WAS A LARGE WEDDING. Tracy looked resplendent in her white, green-and-gold bordered Ethiopian dress. Ray was well enough to give away the bride. And Kirk Russell senior congratulated his son on an excellent choice of a helpmate.

At the reception Irma whispered to Tracy that this was the happiest day of her life. Esperanza warned Tracy to be a little more tolerant this second time around.

Bill had come back from Ethiopia, but only for a brief visit. The Ethiopian Relief Commission had contracted Westwind's services for another year, and along with the purchase of six *Pegasus* planes, Bill was to go back to train a team of Ethiopian pilots assigned to him. Of course he and Helga planned to marry as soon as he returned there. Under his contract Bill could even bring his children to Ethiopia for visits a couple of times during the year, so he was beaming with happiness.

Judy and Kenny came to the wedding hand in hand and Judy whispered into Tracy's ear that she and Kenny were going on their second honeymoon as soon as their new baby was born and old enough to be left with a nanny.

Even Anne pulled in her usually sharp nails in honor of the occasion and went around sweetly chatting with the guests.

After the wedding cake was cut, Ray asked the guests to gather around so that he could make an announcement.

"I've asked myself," Ray said, "what I could give my only daughter that would enhance her new life with her husband, Kirk, and I believe I have finally found the perfect present." He handed Tracy a scroll tied with a blue ribbon.

Tracy unfolded it and let out a great shout of joy and disbelief. It was a Deed of Grant to the ownership of Westwind Airlines. Deeply moved, Tracy read the text aloud to the assembled guests. It gave her title to one half of both the Commuter Line and the Experimental Branch.

Enthusiastic applause followed Ray's announcement. Then the band started to play for Tracy and Kirk to begin the dancing with a waltz.

Just before it was time for her and Kirk to leave the reception, Tracy sought out her father. "But what about your income from Westwind?" Tracy asked.

"You didn't read the small print on the next document," Ray said, winking at her. "Westwind is obligated to pay me a percentage of its profits for the rest of my life."

"That's a wonderful vote of confidence, dad." Tracy hugged her father. Then she looked at him. "Did you know all along that you were going to do this?"

"Of course." Ray's eyes twinkled.

"Then why did you let me pass so many hours in agony?"

"Because Kirk asked me not to tell you, till after the wedding."

"Why on earth not?"

"Kirk told me that otherwise he could never be sure of your motives. He wanted to feel you were marrying him for love—not for your wedding present," Ray said, laughing.

"So YOU WEREN'T sure of my love," said Tracy, turning to Kirk as he locked the canopy down over their honeymoon plane. "Just get up in the air and put us on automatic."

Kirk laughed, for Tracy's husband knew that their flight was going to keep them up in the clouds indeed.

ABOUT THE AUTHOR

Erika Fabian has led a life more vivid than most of us even dream of. Born in Hungary, Erika grew up under a Communist government, and she can recount a number of harrowing stories about trying to escape her homeland before she was able to leave during the 1956 uprising. After finding freedom and a new home in the United States, Erika studied dance and mime, which she later taught in Lima, Peru—one of the many countries to which she has traveled.

Erika has also been a model, an actress, a theater director, a magazine journalist and a photographer-cum-researcher-cum-field producer for *National Geographic*, working with her husband, photographer-writer Albert Moldvay. Plus, she has written stage plays, a screenplay and a television short for children, published eight travel/photo books and co-authored a book on relationships, *Making Love Work*.

Sky Riders is Erika's first romance, inspired by her own experiences flying through Ethiopia with a legendary Swedish pilot while she was on photographic assignment. In her own words, Erika's Superromance is about "two strong, sexy people, who, in the pursuit of their goals, find each other."

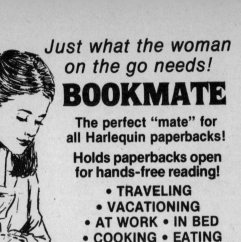
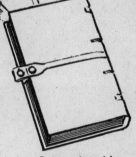